Bound by Darkness

TARA CONRAD

HIS ONE HER ONLY PUBLISHING

Published by: His One, Her Only Publishing

Cover Art by: 100 Covers

Formatting by: Mr. George Conrad III

For every woman who was underestimated, overlooked, or told to stay in her place—this is your reminder that you were meant to be seen, to lead, and to never apologize for it,

Contents

Prologue

AOIFE

I SHOULD FEEL GUILTY.

The blade rests in my palm. Its cold weight is a reminder of what I've chosen to do. What I've become. The room smells of damp stone and fear, the air so thick I can almost taste the tension. Ruairi sits bound in the chair before me, his head slumped forward, his breathing ragged. My twin. My blood. The other half of me, whose shadow I've spent my entire life living in.

And here I am, about to prove once and for all that I'm just as worthy.

The pendulum swings in the shadows above us. Its steady rhythm echoes the pounding in my chest, a reminder of how little time I have. I trace the edge of the blade with my thumb, watching the light flicker across its surface. One slice. One mark to prove that I'm not the same girl he's always underestimated.

"Do it," Eamon murmurs from the corner. Smooth, steady, unrelenting. He's the devil on my shoulder, the man who saw in me what Ruairi never would.

Strength. Ambition. Fire.

Ruairi lifts his head slowly, his bloodshot eyes locking onto mine. He doesn't plead. He doesn't flinch. He merely stares at me with that infuriating mix of defiance and pity, like he still thinks I'm a child playing a dangerous game.

"You don't have to do this, Aoife," he says, his voice hoarse but steady. "You're not like him."

I laugh, though it tastes bitter on my tongue. "And what am I like, Ruairi? A good little girl? The obedient twin? The one you keep locked away while you play king?"

His jaw tightens, and I see the crack in his armor. My words hurt more than the blade ever could.

"You're better than this," he whispers, his voice softer now. Almost pleading.

But I'm not.

I press the blade against his skin. He winces, though he doesn't try to pull away. My hand trembles. Not because I can't do it, but because I know this moment will change everything.

"Better?" I whisper, my voice breaking. "Better doesn't survive in our world, Ruairi. You taught me that."

The pendulum swings lower, its hiss slicing through the silence. Eamon shifts in the shadows, waiting, watching.

But tonight, I'm not here to be his equal. I'm here to take the throne.

I tighten my grip, my voice steadier. "You're right, Ruairi."

He blinks, his expression caught between shock and confusion.

"I'm not like him. And I'm not like you either."

THE MALDIVES WASN'T A LIFELONG DREAM OR A bucket list destination. It was just *next*.

After weeks of shivering through the cold streets of Prague and Helsinki, I craved warmth. Sunlight. Something that didn't feel like a punishment for stepping outside. And so, here I am, soaking in paradise.

From the deck of my villa, the turquoise water stretches endlessly, shimmering under the afternoon sun. The private infinity pool glistens, a perfect mirror of the sea. Every detail is designed to soothe, to make me forget the chaos of the world outside this tiny pocket of perfection.

And for a few moments, it works.

Traveling is what I do—what my father lets me do. He calls it freedom, a way to see the world, to live a life untouched by the darker corners of his empire. But I know better. It's a distraction. A gilded cage designed to keep me out of trouble, out of his business, and above all, safe.

That's why he funds it all without question, from the penthouse suites in Paris to the remote retreats in the Himalayas. "Go anywhere, Aoife," he told me. "You can do anything except within the Quigley Syndicate."

Da believes I'm too fragile for his world, too good for it. But what he doesn't see is how this life, this constant moving, learning, and adapting, is preparing me for the day I'll step into his world, whether he wants me to or not.

While he thinks I'm sipping champagne and collecting pretty postcards, I've been training. Shooting in Moscow, sparring in Bangkok, grappling in Amsterdam. Every skill I've picked up is a weapon he doesn't know I'm forging. One day, I'll walk into his office and prove to him that I'm not a delicate little girl. I'm every bit as strong and capable as my twin brother, Ruairi.

But today isn't about planning my next move. Today's about relaxing. I lean back in my lounge chair, the warm sun on my skin, and let the soft crash of the waves dull the edges of my thoughts.

The resort's beach party starts at sunset, and I've already decided I'll go. It'll be an easy way to pass the evening, maybe even fun if the cocktails are strong enough.

By the time I make my way to the beach, the sun is dipping low, painting the horizon in fiery hues of gold and orange. The resort staff have gone all out. Tiki torches line the sandy paths, the soft hum of music drifts through the air, and the bar is already swarmed with guests holding elaborate, colorful drinks.

I tug my sheer cover-up tighter around my white bikini as the breeze picks up. The soft sand is cool against my bare feet. It's the perfect evening. Quiet enough to think, lively enough to get lost in the crowd.

With my Tequila Sunrise in hand, I start toward the quieter edge of the gathering. I barely take three steps before a solid wall of muscle slams into me.

My drink flies out of my hand, bright orange liquid splashing all over me and the sand. My purse slips from my shoulder and spills onto the ground, its contents scattering like confetti.

"Jesus," I curse. "A *dhiabhal.*"

"I'm so sorry." The voice is smooth—controlled.

I look up to see the man responsible. He's tall, dressed in an expensive suit that immediately stands out against the laid-back crowd. A cell phone is in his hand.

His blue eyes, vivid and piercing, hold mine with an intensity that's both unsettling and magnetic. They're framed by impossibly thick lashes that seem to shift with the light. They aren't just striking. They're assessing, as if he's stripping away every layer I thought I could hide behind.

His jawline is sharp, framed by the shadow of a day-old beard that gives him a dangerous edge, softened only by the faint curve of his lips like he knows exactly what I'm thinking.

My gaze shifts, taking in the way the fabric fits him perfectly, hugging his broad shoulders and tapering down to a lean waist. His athletic build speaks of someone used to relying on precision over brute force.

Beneath the crisp white shirt, unbuttoned just enough at the collar, I catch the faintest glimpse of tattoos—dark ink teasing at his skin, disappearing beneath the pristine fabric. It's a stark contrast, this blend of refinement and rebellion, and I can't help but wonder how far the tattoos extend.

The suit sleeves are smooth and flawless, ending just above strong hands that look like they'd be equally skilled at delivering pain or pleasure. I shiver at the thought before I can stop myself.

This man isn't just attractive. He's devastating. The kind of handsome that's effortless and entirely lethal.

He tilts his head slightly, and I realize I've been caught. Heat blooms in my cheeks, but he says nothing. Instead, he crouches down, scooping up my spilled belongings and brushing sand off them.

"My fault," he says as he straightens, handing me a lipstick tube. "I wasn't looking where I was going."

"You think?" I snap, wiping the sticky drink off my arm. My cover-up clings uncomfortably to my skin, the fabric soaked.

"I'll replace the drink," he says, his tone calm and unbothered, as if it's already a done deal. "And anything else I ruined."

"You can start with my outfit," I mutter, glancing down at the mess he's made.

He chuckles softly, the sound deep and rich, and holds out his hand. "Eamon."

I hesitate. There's something about him, something deliberate in the way he holds himself. He doesn't look like someone who should be at a beach party in the Maldives.

"Eve," I reply, using the name I've been going by since I left Ireland.

He glances at the orange drink now soaking into the sand. "Let me get you another drink, *Eve*," he says, his name clashing oddly with the lack of an accent. His voice is smooth, low, and unhurried like he has all the time in the world. "It's the least I can do."

A shiver of heat travels down my spine, and I hate how much I enjoy the way his perusal seems to claim parts of me without even touching them. My pulse quickens, a mix of discomfort and thrill, and I find myself holding my breath, caught between the urge to hide and the desire to let him look.

"You're far from home." The intensity of his eyes makes me feel exposed. Instinctively, I want to cross my arms. Still, something about the way his gaze lingers, deliberate and undeniably appreciative, keeps me rooted in place.

"So are you," I reply, my voice steady, though I can feel the tension crackling between us.

His smile is faint, more a suggestion than an expression, but his sapphire eyes never leave mine, holding me in place. "Am I?" he asks, his tone teasing, challenging, like he's waiting for me to catch up to some game I didn't know we were playing.

The words hang between us, making me wonder what else he

sees when he looks at me. What secrets he's already piecing together.

He steps closer, the scent of his cologne mingling with the salt air. It's warm and inviting, with hints of amber and sandalwood wrapped in a subtle spice that's intoxicating and undeniably male. It suits him—confident and rich, with a complexity that promises more than meets the eye.

"Come on," he says, gesturing for me to follow him. His voice drops just enough to make the invitation feel intimate, almost dangerous. "Let's fix this mess."

And for reasons I can't entirely explain, I follow him. Maybe it's the way his fingers brush my elbow, barely there but electric, or the way his gaze lingers like he's imagining things he has no right to.

I fall into step beside him, my pulse quickening, every nerve in my body on high alert. Whatever this is, whoever he is, I know I should walk away.

But I don't.

Eamon

The Maldives.

A paradise for the rich, the reckless, and the desperate. I fit none of those categories—or so I tell myself. This place is a long way from Dublin, from the cold streets where my life is carved into stone, every move planned, every decision calculated. But some jobs aren't about strategy. Some jobs are personal.

That's why I'm here.

The deal isn't complicated. A meeting to exchange money for information. No weapons, no bloodshed, just cold, hard leverage. It's a simple enough task that one of my men could've handled. But this isn't about efficiency. It's about making sure the message is delivered face-to-face. They need to know I haven't forgotten. That no one crosses me without consequence.

I should've finished hours ago. But nothing about this trip has gone as planned. First, the local contact was late. Then, their price went up. And now, the final confirmation is taking its sweet damn time to come through. My patience is wearing thin.

The resort around me feels like a mockery. Everything is pristine, artificial. The kind of place where couples sip champagne in infinity pools and pretend they're happy. The type of place where people think they can escape their problems because they paid enough to leave reality behind.

Not me. I don't drink the champagne, don't watch the sunsets, and definitely don't attend the nightly beach parties. But my business brought me here, and until it's finished, I have to endure the noise.

The glow of torches and the thrum of music spill across the sand as I cut through the edge of the party. It's unavoidable as its the fastest way back to my villa, where I can finally get some goddamned quiet. My phone buzzes in my hand—a message from one of my lieutenants confirming the transfer is complete. About bloody time.

This deal has been a thorn in my side for weeks. But instead of satisfaction, I feel the familiar hum of tension, a sense that nothing is ever truly finished, not in my world.

I glance down at my phone to reply, the glow of the screen illuminating my hands. The music from the party thumps in the background, a mix of bass and laughter, and I remind myself I shouldn't be this close to the crowd.

My eyes stay fixed on the screen as I type out my reply, not bothering to look up as I cross the packed pathway. And that's when it happens.

It's not a subtle bump or a brush of the shoulders. It's a full-on, body-to-body collision that jolts me out of my focus.

"Jesus," she curses, the frustration spilling over as a Gaelic curse slips past her lips. "A *dhiabhal*."

"I'm so sorry." I look up, and whatever else I'd planned to say dies in my throat.

She's stunning, though that feels like too simple a word. Long red hair cascades over her shoulders, catching the torchlight and gleaming like liquid fire. Her green eyes, wide with surprise, burn brighter than any emerald, holding me in place longer than they should. She's curvy but toned, the kind of figure that suggests strength and softness in equal measure.

Her purse has spilled onto the sand, its contents scattered.

Keys, lipstick, and a small wallet, but my attention doesn't linger there. Her drink, a vivid orange concoction, has tipped, spilling down the front of her barely-there white swimsuit. The liquid clings to the thin fabric, highlighting every curve as it soaks through.

My first reaction is irritation, the kind that flares hot and fast. But the second? Pure, unfiltered desire. She's angry, and somehow, that only adds to the effect.

"You've got to be kidding me," she mutters, brushing at the mess as she glares up at me.

I crouch down without thinking, scooping up a lipstick tube and brushing sand off it before handing it back to her. "My fault," I say, straightening to my full height. "I wasn't looking where I was going."

Her gaze flickers over me, sharp and assessing, but she doesn't seem intimidated. "You think?" she snaps, wiping her arm with a futile swipe.

"I'll replace the drink," I say, unaffected, slipping my phone into my jacket pocket. "And anything else I ruined."

"You can start with my outfit," she says, glancing down at the sticky mess on her cover-up.

A soft chuckle escapes me before I can stop it, the sound deep and low in my chest. Her fire amuses me.

"Eamon," I say, holding out my hand.

She hesitates, her sharp green eyes narrowing slightly as though she's trying to figure me out. I can tell she's suspicious. She should be. After a moment, she takes my hand. Her grip is firm, her skin warm against mine.

"Eve," she replies.

"Let me get you another drink, Eve," I say, my voice dropping lower. There's no rush to my tone, no urgency. Just a calm, deliberate invitation. "It's the least I can do."

She doesn't respond immediately, but her body betrays her silence as her nipples pebble under the thin fabric of her bikini. I catch the subtle hitch in her breath. It's faint, barely there, but I see it. Her eyes never leave mine, though, steady and defiant, even as I sense the tension rolling off her in waves.

"You're far from home," I add, my tone softer though no less deliberate.

"So are you," she counters, her pulse fluttering at her neck, a subtle but telling sign.

Her gaze doesn't falter even as the tension crackles between us, an invisible thread pulling tighter with every second.

"Am I?" My voice is laced with challenge.

Her lips press together, but there's a flicker of amusement in her eyes now, almost as if she enjoys this verbal sparring.

The faint scent of her perfume drifts toward me, soft and floral with an edge of something sharper. It suits her. Confident. Intriguing. The kind of scent that lingers, refusing to be forgotten.

"Come on," I say, motioning for her to follow. "Let's fix this mess."

She doesn't move immediately, her gaze holding mine for a long moment. Then, without a word, she steps forward, her chin lifted in quiet defiance as she falls into step beside me.

The night stretches out ahead of us as the music from the party begins to fade into the background. Whatever business brought me here feels a million miles away now. Because I already know this woman isn't just another passing stranger.

She's something else entirely.

Aoife

WHAT THE HELL AM I THINKING FOLLOWING THIS MAN away from the safety of the crowd? Danger oozes from him, yet I continue walking. The music and the noise of the party fade into the distance, replaced by the rhythmic sound of the waves lapping against the shore. The only light is from the moon shining overhead, casting silvery shadows that stretch across the path.

"Where are you staying?" he asks, his voice low, breaking the silence.

I hesitate for a moment before gesturing ahead. "In a private villa," I say, my tone clipped, as if that will somehow mask the fact that my pulse is racing.

"Of course you are," he murmurs, a hint of amusement in his voice.

We walk side by side, the tension between us palpable. Every step closer to the villa feels like a step away from reason. My body hums with awareness, my skin prickling under his steady gaze.

When we reach the villa, he stops just outside the door, turning to face me. "Your key card?"

I narrow my eyes, gripping the slim card tighter in my hand. "Why should I give it to you?"

The corner of his mouth curves into a slow, wolfish grin.

"Because, love, if I were the big bad wolf, I wouldn't be asking. I'd already have eaten you."

The audacity of his response sends a shiver down my spine. Against every ounce of common sense I have left, I hand over the card, my fingers brushing his for the briefest moment.

He slides it into the slot, the electronic lock clicking open with a soft beep. He doesn't step in right away. Instead, he holds the door open, tilting his head slightly as he looks at me. "After you."

I step inside, and the awareness of his presence steals my breath. The villa is quiet. The soft glow of the moon filters in through the sheer curtains, casting the room in muted silver tones.

The moment the door shuts behind him, the air shifts.

It's not just tension anymore—it's a storm, crackling with heat and intensity. Building with every shared glance, every unspoken word.

What the hell am I doing? The question flashes through my mind again, but it's drowned out by the pounding of my heart. My body responds to him in ways I can't control. The magnetic pull between us is impossible to resist.

He steps closer, his presence overwhelming, and I feel the heat of his body even before his fingers brush a stray strand of hair from my cheek.

"Careful, Eve," he murmurs, his voice a rasp that seems to ignite something deep inside me. "You don't want to get burned."

His words are meant to be a warning, but they only make me want to play with fire. A slow smile spreads across my lips, desire pooling in my core as I meet his gaze head-on.

"Maybe I like the heat," I say, my voice low and sultry, daring him to push me further.

His eyes darken, the blue deepening into something stormy and wild. He steps closer, erasing the last inch of space between us. His hand lifts, fingers brushing against my jaw as he tilts my face up to his.

"You don't know what you're inviting," he whispers, his tone laced with danger and promise.

"Don't I?" I counter, my breath hitching as his thumb grazes the corner of my mouth.

For a heartbeat, we hover there, the tension between us coiled tight, ready to snap. And then it does.

He kisses me.

It's not soft or hesitant. It's raw, consuming, and utterly unapologetic as he devours me like he's starving. His hand tangles in my hair, pulling me closer, while the other settles on my waist, anchoring me against the solid heat of his body.

I taste the faintest hint of whiskey on his lips as his tongue slides against mine, coaxing a moan from deep in my throat. My hands find his chest, fingers curling into the crisp fabric of his shirt, feeling the hard muscle beneath.

The kiss deepens, and the world around us fades into nothing. It's just him. His touch, his heat, the way he makes every nerve in my body come alive.

When we break apart, I'm breathless, and my lips are swollen.

The look in his eyes sends a fresh wave of desire through me. His thumb brushes over my lower lip. "You taste like trouble," he says, his voice low and rough, the sound of it unraveling what little control I have left.

"Then stop wasting time," I breathe.

He doesn't need any more encouragement. In one fluid motion, he lifts me, his hands strong and sure as they grip my thighs. I wrap my legs around him instinctively, my back pressed against the cool wood of the door as he pins me there.

His mouth moves to my neck, lips and teeth teasing the sensitive skin just below my ear. A shiver courses through me as he nips at the delicate spot, soothing it with his tongue.

The attraction between us is electric. Every touch, every kiss stoking the fire higher. Eamon's hands roam my body, exploring every curve, while my own slide under his shirt, desperate to feel the warmth of his skin.

"Tell me to stop," he murmurs, his voice thick with restraint, though his body says he's already lost the battle.

"Don't you dare," I reply, threading my fingers through his hair and pulling him back to my mouth.

He growls low in his throat, a sound that sends a jolt of pure desire straight through me. The last shred of control between us shatters. In an instant, he tears my bikini top, the thin straps giving way under his strength, freeing my breasts. His hands are on me immediately, rough yet reverent, his touch igniting sparks across my body.

A gasp escapes me as his lips capture a sensitive peak in his mouth. I arch into him, my fingers digging into his shoulders.

"You're fucking perfect," he murmurs. His hands slide down my sides, firm and sure, as though he's learning every curve, every inch of me, and committing them to memory.

The door at my back is suddenly gone as he carries me deeper into the villa, his movements purposeful yet frantic, like he's barely holding himself together. He lowers me onto the bed, the soft fabric cool against my heated skin.

He stands for a moment, towering over me, his blue eyes dark and predatory as they roam my body. Slowly, deliberately, he shrugs off his suit jacket and tosses it to a nearby chair, the motion fluid and unhurried, like he has all the time in the world.

"You're going to ruin me, Eve," he says, his voice full of both frustration and reverence.

I sit up slightly, resting on my elbows. "Maybe I like the idea of being your undoing."

That's all it takes.

He's on me again, his mouth crushing mine as his hands explore, leaving trails of fire in their wake. My legs part instinctively to welcome him, and the weight of his body presses me into the bed, grounding me even as every nerve in my body feels like it's about to combust.

His lips leave mine to trail down my throat, over my collarbone, and lower still. When his mouth closes over the peak of my breast again, I cry out, my back arching off the bed as pleasure courses through me.

He growls in response, his hands sliding lower, finding the tie at my bikini bottom. Making quick work of the strings, the fabric slips away, leaving me bare beneath him. His gaze drops, and the raw hunger in his eyes is enough to steal the breath from my lungs.

"You're stunning," he says, his voice almost reverent, though the heat in his gaze tells me he's anything but saintly.

His fingers trail along the curve of my hip, teasing, testing, as though savoring the moment before he takes what he wants. My body trembles under his touch, every nerve alive, every inch of me aching for him.

The corner of his mouth lifts, cocky and deliberate, but there's nothing teasing in the way his hand moves, his fingers sliding between my thighs to find my slick heat. I gasp, my head falling back against the pillow as he touches me with a skill that feels maddeningly precise.

"Tell me what you want, Eve," he murmurs, his voice low and dark.

"You," I breathe. "I want you."

Eamon

Her words undo me.

"I want you."

They're simple, barely a whisper, but they ripple through me hot, heady, and impossible to ignore. Eve's sprawled beneath me, her body a masterpiece of curves and softness, her green eyes dark with need. Her fiery defiance has melted into something just as powerful—desire.

I should savor this. Take my time. But there's nothing patient left in me. She's set me ablaze, and I feel myself unraveling under the weight of her words, the look in her eyes, the way her body responds to my every touch.

I lean over her, bracing myself with one hand on the bed as my other trails down her side, my fingers tracing the curve of her hip. Her skin is warm, soft, and impossibly smooth, and I can't resist dipping my head to capture her lips again.

She moans into my mouth, her hands sliding up my chest and over my shoulders, tugging at the buttons of my shirt with a desperation that matches my own. I chuckle against her lips before pulling back just enough to shrug out of my shirt, letting it join her swimsuit on the floor.

Her gaze sweeps over me, and the heat in her eyes makes my

17

chest tighten. She doesn't say anything, but she doesn't have to. The way she looks at me, hungry, captivated, is enough.

"You're incredible," I murmur as I trail kisses down her neck, across her collarbone, and lower still.

My hand slides between her thighs again, teasing her, testing her. She's soaked—ready. The sound she makes when my fingers find her most sensitive spot drives me wild.

"Eamon," she gasps, my name tumbling from her lips like a prayer, her hands fisting the sheets as her body trembles beneath me.

My fingers move in a rhythm that has her writhing, desperate for more. "Tell me what you need," I murmur, my lips brushing her ear.

Her breath hitches, but she doesn't falter. She turns her head slightly, her lips grazing my jaw as she meets my gaze, her eyes steady and blazing with intent. "I need you to stop teasing and fuck me," she says, her voice full of fire.

Her plea snaps the last thread of control I'm clinging to. I shift, positioning myself between her thighs, and pause for just a moment, taking in the sight of her—flushed, breathless, and utterly captivating.

"You're sure?" I ask, my voice low, though I already know the answer.

She nods, her eyes locking onto mine, and I see everything in that look. Her defiance, her surrender, her trust.

"Good girl," I murmur, leaning down to claim her lips again.

The world narrows to just us. The way she gasps, the way her body molds to mine, the way her nails dig into my back as she matches my every movement. She's fiery and untamed, and it only fuels me further, driving me to give her everything.

Her breath catches as I shift, trailing kisses along her jawline, down the column of her throat, and over her collarbone. Her skin is impossibly smooth under my lips, and I savor the way she shivers at each touch. My hands follow, exploring every curve, every dip.

I continue my descent, my mouth leaving a heated trail down the valley between her breasts, lingering just long enough to draw a soft moan from her. Her fingers tangle in my hair, tugging gently. I glance up, catching her gaze. Her lips are parted, her cheeks flushed, and the look in her eyes, equal parts trust and need, drives me mad.

I press a kiss to her stomach, my hands sliding down her thighs as I settle between them. Her legs part instinctively, and I run my palms along her soft skin, holding her open for me. She's breathtaking like this—laid bare, vulnerable, yet completely in control.

"You're fucking stunning," I murmur, my voice hoarse with desire.

Her only response is a sharp inhale as I lower my head, my lips brushing over the sensitive skin of her inner thigh. I take my time, teasing her, tasting her, until she shifts her hips, silently begging for more.

When my tongue finally finds her, the reaction is instant. She cries out, her voice raw and unfiltered, the sound rolling through me like a challenge I'm more than ready to meet. Her hips buck against me, instinctive and needy, but I hold her steady, my hands firm on her thighs as I spread her open.

She's soaked, and it drives me to the edge of control as I lap at her, slow and deliberate, dragging my tongue through every inch of wetness. Her taste is addictive. Intense and all-consuming. I take my time, savoring every drop.

My tongue circles her clit, teasing her with featherlight flicks that draw the sweetest sounds from her as her hands twist in the sheets.

I press harder, flattening my tongue against her as I build a rhythm that has her writhing, her hips lifting off the bed to chase the pressure. She's fucking perfect like this—wild and uninhibited, every moan and gasp proof of just how much she's losing herself to me.

"More," she demands, her voice breathless. I obey without

hesitation, sucking on her clit and rolling my tongue over it in slow, torturous circles. Her reaction is immediate. A sharp, broken cry that echoes through the room as her hands fly to my head, her fingers tangling in my hair to pull me closer.

I growl against her, the vibration drawing another moan from her lips as I bury my face deeper between her thighs. My fingers dig into her skin, holding her exactly where I want her as I devour her, my tongue flicking and stroking with relentless precision.

Her body responds to me like it's mine, her movements frantic and her cries desperate as she teeters closer to the edge.

"That's it, love," I murmur against her. "Come for me. Let me hear you."

Her head tilts back, her red hair a wild halo against the pillows as her back bows off the bed. She's close, so fucking close. I push her further, my tongue working her clit mercilessly as I slide two fingers inside her, curling them just right.

The combination is her undoing. With a sharp, almost guttural moan, she comes undone, her body shuddering violently as her climax crashes over her. Her thighs clamp around my head, her hands tug at my hair as wave after wave of pleasure wracks her body.

I don't let up, my tongue and fingers coaxing her through every tremor, every aftershock, until she collapses back onto the bed, spent and gasping for air.

Kissing my way back up her body, my lips linger on her flushed skin as I settle over her once more. Her eyes flutter open, and the way she looks at me, sated but still burning, nearly undoes me.

I'm painfully hard, my body taut with the need to bury myself inside her, to claim her completely.

"You're dangerous," she whispers.

I smirk, brushing my lips against hers. "And you're addictive, love. A deadly combination."

I brace myself on my forearms, caging her in, my body pressing into hers, the unmistakable evidence of my arousal settling against her thigh. Her lips curl into a slow, wicked smile, her fingers trailing down my chest until her nails scrape lightly over my stomach.

She pauses at the waistband of my trousers, her wicked smile deepening as she hooks her thumbs under the fabric. Slowly, deliberately, she tugs at the button, her eyes locked on mine as though daring me to stop her.

I don't.

The sound of the zipper fills the charged silence. Her hand finds me, and the second her fingers close around my cock, a shudder rolls through me—sharp, uncontrollable. Everything in me goes still, like my body's bracing for the storm her touch brings.

I shift, kicking off my trousers and briefs in one swift motion, the cool air hitting my skin, a stark contrast to the heat radiating between us.

Before I can move, she does, crawling over me with a grace that's all sin and intention. Her eyes stay locked on mine, dark with purpose, as she slides lower. Her hair brushes my stomach, a whisper of silk against my skin. Her breath ghosts over the tip of my cock. The anticipation coils tight in my gut, and the groan that rips from me is anything but restrained.

Then her mouth is on me.

The wet heat of her lips and the deliberate pressure of her tongue is overwhelming. It's the kind of pleasure that steals the air from my lungs.

"Christ, Eve." My voice breaks as she takes me deeper, her movements unhurried but devastatingly effective.

She hums softly, the vibration sending a jolt of electricity through me as her hand works in tandem with her mouth, stroking and teasing in perfect rhythm. She's relentless, confident, and utterly in control.

Grabbing her wrist, she stills as I shift my body. Before she can react, I grip her hips and flip her over in one swift motion. Her gasp echoes through the room as she lands on her hands and knees. She glances back at me over her shoulder. The wicked curve of her lips sends a jolt of heat straight through me.

"Decisive," she says, her voice low, teasing, and full of challenge.

"You've no idea," I growl as I drink in the sight of her like this, open, waiting. The smooth arch of her back leading down to her perfect ass has every ounce of control I've clung to slipping away.

I kneel behind her, my chest brushing against her back as I press my lips to the nape of her neck, tasting the salt of her skin. My hands explore her, sliding over her thighs, up her sides, teasing the curve of her breasts before I lean back, gripping her hips once more.

When I position myself at her entrance, the heat of her is almost too much. I slide in slowly, savoring every inch, my groan mixing with the breathy moan that escapes her lips.

"Fuck." My grip tightens as her body adjusts to mine, her heat drawing me in completely.

She pushes back against me, taking me deeper, her movements bold and deliberate. "Harder," she commands, and I'm more than happy to oblige.

My thrusts grow stronger—deeper. The sound of our bodies colliding fills the room. Each movement draws her closer to the edge, her breathy moans turning into desperate cries that spur me on.

"You feel fucking incredible," I growl, sliding a hand up the curve of her back. My fingers thread through her hair, gripping just enough to tilt her head back as I drive into her, each thrust harder and deeper than the last.

Her body trembles, the tight heat of her pulsing around me as her climax builds. I reach around to stroke her, my fingers finding the spot that makes her cry out.

She shatters beneath me, her release hitting her with a force that leaves her gasping, her body clenching around me. The sensation of her, the way she feels, and the way she sounds push me closer to the edge. With a few more erratic thrusts, the tension inside me snaps. My release crashes over me like a storm as I bury myself deep, whispering her name like a vow.

For a moment, the room is filled with nothing but the sound of our ragged breathing, the quiet rush of waves outside the villa the only reminder that the rest of the world still exists. Slowly, I pull out and collapse onto my back beside her.

She doesn't move at first, her chest rising and falling as she catches her breath. Then she shifts, turning her head to look at me. Her green eyes, still dark with satisfaction, meet mine, and for the first time, I see something I can't place. Something that digs under my skin and refuses to let go.

Eve's just unraveled me in a way I've never experienced. I know nothing about her other than her first name, yet I feel like I've been searching for her my entire life.

And that thought terrifies me.

Who the hell is this woman? And why can't I look away?

Aoife

I've hooked up with men before, but I've never taken them back to my room. Never allowed them to sleep in my bed. It's reckless. But I couldn't stop myself.

Why this man? Who is he?

The question plays in my mind as I stare at him, sprawled across my sheets like he owns the place, his chest rising and falling in the steady rhythm of sleep. The moonlight streaming through the window casts soft shadows across his sharp features. For a moment, I can almost forget how dangerous this feels. Almost.

Carefully, I ease out from under his arm and slide out of bed. My feet are silent on the cool tiled floor. Slipping into my silk robe, I cinch it at the waist, then glance over my shoulder. He's still asleep, breaths deep and steady, sprawled across the sheets like sin in human form.

As I move toward the chair, my eyes catch on his clothes. Earlier, he folded them with deliberate precision, as if he hadn't just fucked me in the shower with the kind of hunger that leaves bruises. It should've been endearing. Instead, it twists something deep in my gut, a knot of suspicion I don't care to examine.

A quick search of his pocket turns up nothing—no wallet, no

clues. Then, my gaze shifts to his phone lying on a nearby table. Bingo. I swipe the screen, but of course, it's locked.

Biting my lip, I debate what my next move will be when the ringing of my own phone startles me. My heart leaps into my throat as I grab it, rushing to the deck to avoid waking him.

As I step outside, I'm greeted by the warm night air and the soft sound of waves lapping against the stilts of the villa, filling the quiet around me. The scent of salt and sea is calming, but it does little to ease the frantic pace of my heart.

I glance at the screen. *Ruairi.*

"Shit," I mutter under my breath before answering.

"Finally," he says, his voice harsh with irritation. "You were supposed to call me hours ago."

"I got distracted," I reply, keeping my voice low as I lean against the railing.

"Distracted how?" he demands, the overprotective edge in his tone unmistakable.

"Relax," I say, rolling my eyes even though he can't see me. "I was at a beach party and lost track of time."

He sighs. "You went dark. Anything could've happened."

"But nothing did happen." The lie slips off my tongue so easily. Something definitely did happen, and it's currently asleep in my bed.

Ruairi is mid-lecture when I feel it—a presence behind me. My body tenses instinctively as I glance over my shoulder.

It's him.

He's completely naked, his body silhouetted in the moonlight, every hard line and muscle on display. His eyes are heavy-lidded, his gaze locked on mine with a heat that sends a shiver down my spine. And he's hard. Impossibly, painfully hard.

"Everything okay?" Ruairi's voice crackles through the phone, breaking the spell.

"Yeah," I say quickly, turning my back to Eamon and gripping the railing tighter. "Just stubbed my toe. I'm fine."

Eamon steps closer, his hands bracketing my hips from

behind. My body betrays me instantly as heat pools low in my belly.

"It's late, and I'm exhausted," I tell Ruairi, my voice trembling just enough to make me wince.

"Aoife—"

"I'll call you in the morning." I don't wait for a response, ending the call and tucking my phone into the pocket of my robe as Eamon presses his chest against my back.

"Making excuses, love?" he whispers, his breath warm against my ear.

"You startled me," I reply, though my voice lacks conviction as his hands slide up my sides, his thumbs grazing the undersides of my breasts.

"Did I?" he asks, his tone teasing as he unties the robe, and it slides off my shoulders, pooling at my feet on the deck. Gently, he kicks it out of the way.

Before I can respond, Eamon spins me around, lifting me onto the railing so that I'm perched precariously, with nothing but his strength keeping me steady. The night air kisses my skin as he spreads my thighs, stepping between them with a confidence that leaves no room for hesitation.

"Someone could see us," I say, though there's no real protest in my voice.

His lips curl into a smile as he leans closer. "Let them."

The heat in his voice sends a shiver through me, and I can't help the soft laugh that escapes my lips. "Are you always this reckless?"

One hand slides to the back of my neck, holding me in place as his other grips my hip, pulling me flush against him. "Only with you." The hard length of him presses against my center. My hands clutch his shoulders as he pushes inside me in one smooth, unrelenting motion.

The sensation steals my breath. The way he fills me is over-whelming and perfect all at once. His movements are fast and rough, each thrust driving me closer to the edge as my legs wrap around him, holding him tighter.

The gentle rhythm of the waves mingles with the cries that spill from my lips as he takes me, his pace unrelenting. His hand moves between us, his thumb finding the bundle of nerves that sends electricity shooting through my body.

"Look at me," he growls, his voice low and commanding as he thrusts harder, deeper.

My gaze snaps to his, and the intensity in his eyes sends me over the edge, my body clenching around him as I shatter in his arms. He follows moments later, his movements faltering as his release crashes over him like a storm, raw and all-consuming.

For a moment, neither of us moves. Our bodies stay locked together, skin slick with sweat, breaths ragged and tangled in the silence. The world feels distant—like it's paused to let us exist in this one breathless moment.

With a final brush of his lips against mine, Eamon steps back, helping me down from the railing, his hands lingering on my hips as if reluctant to let go. My legs tremble as I find my footing, my body still humming from the intensity of what just happened.

When his hands finally fall away, it's like coming down too fast from a high I didn't know I was chasing. The space between us feels too wide, too cold. There's something about him I can't shake. He's a stranger, yet it feels like he sees a part of me I've always kept hidden. Like he's touching a place I'm not sure I want exposed.

"Who are you?" I ask, the question slipping out before I can stop it.

He tilts his head slightly, his lips curving into a slow, deliberate smile. "Someone you'll wish you never met," he says, his voice deep and velvety. A chill skitters down my spine.

I narrow my eyes, frustration warring with the undeniable pull he has on me. "That's not an answer."

"It's the truth," he counters, stepping closer, his eyes locked onto mine. His hand lifts, his knuckles brushing against my jaw, lingering there as if daring me to push him away. "You should be running from me, Eve."

"Yet you're the one who can't seem to let go," I say my voice thick with defiance.

His smirk deepens, a dangerous glint in his eyes as his hands slide to the back of my neck, pulling me a fraction closer. "Perhaps I don't plan to."

The words hit harder than I expect. It's a confession cloaked in something darker, something that sets my pulse racing all over again. I open my mouth to respond, to throw his words back at him, but nothing comes out. He's stolen every thought, every breath, leaving me standing here, exposed.

"You don't trust easily," he says, his voice softer now, though no less intense. "But you let me in."

"I wanted to see who you are when you think no one's watching," I counter.

He chuckles softly, the sound low and rich, his thumb brushing along my jaw. "Careful, love. You might not like what you find."

"I'm not afraid of you," I whisper, though the tremor in my voice betrays me.

His eyes flash with something that feels like both a warning and a promise. "We all have our demons," he murmurs, the words a dark caress. "The real question is, what happens when they recognize each other?"

Eve is still sound asleep, her red hair fanned out on her pillow. When my eyes opened, and I realized last night wasn't a dream, that her naked body was pressed up against mine, I wanted to sink inside her and lose myself all over again.

I don't know what's gotten into me. I never spend the night with a woman. I fuck them and leave them—no strings attached. But there's something different about Eve. Something mysterious that makes me want to unravel her. To learn all her secrets.

I'm confident it won't last. We'll have some fun for a few days. I'll fuck her until she's out of my system, and then I'll be on my way home. Speaking of home, I need to check-in.

Sliding my pants on, I grab my phone. The morning air is warm. The salty tang of the ocean lingers on the breeze as I step onto the deck. The water below glistens, a vast stretch of turquoise that would be almost peaceful if my mind weren't already spinning.

I glance toward the villa. She's still asleep. I should leave her there and slip away for a while to clear my head, but something pulls me back. I find myself dialing room service and ordering everything on their breakfast menu. The absurdity of it doesn't hit me until I hang up, but even then, I can't bring myself to care.

My thumb hovers over the screen before I scroll to Seamus's name and hit call. It rings twice before his gruff voice comes through.

"Boss."

"How's everything back home?" I ask, keeping my voice low as I glance over my shoulder into the bedroom. The last thing I need is Eve overhearing any part of this conversation.

"Quiet for now. No signs of movement. But I don't trust the silence," Seamus replies.

"Neither do I," I mutter, running a hand through my hair. The Callahan's have been a thorn in my side for months. Their constant skirmishes on the edge of my territory are a calculated game meant to test my patience.

"You think they'll make a move while you're gone?" Seamus asks, the question loaded.

"They're not that stupid," I reply, though the thought lingers at the back of my mind. "Keep the boys on high alert. If the Callahan's make a move, handle it. Make sure they know where the boundaries are."

Seamus grunts in acknowledgment. "And you? Still in paradise?"

I glance out at the endless water, but it's not the view I'm thinking about. It's her—her green eyes and fiery hair that matches her temperament. The way her body welcomed mine as if she was made for me. "For now."

"Will you be returning tomorrow?"

"No," I say curtly. "I've delayed my flight home."

"Anything I should know?" Seamus presses, his voice dipping into that careful tone that tells me he's prying without wanting to seem like he's prying.

"Nothing that concerns you," I snap, sharper than intended. The tightness in my chest comes out of nowhere. It's unwelcome and hard to ignore. I don't owe Seamus an explanation. I'm the one in charge. And yet, the fact that he even asked grates more than it should.

Especially when I don't have a damn answer myself.

"Understood," Seamus says. "Anything else?"

"Not for now. I'll check in later."

I end the call, tucking my phone into my pocket as I lean against the railing. My jaw tightens as I consider the implications of staying here longer than planned. This was supposed to be a quick stop. Business, and nothing else. But then I met Eve. She's an unexpected complication.

Once again, I tell myself it's nothing. A few days, and I'll be on a plane home. And Eve? She'll be nothing more than a memory. Even as I say those words, I know they're nothing but a lie. The truth is, she's already under my skin, and I don't know how to stop it.

A sharp chime breaks the silence. Room service.

I drag a hand down my face and force myself to move, grateful for the distraction. Because if I sit in this feeling any longer, I might admit just how deep it already runs.

When I open the door, I find the attendant standing there with a polished smile, a cart piled high with silver-domed plates and fresh fruit arranged like art. He offers a quiet greeting I barely register, then pushes the cart inside and begins setting everything up with practiced efficiency.

The soft shuffle of footsteps from behind catches my attention. When I glance over my shoulder, Eve is standing in the doorway of the bedroom. She's slipped back into the silk robe, the one that barely skims the tops of her thighs. The same one she wore last night.

The morning light pouring through the windows wraps around her like a spotlight, highlighting every curve beneath the delicate fabric. Her nipples are visible through the thin silk, a quiet invitation she doesn't even realize she's giving.

The room service attendant notices, too. His gaze drifts toward her, lingering a beat too long.

Jealousy flares hot and sharp in my chest. Unreasonable. Immediate. Mine.

"Focus on the food," I snap, my tone cold and cutting as his head jerks back toward the cart.

"Apologies, sir," he mumbles, shifting uncomfortably as I step closer, taking the receipt and pen from his hand with deliberate force.

"Make sure it doesn't happen again," I add, my voice low and dangerous as I sign the slip and shove it back at him. "Or next time my reminder won't be only words."

The tension hangs heavy as I step between him and Eve, positioning myself in a way that leaves no room for misinterpretation. He quickly finishes his task and exits the villa.

"Everything alright?" she asks, her voice soft and still tinged with sleep as the door clicks shut behind me.

"Perfect," I reply, though the edge in my voice betrays me.

"What's all this?"

"Breakfast," I say, gesturing to the feast.

"Breakfast?" she repeats, her lips twitching like she's fighting a smile. "You do realize there's enough food here to feed a small army?"

I shrug as I sit at the table. "I didn't know what you'd want, so I got everything."

She watches me for a moment, something flickering in her green eyes before she pads over to the table.

"So," I say, leaning back slightly as I watch her pile fresh fruit onto her plate. "What does Eve do when she's not sunbathing in the Maldives?"

She hesitates for a fraction of a second before answering. "I travel," she says, her tone breezy, almost rehearsed. "My parents are big believers in self-discovery or whatever you want to call it." She waves her hand. "So, I figured I'd see the world before getting pulled into the family business."

"And what business is that?" I ask, keeping my voice casual.

"Acquisitions," she says quickly. Before I can press further, she glances up at me with a pointed look. "What about you? What brings you here?"

I mirror her evasive smile, leaning forward slightly. "My family is in the hotel business. I'm here checking out some property. Expansion plans."

"Family business," she says, her tone teasing as she takes a sip of her coffee. "Guess we've got that in common."

"Guess so," I reply, matching her tone. "So, this traveling of yours. Is it always solo?" I ask, trying to find out if she picks up men everywhere she goes.

"Mostly," she replies. "I like the freedom. No schedules to follow, no one to answer to."

"Sounds lonely."

"Not really. It's liberating, actually. I go where I want when I want. What about you?" she counters. "Does the hotel business keep you tethered to one place, or do you get to travel, too?"

"Usually, I stay in one place," I answer with a shrug. "This trip turned out to be a good excuse to mix work with a little pleasure."

"Sounds convenient," she says, lifting a fresh strawberry to her lips. She takes a slow bite, tongue catching a bead of juice before it can slip down her chin.

It shouldn't be erotic, but it is. Far too much.

"You could say that." It's all I can manage, my attention glued to the curve of her lips.

The conversation stalls for a moment, the air between us thick with unspoken truths and the weight of everything we're both holding back.

Her eyes flick to mine, steady and unreadable. "What are we doing here?" she asks suddenly.

I hold her gaze, unsure how to answer. Tension lingers as the unspoken question hangs between us.

What does happen next?

THE TABLE IS LADEN WITH FAR TOO MUCH FOOD, BUT the sheer absurdity of it has sparked an ease between us. Eamon seems at home in this setting, leaning back in his chair as he casually picks at a croissant, his movements relaxed, almost lazy.

I, on the other hand, can't seem to settle. My plate is half full, my coffee barely touched, and I find myself hyperaware of every glance he throws my way.

"So, this traveling of yours," he says, breaking the silence. "Is it always solo?"

"Mostly," I reply, spearing a piece of fruit with my fork. "I like the freedom. No schedules to follow, no one to answer to."

His brow arches slightly, the ghost of a smirk tugging at his lips. "Sounds lonely."

I shrug, keeping my tone breezy. "Not really. It's liberating, actually. I go where I want when I want."

It's not a lie, not exactly. But the truth, the *real* truth, is buried beneath layers I have no intention of uncovering.

"What about you?" I ask, deflecting the attention back to him. "Does the hotel business keep you tethered to one place, or do you get to travel, too?"

"Usually, I stay in one place," he says, his tone giving nothing away. "This trip turned out to be a good excuse to mix work with a little pleasure."

His deliberate vagueness is frustrating. "Sounds convenient."

"You could say that."

Silence stretches between us, thick and humming with something neither of us names. The waves outside lap gently against the villa, a soft rhythm that only makes the charged quiet feel louder. His eyes are on me. I can feel them. Watching. Waiting. Wanting.

I shift in my seat, suddenly too aware of the silk clinging to my skin, of the lingering taste of strawberry on my lips. My tongue darts out to catch a drop of juice at the corner of my mouth, and when I glance up, I find his gaze hasn't moved.

The question pounds in my mind, unrelenting, until it spills out before I can stop it. "What are we doing?"

His gaze sharpens, and he leans back slightly in his chair, studying me with that unreadable expression that I'm beginning to recognize as his default. "Enjoying ourselves," he says smoothly. "Isn't that enough?"

It *should* be. It *has* to be. Because I'm not interested in anything more. I have plans—plans that don't involve entangling myself with a man.

My focus is on something far more important. Proving to my father that I'm more than just the Quigley family's untouchable daughter. That I'm capable, ruthless, and worthy of stepping into the Syndicate he refuses to let me touch.

A relationship doesn't fit into that picture. Love doesn't fit into that picture. And yet, as I sit here with Eamon's dark, penetrating gaze fixed on me, I can't help but feel like I'm teetering on the edge of something I can't control.

"Maybe it is," I say, shrugging as if I'm as unaffected as he is. But the flutter in my chest betrays me, and I can't help but wonder if he notices.

His lips curve into a smile, but it's softer this time, almost teasing. "So, what do you say, Eve? No strings. No questions. Just this."

The idea is tempting. Too tempting. And I hate how much I want to say yes. I search for any cracks in the calm mask he wears. If he feels the pull between us as strongly as I do, he doesn't let it show.

"Just this," I repeat, my tone firmer now.

"Good," he says, leaning forward slightly, his eyes locking onto mine with a fierce, unrelenting intensity. "Because I'm not done with you, Eve. Not even close."

Something tightens low in my belly, but my face stays unreadable.

"Who said I'd let you walk away?"

The air between us feels lighter now, the tension shifting into something less daunting and more thrilling. I take a sip of my coffee, the warmth grounding me, even as my mind races with questions I know I'll never ask.

"So," I say, tilting my head, my voice light and teasing. "What's next on the agenda?"

His smirk returns, a spark of mischief lighting his eyes. "Oh, I have a few ideas."

The sun beats down on us as the private yacht speeds across the crystal-clear waters. Eamon stands at the bow, the wind tousling his dark hair as he casts a sidelong glance at me, his lips curving into a maddening smile.

"I'm starting to think you're showing off," I tease, leaning back against the plush seating with a glass of champagne in hand.

He chuckles, the sound low and rich. "If I wanted to impress you, I'd be the one piloting."

"Oh, please. Like you know how to drive this thing," I say as I set my glass on the small table beside me.

"Do you want me to prove it?" he challenges, his eyes narrowing in mock offense.

Before I can fire back, the yacht slows, and the captain announces that we've arrived at the sandbar. I lean over the side to catch a better view. My breath catches at the sight before me—a stretch of pristine white sand rising out of the endless cyan water, like something out of a dream.

A cabana has been set up, complete with loungers, a small bar, and snorkeling gear. I've seen many places in my travels, but this is the most breathtaking yet. For a moment, I forget myself, captivated by the scene.

Eamon steps up beside me, his arm brushing against mine. "Speechless?" he murmurs.

I glance up at him, rolling my eyes even as I smile. "Don't let it go to your head."

We wade into the warm, shallow water, laughing as the gentle waves lap at our legs. The sun glints off the surface, casting dappled reflections onto our skin.

Eamon moves closer, his hands skimming my waist, the heat of his touch sending a pleasant shiver through me. His lips brush against my ear as he whispers, "This better than your usual solo travels?"

"Maybe," I admit, trying to suppress a grin. "The company isn't half bad."

"Not half bad?" he repeats, as his hands tighten on my waist. Before I can react, he lifts me into the air, spinning us both as I shriek.

"Put me down," I laugh, though my arms instinctively wrap around his shoulders.

"Only if you admit you're having the time of your life," he says, his voice low and teasing as he finally sets me down.

"Fine," I reply, still catching my breath. "You're tolerable. Happy?"

"Not even close," he says, his fingers lingering on my bare skin. "I'll be happy when you admit that no one else will ever touch you the way I do. When you realize you're mine, whether you like it or not."

I arch a brow, refusing to let him see how his words make my pulse race. "Yours?" I repeat, my voice laced with challenge. "That's awfully confident for a man who hasn't proven he's worth keeping around."

My words are sharp, calculated, and meant to throw him off balance. But the truth is, I'm trying to regain my footing. Every look, every touch, every word from him feels like a tether pulling me closer, wrapping me tighter, and I can't afford to let that happen. Not when my world doesn't allow for distractions like this.

His grip tightens just enough to send a shiver through me. His gaze deepens, dark and full of intent. "Oh, love," he murmurs, leaning in until his lips are just a breath away from mine. "By the time I'm done with you, no one else will ever come close."

The way he says it, low and rough, a promise and a threat all at once, makes my pulse race. My body betrays me, leaning into him before I can stop myself. I hate how easily he makes me want more. What he doesn't realize is I won't give in to his panty-melting smiles or smooth words. This is fun and nothing more.

The hours pass in a blur of sun-soaked moments that feel too easy, too perfect. We snorkel through coral reefs as vibrant fish dart between us. Eamon playfully nudges me, pointing out the most colorful ones.

Later, we lounge under the cabana with icy drinks in hand. Eamon leans back in his chair, shirtless and far too smug, as we tease each other about who swam better.

"You cheated," I accuse, taking a long sip of my cocktail.

"Cheated?" he repeats, his brows lifting. "How does one cheat at snorkeling?"

"You splashed me on purpose," I say, narrowing my eyes. "You threw me off my game."

"Your game was questionable to begin with," he counters, his grin wide and unapologetic.

I toss a grape at him, laughing as he easily catches it in his hand. The banter feels effortless and natural. At some point, I realize I'm not just having fun—I'm enjoying *him*. The thought unsettles me, twisting my chest in a way that feels both foreign and dangerous.

I push it aside, blaming the intoxicating beauty of the Maldives.

This is temporary. A fleeting escape. It has to be.

<h1 style="text-align:center">Aoife</h1>

BACK AT THE VILLA, THE AIR FEELS CHARGED, THICK with the remnants of the day—salt, sun, and the undercurrent of the undeniable chemistry we share. I set my bag on the table, grabbing my phone, and immediately notice the string of missed calls and texts lighting up the screen.

Ruairi. Da.

The phone unlocks with a soft click, and a scroll through the messages reveals Ruairi's usual style—short, clipped, every word edged with frustration.

I clear my throat, forcing my voice to stay casual. "I need to make a phone call."

He turns to me. "Is everything okay?"

"Just something I need to handle," I say, avoiding his gaze. "It won't take long."

For a moment, he doesn't move, his sharp eyes studying me with a calculating intensity. But then he nods and motions toward the door.

"I'll give you some privacy," he says, his tone casual but edged with curiosity. He takes his drink and steps out onto the deck, sliding the glass door shut behind him.

I let out a breath I hadn't realized I was holding and scroll through the missed calls and texts one more time. My chest tightens as I open the most recent voicemail and press play.

"Aoife," my father's voice booms, his Irish lilt harsher than usual. "I haven't heard from you, and neither has your brother. You were supposed to call home this morning. If I don't hear back from you by tonight, I'll send my men to find you. Do not make me do that."

My stomach twists as his words echo in my head. *Do not make me do that.* The unspoken threat is clear. He'll use this as proof that I'm not capable, that I don't belong in the Syndicate. I've been working hard to prove that I'm strong and independent— that I can handle myself. I won't let a single mistake unravel my carefully constructed plan.

I glance toward the deck, where Eamon's looking out over the water, his broad shoulders illuminated by the soft hues of the setting sun. For a moment, I'm tempted to follow the pull he seems to have on me, to lose myself in the easy distraction he offers. But this isn't a conversation I can avoid.

Slipping into the bedroom, I close the door behind me and press the phone to my ear.

"Hi, Da."

"Aoife," he says, his tone warm but threaded with irritation. "You vanished. No calls. No texts. Do you have any idea what kind of risk that puts you in?"

"I'm sorry," I say quickly, keeping my voice low. "I got caught up in sightseeing."

There's a pause on the other end. "You're alone, right?" he asks.

"Of course," I lie, glancing around the room. It's then I notice them—Eamon's suitcases. They're neatly stacked in the corner of my bedroom. My heart skips a beat, my mind racing with so many questions. When did he do this? How did they get here?

"Aoife?" my father prompts, his voice cutting through my thoughts.

"Yes," I reply quickly, forcing my focus back on the call. "No one's here but me."

His skepticism is almost tangible, but he doesn't press. "Alright," he finally says, though his tone is far from convinced. "But call your brother tomorrow. He's worried, and you know how he gets."

"I will," I promise, forcing my voice to sound light and unconcerned.

"Do not make me rethink allowing you to continue traveling *alone*," he warns. His emphasis on the word alone doesn't escape me.

"I won't. Talk soon."

I hang up and let out a shaky breath, my eyes flicking back to the suitcases. Why are they here? Eamon hadn't mentioned staying longer—or staying at all, for that matter.

This double life I've crafted, balancing who I am and who I pretend to be, is beginning to feel like a house of cards. And Eamon? He's the wild card I can't predict. One wrong move and it'll all come crashing down.

When I return to the deck, he's leaning casually against the railing, his arms crossed over his chest. "Everything okay?" he asks, his voice low.

"Fine," I say lightly, brushing past to lean against the railing beside him. "When were you planning on telling me you moved in?"

He turns to look at me, the fading sunlight catching the mischievous glint in his eyes. "I thought it was obvious."

"Obvious?" I repeat, arching a brow. "You don't think that's something you should've run by me first?"

Eamon shrugs, unbothered. "I had my things sent here while we were out. Figured it'd save me the trouble of doing it myself now."

My pulse kicks up, a mix of indignation and something far more dangerous—excitement. "You figured?"

His hand brushes against mine on the railing. "You're not complaining, are you?"

I open my mouth to retort, but before I can get a word out, he grips my waist and pulls me onto his lap as he sits down on one of the cushioned deck chairs. My breath catches as I settle against him, his hands firm and possessive on my hips.

"Eamon," I say, trying to keep my voice steady, though the heat of his body against mine is already making my thoughts scatter. "You can't just—"

"I can," he cuts me off, his voice low and commanding, his lips brushing against the shell of my ear. "And I will."

His words send a shiver through me, and I can't help the way my body reacts by leaning into him, even as my mind protests.

"You're impossible," I murmur, my hands resting on his chest, feeling the steady thrum of his heartbeat beneath my palms.

"And you love it," he counters, his lips trailing down my neck, his hands sliding beneath the hem of my dress.

I want to argue, but the words die on my tongue as his fingers skim the bare skin of my thighs, the heat of his touch igniting a fire that spreads through me.

His lips claim mine in a kiss that's all heat and possession, his hands pulling me closer until there's no space left between us. I gasp against his mouth as his fingers slide higher until they find exactly what they're looking for.

"You're already wet for me," he growls, his voice rough with desire as his fingers delve into my heat.

I bite my lip, refusing to give him the satisfaction of a moan, but he's relentless. His other hand tangles in my hair as he tilts my head back to meet his gaze.

"Don't hold back, love," he says, his voice low and demanding, his fingers moving with a rhythm that has me trembling in his lap.

The sound that escapes me is raw and unrestrained. It only seems to spur him on. His teeth graze my skin as his fingers work me with a precision that leaves me breathless.

I grip his shoulders, my nails digging into his skin as the pleasure builds, sharp and all-consuming. "Eamon," I gasp, my voice breaking as my body arches against him, chasing the release that's just within reach.

"Let go," he murmurs, his lips brushing against my ear. "I want to hear you come for me."

His words push me over the edge. My body shudders in his arms as waves of pleasure crash over me. Eamon holds me through it, his grip steady and unyielding as I come undone.

But he doesn't stop. He adjusts his grip, lifting me slightly while his fingers work quickly between us. The shift of fabric and the heat of his touch sends a jolt of desire straight through me.

It doesn't make sense how I can still want him like this seconds after falling apart. But my body doesn't care. It answers him anyway, aching all over again.

He positions me over his hard length, and in one smooth motion, he's inside me, the sudden fullness stealing my breath.

"Christ," he groans, his head tipping back as his fingers dig into my hips. "You're fucking perfect. Like you were made for me."

His intensity and the way he fills me leave me reeling. I move instinctively, my hands braced on his shoulders as I ride him, the rhythm building between us until it's all I can focus on.

His lips find mine again, the kiss messy and desperate as our movements grow more frantic. My release builds again, more intense this time, and when it hits, it pulls a choked cry from my lips.

Eamon follows moments later, his hands gripping me tightly as he thrusts into me one last time.

We stay like that for a moment, tangled together in the fading light, our breathing heavy as the sound of the waves fills the silence around us.

"You're still impossible," I murmur, my voice shaky but teasing as I rest my forehead against his.

"And you're still mine," he replies, his tone softer now but no less possessive.

Eamon

She stays in my arms for a few moments, her body soft and relaxed against mine. It's a sensation I can't quite describe. Comfort, maybe, but also something deeper, something I've never felt with any other woman. Usually, once it's over, I'm already thinking about what comes next, about moving on. Instead, my mind is quiet—content.

Eventually, she shifts, leaning back against the lounger, her hair a wild mess that somehow makes her look even more beautiful. I grab the blanket draped over the chair and settle it over us, the night air cooling slightly. "I'm starving," she finally says, breaking the silence.

I glance at her, smiling. "Didn't the five-star dinner at the sandbar do it for you?"

"It did," she admits with a laugh. "But that feels like hours ago. Plus, I've worked up an appetite."

She shoots me a playful look, and I can't help but laugh. "Alright, what are you in the mood for?"

"Something easy," she says, shrugging. "Pizza, maybe?"

"Pizza?" I echo, arching a brow. "Here?"

"Don't tell me you're too sophisticated for pizza," she teases, her green eyes sparkling.

"I didn't say that," I reply, pulling out my phone to order. "But I'm pretty sure the resort doesn't have a greasy takeaway menu lying around."

"Then you're not looking hard enough," she quips.

I call room service, asking for their best attempt at pizza and a bottle of wine. By the time I hang up, Eve has folded the blanket and is leaning against the doorway, her arms loosely crossed and a knowing smile playing on her lips.

"You're quick to take charge," she says, her voice edged with challenge.

I step closer, drawn in by the way her gaze holds mine. "Is that a complaint?"

"Not yet," she replies, her smile widening. "But I'm trying to figure out if you're always this decisive."

I stop a few inches from her, letting my eyes roam over her face before meeting her gaze again. "When it comes to getting what I want, yeah."

Her green eyes sparkle. "And what exactly do you want?"

"You'll figure it out, Eve. I'm good at making things obvious."

"Is that your idea of seduction?"

I lean in, my voice dropping low. "If I were trying to seduce you, you'd already know."

Her composure falters for just a moment before she recovers. "You talk a big game."

I chuckle softly, the sound rumbling between us. "I don't play games," I say, my voice a quiet promise. "And I don't stop until I win."

Her cheeks flush, but her defiance remains. "Lucky for you, I'm not the kind to walk away from a challenge."

I grin, stepping even closer, close enough to feel the heat of her body. "Good," I murmur. "Because I'm just getting started."

Eve's lips part slightly, and for a moment, the space between us feels electric. "Is that so?" she purrs and slides her hands up my chest, her fingers trailing deliberately slow until they reach the collar of my shirt. She tugs me down just enough to bring her lips to my ear. "Prove it," she whispers, her breath warm against my skin.

Before I can react, she presses a fleeting kiss to the corner of my mouth, a tease, a challenge, and then steps away, brushing past me as her fingers trail down my arm. She pauses at the doorway to the bedroom, her gaze lingering on me with a wicked glint in her eyes before disappearing inside.

I exhale slowly as I pour myself a glass of water, letting the cool liquid chase away the fire she ignited. But when she steps back out, all rational thought vanishes.

Eve's changed into tiny shorts that cling to her hips, her legs on full display like a fucking invitation. Her half-shirt rides up just enough to tease a glimpse of her toned stomach. The fabric clings to the curve of her breasts, daring me to look and making it impossible not to.

My body reacts instantly, heat surging low in my gut, my blood thrumming with the kind of need that demands release. I grip the glass in my hand tighter, the condensation slick against my skin, as I fight the urge to close the distance between us and pin her against the nearest wall.

She moves with an easy confidence, her every step a slow torment. The way her hips sway, the way her hair tumbles over her shoulders. Everything about her seems designed to undo me.

And the worst part? She has to know. She must see the way my eyes follow her, the way my body reacts in her presence. Or maybe she doesn't, and that thought alone drives me even closer to the edge.

A sharp chime breaks the moment, and I snap my head toward the door. Damn room service again.

"Saved by the bell," she teases.

I grunt, straightening and running a hand through my hair as I move to answer the door. A young attendant wheels in a tray topped with two pizzas and a bottle of wine. He glances once at Eve, his gaze lingering a fraction too long on her bare legs and my body tenses.

Another one. It's the same as yesterday. The same lingering look that stirs something dark and territorial in me. If every man here keeps staring at her like that, I might have to start making examples. I can't kill every bastard on this island before we leave, but the thought isn't entirely unappealing.

"Right there," I say, my voice clipped as I gesture toward the table.

He places the tray carefully, muttering a polite, "Enjoy your meal," before retreating. My eyes follow him until the door closes, the tension in my chest easing once he's gone.

"Territorial, are we?" Eve quips from behind me, her green eyes bright with amusement as she saunters over to the table.

Grabbing the wine, I pop the cork. "Just making sure people know their place."

"Mhmm," she hums, picking up a slice of pizza and taking a bite, her expression turning blissful. "You might have just earned a few points with this."

"Only a few?" I ask, pouring two glasses and handing her one as she settles onto the plush sofa.

She grins, patting the cushion beside her. "Guess you'll have to work for the rest."

I shake my head and sit next to her. The pizza isn't half bad, but the way she digs into it, making a satisfied hum, makes it taste even better.

"See?" she says, pointing a slice at me. "Pizza solves everything."

I chuckle, shaking my head. "I'll give you this one."

While we're eating, Eve grabs the remote and begins searching the guide on the big-screen television. "Do you watch movies?" she asks, scrolling through the options.

"Not often," I admit, leaning back and nursing my glass of wine.

She pauses, glancing over her shoulder at me. "What kind of person doesn't watch movies?"

"The kind with a lot of responsibilities," I say. "But I'll let you pick."

"Careful," she warns. "I could make you sit through a rom-com."

"Try it," I say, my tone low, teasing. "And I'll make you regret it."

She laughs, finally settling on a classic action movie. "Compromise," she says, tucking her feet under her.

She dims the lights as the movie starts, and I expect my mind to wander back to work, back to the Callahan's, back to anything but this moment. But it doesn't. Instead, I find myself drawn to her laugh, the way she reacts to the explosions on the screen, and her teasing commentary about the absurdity of the plot.

At some point, she leans into me, her head resting on my shoulder. It feels natural, her warmth seeping into me as I drape an arm around her.

"You're quiet," she says softly, glancing up at me.

"I'm just enjoying the moment," I reply.

Her lips curve into a small smile, one that feels more genuine than anything I've seen from her before. "You're full of surprises, you know that?"

"You've mentioned," I say, smirking.

Halfway through, her phone buzzes on the table. She picks it up, shielding the screen slightly as she unlocks it. Her expression softens almost immediately, her lips tugging into a small, wistful smile as she scrolls through whatever has her attention.

I glance over. "Should I be jealous?"

"It's just some family stuff," she says quickly, locking the screen and setting the phone down.

Eve doesn't elaborate, but her mind seems elsewhere now, her gaze distant even as she leans into me.

"What'd I miss?" she asks, nodding toward the screen.

"Explosions. Car chases. The usual," I reply, studying her for a moment before turning back to the movie.

What are you hiding, Eve? Before we leave this island, I plan to unravel all of your secrets.

51

Aoife

Eamon's arm rests across my shoulders, his fingers tracing slow circles on my skin. I sink against him, feeling the steady rise and fall of his chest beneath my cheek. It's comfortable—too comfortable as if we've done this a thousand times before.

The realization makes my chest tighten. This feels normal. Like a moment between two people who know each other. Who belong to each other. Except that we don't.

He's practically a stranger. A devastatingly gorgeous stranger I can't seem to keep my hands off, but still a stranger. Having insanely good sex with someone doesn't equate to this. Whatever *this* is.

I swallow hard, pulling myself back from the ridiculous thought. This is fun. No questions. No strings. That's what we agreed on, and that's all it needs to be. I can't allow myself to fall into the trap of pretending this is anything more.

A soft sigh escapes as I shift slightly to get more comfortable. The wine is smooth, and the movie is forgettable, but I'm aware of every point of contact between us. Eamon's arm around me, the warmth of his body, the steady brush of his fingers. The lie plays on repeat—just a harmless distraction, nothing more. Now if only my traitorous heart would get the message.

The buzzing of my phone pulls me out of the moment. My sister-in-law's name flashes across the screen, and a quiet smile pulls at my lips. I swipe it open to read her message.

Bridget: Saoirse misses her Aunt Aoife. Look at this little face. She's begging you to come home for her birthday next month.

Attached to the text are a few new photos of my niece. Saoirse's tiny face is lit with a wide grin, her red curls sticking out in all directions as she clutches the *Rakosníček* I sent her from Prague. As soon as I saw it in that quiet little shop, I knew she'd love it. Now, seeing it in her chubby hands, it's like I'm right there with her, and yet I'm so far away.

Another message follows.

Bridget: She's almost walking now. You don't want to miss it.

Warmth floods my chest as I stare at the screen. Saoirse is perfection. Innocent, untouched by the weight of our family's name. Her wide green eyes sparkle with Ruairi's stubbornness. I hope that everything I'm trying to do now makes her future easier.

"Should I be jealous?" Eamon asks as his arm tightens around me slightly.

I glance up at him, startled to find him watching me. His blue eyes hold a quiet curiosity that makes my stomach twist even more.

"It's just some family stuff," I say, forcing a faint smile as I lock the phone and set it aside. "What'd I miss?"

"Explosions. Car chases. The usual," he replies.

I refocus my attention on the television, but I can feel his gaze lingering on me for a moment longer before he relaxes. His fingers resume their slow, lazy circles on my arm, and the warmth of his touch pulls me back to the present.

For now, I let myself sink into the moment, letting the guilt and the complicated realities of home drift further away.

As the movie ends, Eamon shifts beside me, his arm tightening around my shoulders. "Ready for bed?" he murmurs, his voice sending a shiver down my spine.

I nod, letting him lead me to the bedroom.

Once inside, he doesn't let go, his hands settling on my arms as he studies me, his blue eyes dark with intent. Slowly, deliberately, he lifts the hem of my shirt, his fingers grazing my skin.

"You won't need this," he says, his voice thick, as he pulls it over my head and lets it fall to the floor.

A smile tugs at my lips as I reach for him, but he catches my wrists, holding them firmly as he leans in, his lips brushing against my ear. "I've got it," he whispers, his tone full of promise.

The world outside ceases to exist as I sink onto the bed beneath him, his touch chasing away everything except the fire simmering between us.

Eamon

THE VILLA IS QUIET NOW. THE ONLY SOUND IS THE rhythmic splash of the waves outside. Eve is curled up beside me, her breathing slow and steady, her red hair fanned out across the pillow. The sight of her like this, relaxed and unguarded, does something to me I don't want to name.

I should feel satisfied. Each time I fuck her, I tell myself it'll be enough. That she'll loosen her hold on me, and I'll finally work her out of my system. But instead, it's the opposite. I'm becoming addicted.

The thought lingers as I watch her sleep. It's not just the way her body feels beneath mine, though that alone is enough to undo me. It's the way she laughs. The way she looks at me like she knows exactly what kind of man I am and doesn't care.

My jaw tightens as I run a hand through my hair, trying to shake the thoughts away. This is temporary. Fleeting. It has to be. But when she shifts closer to me, her hand brushing against my chest, all my resolve crumbles. I press a kiss to the top of her head, allowing myself one stolen breath of peace even as I feel the chains tightening.

For now, I let her stay. For now, I let myself want her.

But reality never stays at bay for long. As much as I'd like to keep losing myself in her, I can't completely ignore the responsibilities waiting for me back home. Cleaning up the mess the Callahan's caused. My Syndicate. The world I've built and fought to hold onto doesn't allow for distractions like this, no matter how tempting.

Seamus will want an update. He's loyal to a fault, but he's no fool. If I don't handle this, the questions will pile up, and the last thing I need is anyone thinking I'm distracted or, worse, weak.

I slip out of bed carefully, not wanting to wake her and grab my phone from the table. Stepping outside, I leave the sliding glass door cracked open. The night air wraps around me as I dial Seamus. The line barely rings before he picks up.

"Boss," Seamus says, his voice rough but alert.

"I'm extending my trip," I tell him, keeping my tone measured. "There are a few loose ends I need to tie up here."

There's a pause, and I can practically hear the wheels turning in his head. "Is this about the Callahan's?" he asks cautiously. "Because if it is, you should be back here. We can't afford to lose ground."

"It's not about the Callahan's."

"Then what is it about?" Seamus presses his tone harder now. "You've been gone longer than planned. The men are starting to ask questions. They need to see you here, running things, or—"

"Or what?" I cut him off, my grip on the rail tightening.

"They're beginning to think you're losing control. That you're distracted," Seamus says bluntly.

My chest tightens, anger flaring hot and fast. "Distracted? I've bled for this Syndicate. Built it from the ground up. Don't mistake me being out of sight for not being in full control."

"Then come back," Seamus snaps, his frustration bleeding through. "Handle things yourself before someone gets the wrong idea. I'm doing what I can, but—"

"You're overstepping." The calm I'd been holding onto slips away, and my voice rises, cutting through the stillness of the night.

"Your job is to keep things running while I'm gone, not question my decisions."

Silence crackles on the other end.

"Are you done?" I press, my tone cold and unyielding.

"Yes, boss," Seamus finally says, his voice clipped.

"Good. I'll be in touch." I end the call without waiting for a response.

A breath escapes as I rake my fingers through tangled hair and turn back toward the villa. But the sight of Eve standing in the doorway stops me cold.

She's wrapped in nothing but the sheet from the bed, her hair tousled, her eyes locked onto mine. "Didn't mean to wake you," I say, softening my voice.

Instead of answering, she steps forward, releasing the sheet. It slips from her fingers and pools at her feet. The air leaves my lungs in a slow, controlled exhale, my gaze locked on her bare form. The call is already a distant memory.

"Is everything okay?" she asks, her voice pointed. Her green eyes narrow slightly, studying me with just enough interest to make my skin prickle.

Heat lingers in my gaze as I close the distance between us in a few steady strides. "Nothing I can't handle," I murmur as my palm presses flat against her lower back, pulling her flush against me.

She arches a brow, clearly unimpressed by the excuse. "Who's Seamus?"

"No one you need to worry about," I reply smoothly, brushing off the question as I lift her effortlessly into my arms.

She loops them around my neck. "You avoid questions too well for my liking."

I chuckle softly, pressing a kiss to her shoulder as I carry her back into the bedroom. "And you're far too tempting for me to care right now."

Her lips twitch into a small smile, but her eyes linger on mine, searching for something I'm not ready to give. There's curiosity there, but I don't let her dig any deeper. Not tonight.

The mattress dips beneath her as I ease her onto the bed. She relaxes back against the pillows as I stand there watching her. The way the dim light catches the red in her hair, the way her gaze never strays from me, calm yet challenging all at once.

"Like what you see?" she asks, amusement dancing in her voice.

"You're dangerous, Eve," I reply as I crawl over her.

She raises an eyebrow, a teasing smile tugging at the corner of her lips. "I'm dangerous?"

"You have no idea," I murmur, trailing my fingers along the bare skin of her thigh. The heat that sparks between us is immediate, a current I can't seem to escape.

"I could say the same about you."

The words hang between us for a beat, her voice quieter now. For a moment, I think about giving her something real, one small piece of who I am, of the things I carry, but the instinct dies before it can take hold.

Instead, I slide my hand higher, leaning in until my lips brush against hers. "Then I guess we're a good match." My voice dips, heat curling in my chest as I tug lightly on her lower lip.

She doesn't argue. Doesn't press for more. She just kisses me back as her fingers tangle in my hair.

I lose myself in her again, in the taste of her, in the feel of her body pressed against mine. It's easier to let this pull between us drown out everything else.

Later, when she's curled against me, her breathing even and slow, I lie awake, staring at the ceiling. I tell myself I'll leave eventually, that this thing between us will burn out just as quickly as it started. But with her in my arms, the lie doesn't feel as convincing as it should.

Aoife

When I wake up, the villa is bathed in the golden glow of early morning, the quiet stillness of this place wrapping around me like a blanket. Waking up with Eamon's warmth beside me, his arm heavy across my waist, has become a familiar routine.

It's been weeks now, the days blurring together into something that feels like a dream. Sun-drenched afternoons on secluded beaches, lazy evenings spent tangled in each other, and nights filled with more heat and passion than I thought possible. I'd call it bliss if I didn't know better.

Because the truth is, we don't talk about anything real. I don't ask questions. Neither does he. It's unspoken—this thing between us. No strings. No complications. Just us, tucked away here where the rest of the world feels like it doesn't exist.

I roll onto my side, propping myself on my elbow as I study him. He's still asleep, his face relaxed. The sharp intensity I've come to know so well is nowhere to be found. Without that smirk or the intense stare he always wears like armor, he almost looks peaceful. Vulnerable. It's disarming seeing him like this, and the attraction I've been trying to ignore digs in deeper, stubborn and unwelcome.

I remind myself that this isn't real. This is temporary. Nothing more than a stolen moment outside the lives we both clearly want to avoid. That any day now, I'll wake up and be ready to move on.

But as I lie here, watching the rise and fall of his chest, I can't shake the feeling that this is starting to feel too comfortable. There's a pull between us, something I can't explain, and I hate that I feel it. This isn't supposed to happen.

We're not anything.

Having great sex with a man doesn't make him yours, and it sure as hell doesn't make him safe. I've lived with secrets my entire life, and I'd bet anything he's keeping his own.

The man is a mystery, and that's all he should ever be.

My phone buzzes on the nightstand. I grab it and glance at the screen.

Ruairi: Call me today.

The knot in my stomach tightens as I swipe the message open. It's short, clipped, and carries the weight of his concern, but there's something else there too—suspicion.

It's getting harder and harder to hide Eamon from him. He knows me too well. *Twintuition* we used to call it when we were younger. I haven't returned his calls in days. He's already been asking too many questions about why I'm still in the Maldives. I usually don't stay in one place for so long and I'm running out of excuses. But Ruairi will continue to push, probe, and demand answers because that's what he does. He never lets things go.

And if Ruairi finds out I'm with a man, he'll shift straight into overprotective brother mode, demanding to know who Eamon is, whether I'm safe, and if I've lost my mind. I can't let that happen. Not when I've worked so hard to show everyone I can take care of myself.

With a heavy exhale, I swipe the message away and set the phone down, forcing the tension in my shoulders to ease. When I roll over, I find Eamon watching me, his blue eyes now awake and alert. "Morning," he murmurs, his voice rough with sleep.

"Morning," I reply.

He stretches, the sheet slipping dangerously low on his hips.

"You're quiet," he says, studying me. "Regretting something?"

I arch a brow, masking the way my pulse quickens. "I don't do regrets."

"Good." He pushes up on one elbow, his gaze locked onto mine. For a moment, I feel like he's about to say something else, something real, but then the corner of his mouth lifts. "Get dressed."

I blink. "Excuse me?"

He throws the covers off and stands, stretching his arms lazily as he glances over his shoulder. "We're going out. Get dressed."

"Where exactly are we going?"

"You'll see," he says with maddening confidence as he disappears into the bathroom.

A half-hour later, I'm gripping Eamon's waist as the jet ski slices through the water. He's reckless, pushing the engine harder than necessary. Every bump sends my heart into my throat.

"This is your idea of a day out?" I shout over the roar, my voice a mix of laughter and protest.

He glances back at me, his grin smug. "You said you wanted fun, didn't you?"

"I didn't say death wish."

He laughs, speeding up until I'm clutching him tighter, torn between terror and exhilaration.

By the time we stop at a secluded stretch of white sand, my legs are shaking as I climb off the jet ski. "You're insane."

"You love it," he replies unapologetically.

I roll my eyes, but I can't deny the truth. Being with Eamon makes me feel alive.

Grabbing a small bag strapped to the back of the jet ski, he nods toward the shore. "Come on."

My curiosity is piqued as I watch him unroll a blanket and

unpack what he brought—champagne, fruit, and cheese. Simple but thoughtful.

"You've got layers, Eamon," I say, popping a strawberry into my mouth. "This almost looks romantic."

He leans back, watching me with that unreadable intensity. "Maybe I do, and maybe it is." I laugh softly, shaking my head, but his gaze lingers on me, serious now. "What happens when you leave?" he asks, his voice low but pointed.

The question catches me off guard, and I pause, the strawberry frozen halfway to my lips. "Excuse me?"

"You can't stay here forever," he says, his eyes locked on mine. "Eventually, you'll have to go home. What's waiting for you there?"

I force a smile, trying to play it off. "Why the sudden interest in my future?"

His fingers drum once against his thigh before stilling. "Because I want to know."

The weight of his gaze presses against me, and I sigh, leaning back on my hands as I glance toward the horizon. "My father runs a business," I say, choosing my words carefully. "He wants me to stay out of it. Says it's not a place for me."

He doesn't move, but something shifts in his eyes, a glimmer of something darker. "And what do you want?"

"I want to work for him," I admit. "Da underestimates me. Always has. I refuse to be someone who sits on the sidelines and lets other people make decisions for me the rest of my life."

Eamon shifts, sitting up straighter as he studies me. "And you think this trip will change his mind?"

"When I get home, I'll show him that I'm capable and can take care of myself. That I'm more than just his little girl," I say, my voice firmer now. "He'll have no choice but to take me seriously."

There's a pause, the weight of my words hanging between us.

"You're stubborn," he says finally, his tone almost amused.

I glance at him, my lips twitching into a small smile. "Takes one to know one."

"You're not afraid of the fight, are you?"

"No," I reply, meeting his gaze. "Are you?"

His smile returns, slow and dangerous, but he doesn't answer. Instead, he picks up the champagne and refills my glass, his eyes lingering on me.

The conversation shifts after that, lightening as we tease each other over who was better on the jet ski. But Eamon's question stays with me, the way he asked it, the way he looked at me like he was trying to figure out more than I was willing to give.

And for a fleeting moment, I wonder if he already knows.

I'm startled awake by the sharp, insistent ringing of my phone. My heart jumps into my throat as I blink into the darkness, disoriented. The room is still, the only light coming from the faint glow of my screen.

Ruairi.

I'll call him tomorrow. The last thing I want is to argue with him right now. I swipe to deny the call and lay back against the pillows, trying to calm the sudden rush of unease.

The phone rings again.

He's not going to give up. I exhale shakily and answer it this time, whispering, "What the hell are you doing calling me in the middle of the night?"

"Why are you whispering?" There's a beat of silence. "Forget it. It doesn't matter."

"Hang on a minute," I say as I slip out of bed, glancing toward Eamon's sleeping form. He's still, his breathing steady. Quietly, I slip out of the bedroom, closing the door behind me. "What's going on that couldn't wait until morning?"

Ruairi's voice comes through, tight and unsteady in a way I've never heard before. "There's been an accident."

I freeze, the words not making sense. "What kind of accident?"

"Mam and Da," he says, his voice thick. "They were on their way back from a fundraising gala. A truck hit them. Head-on. They didn't make it."

The floor feels like it drops out from under me, and I grip the arm of a nearby chair for balance. "That's not funny."

"Do you think I'd joke about something like this?" he snaps.

I stumble onto the sofa, the phone trembling in my hand. "You're wrong. They can't be—"

"They're gone, Aoife," he says quietly, his voice breaking.

The words hit like a physical blow, knocking the air from my lungs. My vision blurs, my chest heaving as I try to process what he's telling me. *They're gone.*

"No," I whisper, pressing the heel of my hand to my forehead like I can somehow stop the spiral of grief swallowing me whole.

Ruairi inhales shakily on the other end of the line. "You need to come home."

I blink, unable to focus through the haze of panic and disbelief.

"The resort's driver is waiting for you," he says firmly. "I've chartered a plane. It's ready for you at the airport."

"Ruairi, I—" My voice cracks. I want to argue, to tell him I don't know what to do, but the words won't come.

"You don't have to do anything except get on the plane," he says, his tone softening, even though I know he's barely holding it together himself. "I'll be waiting for you when you land."

The call ends, and I sit in the darkness for a moment, staring at nothing. I'm numb.

The words replay in my mind, over and over, a cruel loop I can't escape. My parents. Dead. Just like that.

A sob threatens to break free, and I press a hand to my mouth to stop it. I can't lose it right now. I don't have time.

Standing on unsteady legs, I quietly walk back into the bedroom. Eamon's still asleep, his face relaxed in the low light. Something in my chest cracks wide open at the sight of him.

This is it. The decision's been made for me. It's over.

I grab a small bag and throw a few things inside—clothes, a phone charger, my passport. My movements are quick and mechanical, my mind working on autopilot as I fight to hold myself together.

When I'm done, I grab a notepad from the desk and a pen. I pause, the pen hovering over the paper as I stare at the empty space. For a moment, I consider leaving Eamon a way to contact me. The thought lingers longer than it should, tempting me. But I quickly push it out of my head.

That's not how this works. I press the pen to the page, steadying my shaking hand.

Eamon,
Thank you for everything—for the time, for the memories. For making me forget the rest of the world, if only for a little while. But I've realized it's time to go back to reality. I won't forget this or you.
~Eve.

After setting the note on the nightstand, I pause, looking at him one last time, committing every detail to memory. He shifts slightly, a faint furrow appearing between his brows, and I turn away before I can change my mind.

With my bag slung over my shoulder, I slip out of the villa as quietly as I can. Outside, the resort's driver is waiting just as Ruairi promised.

I slip into the car and close the door softly behind me, the sound echoing like a final goodbye. As we pull away, I stare straight ahead, refusing to look back. I don't need to see the villa disappearing to feel the loss of the man I was never meant to fall for.

I tell myself this is for the best. That once I'm home, I'll forget him.

But as the distance grows, I already know I'm lying.

Eamon

A LOW RUMBLE OF THUNDER JOLTS ME AWAKE. FOR A moment, I lie there, disoriented, staring at the ceiling as the distant rumble rolls through the air. Rain patters faintly against the villa's windows, a sharp contrast to the usual stillness of the Maldives.

I shift, instinctively reaching for Eve, but my hand is met with nothing but an empty space. My brows pull together as I sit up, the faint glow of early morning spilling into the room. The sheets are cool as if she hasn't been there for hours.

"Eve?" My voice is rough, sleep still clinging to it. I scan the room, expecting to find her slipping out of the bathroom or perched on the deck like she sometimes does when she wakes before me. But there's nothing.

A sinking feeling settles deep in my gut as I stand and check the rest of the villa. The silence presses in. There's no sign of her anywhere, and for a moment, the absence of her presence feels more real than anything else.

And then I see it.

A single sheet of paper sits on the nightstand, folded neatly, my name written across the front.

I hesitate for a fraction of a second before picking it up, my fingers brushing the paper like it might burn me as I unfold it and read.

Eamon,
Thank you for everything—for the time, for the memories. For
making me forget the rest of the world, if only for a little while.
But I've realized it's time to go back to reality. I won't forget this
or you.
~Eve.

The words blur in front of me, but not because I don't understand them. I do. Eve's gone.

I crumble the note in my hand, my chest tightening in a way that's unfamiliar, unwelcome. I've woken up alone before countless times, in fact. But this is different. The loss of her is like a blade to the gut, sharp and immediate.

Dragging a hand down my face, I pace the room as the note burns in my fist. My jaw tightens, the ache in my chest refusing to ease. I let myself get attached to her. The woman who never asked for my last name, just like I never asked for hers. We were playing a game, but somewhere along the way, I stopped pretending.

Because the truth I didn't want to admit is staring me dead in the face.

I was falling in love with her.

And now she's gone.

Staring at nothing, I try to make sense of what I'm feeling. Weeks. It's been weeks of waking up beside her, of letting myself believe, if only for a fleeting moment that this could be something more.

I should've known better.

No strings. No questions. I remind myself bitterly. That was the deal. And now, without so much as a goodbye, she's walked out of my life.

I sink into the chair beside the window, staring out at the rain-slicked horizon as I pull the airline website up on my phone. It's time to go home.

After I book the first available flight back to Dublin, I text Seamus.

Me: Flight info attached. I'll be home tonight.

Seamus: I'll be there to pick you up.

Sitting in first class, my gaze drifts out the window as the plane climbs into the sky, the Maldives shrinking beneath me. Weeks ago, this place felt like a paradise, removed from the weight of responsibility, from everything I'm supposed to be. Now, it feels like a mistake. A beautiful, dangerous mistake wrapped in fire-red hair and mesmerizing green eyes.

I've always been good at compartmentalizing, at shutting things out. It's what's kept me alive, what's kept me in control. I try to shut her out. To focus on anything else, numbers, business, the issues I know will be waiting for me when I land, but my thoughts circle back to her every damn time.

Why did you leave me without so much as a goodbye, Eve?

I replay our last day together, the way she laughed when I pulled her into the water, the way her eyes softened when she thought I wasn't looking. The moments were small, but they linger, taunting me. I thought I'd figured her out, at least enough to know what to expect, but she slipped away before I could hold on.

And that's what bothers me most. I didn't see it coming.

The cabin lights dim, and the hum of the engines fills the silence as the flight drags on. I lean my head back against the seat, clenching my jaw as I wrestle with my thoughts.

Her face is there every time I close my eyes—her smile, her laugh, the way she looked at me like she could see past the parts of me I've spent years burying. I told myself it was just fun, but somewhere along the way, it became something else.

You let her get too close, I think bitterly, gripping the armrest. I let myself believe, even for a second, that she was mine.

I've spent years knowing what people want from me—respect, fear, power. I've been with women before. More than I care to count. None of them ever got under my skin. None of them ever made me wonder what it would be like to stay. With her, it was different. She didn't ask for anything, and maybe that's why I let her in.

By the time the wheels touch down in Dublin, my body aches from sitting still for too long, and my mind feels even worse. I grab my bag, ignoring the exhaustion and the gnawing emptiness I can't seem to shake.

Seamus is waiting for me when I step through the terminal, hands shoved in his coat pockets, his usual scowl firmly in place. The cold Dublin air smacks me in the face. It's a far cry from the golden sun and heat I've been living in, but I welcome it. Maybe it will help me clear my head.

"Welcome home, boss," he greets, falling into step beside me.

"Seamus," I say, my voice gruff as I toss my bag into the boot and climb into the passenger's seat.

He slides in behind the wheel, giving me a quick glance before he starts the car. "You look like hell."

"Long flight," I mutter, staring out the rain-streaked window.

Seamus snorts. "We'll call it that." He pauses as if debating something before launching into business. "The Callahan's have been pushing again. There have been more delays at the docks, and shipments are getting flagged. I sent a few mates to remind them we're still in charge, but it's getting messy. Then there's the issue with—"

I let his voice wash over me, hearing but not listening. My mind drifts back to the villa, to the sight of the note sitting on the nightstand. To the way she looked at me when she thought I wasn't paying attention like I was something more than I am.

"Eamon." Seamus's tone sharpens. "Are you even listening?"

"Yes," I snap, though I know it's a lie.

"No, you're not," he presses, undeterred. "I don't know what the hell happened to you over there, but you better pull your head out of your ass before everyone starts thinking you've gone soft."

"Enough, Seamus." My voice drops, low and dangerous.

He doesn't flinch. "We've got problems here. Real ones that won't wait for you to sort your shit out."

I glare at him, but there's nothing I can say to refute it. He's right, and we both know it.

"Don't worry about me," I say finally. "I'm back. That's all that matters."

Seamus doesn't look convinced, but he doesn't push either. The rest of the drive passes in silence, the city blurring past the window as I try and fail to bury my thoughts of her.

She's gone, I remind myself again, the words cold and final.

But no matter how hard I try to shut her out, I know one thing for certain.

This isn't over.

Aoife

THE PLANE'S WHEELS HIT THE TARMAC, AND MY stomach flips, not from the landing but from the reality waiting for me. I grip the armrests tightly, my breath shallow as the plane slows to a stop.

My parents are gone.

The words echo in my head, hollow and cruel. I've replayed Ruairi's voice over and over during the flight, his grief barely concealed as he told me what happened. But it still doesn't feel real.

When I step off the plane, the cold Belfast air bites at my skin, a sharp contrast to the Maldives' warmth. Ruairi's there, waiting near the private terminal, his shoulders squared, his expression guarded.

The moment I see him, the grief I've been holding in breaks free. His arms open, and I rush toward him, collapsing into his embrace.

"Ruairi," I whisper, my voice cracking as the tears come. "Tell me it's not true. Please."

He holds me tightly, his hand cradling the back of my head as I sob into his chest. "I wish I could. God, I wish I could," he murmurs.

I cling to him, my fingers curling into the fabric of his coat as a sob wracks my body. "It doesn't feel real," I whisper.

"It doesn't," he agrees, his voice thick with grief. "I keep waiting for the phone to ring, for them to walk through the door. But they're not coming back."

His words hit like a blow, the finality of them sinking in as my knees give out. He holds me tighter, his hand steadying me.

"I've got you," he says softly.

Pulling back slightly, I look up at him through blurred vision. "Are you sure it wasn't a hit? No one... no one was targeting them?"

His jaw tightens, his grief momentarily eclipsed by anger. "I had it checked out. Every angle. It was nothing more than a drunk driver who shouldn't have been on the road." His voice falters as he adds, "The other driver didn't make it either."

I nod slowly, though it does little to ease the ache in my chest. "I can't believe they're gone."

"Neither can I," he admits, his voice quieter now. "But we'll get through this. Together."

The drive to Ruairi's house is silent, the finality of our loss filling the space between us. When we pull up, the porch light is on. Bridget stands in the doorway, Saoirse balanced on her hip.

The sight of them sends a fresh wave of emotion crashing over me.

Bridget hurries down the steps, her eyes wide as I step out of the car. "Aoife," she says, wrapping me in a warm hug, her voice thick with unshed tears. "I'm so sorry."

I hug her back tightly, my throat too tight to speak. Saoirse reaches out to me, her tiny hands grabbing at my coat, and something in me shatters all over again.

"She's been asking for you," Bridget says softly, handing her over.

I hold my niece close, her little arms wrapping around my neck as she babbles softly, completely unaware of what's happened. Her red curls tickle my cheek, and for a brief moment, the warmth of her presence steadies me.

Inside, the house is quiet but feels full of unspoken grief. Bridget has tea waiting, but it goes untouched as we sit together, trying to process what comes next.

"Did they leave any instructions?" I ask, my hands gripping the warm mug tightly.

"They did," Bridget says gently. "Your father wanted something small and private. For family and close friends. Nothing public."

Ruairi nods. "I'll handle everything."

I shake my head, sitting up straighter. "No. I want to help. I need to."

"Can you give us a minute?" Ruairi asks. "I need to speak with Aoife alone."

Bridget glances at me, her expression softening with understanding. "Of course. It's time for Saoirse to go to bed anyway." She presses a gentle kiss to my cheek and whispers, "Let me know if you need anything."

I nod silently and watch as she heads upstairs, her voice low as she soothes the baby.

When the sound of her footsteps fades, Ruairi leans forward, his elbows resting on his knees and his face set in the grim determination I know too well.

His jaw tightens as he pins me with a look that's both protective and unyielding. "This isn't something you need to carry, Aoife. As the head of the family, this is my role now."

"Head of the family?" I echo, my voice sharper than I intend. "I'm part of this family too, Ruairi."

"You are," he agrees, his voice steady but firm. "But it's not the same, and you know it. Da would've wanted me to handle this. Alone."

I scoff, my frustration bubbling to the surface. "Da wouldn't have wanted you to shut me out. He—"

"He wouldn't have wanted you dragged into this," Ruairi

interrupts. "He spent his entire life keeping you away from the mess. I'm not about to change that now." His tone is edged with finality.

His words hit like a slap, and for a moment, I'm too stunned to respond.

"This isn't just about the Syndicate," he continues, his voice softer now but no less resolute. "This is about family. About doing what Da and Mam would've expected of me. Let me do this for them. For us."

The room falls silent. I know he's trying to protect me, just like he always has, but it doesn't make it any easier to accept.

Finally, I exhale shakily and nod, the fight draining out of me. "Fine," I say quietly. "But after the funeral, we're revisiting my place in the family. This conversation isn't over."

His expression hardens, his frustration evident, but then it softens just slightly. He nods once. "We'll talk," he says, though his tone makes it clear he doesn't plan to budge.

The funeral is held three days later. True to my father's wishes, it's a small, private gathering with only family and a few trusted associates from the Syndicate. The chapel is quiet, its stone walls and vaulted ceilings casting long shadows in the flickering candlelight.

I sit in the front pew, my hands clasped tightly in my lap. Ruairi is beside me, his jaw set in a way that's both protective and unreadable. Bridget sits on his other side, Saoirse in her lap, mercifully quiet as if even she can sense the gravity of the moment.

The priest speaks in soft, measured tones, his voice echoing faintly through the chapel as he talks about the importance of family, legacy, and love. But the words fade into the background as my focus drifts to the polished mahogany caskets at the front of the room, each adorned with a spray of white lilies and roses.

This is it. The final goodbye.

For a fleeting moment, my thoughts drift to Eamon. I picture him here beside me, his presence steady and unwavering in a way that could make this unbearable moment feel just a little less heavy.

But he's not here. He can't be. And even if he were, he'd never belong in this world. *My* world.

The ache sharpens as I push the thought aside, forcing myself to focus on the present. This isn't about what I want or what I wish. It's about honoring them.

When the service ends, we move outside to the small graveyard behind the chapel. The air is crisp, the kind of biting cold that turns your breath into visible clouds. I wrap my coat tighter around me, but it does little to shield me from the chill seeping into my bones.

As the caskets are lowered into the ground, the priest says a final prayer. I bow my head, my tears spilling silently down my cheeks.

"They loved you, you know," Ruairi says softly beside me.

I glance at him, his face pale against the black of his coat. "I know," I whisper, though it doesn't make the loss any easier.

When the burial is complete, Ruairi steps forward, his hand shaking as he drops a single white rose onto each casket. Bridget follows, her movements steady.

I'm the last to stand over them. The petals of the roses I hold are soft and fragile between my fingers before I let them fall into the open grave.

"I'll make you proud," I whisper, my voice catching. "I promise."

Back at Ruairi's house, the silence is heavier than it's ever been. The guests are gone, and the house is empty except for us. Bridget busies herself in the kitchen, her grief manifesting in quiet movements as she cleans and prepares tea. Saoirse is down for a nap the faint sound of her breathing comes through the baby monitor.

Ruairi and I sit in the living room, the same place we'd talked that first night I came back.

"They'd be proud of you, you know," he says, his voice low.

I glance at him, my eyes still red from crying. "Would they? Da spent his whole life keeping me away from the Syndicate. Keeping me out of his world."

"He did it to protect you," Ruairi says firmly. "Not because he didn't think you were capable."

I scoff softly, shaking my head. "We'll never know now, will we?"

Ruairi's jaw tightens, and for a moment, I think he's going to argue. But instead, he sighs, rubbing a hand over his face. "We'll revisit this," he says, his tone resigned. "After things settle."

I nod, though the fire inside me hasn't dimmed. I've spent my entire life waiting for my moment, and I won't let grief, or Ruairi, keep me from taking my rightful place in the Syndicate.

For now, though, I let the silence settle between us, the weight of the day enough to keep my fight at bay.

Eamon

THE WHISKEY BURNS AS IT GOES DOWN, BUT IT DOESN'T chase away the restlessness knotting my chest. I lean back in my chair, staring at the map of Dublin spread across the table in front of me. It's marked with red pins—territory disputes, shipments, and other business dealings that should have my full attention.

But my focus drifts, as it has every day since I got back.

Eve.

Her voice echoes in my mind, the way her words carried that distinct Belfast lilt. It wasn't purely Irish, but not entirely foreign, either. It was unique, like her.

It's been months, and I still can't get her out of my head. I've spent hours tracking down every lead I can think of, but I've got nothing. Just the vivid memory of her fiery red hair, green eyes, and the way she could make me forget everything else with a single look.

I've turned to every connection, and every resource I have, but it's all led to dead ends. The resort in the Maldives had no record of her booking. No surprises there, considering she'd probably used an alias.

And the worst part? The not knowing.

No pictures. No last names. Who Eve really was. Where she is now. Whether she's thinking about me the way I can't stop thinking about her.

The door to my office creaks open, and Seamus steps inside, his face a mix of irritation and concern. "We need to talk."

I glance up, my expression flat. "If it's about the Callahan's, I've already—"

"It's not the Callahan's," he cuts in, crossing his arms. "It's you."

My jaw tightens, and I set the glass down slowly. "What about me?"

Seamus exhales sharply, running a hand through his hair. "The men are talking. They're saying you've changed since you came back. That your head's not in the game anymore."

"That's bullshit."

"Is it?" His gaze sharpens. "You've been distracted for months. You're handling things, sure, but it's like your fire's gone. And the men notice. They're questioning your commitment. And frankly? So am I."

Anger flares instantly, sharp and hot. I stand, the chair scraping back against the floor. "I haven't dropped the ball on anything. Business is running smoothly, and no one's stepping out of line."

Seamus doesn't back down. "Not yet. But they will if they think you're slipping. This isn't just about keeping the trains running. It's about power. Control. Perception. If they think you're not the same man who left, they'll take advantage of it."

The truth in his words stings more than I want to admit.

"What do you want me to do?" I snap. "Throw someone off a building to remind them who I am?"

"If that's what it takes," Seamus says bluntly, his voice steady. "You need to remind them you're not just present, but that you're still the ruthless leader they fear and respect."

The silence between us crackles.

Finally, I exhale sharply, dragging a hand down my face.

"What about Liam O'Connor?" I say, my voice cold and measured. "He's been encroaching on our territory, hasn't he?"

Seamus raises an eyebrow, surprise flashing briefly across his face. "We've had reports he's been making moves, trying to undercut our operations in the Docklands. Nothing definitive yet."

I fix him with a hard stare. "Definitive or not, he's testing us. If the men need a reminder of who I am, then Liam's the perfect example."

Seamus hesitates. "You want me to send someone to deal with him?"

"No," I snap. "I'll deal with him myself. Arrange a meeting. Somewhere neutral enough to keep this controlled but public enough to make an impression."

"You want to go face-to-face with him?" He shakes his head, incredulous. "You know he's the kind of rat who'll have backup waiting."

I lean forward, my tone sharp. "Let him. I'm not walking into this unprepared. But the message has to be clear. Anyone who crosses me doesn't get to walk away."

Seamus exhales, nodding slowly as the realization sinks in. "Alright. I'll set it up and make sure word gets out. Everyone will know you're handling this personally."

"Good," I say, leaning back. "And make it clear to Liam that this isn't a negotiation. It's a warning."

Seamus smirks faintly, the tension between us easing slightly. "He won't know what hit him."

As he leaves the room, I stare at the map on the table, my focus narrowing on the Docklands. Dealing with Liam O'Connor isn't just about business. It's about reasserting control. The men need to see me at my best or, more accurately, at my worst.

Every time I try to focus on business, on the next move, I feel her pulling at the edges of everything, like a wound that won't close. Her absence aches in places I didn't know could hurt.

One part of me wants to hunt her down, to demand answers, to figure out why the hell she left. The other knows I've got a job to do. A life that doesn't have room for someone like her. No matter how hard I try to compartmentalize, she keeps bleeding into the parts of my life I swore would stay untouched.

But I can't let her go. Not yet. Not until I know who she really is.

Aoife

THE SHARP CRACK OF GUNFIRE ECHOES OFF THE WALLS as I squeeze the trigger again, the recoil kicking lightly in my arm. Another clean shot, center mass.

I lower the pistol, satisfaction warms my chest as I take in the target riddled with precise hits. I started training while I was traveling, studying with some of the best sharpshooters in the world. Each shot feels like proof that I'm capable of more than my father and Ruairi have ever given me credit for.

"You're good," his voice cuts through the stillness.

I set the pistol down and remove my ear protection.

Turning around, I find Ruairi leaning casually against the doorway of the shooting range, arms crossed over his chest. His expression is somewhere between impressed and curious. "Almost scary good," he adds, pushing off the wall to approach me.

"Isn't that the point?" I quip, raising an eyebrow.

He stops a few paces away, his gaze flicking to the target before settling back on me. "What's got you in here?"

I shrug, keeping my tone light. "Thought I'd make myself useful."

He studies me for a long moment, his sharp eyes seeing more than I'd like. I've been home for months, biding my time and planning how to approach him about the one thing I've been working toward for years. Now, the moment feels closer than ever.

"Can we talk?" I ask, tilting my head toward the door.

His brow furrows slightly, but he nods. "Alright. I'll meet you in my office in fifteen minutes."

"Perfect," I say, my voice clipped as I turn back to my weapon. My hand brushes over the pistol, methodically unloading and cleaning it before setting it back in its case. Every movement is precise, almost mechanical, a way to keep my nerves in check.

Once everything's in order, I leave the shooting range and head to my room.

The familiar weight of the folded paper in my bedside drawer is a comfort I've clung to for years. Sitting on the edge of my bed, I carefully unfold it. The creases are worn, the ink slightly faded, but the words are still as clear as the day we wrote them.

We were seven years old, sitting cross-legged on the floor of the old treehouse in the back garden. The summer air was thick with the smell of grass and sunshine. Ruairi was already trying to boss me around, even then.

"Da says I'll run the Syndicate one day," Ruairi declares, puffing out his chest in the way he always did when he wanted to sound important.

"You mean we'll run the Syndicate," I correct, crossing my arms.

His mouth pulls into a small frown, and he scrunches his nose but, after a moment, gives a quick nod. "Fine. We'll run the Syndicate."

"Together," I add.

"Together," he agrees.

I grab a scrap of paper from the small desk in the corner, and with my tongue sticking out in concentration, scrawl the words:

We promise to run the Quigley Syndicate together, side by side.

I push the paper toward him. "Sign it."

"Wait," he says, flashing a small pocketknife he isn't supposed to have. "If we're making promises, it has to be real."

I don't hesitate, holding out my hand as he makes a tiny slice on the tip of my finger. The sting is sharp but quick, and after he does the same to his finger, we press them to the page, smearing tiny drops of blood over our signatures.

"There," he says, grinning. "Now it's official."

I smile back, tucking the paper into my pocket like it's the most important thing in the world.

The sound of footsteps in the hallway pulls me back to the present. I refold the note carefully, slipping it into my pocket.

This isn't just a childhood promise. It's a pact we made together. And it's time for my brother to keep his end of it.

Standing, I square my shoulders and head toward Ruairi's office.

Stepping inside, it's just as I remember it. Dark wood, shelves lined with books. The faint scent of our father's cologne lingers in the air. Ruairi sits behind the desk, motioning for me to take the chair opposite him.

"What's on your mind?" he asks, leaning back slightly.

I reach into my pocket, fingers brushing the worn paper. My stomach knots as I pull it out, but I force myself to stay composed.

"I want to take my place beside you," I say firmly, meeting his gaze.

He groans, rolling his eyes. "Not this again."

The dismissal stings, and I sit up straighter. "Yes, this again. I've spent years preparing for this. While I was traveling, I wasn't just sightseeing—I was training. I've studied Krav Maga, Brazilian Jiu-Jitsu, and Muay Thai. I've learned how to shoot, as you've seen for yourself."

His lips press into a thin line, but he doesn't interrupt.

"I've been working for this," I continue, my voice rising. "I'm not asking to jump into something big. Let me start small. Anything."

He shakes his head, leaning forward. "No. It's not happening."

Anger flares in my chest. "Why not?"

"The Syndicate isn't a game, and it's no place for a girl."

My hands ball into fists at his words, the condescension igniting every ounce of frustration I've been holding back. "You're unbelievable," I snap. "You're so stuck in your own head you can't see past this archaic, sexist bullshit."

Ruairi sighs, pinching the bridge of his nose. "Aoife, listen. I've already been thinking about your future. There's someone I want you to meet. Cian O'Leary. He was one of Da's most trusted associates. Smart, dependable, and—"

I'm out of my chair before he can finish. "You're trying to marry me off?"

He raises his hands defensively. "I'm trying to look out for you."

"You're unbelievable," I repeat, my voice shaking with anger. I reach into my pocket again, this time slamming the worn paper onto his desk. "Read it."

Ruairi's brows knit together as he picks it up, unfolding it carefully. A small smile tugs at his lips as he reads, the memory clearly hitting him. "We were barely out of nappies," he says softly, shaking his head.

"We promised," I say firmly. "You agreed that we'd run this Syndicate *together*. You remember, don't you? Slicing our fingers, signing it in blood? It meant something to me, Ri."

His smile fades as he slides the paper back toward me. "We were kids, Evie. It was silly."

"It wasn't silly to me," I snap, my voice breaking. "It was a promise. One I've held onto all these years. And now it's time for you to honor it."

He leans back, exhaling heavily. "It changes nothing. I won't let you do this. Working in the Syndicate is no place for you."

"I've been kept in the dark for years," I argue. "I refuse to stand on the sidelines anymore."

His jaw tightens. "This conversation is over."

Fury burns through me as I glare at him. "This isn't over," I hiss, spinning on my heel and storming out of the office.

I nearly collide with Bridget in the hallway. Her eyes widen as she steadies me. "What's wrong?"

"Your husband is being a stubborn ass," I snap, pushing past her.

Bridget chuckles softly, following me. "And what else is new? What's it about this time?"

I stop, turning to face her. "I want to work in the Syndicate. But he won't even listen."

Bridget's expression softens. "He just wants what's best for you."

"Best for me?" I scoff. "He wants me to meet some associate and settle down like a good little wife."

Bridget smiles faintly. "Cian O'Leary, right? He's a good man. And Saoirse would love a cousin to grow up with."

I roll my eyes, throwing my hands up. "You're as bad as he is."

She places a gentle hand on my arm. "I'm not saying you should do what he wants. But try to understand where he's coming from. He only wants to protect you."

I shake my head, stepping back. "I don't need his protection. Or yours."

And with that, I walk away, my resolve burning stronger than ever.

Ruairi

Aoife's words echo in my ears as I stare at the crumpled note she slammed down in front of me. The audacity of her dragging out some childhood promise we made when we were seven, as if that holds any weight now.

I pinch the bridge of my nose and lean back in my chair, exhaling sharply. I can't wrap my head around why she's so insistent on this. She has no idea what she's asking for.

The door creaks open, and Bridget steps inside, her expression soft but curious. "I bumped into Aoife in the hallway."

I snort as I sit up, patting my knee to invite my wife closer. "Come here, then. Might as well sit while you tell me what an *amadán* I am."

Bridget chuckles softly as she crosses the room, her smile teasing. "You said it, not me."

"Don't hold back on my account," I mutter as she settles into my lap.

Bridget rolls her eyes as she sinks into my lap. Her arms loop around my shoulders, calming some of the storm inside. "She told me she asked you to let her work in the Syndicate."

"She brought this," I say, holding the note up for her to see.

"What is it?" she asks.

"It's a promise we made when we were kids barely old enough to tie our shoes. We wrote it in a *shite* little treehouse and signed it in blood, for Christ's sake. And here she's kept it like it's some sacred contract."

Bridget takes the note from my hand. Her lips twitch into a smile as she reads it. "You two were adorable," she says, handing it back.

I groan, running a hand through my hair. "It was a game, Brie. Kids' stuff. But my sister is acting like it's the bloody Proclamation of the Irish Republic."

"She's serious about this," Bridget says gently.

"I know she's serious," I snap, though the anger in my tone is more frustration than anything else. "That's what worries me. Aoife doesn't understand what she's asking for. This life is dangerous. It's brutal. It's not a place for a girl."

"Aoife's not a child anymore. She's a grown woman, and she's determined." My wife's gaze softens as she rests a hand on my arm. "You can't protect her from everything."

I shake my head. "I can try."

"Be patient with her," Bridget says. "She's trying to figure out where she belongs now that your parents are gone. She's still grieving."

I exhale heavily. "I get that she's grieving. I am, too. But this obsession with the Syndicate? It's not about finding where she belongs. It's about proving something, and I won't let her do that."

"She mentioned Cian O'Leary," Bridget says, changing the subject. "Maybe now isn't the best time to introduce them."

I let out a humorless laugh. "It's too late for that. He's coming to dinner tonight."

Her brows lift in surprise. "Does Aoife know?"

"No," I admit. "I didn't think it was necessary to mention it."

My wife sighs, shaking her head. "You're playing with fire, Ruairi."

"She'll get over it," I say, though I'm not entirely convinced.

Aoife's temper is as fiery as her hair, and I know this will only stoke the flames. Whether she likes it or not, she needs to understand that I'm doing this for her.

Bridget stands, smoothing her hands over her dress. "Don't push her too hard. She's not as fragile as you think, but she's not unbreakable either."

I nod, though my resolve remains firm. Aoife doesn't see the danger she's walking into, but I do. And as long as I'm in charge, I'll do whatever it takes to keep her out of it. Even if she hates me for it.

<h1 style="text-align:center">Aoife</h1>

Saoirse kicks her little legs happily on the changing table, her tiny hands waving in the air as I carefully fasten her nappy. "You're so lucky, you know that?" I tell her, smiling as her green eyes twinkle up at me. "Your biggest problem right now is what color onesie to wear. Meanwhile, your da is trying to marry me off to some stranger."

Saoirse gurgles in response, her chubby fists grabbing at the air, and I can't help but laugh softly. "Exactly. He's being ridiculous, right? As if I don't have enough on my plate."

She giggles, her laughter so pure and infectious that it softens some of the frustration I've been carrying since my argument with Ruairi. "Don't get me wrong," I continue, pulling a soft pink onesie over her head. "I might want kids someday. But not now. I have things I want to do first. A life I want to live. And settling down with some guy my brother's trying to set me up with isn't in the plan."

My hands still for a moment as I think about Eamon. His piercing blue eyes. The way his touch made me feel like the most important person in the world. I should've told him who I was. Left him my number. Something.

I shake my head, trying to push the thought away. "See what I mean, Saoirse? Men only complicate things."

She coos softly, her small hands patting my arm, and I lean down to kiss her head. "Come on, love. Let's get you to dinner."

When I step into the dining room with Saoirse on my hip, I immediately spot Ruairi and Bridget, who are already seated. Bridget smiles warmly, but when Ruairi stands, I immediately know something's off.

"There you are," Ruairi says, his expression softening as he moves toward me. "I was wondering when you and my little princess would arrive."

I'm about to respond when a deep, unfamiliar voice cuts in. "And who's this beautiful little one?"

I freeze, my eyes snapping to the man sitting at the table. He's older, probably in his late forties, with dark hair that's starting to silver at the temples. His tailored suit fits perfectly, and the way he carries himself screams wealth and power.

Ruairi steps beside me, taking Saoirse from my arms. He leans in close, lowering his voice. "Please be on your best behavior," he whispers, his tone clipped but pleading.

He presses a kiss on the baby's temple. "This little one," he says warmly, his tone softening in a way it rarely does. "Is my daughter, Saoirse."

The man's expression shifts, a genuine smile breaking across his face. "A beauty, like her mother, no doubt," he says, nodding to Bridget, who smiles in return.

Holding Saoirse as if she's a buffer between us all, Ruairi says, "And this is my sister, Aoife." Ruairi shifts beside me, nodding toward the man at the table. "Aoife, this is Cian O'Leary."

Cian stands, extending a hand toward me. "And here I thought I'd never see little Aoife Quigley all grown up," he says smoothly, his smile polite but assessing. "It's a pleasure to meet you."

"Likewise," I reply, my tone cool as I take his hand briefly before sitting down.

Over the course of dinner, the conversation remains polite, almost painfully so. Cian asks about my travels, where I've been, and what I've seen. I keep my answers short but cordial, though my mind churns with fury at Ruairi.

He planned this. Springing this dinner on me without so much as a warning, and now he's sitting there as if this is the most natural thing in the world. The heat of anger simmers under my skin. Ruairi doesn't just want to control the Syndicate. He wants to control *me*. He refuses to acknowledge that I'm not someone who needs his protection or his permission.

"I imagine you've had some incredible experiences," he says, swirling his wine.

"I have," I reply.

"Do you have a favorite destination?" he asks.

"The Maldives," I answer quickly.

Ruairi, clearly growing impatient with the small talk, clears his throat. "Cian and I were discussing earlier how nice it would be for the two of you to get to know each other better. Maybe over dinner sometime."

Without thinking, I blurt out, "Actually, I'm not sure how long I'll be in town."

The room goes quiet.

Ruairi sets down his wine with a little more force than necessary. "Excuse me?" I straighten, refusing to look away. "I said I don't know how long I'll be here."

His eyes narrow. "Funny, considering we were under the impression you planned to stay." His tone has that edge I remember too well. Disbelief wrapped in control.

"You don't get to make that call for me," I reply, sharper than I intended, but I don't take it back.

Bridget's gaze bounces between us, concern tightening her features. Cian remains silent, but I feel his eyes on me—curious, calculating.

The rest of dinner is awkward, filled with stilted conversation and forced politeness. When Cian finally excuses himself, thanking Ruairi for the invitation, I practically feel the tension in the room ease.

As soon as the door closes behind Cian, Ruairi turns to me. "Care to explain what that was about?"

"What?" I ask, feigning innocence as I start clearing the plates.

"You've done nothing but dodge questions about how long you're staying since you've been home. Now you're brushing off dinner like it's nothing." His voice is low but tight with control. "What aren't you telling me, Aoife?"

The plate hits the table harder than I intend. "I don't owe you an explanation."

His jaw tightens, and he steps closer. "I'm only trying to protect you. You don't know the players or how dangerous they can be."

"So, it's fine for you to dictate my future, but I can't make my own choices?" I argue. "Is that it? I should sit quietly and let you marry me off like some business transaction?"

"Cian's a good man," Ruairi argues, bristling. "You'd do well to get to know him."

"Did you bring me here to reconnect with family or to shove me into your version of what my life should look like?"

"I'm trying to look out for you," he says, voice rising with frustration. "You're acting like I'm the enemy for wanting you safe."

"No," I say, my voice cold. "You're treating me like I'm a child. But I'm not. And I don't have to answer to you. You're my brother, not my father.

Bridget steps forward, placing a calming hand on Ruairi's arm. "Ri, just let it go," she says softly.

He shrugs her off, his eyes locked on mine. "I'm not letting it go. She's hiding something. I know it."

I cross my arms, matching his stare. "You're right. I am. Because you don't get access to every part of me just because we share blood."

Ruairi's expression hardens, his tone biting. "You think you can handle this world on your own? You have no idea what you're walking into, Evie."

"Enough," Bridget cuts in, her voice firm but calm as she steps between us. She places a hand on Ruairi's chest and looks at me, her expression exasperated. "Both of you. Stop arguing in front of Saoirse."

I glance at the baby, who's still sitting in her high chair, her big green eyes darting between us with a hint of confusion. Guilt prickles at the edges of my anger, but I refuse to back down completely.

Ruairi rakes a hand through his hair as he steps back. "We're not done with this," he mutters, his tone simmering with frustration.

Bridget turns to me, her voice softer now. "Aoife, maybe we can all take a breath and talk about this later. Without an audience."

Ruairi exhales sharply before storming out of the room. Bridget lingers for a moment, her gaze shifting between me and the baby.

"Do you mind staying with Saoirse for a bit?" she asks, her tone careful, almost apologetic. "I should go check on him."

I nod, managing a tight smile. "Of course."

She hesitates, her hand brushing Saoirse's head gently before she leaves.

Saoirse begins babbling happily. I pick her up, holding her close, her tiny hands clutching at my necklace.

"You've got it easy, you know that?" I murmur, pressing a kiss to her soft curls. "No overbearing brothers telling you what to do."

She gurgles in response, and despite myself, I smile.

But as I hold her, my mind churns. Bridget's words echo faintly about my brother wanting what's best for me and about patience.

How much longer am I supposed to wait? How many more

dinners like this, where my choices and my future are discussed like I'm not even in the room, am I expected to endure?

As Saoirse rests her head on my shoulder, the soft weight of her trust and innocence settles over me. For her sake, I'll let it go tonight.

But this isn't over. Not by a long shot.

Eamon

The restaurant is quiet at this hour, tucked just off one of Dublin's busier streets. Neutral ground—but public enough to make a point. The soft murmur of conversation from the few remaining diners barely touches the private corner where I sit. Across from me, Liam O'Connor shifts in his seat, fingers tapping a nervous rhythm against the edge of the table.

I swirl the whiskey in my glass, watching the amber liquid catch the dim light as I let the silence stretch. He hates silence. It makes him nervous. Makes him talk. I've always used that to my advantage.

"Liam," I say finally, my tone calm but cutting through the tension like a blade. "Do you know why I called you here tonight?"

He forces a smile, though it falters at the edges. "I have an idea," he says, his voice tight.

I set my glass down, the sound of it hitting the table louder than it should be. "Enlighten me."

His throat bobs as he swallows, glancing around the room as if looking for support. There's none to be found. My men are scattered throughout the restaurant, subtle but present. He knows that.

"Eamon, if this is about the Docklands—"

"It's about you trying to take something that doesn't belong to you." I cut him off, my voice dropping lower. "It's about you thinking you could steal from me and get away with it."

"It wasn't stealing," he blurts out, leaning forward in his chair. "It was a business opportunity. I saw a gap and—"

"You saw a gap?" I interrupt, my voice cold. "The Docklands are mine. There are no gaps. Everything that moves through there, every shipment, every deal, is accounted for. You don't take a *business opportunity* without going through me first."

"I didn't mean any disrespect," he says, holding up his hands in a placating gesture. "You know I've always been loyal."

I lean forward, my elbows resting on the table as I lock eyes with him. "Loyalty has nothing to do with what you say. It's what you do. And what you did was disrespect me and my Syndicate."

His face pales, and he stumbles over his words. "Eamon, please—"

I hold up a hand, silencing him. "You thought I wouldn't find out? That I wouldn't notice? Do you think I got to where I am by being blind?"

The table between us feels like a thin line separating predator from prey, and he knows it. His hands tremble as he reaches for his glass of whiskey, knocking it back in one gulp.

Right on cue, his phone buzzes on the table between us. He doesn't move to check it.

"Go on," I murmur, gesturing toward it. "I think it's something you'll want to see."

Liam hesitates, then snatches the phone with a huff of annoyance. His eyes drop to the screen. Unlock. Tap. The moment the video starts playing, the color drains from his face.

I don't need to look. I know what he's seeing.

His house is engulfed in flames. The camera's steady, too steady to be accidental. A slow pan across the property as fire devours everything. Windows shattering. The roof caving in. Smoke billowing into the sky.

Controlled chaos. Precision-wrapped panic.

Liam's hand trembles as he lowers the phone. "What the hell is this?"

I take a sip of my drink before answering. "Heard it was a gas leak. Very unfortunate."

He stares at me, stunned into silence, trying to decide if he's angry, afraid, or both.

"You son of a—" he starts.

"Here's how this is going to go," I cut him off, my voice laced with menace. "You're going to pull out of the Docklands completely. Every deal you've made, every contact you've established, you sever them all. And you're going to make sure everyone knows exactly why."

Liam leans forward, jaw tight. "You're asking me to walk away from everything I've built there. Do you know how long I've worked on those contacts? If I pull out now, I lose face. I lose money."

I don't respond. Instead, I slide my phone across the table. The screen lights up with a photo of his wife and two children walking hand-in-hand along a quiet seaside path. The kind of place meant for peace. The timestamp is from this morning.

Liam freezes. Then he snatches the phone, staring at the image like it might change if he blinks enough. "How the hell did you—"

"It's a lovely neighborhood," I say calmly. "Hope they're enjoying the holiday. It's a quiet little rental. Right near the beach, yeah?"

His face pales, the color draining fast.

"Nothing happens in my territory without me knowing," I continue, voice dropping. "No one moves, no one breathes, without it crossing my radar. You should've known that before you started making moves that weren't yours to make."

He says nothing. Doesn't have to. I see it in the way his hand tightens around the phone, in the way his confidence collapses in on itself.

"Unless you'd prefer I drop in on their holiday," I murmur, leaning forward, "I'll assume you're ready to do it my way."

He nods quickly, his head bobbing like a puppet. "Yes, of course. Consider it done."

My gaze never leaves his as I lean back. "And if I so much as hear your name in connection with the Docklands again, I won't be as generous as having this conversation. Do you understand me?"

"Yes, Eamon," he whispers, his voice barely audible.

"Good," I say, finishing my drink. "Now, get out."

He stumbles to his feet, mumbling something that might've been gratitude, and practically runs for the door. The tension in the room eases slightly, but only just.

Seamus steps forward, his expression unreadable as he watches Liam's retreating figure. "Think he got the message?"

I smirk faintly, adjusting the cuffs of my jacket. "If he didn't, he'll wish he had."

I'm about to signal for another drink when I hear a familiar voice behind me.

"Well, well. Eamon O'Sullivan in the flesh."

I turn slowly, my eyes landing on a blonde in a fitted red dress that clings to every curve. She moves toward me with the confidence of someone who's used to turning heads, her lips curling into a sly smile.

"Maeve," I say evenly, nodding as she steps closer.

She slides into the chair Liam vacated, crossing her legs in a way that's clearly meant to draw my attention. "It's been a while," she purrs, her tone dripping with suggestion. "What's it been? Six months? A year?"

"Something like that," I reply, casually leaning back in my chair.

She studies me with her sharp blue eyes. "I heard you were in the Maldives. What were you doing out there?"

"Business," I say, voice flat.

"Hmm," she hums, swirling her drink before taking a sip. "You look distracted. That's not like you."

I don't respond.

She leans forward, her perfume wafting toward me, a scent I once found enticing but now barely registers. Her gaze flicks briefly to Seamus, and the smirk that follows tells me everything I need to know. He's responsible for her presence here this evening.

"I know how you like to unwind after handling business," she purrs, her voice low and sultry. "What do you say, Eamon? Come back to my flat, and let me take care of you."

For a moment, I try. I try to feel something, anything.

Maeve is stunning, confident. I know exactly how good it was between us. The way her body fit against mine, the heat of her skin, the way she'd moan my name like she couldn't get enough. She's the kind of woman I never thought twice about taking to bed.

What I used to crave.

I shake my head, pushing back from the table. "Not tonight."

Maeve blinks, her surprise quickly morphing into irritation. "Really? That's it?"

"That's it," I say firmly before standing.

Her lips twist into a smirk, but there's no humor in it. "Didn't think I'd see the day Eamon O'Sullivan would lose his appetite. Maybe you're not the man I remember after all."

Seamus whistles low, leaning back slightly. "That's a hell of a parting shot."

I glance at him, then back at Maeve, my expression cold. "She's all yours," I say dryly, the corner of my mouth lifting in a humorless smirk.

Maeve's eyes flash with indignation, her jaw tightening as if she wants to fire back, but I don't stick around to hear it. I walk out without a backward glance.

The night air hits me, but it does little to settle the storm inside. Maeve's words were meant to sting, to cut at my pride, but they barely register.

Because all I can think about is Eve.

The way her green eyes sparkled when she laughed. The way her hair felt like silk in my hands. The way our bodies fit together as though we were made for each other. The way she left without a trace and took a part of me with her.

I clench my fists, trying to will her image away, but it's useless. She's in my head, under my skin, and nothing—not Maeve, not anyone compares.

<h1 style="text-align:center">Aoife</h1>

I TOSS ANOTHER PAIR OF HEELS INTO MY SUITCASE, THE faint thud barely audible over the sound of my thoughts. I try to focus on the task at hand, but my mind keeps circling back to my argument with Ruairi. The tightness in my chest hasn't eased since last night, making every item I pack feel like a small rebellion.

The door creaks open, and I glance up to see Bridget, concern etched on her face. "You're packing?"

I nod, folding a dress and placing it neatly on top of the other items. "I need a change of scenery."

Her frown deepens as she steps into the room. "You can't just take off every time you and Ruairi fight. You're home now."

I sigh, turning to face her. "I'm not running away."

She glances at the half-packed suitcase. "Where are you going?"

"Dublin," I say, zipping the suitcase closed. "Erin, my flatmate from college, is turning twenty-six. She's throwing a big party, and I promised I'd go."

Bridget relaxes slightly, the tension in her shoulders easing. "Good. I was worried you were planning to disappear again. Ruairi wouldn't handle that well."

I let out a short laugh. "Oh, please. He'd probably be glad if I disappeared and stayed out of his hair. Less for him to micromanage."

"You think so? You're his favorite person to boss around, you know."

"Don't remind me."

Bridget exhales, leaning back on her hands. "You know he's just trying to protect you, right? He's worried about you. This isn't some power play for him. It's fear."

"I know," I say, pausing to meet her gaze. "But I'm not a child anymore. I've traveled the world and learned skills he doesn't even know I have. I've prepared for this. I need him to see me for who I am now, not who I was when we were kids."

Bridget's brow furrows slightly, her tone softening. "I get it, Evie, I really do. Please don't let this trip make things worse between you two. You leaving might feel like you're walking away from him."

"I'm not," I insist, shaking my head. "I need some time, and so does he. Maybe if I give him some space, he'll reconsider letting me have a role in the Syndicate."

She watches me for a moment, then nods. "Alright. Just don't push him too far, okay?"

I smile faintly. "I won't. I promise."

Bridget hesitates, then leans forward slightly. "Okay, enough about Ruairi. Is there something you're not telling me?"

I blink. "Like what?"

Her eyes narrow just enough to be playful. "Have you met anyone interesting lately?"

I let out a small laugh, shrugging. "Not exactly."

"Not exactly," she repeats, arching a brow. "That sounds like there's a story."

"We met while I was in the Maldives," I admit, fiddling with the edge of the duvet.

Bridget perks up instantly. "The Maldives? That already sounds romantic. Go on."

"It wasn't anything serious," I say quickly. "It was just something fun without all the baggage and expectations."

Bridget watches me carefully. "And what about the guy? What's his story?"

I shrug. "All I know is his name's Eamon. We didn't exchange numbers or talk about our lives. No strings. No questions," I murmur.

Her mouth drops open slightly. "You're telling me you spent how long with this man, and you don't know his last name or where he's from?"

I laugh lightly, the sound hollow. "Yeah, well, we weren't exactly sitting around swapping life stories. It was fun while it lasted, and now it's in the past."

"Except you didn't leave it behind," she says softly.

The statement lands harder than I expect, and for a moment, I don't have an answer.

"No," I whisper. "I can't stop thinking about him. I don't even know why. It's not like we had some grand romance. It was just..." I trail off, searching for the right words.

"Special?" Bridget offers.

"Yeah," I admit. "And now it feels like unfinished business."

She gives me a pointed look. "If it's unfinished business, maybe you should find him. You know your brother has connections," she says with a knowing smile. "Tell him about this guy and see what he can dig up."

"Yeah, right. Ri would love me asking for his help to track down some guy I met while I was traveling. He'd lose his mind," I say and shake my head.

"I know my husband can be overbearing and stubborn, but if this Eamon really meant something to you, maybe you should try."

"I'm not chasing after a guy I barely know. And this trip is about giving Ruairi space, not about Eamon."

"Fair enough," she says, standing.

"Besides, he's probably forgotten about me already. I was a

coward," I confess. "I left him a note in the middle of the night. No real goodbye. No way for him to find me. Why would he even think about me now?"

Bridget tilts her head, her expression softening. "Because you're unforgettable, Aoife. Whether you believe it or not."

"You're biased."

"Perhaps," she says with a slight shrug. "But I'm also right."

She moves toward the door, but before she leaves, she glances back. "You deserve to be happy. Don't let anyone, including yourself, convince you otherwise."

Her words linger long after she's gone, leaving me alone with my thoughts and the quiet echo of what might have been.

Aoife

THE CAB WINDS THROUGH DUBLIN'S STREETS, THE blend of red-brick buildings and glassy modern storefronts passing by in a blur. It's been years since my last visit, long enough that the city feels distant but not unfamiliar. A place I recognize without truly knowing.

My phone buzzes in my lap. Erin's name flashes on the screen, accompanied by yet another message.

Erin: How far out are you?

Aoife: 5 mins, max. Relax, I'm not standing you up.

Erin: You better not. I've been cooking. Like actual cooking.

Aoife: Should I be worried?

Erin: Watch it, world traveler. Some of us didn't have unlimited Michelin stars to sample.

A quiet laugh escapes as I tap out a reply.

Aoife: Touché. I'll try to survive whatever you've got waiting.

The cab slows, pulling up outside a stone-faced building with ivy creeping up the edges, its weathered exterior softened by window boxes spilling over with cheerful blooms. I toss a quick thanks to the driver, grab my suitcase from the seat beside me, and text Erin again.

Aoife: Outside.

Before I reach the front door, it swings open, and Erin's face lights up like it's Christmas.

"Evie," she squeals.

"Hey, stranger," I call as I head up the short path.

She practically bounces down the steps to meet me, pulling me into a tight hug. "You're really here."

I laugh, hugging her back. "Told you I wouldn't stand you up."

She pulls back, giving me an exaggerated glare. "Yeah, after about a million, *I swear I'll visit soon texts,* I was beginning to think you were avoiding me. And video chats don't count, you know. I need the real Aoife experience."

"I don't think it was quite a million," I say with a smirk.

"Come on, lunch is ready," she says, looping her arm through mine and steering me toward the door.

The moment we step inside, the warm, savory aroma of butter and scallions fills the air, rich and comforting. It's the kind of scent that wraps around you, making the entire apartment feel like a hug. There's a faint hint of salt and cream in the mix, and my stomach growls in anticipation.

"You made champ?" I ask, grinning as I drop my bag near the couch.

"Of course," she says, puffing up with mock pride. "It's an Erin specialty. Potato perfection, thank you very much."

A pot of mashed potatoes sits on the stove, still steaming. Fresh rolls rest on a cutting board nearby, their golden crust dusted lightly with flour. Two plates and cutlery are already laid out on the small table.

"Help yourself," Erin says, gesturing toward the pot.

I scoop a generous helping of champ onto my plate, the creamy texture practically inviting me to dive in. The smell of the buttery scallions wafts up as I serve myself, making my stomach rumble again.

"Don't hog all the butter," Erin says, nudging me with her hip as she grabs a roll.

"Can't make any promises," I reply, but the laughter between us makes everything feel light and comfortable.

While we eat, Erin peppers me with questions, zeroing in on one location in particular. "Okay, so, the Maldives," she begins. "You said it was going to be a quick layover before you went back to Paris. But you stayed for almost two months." She raises an eyebrow. "Anytime I ask about it, you barely tell me anything. What gives?"

I shrug, taking a bite of champ to buy myself a second. "What's there to tell? White sand, blue water, postcard perfection. Just as amazing as I imagined."

Her eyes narrow, and she sets down her fork. "Uh-huh. You went from sending me constant updates, pictures of your meals, your beach reads, and even random sunrises to radio silence halfway through. Did something happen?"

"Nothing happened," I say too fast. "I decided to take advantage of island life and unplug for a bit instead of documenting every second of it."

She arches an eyebrow, clearly unconvinced. "The queen of *look at this amazing view* photos wanted to unplug?"

I laugh, keeping my tone light. "Even queens need a break sometimes."

"Right," she says, drawing out the word, her eyes narrowing as suspicion settles in her gaze.

I deflect with a joke, pointing at her plate. "You're going to overthink this so much you'll forget to finish your champ. That would be a tragedy."

"Fine," she says, rolling her eyes, but picks up her fork again. "But I will get the full story eventually."

"Good luck with that," I say, taking another bite and steering the conversation to safer territory.

The afternoon passes in a haze of laughter and stories, the kind of easy companionship I hadn't realized I'd missed. By the time Erin's boyfriend, Ryan, arrives, the apartment is alive with warmth and energy.

Ryan is tall and broad-shouldered. His solid, athletic build, paired with an easygoing smile, immediately puts me at ease. Beside him stands another man, slightly shorter but no less imposing, with sandy hair and sharp blue eyes that seem to take everything in. He carries himself with quiet confidence, his presence calm but undeniably self-assured.

Erin ushers them in, all smiles. "Aoife, you remember Ryan. And this is Shane, his flatmate. I thought you might appreciate some extra company tonight," she adds.

I shoot her a look that says *we'll talk about this later* but manage a polite smile for Shane. "Nice to meet you."

"Likewise," he says, flashing me a smile that reveals a faint dimple.

Before I can say much else, Erin grabs her purse, announcing, "Let's get moving. I refuse to be late to my own party."

Ryan laughs, shaking his head as he follows her out the door.

Shane and I trail behind, his gaze briefly meeting mine before he looks away without a word. When we reach the car, Ryan takes the driver's seat, and Erin slides into the passenger side. I hesitate for a split second before climbing into the back.

Shane follows, settling beside me with an easy, unhurried motion. The car is spacious, but his presence feels closer than it should, his broad frame taking up more space than I expected.

"So," he says, his tone casual but polite as Ryan starts the car. "Erin tells me you've been traveling a lot."

I glance at Erin's reflection in the rearview mirror, her eyes practically twinkling with excitement.

"I have," I reply. "Spent the last year or so bouncing around Europe and Asia. It was nice to get away for a bit."

"Any favorites?" he asks, turning slightly to face me. His voice is calm steady—no pressure, just curiosity.

"Hard to choose," I say, smiling faintly. "But I'd say the Maldives was pretty high on the list."

"The Maldives?" he repeats, a hint of surprise in his tone. "That's a bit of a leap from Belfast."

I shrug. "White sand and blue water are hard to beat."

"You don't miss home when you're gone that long?"

The question hangs in the air for a moment, and I notice Erin shift slightly in her seat as if listening in. "Sometimes," I admit. "But there's a freedom in being somewhere new. No expectations, no familiar faces."

Shane nods, his gaze thoughtful. "Fair enough. Sounds like you've had some incredible experiences."

"Definitely," I say. "And what about you? Do you travel much?"

"Not as much as I'd like," he replies with a small chuckle. "Work keeps me busy."

Before I can ask what he does, Erin cuts in from the front. "Shane's being modest. He runs his own business."

"Oh?" I say, raising an eyebrow.

"It's nothing fancy," he says, brushing off Erin's praise. "Just a tech startup. Keeps me out of trouble, mostly."

"He's downplaying it," Erin interjects, glancing back at me. "It's one of those app things that everyone's obsessed with."

Shane chuckles, shaking his head. "It's just software for streamlining small business operations. Not exactly ground-breaking."

Erin snorts. "Don't let him fool you. He's got investors and everything."

"Sounds impressive," I say, though I catch the faintest trace of discomfort in his expression as if he's not used to the spotlight. "What kind of businesses use it?"

"A mix," he replies, his tone easy. "Retail, hospitality, some independent contractors. Basically, anyone who needs to stay organized without the headache of spreadsheets."

"Smart," I say, genuinely intrigued. "You must be good at solving problems."

He shrugs, a small smile tugging at his lips. "I try."

"Don't let him fool you. He's annoyingly good at it," Erin adds.

The conversation shifts to lighter banter as we pull up to The Emerald Briar, its elegant stone façade glowing softly in the evening light. Erin claps her hands together, practically bouncing in her seat. "Right, let's get this party started."

Shane steps out first, holding the door open for me with a polite nod. "After you," he says.

"Thanks," I reply, straightening my dress.

As we head inside, I can feel Erin's satisfaction radiating from her. She planned this perfectly, maybe too perfectly, and I can already tell the night is going to be anything but simple.

The private room at The Emerald Briar is cozy but stylish, with warm wood paneling and several tables set for Erin's party. Fairy lights hang along the walls, giving the space a soft, intimate glow. The hum of conversation fills the air as we step inside.

Erin takes my arm and immediately flits from one group to another, introducing me to her friends. I recognize a few faces from our college days, but there are plenty of new ones, too. They all greet me warmly, their curiosity polite but persistent as they ask about my travels. Erin loves to make me the center of attention, a habit I've tolerated over the years, but tonight, it feels heavier.

Shane sticks close to me, which I can't decide if I appreciate or not. His quiet presence feels steadying, a barrier between me and the room's buzz, but it's also unnerving. I'm not used to being watched so closely, even if it's done with polite interest.

As the group settles in, I do my best to stay engaged, laughing in the right places and answering questions when asked. But my thoughts keep wandering, drifting to places I wish they wouldn't.

"So, world traveler," Shane says, leaning in slightly as we linger by the drinks table. "Does this kind of thing feel mundane to you now?"

I glance at him, startled out of my thoughts. "What do you mean?"

"You know," he says, gesturing toward the room. "Hanging out here. Compared to everything you've seen, this must feel so ordinary."

I hesitate, swirling my drink in its glass. "I wouldn't say ordinary. There's something nice about coming back to the familiar. It's easier in some ways."

He nods, studying me for a moment. "Fair point. But you seem a bit distant."

I force a smile, deflecting. "It's been a long day of travel."

My phone vibrates in my pocket. I pull it out and glance at the screen.

Ruairi: You never called to say you got there.

I sigh, slipping the phone back into my bag, determined to ignore it.

"Is everything okay?"

"Yeah," I reply quickly. "Just my brother checking in. He worries too much."

Shane raises an eyebrow. "Older brother, I'm guessing?"

"My twin, actually."

"Twins, huh?" He chuckles, shaking his head. "That explains the extra layer of protectiveness."

I roll my eyes, leaning back slightly. "I guess. He likes to pretend I can't manage without him."

Another buzz cuts through the conversation.

Ruairi: Aoife. Are you there?

I stifle a groan, standing and excusing myself as casually as I can. "I have to take this. Please excuse me," I say, flashing Shane a quick smile as I step out of the room.

The hallway is quieter, the low hum of the hotel's music filtering through the space. I tap out a quick reply as I walk, my fingers flying over the screen.

Aoife: I'm here. I'm fine. Stop hovering.

I hit send, distracted by the familiar push and pull of Ruairi's need to check on me. So distracted, in fact, that I don't see the man coming toward me until I collide with him.

Hot liquid splashes against my arm and the unmistakable aroma of coffee hits me as I stumble back, my phone nearly slipping from my fingers.

"*Dia ár sábháil*," the man mutters, his voice rough with irritation.

I freeze, recognition slamming into me as I look up. Standing there, scowling down at the coffee stain spreading across his shirt, is Eamon.

For a second, I can't speak. My mind reels as his gaze lifts from the mess to meet mine. The piercing blue of his eyes is like ice, sharp and unrelenting, locking onto me with the same intensity they always had.

"Eve?" he asks, his tone incredulous.

"Eamon." His name leaves my lips in a breathless whisper. "What are you doing here?" I ask, the words slipping out before I can stop them.

He gestures vaguely around us, his tone calm but firm. "This is my hotel."

That takes a second to register. "You own The Emerald Briar?"

His smirk tugs at the corner of his mouth. "Surprised?"

I don't answer. My thoughts are too jumbled to form a coherent response. He told me his family-owned hotels, and this is exactly the kind of empire he'd run—polished, successful, untouchable.

"What about you?" he asks, his voice cutting through my thoughts. "What are you doing here?"

"A friend's party," I manage, keeping my tone neutral.

His gaze sharpens, scanning my face for something I'm not willing to offer. "And are you staying?"

I shake my head, my answer coming quickly. "No. I'm only here for the evening."

Before the silence stretches too long, I notice a subtle shift in

Eamon's posture. His shoulders stiffen, and his jaw tightens as his eyes focus on something behind me.

The change is so sudden, so sharp, that it sends a prickle of unease down my spine. I glance quickly over my shoulder and spot Shane approaching. His gaze is steady, curious but relaxed, as he closes the distance.

When I turn back to Eamon, his expression is harder, and the faint smirk on his lips is gone entirely. His piercing blue eyes have turned cold, his shoulders stiffening as he watches Shane approach. It's not only anger.

It's jealousy—pure and unmistakable.

The air feels heavier, the tension between us palpable. My heart pounds in my chest as I meet Eamon's gaze, the unspoken tension in his expression enough to make my breath hitch.

This isn't going to end well.

Eamon

I SEE HIM BEFORE SHE DOES. A TALL MAN WITH DIRTY blond hair, his easy stride carrying him toward us like he doesn't have a care in the world. But I care. My jaw tightens as I watch his gaze dart between me and Eve.

"There you are," he says as he sidles up beside her. "I thought I lost you for a minute."

The tension in Eve's posture is immediate, her shoulders stiffening as she glances at him, then back to me. There's a flash of panic in her eyes before she masks it, but I see it.

"And you are?" I ask, keeping my tone calm, though the fury simmering beneath it is anything but.

He extends a hand, his smile disarming. "Shane. Aoife's date."

Aoife. The name catches me off guard. It's unfamiliar, yet undeniably her. I've called her Eve for so long that hearing something different feels like a betrayal and a revelation. It pulls at something deep, something raw.

But then *date.*

That single word twists the knife. I barely stop myself from reacting, my hand curling at my side before I force it to relax. I've spent too long looking for her. Spent too many nights wondering where she was or who she might be with. And now she's here, and this man thinks he can lay claim to her?

"A pleasure," I say, my voice tight as I grip his hand briefly before letting go. "Eamon. Owner of The Emerald Briar."

Shane nods, oblivious to the storm brewing under the surface. "Nice place."

Aoife glances at me, her expression a mix of guilt and unease. Good. She should feel it.

"Anyway," Shane continues, turning back to her, "they're waiting for you to sing Happy Birthday. You ready to head back?" He places a hand lightly on her arm. The movement makes my blood boil.

"She's not going anywhere," I say, stepping closer to her.

Shane looks confused, his brow furrowing. "Sorry?"

Aoife jumps in quickly, her voice unsteady. "You go back without me. I'll be there in a minute."

He hesitates. "You sure?"

"Yes," she says, her voice firmer now. "I'm fine. Go on."

Still, he lingers, clearly unsure whether he should leave her alone with me. Wise.

I force a polite smile, though it's the last thing I feel. "She said she'll be along shortly."

After a long pause, Shane nods reluctantly. "Okay. I'll see you inside." He shoots her one last questioning look before walking away.

The moment he's gone, I take her by the arm. "We need to talk," I say, my voice low and controlled.

"Eamon—"

"Now."

I steer her into the nearest empty room, my grip firm but deliberate. The door clicks shut behind us. Without hesitation, I reach back and turn the lock. The sound reverberates between us like a thunderclap.

The room is small, lit only by a single desk lamp in the corner. An oak desk sits against one wall, cluttered with papers and a closed laptop. Shelves line the walls, filled with ledgers, books, and binders. It smells faintly of leather and dust. The air is thick with tension that crackles between us.

Aoife backs up instinctively, her shoulders meeting the wall. Her wide eyes dart to the door, then back to me. She isn't afraid. That's not her. But she's uneasy, and she should be.

"What the hell are you doing?" she snaps, her voice sharp, though I catch the slightest tremble underneath.

"What am *I* doing?" I growl, stepping closer, my voice low and unforgiving. "I should be asking you the same thing."

Her chin lifts, defiance flashing in her eyes even as her chest rises and falls too quickly. "I told you. I'm here for a party."

"And that guy? Shane," I say, his name dripping from my lips like venom. I take another step, closing the distance between us pinning her with my gaze. "Who the hell is he? And why are you here with him?"

She hesitates, her lips parting as if to answer, but nothing comes. Her gaze drops momentarily before she looks back up to meet mine.

"It's nothing," she says finally, her voice softer now, almost pleading.

"Nothing?" I echo, my tone razor-sharp. I plant my hands on the wall on either side of her, caging her in. "Try again, *Aoife*," I say, testing out the feel of her real name.

She flinches slightly but doesn't argue. Doesn't deny it. That silence, that damned silence, is the final straw.

I lean in and kiss her, hard and unforgiving, pouring every ounce of my frustration, fury, and longing into it. She gasps against my lips, the sound both soft and sharp, and then she kisses me back. Her hands clutch at my shirt, her fingers curling into the fabric like she's trying to hold herself together.

It's still there. That undeniable pull between us.

When I finally break away, we're both breathing hard.

"Who is he?" I demand. "And who the hell are you really?"

She presses her palms against my chest, not to shove me away but to create space, to anchor herself. "It's a long story," she says, her voice trembling.

I nod, brushing a strand of hair from her face. "We've got all night."

Her eyes widen, but she holds her ground. "If I don't check in with my friend Erin, she's going to worry. I don't know what Shane's already told her."

"Fine," I say, stepping back, my voice tight with barely restrained anger. "Let's go."

"You're coming with me?" she asks, her voice edged with disbelief.

"I'm not letting you out of my sight again," I reply, my tone low and resolute, leaving no room for argument.

Opening the door, I gesture for her to lead the way.

We walk into the party that's humming with energy and laughter. Chatter fills the room as plates of cake are already being passed around, the sweet scent mingling with the buzz of celebration. From across the crowd, Shane leans toward Erin, nudging her arm and murmuring something. Her gaze follows his, and when she spots us, her expression shifts to confusion.

She hesitates for a moment before she begins to make her way over, her steps quick and deliberate.

"Is everything okay?" Erin asks, stopping in front of us. Her eyes dart to mine before settling on her friend.

Aoife hesitates. "I'm sorry," she says quickly. "But I need to leave early."

"What?" Erin's face falls. "You're leaving? But—"

"I'll explain later," Aoife says, her voice soft but urgent. "Please, apologize to Shane for me."

Erin looks like she wants to argue, but then her gaze shifts to me, suspicion clouding her features. "Who is this?"

I step forward, extending a hand. "Eamon," I say smoothly. "Aoife's boyfriend."

Erin blinks, her mouth opening slightly in shock as she looks back at Aoife. "Boyfriend?"

Aoife gives her a tight smile. "It's complicated. I'll explain everything later, I promise."

Erin looks uneasy but nods reluctantly. "Okay. But your suitcase is still at my apartment."

"I'll handle that," I say, my tone leaving no room for argument. "One of my men will get the address, and I'll have it picked up tonight."

Aoife looks at me but doesn't argue. Erin, however, steps forward, her unease now edged with desperation.

"Wait, Aoife," she says quickly, glancing between us. "Are you sure about this? Maybe you should call your brother first. Doesn't he usually—"

"He already knows," Aoife cuts in, her tone calm but firm. "He's aware that my plans have changed."

Erin's eyes narrow as doubt clouds her face. "You're certain? Because I could—"

"Erin," Aoife says softly, reaching out to touch her arm. "It's fine. Really. Don't worry about me, okay?"

The girl looks anything but reassured, her gaze shifting back to me. "And you're just going to take her without any explanation?"

I smile, though my patience is wearing thin. "She doesn't need to explain herself to you. Or anyone else, for that matter."

She opens her mouth to argue, but Aoife steps in again, her voice more insistent now. "Erin, please. I'll explain everything later. But I have to go."

Erin hesitates, clearly torn, before stepping back, her shoulders slumping slightly. "Fine. But you better explain this, Aoife. *All* of it."

Aoife nods once before turning toward me, her expression unreadable. Erin stands rooted to the spot, her confusion and unease heavy in the air as she watches us.

We're nearly at the door when I pause, turning back to Erin. "I'll cover the cost of the party," I say, my tone casual but deliberate. "Consider it my contribution to the celebration."

Erin's eyes widen slightly, her lips parting as if to respond, but I don't wait for her answer. I guide Aoife out of the room, my hand firm but not harsh at the small of her back.

As we walk through the quiet hallway, I glance down at her, my voice low and simmering with unresolved anger. "You've got a lot of explaining to do, *Eve*," I say, the old name slipping from my tongue like a warning. "And I'm not going anywhere until I hear it all."

Aoife

There's a tense silence between us as Eamon leads me through the hallways of The Emerald Briar. His hand rests at the small of my back, steady and unyielding. I can't decide if it's meant to guide me or keep me from running.

I still can't wrap my head around it. Eamon. Of all the places, all the people I could've crossed paths with. How is it possible that I just happened to walk into *his* hotel and bump into him? My chest tightens as the realization settles in.

This isn't chance. It can't be.

I've spent so long thinking about him. Dreaming about him. Wishing I hadn't left like I did. And now he's here, and I'm following him like it's the most natural thing in the world.

We reach the elevator, and he pulls a sleek black card from his pocket, swiping it before pressing the button for the penthouse.

I glance at him, my voice hesitant. "Where are we going?"

"To my apartment," he replies, his tone calm and matter-of-fact as if that answers everything.

"You live at the hotel?"

"I do," he says, his gaze fixed forward as the elevator hums to life.

The ride feels endless, the tension in the air coiling tighter with each passing second. When the elevator finally stops, and the doors slide open, my chest tightens at the sight of two men waiting outside.

They're dressed in dark suits, standing tall and alert, their gazes scrutinizing as they assess me briefly before focusing back on Eamon.

Guards? My pulse quickens. Why does he have guards?

I don't know what I expected, but it wasn't this. A harsh realization cuts through me—I don't really know him. Not the way I thought I did.

Eamon doesn't spare me a glance as he speaks to one of the men. "Her friend's hosting a party in the ballroom. Get the address and arrange for her belongings to be picked up."

The man nods without hesitation. "Yes, sir."

I swallow hard as Eamon steps forward, his hand brushing against mine to pull me along.

The doors to his penthouse swing open, and I stop just inside, my feet planted. The space is sprawling, luxurious but not ostentatious, with sleek furniture in neutral tones and floor-to-ceiling windows that offer a breathtaking view of the River Liffey.

I hesitate, suddenly unsure of myself.

"Come in and make yourself at home," he says, his tone even as he strides toward a built-in bar along one wall. Eamon pulls out a bottle of red wine and pours two glasses, the deep ruby liquid catching the light as it swirls in the crystal.

He turns, handing me one of the glasses, his movements calm and deliberate. "Sit," he says, gesturing to the sofa.

I take the glass, my fingers tightening around the stem as I cross the room. He waits until I settle on the soft leather before sitting beside me, his gaze steady and unreadable.

"Start talking," he says, leaning back, his posture deceptively relaxed.

I stare at the wine for a moment, then glance up at him. "I don't know where to begin."

"At the beginning," he replies, his voice low but firm.

The words stick in my throat, refusing to budge. Only after a deep breath do I manage to speak. "My name is Aoife Quigley."

His expression doesn't change, but I see the faintest trace of something in his eyes—recognition, maybe.

"My father was Patrick Quigley," I continue, the words barely above a whisper.

This time, there's no mistaking the shift in him. His brows draw together, his body going still as the name sinks in.

"You've heard of him," I say softly, more a statement than a question.

Eamon nods once, his voice calm but pointed. "Everyone in our world has."

I frown, the phrasing catching me off guard. *Our world?* What does he mean by that? But I push the thought aside and continue telling my story.

"I was traveling because of him," I begin, the words careful, deliberate. "He didn't want me involved in the Syndicate. Every time I brought it up, he shut me down. Wouldn't hear of it."

Eamon stays silent, his expression unreadable as I take another sip of wine.

"Instead of arguing with me, he suggested I travel. See the world," I pause, my lips twisting into a faint, bitter smile. "He was hoping that I'd change my mind. That I'd decide a different life was better."

"And did you?" Eamon asks his tone even.

I meet his gaze, my voice firm. "No. I traveled, but not for the reasons he hoped. Everywhere I went, I trained. Martial arts, hand-to-hand combat, shooting, whatever I could learn. I wanted to return home stronger. To prove to my father that I wasn't a little girl that he needed to protect. I needed him to see I was capable."

Eamon leans back slightly, swirling the wine in his glass, his eyes fixed on me.

"My father had me go by Eve my whole life," I explain. "It was safer that way. It was meant to keep my real identity hidden. To keep me safe."

The silence that follows is suffocating, the weight of the admission settling heavily between us. Eamon doesn't speak, but his gaze never leaves mine.

"And the night you left?" he presses, his voice sharp.

"My brother called to tell me our parents had been killed..." My voice falters, the words choking in my throat. I swallow hard, the memory bitter. "I packed my things and left. I didn't know what else to do."

"You should've woken me," he says, his tone quiet but brimming with restrained anger. "I would've gone with you. You shouldn't have had to travel alone after learning that."

"I couldn't have shown up with you. My brother would've lost it." I shake my head, my fingers tightening around the glass. "And by now, I'm sure Erin's called and told him I left with you. He's probably on his way already."

"Let him come," Eamon says, settling back with the kind of calm that feels more like a challenge than comfort. A faint smirk tugs at the corner of his mouth, but his gaze doesn't waver. "You have nothing to worry about," he adds, his voice low and steady. "You're in my territory now, Aoife."

His territory. The words are meant to soothe, but I know better. This isn't just a place—it's a choice.

And when Ruairi finds out where I am, who I'm with... there won't be a way to walk this back.

Still, I don't move. I don't argue.

And maybe that says everything.

Eamon

Sitting on my sofa, swirling a glass of wine, completely unaware of how much her presence alone has turned my world upside down. *Aoife*. Her name rolls through my head, unraveling months of frustration. It makes sense now why I couldn't find Eve. It was nothing more than a nickname, a deliberate mask to keep her hidden.

And hidden she was. Patrick Quigley's daughter. Ruairi Quigley's twin.

The revelation hits harder than it should, considering the tension already thrumming through me. Patrick Quigley was one of the most powerful men in Ireland—sharp, ruthless, and untouchable. The stories about him are legendary, but the whispers about his daughter? Those were rarer, quieter, and far more intriguing.

The daughter no one had ever seen. The one he kept out of sight, away from his world.

In today's society, where privacy is a luxury even the rich and powerful can't afford, the fact that Patrick managed to shield her identity entirely is staggering. No photos. No accidental mentions. Nothing. It's a testament to the kind of power he wielded, the respect and fear he commanded. Keeping Aoife

Quigley hidden from the eyes of his enemies and his allies must have been his greatest act of protection.

And now, she's here.

With her name finally revealed, her guarded exterior is showing the slightest cracks. It all makes sense—the secrecy, the carefully built walls around her. This is what it took to survive as Patrick Quigley's daughter.

I glance at her again, watching as she traces the rim of her glass absently. She's distracted, probably still trying to figure out how the hell we found one another again. But my thoughts drift elsewhere to her brother, Ruairi.

Ruairi Quigley hasn't been in power long. His father's death put him at the head of their Syndicate less than a year ago, but he's wasted no time making moves.

The lines between our territories had been clear for years. Dublin was mine. Belfast was theirs. But since Patrick's death, Ruairi has been pushing south, testing boundaries, trying to claim more. The Midlands, those critical trade routes connecting ports on both coasts, have become a battleground. Whoever controls them doesn't just control smuggling. They control influence, wealth, and alliances.

It's a bold play, especially for someone so new to power. And though we've exchanged more than one warning shot, I've kept my retaliation measured. For now.

But the fact that Ruairi's sister is sitting in my penthouse? That's a new kind of weapon. This changes everything.

The idea of Ruairi storming in here, realizing his precious, sheltered sister is with me—it's not a fantasy. It's a certainty. Her being here will escalate things between us and push a fragile balance closer to collapse. And I should care more than I do.

But I spent too long looking for her. Too long, wondering where she'd gone and if I'd ever see her again. Every part of me knows she's a complication I can't afford, a line I shouldn't have crossed. She's not just temptation—she's the Quigley Syndicate's untouchable daughter, the one girl who was never meant to be part of this world.

Now she's here, flesh and fire and defiance, and I won't let her go. Not when I've already tasted what it feels like to have her close.

I take another sip of my wine, leaning back in my chair as I fix my gaze on Aoife. "So," I say, breaking the silence, "tell me about Ruairi."

She frowns, her shoulders tensing slightly. "What about him?"

"Anything you haven't already mentioned," I reply smoothly. "You said he won't let you work in your family's Syndicate. Why?"

Her lips press together for a moment before she sighs. "I'm a girl," she says bluntly. "In his eyes, that makes me a liability. He keeps saying I need to stay out of it, that it's not my place."

I scoff, setting my glass down on the table. "And what do you think?"

Her gaze snaps to mine, fire sparking in her eyes. "I think he's wrong."

"Good," I say with a faint smirk. "Then we're on the same page."

She arches a brow, cautious. "What do you mean?"

Studying her, I let the silence stretch between us. When I finally speak, my voice is calm. Certain. "Us. This." I motion between us. "That's how I'll get to him."

Her expression shifts, guarded now. "So I'm bait?"

"You're leverage," I correct, tone even. "Your family kept you hidden your entire life. You watched from the shadows while you were whispered about behind closed doors. All the while, they told themselves it was to protect you." I lean in, gaze locked on hers. "But we both know better."

Her breath catches. She knows I'm right.

"They kept you out of something you were born to be part of. Shut you out of the world they built while expecting you to stay silent, stay small." I let the next words fall like a quiet verdict. "And now you're with me."

She doesn't flinch. Doesn't look away. But I feel the storm building behind her eyes.

"He won't take that well." Her mouth opens like she wants to argue, but she quickly corrects herself. "Ruairi thinks he owns your loyalty," I continue. "And when he finds out you've given it to me, it'll gut him."

She doesn't speak. Doesn't move. But I can feel the energy shift between us.

Because it's not just that she's with me. It's that she chose to be. Her family kept her locked outside the game her whole life. But now? She's inside. And she's sitting across from the enemy.

Aoife doesn't speak. Doesn't move. The moment stretches between us, taut and heavy, like a breath held too long.

She's no prisoner. There are no chains. Just a quiet, beautiful stillness—like a woman standing beneath the slow descent of the blade, daring it to fall. And maybe, just maybe, hoping it will.

That tells me everything I need to know. Aoife's hesitation is palpable, but I see the intrigue in her eyes.

She's already in it.

"How?" she asks, her voice low and cautious.

"We dismantle him," I say, my voice quieter now. "From the inside out. Not with bullets or bloodshed. With doubt. With fear."

I pause, letting the words hang. Letting her breathe them in.

"We'll make him question everything he thinks he knows about you, about himself, about the grip he believes he still has. Every truth he's ever relied on? We'll twist it until it cuts."

She stares at me, breath catching just slightly. "And if it doesn't work?"

I lean closer, slow and deliberate, brushing a strand of hair behind her ear.

"It will," I whisper. "Because we won't give him a choice."

The silence stretches between us, charged and electric. Her

lips part slightly, her breathing uneven. I know I'm pushing her boundaries, testing the line between her defiance and her trust.

"You're insane," she murmurs, but there's no conviction behind her words.

"You already knew that," I reply, my voice low and deliberate.

And then I kiss her.

It's not soft or tentative. It's raw, consuming, a clash of anger, desire, and unspoken promises. Aoife's hands tangle in my shirt as she pulls me closer, meeting my intensity with her own.

The wineglass in her hand slips to the floor, shattering as it hits the polished wood, but neither of us acknowledges it. Her gasps melt into a moan as I lift her off the sofa, her legs instinctively wrapping around my waist. I carry her toward the bedroom, the heat between us drowning out everything else.

There's nothing gentle about this—no slow burn or hesitation. Its passion and fury and the weight of months of longing snapping all at once. She clings to me like gravity itself is failing, tugging me closer like she can't stand the thought of even an inch between us.

I push the bedroom door open with my shoulder. The soft light from the city spills through the windows, casting shadows across the dark wood floors and the king-sized bed that dominates the space. I don't hesitate, lowering her onto the mattress.

Our lips never part, the kiss frantic and raw, all-consuming. My hands slide down her back, fingers finding the zipper of her dress. There's an urgency I can't control. I need her bare, her body beneath mine.

The zipper gives way under my touch, the fabric loosening and slipping from her shoulders as I push it down to her waist. My eyes drop to her breasts, full and perfect, barely contained by the delicate black lace of her bra. The sight alone sends a surge of heat through me, tightening every muscle in my body.

I dip my head, pressing my lips to the curve of her collarbone, trailing lower as my hands slide up her sides. My thumbs glide over the lace, teasing her hardened nipples through the delicate fabric. She gasps, her body arching into me.

"Missed this," I say as my tongue traces the edge of the lace.

I've craved this, craved *her*, every inch of her bare skin, the way her body moves beneath mine. Her dress slips lower as I shift, pulling it the rest of the way off, leaving her in nothing but black lace.

I pause for a moment, drinking her in, the curve of her hips, the swell of her breasts framed by the delicate fabric, her flushed skin begging for my touch.

"You're fucking perfect," I murmur, my voice rough and thick with need.

Her eyes meet mine, dark with desire, and she pulls me closer, her voice low and breathless. "Then stop looking and touch me."

Her words snap the last thread of my restraint. My hands are on her instantly, sliding over her hips, tracing the curve of her waist as I press my body against hers. My lips find hers again, the kiss fierce and consuming, a collision of hunger and desperation.

I tug the lace straps off her shoulders, trailing my mouth down the line of her neck, over her collarbone, and lower. My fingers slip beneath the edge of her bra, pulling it away to expose her completely. She gasps as I take her nipple into my mouth, my tongue circling the sensitive peak while my hand moves to her other breast, teasing it with slow, deliberate strokes.

Her back arches, pressing into me, her fingers threading through my hair, tugging just enough to send a jolt of heat through me. "Eamon," she breathes. The sound of my name on her lips is enough to push me further.

I shift, pressing kisses down her stomach, savoring the way her body trembles beneath me. Her thighs part instinctively, and I can feel the heat radiating from her. Pausing, I glance up at her before my hands glide up her legs, spreading them wider.

"You're mine," I say, my voice low and rough, claiming her as I lower myself between her thighs.

Her breath hitches, her body tightening beneath me as I taste her for the first time in months. I take my time, savoring every sound she makes, every shiver that ripples through her.

My tongue moves in slow, deliberate strokes, teasing her. Pressing her thighs open wider, the tension builds until her hips begin to lift. Her moans grow louder, more desperate. But I don't let her fall. Not yet.

Instead, I change the pace, alternating between slow, deliberate movements and faster, relentless strokes, keeping her suspended in that perfect, torturous moment. Her breathing grows ragged, her hands clutching at the sheets like they're the only thing anchoring her.

When she finally shatters, her cry echoes through the room, her body arching off the bed, her thighs quivering against my shoulders. I don't stop, coaxing every last wave of pleasure from her until she collapses back onto the mattress, her chest heaving, her skin flushed and glistening.

I move back up her body, my lips tracing a path over her skin, savoring every shiver, every soft gasp that escapes her lips. I don't stop until I'm hovering over her again, my weight braced on my forearms.

Her eyes meet mine, wide and full of desire. Her lips part slightly, and she reaches for me, her fingers trailing up my arms, pulling me closer.

"I want you," she whispers, her voice low and thick with need. "I need to feel you."

Her words ignite something primal, a hunger that I've kept buried for too long. The space between us feels electric, charged with everything we've been holding back. I lower myself until my lips brush hers. The kiss is slow and teasing as I let the tension between us stretch for a moment longer.

"You have me," I murmur against her lips. "Every part of me."

The world falls away as I push into her in one smooth, deliberate motion. Her gasp melts into my groan as I bury myself fully inside her. It's raw, consuming, a perfect storm of passion and fury, every touch igniting a desire that burns hotter with each second.

She matches me movement for movement, her legs wrapping tightly around me, pulling me deeper. Aoife's nails rake down my back, a delicious sting that only fuels the fire raging between us. Her moans grow louder, raw and unrestrained, each sound driving me further, harder as if I can't get close enough to her.

"You're mine," I growl against her ear, claiming her with every word, every movement. "Say it."

Her breath hitches as her hips meet mine, desperate and demanding. "I'm yours," she gasps.

The words ignite something feral inside me, the need to possess her completely, to leave no doubt in her mind that she belongs to me. My pace quickens, my hand sliding down to grip her thigh, spreading her wider beneath me.

Her body trembles beneath mine, her head tilting back as my lips find her throat, pressing kisses along the delicate line of her neck, my teeth grazing her pulse.

I press deeper, my movements deliberate, every thrust meant to remind her of exactly what she's done to me. "I've thought about this every damn night," I confess, my voice low and rough. "The way you feel, the way you sound, the way your body moves under mine. I couldn't forget it, even when I tried."

Her eyes lock with mine, the vivid green darkening, swirling with desire and an intensity that holds me captive, daring me to take everything she's offering. "You don't have to forget. I'm here now."

The words hit me harder than I expect, unraveling me from the inside as I drive into her harder, faster, claiming her in every way I've craved since the moment she disappeared.

Her hands tangle in my hair, pulling me closer as the intensity between us builds, a tidal wave threatening to crash. She's close, teetering on the edge. I'm relentless, driving her higher and higher, determined to take her with me as the tension between us spirals to its breaking point.

"Come for me," I command, my voice rough and possessive. Her response is immediate. Her body clenches around me, her cry raw and unrestrained as she gives herself over completely.

The sight, the sound, the feel of her unraveling beneath me is enough to tip me over the edge. A guttural groan tears from my throat as I bury myself deep, my body shuddering with the force of my release. It's raw and consuming, a wave of pleasure so intense it leaves me breathless. For a moment, everything else fades —there's only her, only us.

I collapse against her, both of us breathing hard, our bodies still tangled as the aftershocks ripple through us. Her arms wrap around me, holding me close, and I press my forehead to hers, the weight of what just happened sinking in.

"You're mine, Aoife," I murmur again, softer this time, a promise rather than a demand.

She doesn't respond, but the way she clings to me says everything I need to hear.

Aoife

I LIE IN THE TANGLE OF SHEETS, MY BODY STILL humming from the intensity of what we just shared. Eamon's arm is draped over my waist, his fingers tracing absent patterns on my hip. The silence between us is comfortable, but my mind is anything but.

"What happens next?" I ask softly, breaking the quiet. "What does this mean for us?"

Eamon shifts, propping himself up on one elbow to look down at me. His gaze is steady. "It means exactly what I said, Aoife. Now that I've found you again, I'm not letting you go."

I sit up slightly, clutching the sheet against my chest. "It's not that simple, Eamon. My life is in Belfast—"

"Not anymore," he interrupts, his voice firm but calm. "Your life is here. With me."

My mouth opens to argue, to tell him it's not that easy, but the sharp trill of his phone cuts through the air.

He leans over, grabbing the device from the bedside table. "Hold that thought," he mutters, swiping to answer the call.

I watch as his expression hardens almost immediately. "Yes, I was expecting him," he says, his tone clipped. "Send him up."

He hangs up and places the phone back on the table, turning to me. "Your brother's here."

I exhale slowly, not surprised but still uneasy. "Of course he is."

Eamon swings his legs over the edge of the bed, standing and pulling on a pair of slacks. "Get dressed," he says, his tone softening slightly. "We'll handle this together."

I slip out of bed, grabbing my dress from the floor and pulling it on. My hands tremble slightly as I smooth the fabric.

"Don't be nervous," Eamon says, stepping closer. He places his hands on my shoulders, forcing me to look at him. "You're with me now, Aoife. No one, not even your brother, is going to take you away from me."

His words are meant to be reassuring, but they only fuel the tension tightening in my chest. "You don't know Ruairi like I do," I murmur. "He won't back down. Not easily."

A knock at the door cuts off any further conversation. Eamon's jaw tightens, and he gestures for one of his guards to answer.

The door swings open, and Ruairi strides in, flanked by two of his guards, their imposing figures lingering just behind him. His green eyes, a mirror of my own, lock onto me with an intensity that feels like a physical blow. His expression is thunderous as his gaze shifts briefly to Eamon, narrowing with barely concealed fury.

"What the hell is going on?" he demands.

I stand tall, refusing to cower. "What does it look like?"

Ruairi's eyes narrow, his jaw tightening as he steps closer. "It looks like you've lost your damn mind," he snaps.

"No," I reply sharply, standing my ground. "I've finally made a decision for myself. I'm with Eamon."

"You're *with* him?" Ruairi's laugh is bitter and humorless. "You must think this is some kind of game? Do you have any idea what you're doing?"

"I know exactly what I'm doing," I shoot back. "I'm making a choice, Ruairi. One you can't control."

"This? Him? You're playing with fire." He turns, jabbing a finger toward Eamon, his voice dropping dangerously low. "And you. What is this to you, O'Sullivan? A game? A way to get under my skin? Because if it is, you've just made the biggest mistake of your life."

Eamon steps forward, unshaken, his expression cold and calculating. "This isn't a game, Quigley," he says, his voice steady and razor-sharp. "Aoife isn't a pawn, and I'm not some fool looking to provoke you for sport. She's with me because she chose to be. Maybe that's what you can't handle, that you don't control her anymore."

His lips curl into a faint smirk, his tone turning deadly calm. "And as for mistakes, I don't make them. But you're in *my* home, in *my* city. You're dangerously close to making one yourself."

Ruairi ignores Eamon's challenge, his gaze snapping back to me. "You go to a party, and somehow, you end up with him?" he says, his tone dripping with disbelief and anger.

I lift my chin, refusing to flinch. "I didn't *end up* with him," I reply evenly. "I met Eamon in the Maldives. We've been together since."

His eyes narrow, a cold fury simmering beneath the surface. "You told Bridget you were coming to Belfast to spend a weekend with a friend."

I falter, my confidence wavering for the first time. "I—"

"Save it," he snaps, cutting me off before I can find the words. "It doesn't matter. We're going home." He steps forward, his hand shooting out to grab my wrist.

"Ruairi—"

Before I can finish, Eamon moves. His fist connects with my brother's jaw.

Ruairi stumbles but recovers quickly, shoving me aside as he lunges at Eamon. "You bastard," he snarls, throwing a punch that Eamon dodges.

The two of them collide, fists flying. The room erupts into chaos. The sound of grunts and thudding impacts mingle with my shouted pleas.

"Stop it," I yell as I try to get between them. "What the hell are you doing? You're going to kill each other."

Neither listens, their focus locked entirely on each other, the fight spiraling into something primal and vicious. I whip toward the guards standing uselessly at the door. "Are you just going to stand there? Do something!"

They shift uncertainly, caught between loyalty and fear, but no one moves.

The fight spirals—raw, brutal, and unrelenting. Ruairi and Eamon are locked in their own world, all violence and betrayal, years of tension exploding in fists and fury.

Then, a sharp click pierces the chaos. The sound of a safety being switched off freezes everyone in place. One of Eamon's guards has drawn his weapon, the barrel trained on Ruairi.

"Enough," the guard says coldly.

I push between them, placing a hand on Eamon's chest to keep him back while glaring at Ruairi. "Both of you need to stop," I say, my voice firm and unyielding. "Beating each other to a pulp isn't going to solve anything."

Eamon's chest heaves beneath my hand like he's holding himself back by nothing but sheer will. I glance at him, and he nods once to his guard, who lowers the weapon but doesn't holster it.

Ruairi rubs his jaw, his glare darting between me and Eamon. "This is what you want, Aoife? To be O'Sullivan's little play-thing? Warming his bed and letting him pay your way through life?"

"Watch yourself," Eamon growls.

"Don't you dare try to reduce me to that," I say, stepping closer to Ruairi, my anger rising to match his. "I'll be paying my own way working for Eamon."

That stops them both.

Ruairi's eyes widen, his composure snapping as his anger boils over. He rounds on Eamon, his voice sharp with disbelief. "You're letting her work in your Syndicate? What kind of man allows a woman to get involved in this world?"

Before Eamon can respond, I step forward, cutting him off. "A man who respects me enough to give me a chance," I say, my voice steady and firm. "Unlike you. You've had every opportunity to let me prove myself, and you refused."

The room seems to darken, the weight of my words settling heavily between us. Ruairi's expression twists, and a storm brews in his eyes.

"You have no idea what you're doing," he says, his voice low. "You think you're in control here, but you're not."

"That's where you're wrong," I reply. "I'm in complete control."

Ruairi's voice drops into a growl. "You're making a mistake, Aoife. A dangerous one."

"And so are you," Eamon cuts in, his voice smooth but edged with steel. "You're in my territory now, Quigley. Tread carefully."

Ruairi's glare burns into him for a long moment before he turns back to me. "Fine," he says, his voice cold. "I'll leave. For now. But this isn't over, Aoife."

His gaze shifts back to Eamon, his tone darkening. "And when I come back, my sister's coming home with me."

With that, he storms out, his guards trailing behind him, the air left heavy with his parting threat.

Aoife

The door slams behind Ruairi, the sound reverberating through the room. I force myself to stand tall, staring at the closed door as though I've won some kind of victory. But my hands betray me, trembling at my sides, the adrenaline coursing through me refusing to settle.

"You're shaking," Eamon says softly.

"I'm fine," I insist, my tone harsher than I intend, but I don't turn to face him. I can't. Not yet.

He steps closer, his presence solid, grounding. "Leave us."

The command is quiet but absolute. The guards don't hesitate. Within seconds, the room empties.

Only then do I turn. The sight of his split lip stops me cold. A smear of blood mars his mouth, the edges already bruising. "You're hurt," I whisper, stepping forward before I can stop myself. "Your lip—"

He shrugs like it's nothing but doesn't stop me when I slip away, wet a cloth, and return to him. He holds still as I press it gently to his mouth, his eyes never leaving mine. There's no flinch, no bravado. Just heat and quiet restraint simmering beneath the surface. The cloth falls away, and before I can say anything, his hands are on me, pulling me in.

His warmth wraps around me, steady and sure, and I let myself sink into him. My face presses to his chest. My breath catches as everything I've been holding in threatens to break free.

"You were incredible," he murmurs, his lips brushing against my hair. "Standing up to him like that, refusing to back down. I've never been prouder of you."

"I don't feel incredible," I admit, my voice muffled against his chest. "I feel like the walls are closing in. Like I'm running out of space to move."

He pulls back just enough to tilt my chin up, his piercing blue eyes locking with mine. "That's because you're playing a game you've never been allowed to play before. You're not used to holding the power."

I shake my head, biting my lip. "I don't want to fight with Ruairi, but I won't be hidden away any longer."

Eamon strokes his thumb across my cheek, his voice low but firm. "This isn't about fighting with him. This is about showing him that the rules have changed. The pendulum swings in your favor now, Aoife. You decide where it stops."

I stare up at him. "What if I can't do it? What if I'm wrong?"

"You're not wrong," he says with absolute certainty, his hands tightening on my arms. "You were born for this. You're stronger, smarter, and more capable than he's ever given you credit for. Your brother doesn't know how to handle that, but he's about to learn."

I swallow hard, leaning into his strength, clinging to his words like oxygen. "I don't know where to start."

He studies me for a long beat, then lets out a quiet breath. "After watching Ruairi lose his composure when you said you'd be working for me, I think employing you at the hotel is exactly the right move."

I glance down, suddenly unsure. "I probably should've asked first. I wasn't trying to speak out of turn. I just..." I trail off, uncertain how to explain the need I felt in that moment to be heard.

"You didn't overstep," Eamon says, "You made a move. And it was the right one." His eyes hold mine. "You already know how to read people, how to listen when others forget you're in the room. You don't need training. What you need is a platform, and this gives it to you."

"But what does it prove?" I ask. "To Ruairi?"

"That you're not under his thumb anymore," he says. "That you've made a choice, and you're not backing down from it. You won't have to spy or dig for secrets. Your presence is the message."

His words stir something in me like flint striking steel, igniting a spark of confidence.

"He doesn't expect this from me," I murmur. "He's always seen me as fragile. Something to protect, not respect."

"Then it's time to show him how wrong he's been. You're going to let him see exactly what you're capable of." Eamon's smile curves slow and dark, his eyes gleaming. "You make him question everything. Show him you're not a woman who needs his protection. That you can not only survive but thrive in our world."

Ruairi

I slam the door behind me, the sound reverberating through the house. My chest heaves as I try to force down the anger boiling inside me, but it's no use. The image of Aoife standing beside Eamon O'Sullivan burns in my mind like a brand.

"Ruairi?" Bridget's voice carries from the sitting room, cautious and expectant. She steps into the hallway, her expression softening when she sees my face. "Where's Aoife?"

"She's not here," I snap, brushing past her and heading toward the kitchen. I grab a glass from the counter and pour a measure of whiskey, the amber liquid sloshing as my hands shake.

Bridget follows, her footsteps light but determined. "What do you mean she's not here? What happened?"

I throw back the drink in one gulp, the burn doing nothing to quell my fury. "She's *with* him." The words taste bitter as they leave my mouth.

Bridget frowns, confused. "With whom?"

"Eamon bloody O'Sullivan," I snarl, slamming the glass onto the counter. "My sister is with the head of the Dublin syndicate."

Bridget's face pales, her hand coming up to her mouth. "Oh,

Ruairi," she hesitates, her eyes darting away. "I knew she met someone, but I didn't know who it was."

My head snaps toward her, the betrayal twisting in my gut. "You knew?" I bark, advancing on her. "And you didn't tell me?"

Bridget doesn't flinch, her expression hardening. "Don't you dare turn this on me," she fires back. "I didn't know who it was, and even if I had, it wouldn't have mattered. Aoife's a grown woman. You can't keep treating her like a child."

"She's my sister," I growl, the words grinding out between clenched teeth. "I'm trying to protect her."

"No, you're not," Bridget argues, crossing her arms. "You're trying to control her, and it's going to backfire on you. She's not the little girl you used to boss around, Ri. She's a capable young woman, and you need to stop underestimating her."

My temper flares again. "So now you're telling me I'm wrong, are you? That I should let her work in the Syndicate?"

"I'm saying I understand why you're against it," Bridget says evenly. "But in Aoife's mind, she has just as much right to lead this Syndicate as you do."

"If you're referring to that ridiculous promise," I scoff, throwing up my hands. "We were children. We didn't know what we were saying."

"Maybe you didn't," she replies, her tone softer but no less resolute. "But Aoife did. And it meant something to her. Maybe it's time you considered things from her point of view."

I shake my head, pacing the room like a caged animal. "So what? You think I should hand her a role? Let her throw herself into this life without a second thought?"

"I'm saying there must be something you can let her do," Bridget counters. "Something small, something that keeps her here. At least then she's safe, and she's not in Dublin with some man."

I meet her gaze, my voice cold. "Aoife made her choice clear. She's with O'Sullivan now. She deserves whatever comes of it."

Bridget's shoulders sag slightly, disappointment flickering

across her face. "Be careful, Ri," she warns. "If he's as dangerous as you say, Aoife's going to need you eventually. Don't slam the door on her completely."

With that, she turns and leaves, the quiet click of the door leaving me alone with my thoughts.

I sink into a chair, rubbing a hand over my face as Bridget's words echo in my head. *Aoife's going to need you eventually.*

My fists clench. I can't think like that. She chose this path. Chose him over her own flesh and blood.

I pull out my phone, scrolling through my contacts until I land on Ronan, my second-in-command. He's dependable and ruthless, the one person I can trust to handle this without hesitation.

When he answers, his voice is calm. "Boss?"

"I want plans in place to take O'Sullivan's Syndicate down," I say, my tone steely.

There's a pause before Ronan responds, his voice measured but curious. "What's this about? O'Sullivan's been on your radar for a while, but we've never gone after him directly."

I clench my jaw, debating how much to share. "He's been pushing for more territory in the midlands, and it's time we remind him where the lines are."

Ronan hesitates. "Pushing how? I haven't seen anything that justifies starting a war."

"O'Sullivan's taken something that belongs to me," I snap.

"What did he take?" Ronan asks, his tone cautious. "And how fast do you want us to move?"

I grip the edge of the desk, my knuckles white. "My sister," I say finally, the words like acid on my tongue. "Aoife is in Dublin with him."

Ronan hesitates, the weight of my admission sinking in. "Aoife's with O'Sullivan?" he repeats, disbelief evident in his voice.

"Yes," I growl. "And while we're dismantling his operation, I want every precaution taken to ensure she's not harmed. Pass that down to every man. Aoife does not get touched. No exceptions."

"Understood," Ronan replies, his tone sharpening with purpose. "Do you want us to target his supply chain first?"

"Ports, routes, businesses. Start where it'll hurt him the most. Hit them clean, make him bleed, but don't overreach. I want this controlled."

"Got it," Ronan says after a pause. "Anything else?"

"That's all for now. Keep me updated," I say, ending the call.

I toss the phone onto the desk, exhaling slowly as my mind races with the weight of what's to come. If Aoife wants to stand by O'Sullivan, then she'll learn the hard way how much it will cost.

Eamon

THE TENSION IN THE PRIVATE MEETING ROOM IS palpable as Seamus shifts uncomfortably in his chair. The faint scent of smoke lingers on his clothes as I scroll through the pictures once more. I scroll through the photos again: blackened debris, twisted metal, the remains of a shipment that was supposed to be untouchable. My jaw tightens as I set the phone down on the table.

"What the hell is this about?" Seamus asks, his voice edged with irritation and confusion. "Why would Ruairi Quigley risk a full-on war with us? It doesn't make sense."

"It's a message," I reply, my tone cold and clipped. Holding up the white envelope, I let the wax seal speak for itself. The Quigley crest, bold and undeniable, was found pinned to the warehouse door. "He's making his intentions very clear."

"A message? For what?" Seamus shakes his head. "Quigley's no fool. He knows we'll retaliate."

I place the envelope on the table, staring at the crest for a moment before breaking the seal. The faint crack of wax echoes in the room as I pull out a folded sheet of thick, cream-colored paper and read the note aloud.

She is blood of my blood, bound by a name you'll never own.
Turn back while you still can,
Or be swallowed whole by the abyss you've chosen.
~R.Q.

"That's a bit dramatic," he mutters.

"Dramatic or not, it's a warning." I set the note down. "And he's not bluffing."

"Eamon, what in the bloody hell's going on?" he asks.

My fingers brush the edge of the table. I don't like having to explain myself to anyone, but there's no point in dancing around the truth. Not after this. Meeting Seamus's questioning gaze, I keep my voice low and steady. "It's about the woman in my penthouse."

Seamus arches a brow, his confusion deepening. "You're telling me this is about a girl?"

I exhale sharply. "Her name is Aoife. Aoife Quigley. Twin sister of—"

"Hold one. Are you telling me she's Ruairi's twin sister?" He leans forward, his voice lowering. "You mean to tell me the woman you're *ag scairteadh léi* is Patrick Quigley's daughter? The one he kept hidden for years?"

I nod once. "Yes."

Seamus lets out a low whistle. "Christ, Eamon. That explains a lot. How the hell did this even happen?"

"It was an accident," I say flatly, not wanting to indulge him but knowing he won't let it go. "We met in the Maldives. I didn't know who she really was, and then she left unexpectedly."

Seamus smirks. "So she's what's had you so twisted up all this time. I didn't have you pegged as the type to lose your head over some pussy."

I glare at him, my voice cutting through his amusement. "You're treading on thin ice."

"Fine, fine." He raises his hands in mock surrender. But still, mate, this is different. The woman's a hot piece of ass, no denying that, but she's not worth—"

I'm on him before he finishes the sentence, grabbing the front of his shirt and pulling him halfway across the table. My voice drops, deadly quiet. "Do not. Talk. About her. Like that. Not ever."

Seamus stares at me, startled, before nodding slowly. I release him as I sit back in my chair. "You will treat Aoife with respect," I say, my tone laced with warning. "I can promise you won't like what happens if you don't. Understood?"

He nods again, straightening his shirt, his focus shifting as he clears his throat. "Fine. So, what do we do about this attack?"

"We strike back," I say. "Quigley just received a critical shipment of weapons. He's planning to move it through the Midlands en route to supply a nationalist faction that's looking to stir unrest in the north. If this deal goes through, he won't just strengthen his Syndicate. He'll position himself as a major player with political factions owing him favors."

Seamus' expression darkens. "The Midlands? If he's running his routes through there, he's not just pushing limits. He's staking a claim."

"Exactly," I reply, my voice tightening. "He's testing the waters, seeing how far he can go before someone pushes back. This shipment isn't just about weapons. It's leverage. If he pulls this off, he'll have power over groups no one should have control of."

"So, we hit it. Hard. Make sure Quigley loses the shipment and the deal. That'll send a clear message."

"And cripple his plans," I add, leaning back in my chair. "We intercept it before it leaves the Midlands. His buyers lose faith, and he loses the foothold he's trying to build."

"And here I thought we'd have a quiet week." Seamus grins, a glimmer of excitement in his eyes. "And Quigley? Do you want me to take him out?"

I shake my head. "No. Ruairi stays unharmed. Make that clear to the men."

Seamus's mouth opens like he's about to protest, but the look I give him silences whatever thought crosses his mind. "You're the boss," he mutters, though the doubt in his voice is unmistakable.

"Good," I say and motion toward the door. "Now get it done."

Seamus hesitates for a moment before nodding and leaving the room, the door clicking shut behind him.

Sitting alone in the silence, the gravity of what's about to transpire weighs heavily on me. Ruairi's not stupid. He knew exactly what he was doing by attacking my shipment. He wanted to provoke me, to test how far I'd go for Aoife. And I know it won't end here.

But I meant what I said to her. She's mine now, and I won't allow anyone, including her brother, to take her from me.

The room feels too quiet, the silence almost mocking as it settles around me. My phone sits on the table, the screen dark. But my mind is already racing ahead, calculating my next move. Ruairi thinks he can send a message, but he'll learn soon enough that I don't play defense. I strike back.

For now, I'll ensure his safety—for Aoife's sake. It's a line I won't cross unless he forces my hand. If that happens, I'll no longer be able to guarantee his survival.

With my decision made, I rise to my feet. If Quigley wants a war, then he'll get one. And when the final move is played, there won't be a shadow of doubt about who holds the upper hand.

Aoife

THE LOBBY OF THE EMERALD BRIAR HUMS WITH LATE afternoon activity. Guests filter in through the revolving doors, the quiet click of polished shoes echoing against marble floors. The soft whir of suitcase wheels trails behind them, blending with low conversation and the occasional chime of the elevator. Sunlight slants in through the tall windows, casting warm streaks across the glossy check-in counter where I stand.

I finish processing a reservation for a couple from Spain, sliding them their room keys with a practiced smile. Their gratitude is polite yet distant. They're already eager to disappear into the elevator and begin whatever version of their escape brought them here.

I've never held a job before this. Not because I wasn't capable but because I wasn't allowed. Da's priority was keeping me hidden, sheltered from the public eye like a secret too dangerous to share. For years, I told myself it was for my own protection. Now, as I stand beneath a chandelier of cut glass and gold trim, I'm anything but hidden.

Working the front desk at the hotel isn't glamorous, but there's something grounding about it—something real. Surprisingly, I like it more than I expected. There's comfort in the structure, the repetition. Here, I'm not a Quigley. I'm just Aoife, and that feels like power in its own right.

Eamon told me he conducts a lot of his Syndicate business here—that behind the elegant facade, this hotel is as much a stronghold as it is a sanctuary. But so far, I've seen nothing out of the ordinary. Just business people, tourists, and whispered conversations in the bar. Everything feels normal.

At least, it does until I sense the shift.

From the corner of my eye, movement draws my attention—deliberate, confident. I glance up just as Eamon strides across the lobby, every step precise, purposeful. His dark suit fits him too well. His mere presence turns heads. Including mine. My stomach flips in that infuriating way it always does when he's near.

"Ms. Quigley," he says as he stops in front of the desk, his tone smooth and teasing. His gaze locks onto mine, his smile lazy but deliberate, like he knows exactly how much attention he's drawing.

"Mr. O'Sullivan," I reply, a hint of a smile playing on my lips. "Is this a professional visit, or are you here to cause trouble?"

His smile deepens as he leans casually against the counter, his eyes never leaving mine. "Can't it be both?"

From the corner of my eye, I catch the two women working beside me freeze in place. They're watching us, their wide-eyed stares bouncing between Eamon and me like they can't believe what they're seeing.

Eamon doesn't seem to notice, or maybe he doesn't care. His full attention stays locked on me. The air between us hums with something that feels far too private despite the public setting.

I arch a brow, playing along. "You'd better be careful. Trouble has a way of backfiring when you least expect it."

"Backfiring, huh?" he says, his tone laced with amusement. "I think I'll take my chances."

"You always do," I shoot back, my voice light but pointed.

He chuckles a low sound that draws even more attention

from the women. I can feel their stares and practically hear what they're whispering to each other.

"I was actually here to check on you," he says, leaning in, his voice dropping just enough to make the moment feel private despite the public setting. "How's the shift going?"

"Fine," I say, shrugging as I glance at the line of guests waiting to check in. "Busy."

He studies me for a long minute. "And here I thought I hired you to keep things under control. Surely you can handle it?"

I smile, folding my arms. "Oh, I can handle it. Question is, can you handle not micromanaging for once?"

His grin sharpens, his eyes gleaming with challenge. "Fair point. But I'm not here to micromanage. I'm here to tell you you're not working late tonight."

I blink at him. "Excuse me?"

"You heard me," he says, his confidence maddening. "You're not working late. I'm taking you out tonight."

"Some of us have responsibilities," I counter, lifting my chin. "One of the girls called off. I'm covering for her."

"There are plenty of people here who can take over," he replies smoothly. "And besides, I'm the boss. That means you have to listen to me."

I narrow my eyes, fighting the urge to laugh. "Pulling rank, are we?"

"Absolutely," he says, leaning back with a satisfied smirk. "Wrap things up. I'll expect you upstairs shortly."

I shake my head, biting back a smile. "Fine, but only because I don't want to hear you whine about it later."

Behind me, my coworkers whisper in clipped, hushed voices. It's the unmistakable sound of scandal being shaped. Of women deciding I didn't earn this job, I fucked my way into it.

"Of course she's sleeping with him," one of them mutters. "She wouldn't have gotten the job otherwise."

"She probably thinks she's untouchable now," the other adds, her voice dripping with venom.

I turn slowly, my lips curving into a sweet, yet dangerous smile. "If you've got something to say, ladies, go ahead and spit it out. I'd hate to think you didn't have the backbone to say it to my face." My tone is calm, almost pleasant, but the edge beneath it is unmistakable.

They both blanch, stammering some excuse about getting back to work. I turn back to the desk, spine straight, their words falling off me like rain on glass.

After making sure the last guests are checked in and that my coworkers aren't left juggling a line, I finally step away from the desk. The polished professionalism I wore all afternoon slips the moment I'm alone in the elevator.

The ride feels slower than usual, each floor crawling by, the soft hum of the machinery too quiet to distract me from the echo of their voices. Whispered judgment. Thinly veiled insinuations. Words not meant for me to hear but designed to cut just the same.

I know I handled it. I didn't flinch. I didn't snap. I stood tall and let their silence say more than any defense I could have offered. And still, it stings.

Because no matter how capable I prove myself to be, there will always be someone waiting to tear me down. To reduce me to gossip. To pretend power was something I was handed, not something I seized.

I'm not fragile. I know that. But tonight, their words burrow deeper than I want to admit.

Eamon is waiting when I step inside, his jacket off, the sleeves of his shirt rolled up.

He looks up, and the moment his eyes land on me, his demeanor changes. "What's wrong?"

"Nothing," I say, shaking my head as I kick off my heels.

"Try again," he says, stepping closer.

I sigh, crossing my arms. "It's nothing worth worrying about."

His brow lifts. "Aoife."

I relent, knowing he won't let it go. "The girls at the desk made some comments after you left."

"What kind of comments?"

"Implying I only got the job because I'm sleeping with you."

"They're fired." His tone is cold, final.

"That'll only make it worse. I handled it, and I'll keep handling it," I say firmly.

"No one disrespects you and gets away with it."

"You will not be fighting my battles for me," I say, meeting his gaze with determination. "I'm not weak."

"No, you're not," he says and lifts me onto the kitchen counter. "You're incredible." His mouth captures mine in a kiss that steals my breath. "And you're mine," he murmurs against my lips.

"Yours," I whisper back, my fingers tangling in his hair.

The tension from the day dissolves as the fire between us takes over, raw and consuming. Nothing else matters. Not the whispers, not the world outside. Just this.

His hands grip my thighs, pulling me closer to the edge of the counter as his lips trail fire down my neck. The roughness of his stubble against my skin sends desire straight to my core. His fingers dig into the soft flesh of my hips, and I gasp as he pushes my skirt up, the cool air brushing against my bare skin.

"God, Aoife," he breathes, his voice low and ragged. His hands slide higher, expecting lace but finding bare skin. "No knickers?" he murmurs, his eyes dark with hunger, drag over me like a slow caress. "Jesus, you're trying to kill me."

The shift in him is immediate—need rising, sharp, and consuming, and all of it aimed at me. His hand slides between my thighs, his finger stroking me with a confidence that leaves me trembling. My back arches, a moan slipping from my lips as his mouth claims mine in a kiss that's all teeth and desperation.

"You're so wet for me." His voice is rough and sends a shiver through me.

His touch is unrelenting as he circles my clit, pressing and teasing until my hips instinctively move toward him, desperate for more. He slides two fingers inside me and curls them just right, hitting a spot that makes me cry out.

His lips graze my ear. "You're fucking perfect, Aoife," he says, his breath hot against my skin. "I could spend all night driving you to the edge just to hear those sounds you make when you fall apart for me."

I can only nod, my hands clutching his shoulders as he increases his pace, his thumb brushing over my clit, making my legs shake and my mind blur with pleasure. My body burns with a need only he can satisfy.

When I can't take it anymore, I tug at his shirt, fumbling with the buttons in my desperation. He pulls back just long enough to shrug out of it. My hands roam over him, tracing the ridges of his defined abs and the lines of his tattoos, my nails scraping lightly over his chest. He shoves his slacks down in one swift motion, his movements precise and brimming with raw, controlled power.

When he's free, he positions himself between my thighs, his hard cock pressing against me, teasing. "I need you," I say as I wrap my legs around his waist, pulling him closer.

"Say it again," he demands, his hands gripping my waist. "Tell me what you want."

"I want you to fuck me, Eamon," I moan, my head falling back as he fills me completely.

He doesn't hold back, his thrusts are hard and deep. His grip on my hips tightens, his fingers digging into my skin as he drives me higher.

"You're mine, Aoife," he growls, his voice low and commanding. "Every inch of you."

I meet him thrust for thrust, my nails raking down his back as the pleasure builds, spiraling out of control. His mouth finds mine again, his kiss all-consuming, as if he's trying to claim me in every possible way.

When I shatter, it's like a dam breaking, the pleasure crashing over me in waves. I cry out his name, my body trembling against his as he continues to drive into me, pushing me through the high.

Moments later, he follows, his rhythm faltering as he groans my name, his release spilling into me as his grip on my hips holds me firmly in place.

We stay like that for a moment, both of us breathing heavily. His forehead rests against mine, his hands softening their grip but still holding me close.

"No one disrespects what's mine, Aoife. Not ever."

The raw promise in his tone sends a shiver down my spine, and as his lips brush mine again, I know he means every word.

"I can handle myself," I whisper, my fingers tracing the tattoos on his chest, trying to hold on to some semblance of control.

"I know," he murmurs, his hand cupping my jaw, tilting my face up to meet his gaze. "But that doesn't mean I won't fight for you. Always."

There's no arguing with the certainty in his eyes, so I don't try.

He presses one last kiss to my lips before easing me down from the counter. "You should get ready. We have reservations for dinner."

"I think we should stay in," I murmur, the words soft but suggestive, more invitation than suggestion.

His gaze darkens as his lips curve into a knowing smile. "Tempting, but no."

"No?" I ask, feigning disappointment.

"We're meeting someone," he says firmly.

"Someone more important than me?"

His lips brush against my ear. "Not possible. But it's important we make a public appearance this evening."

That gets my attention, though I don't let it show. Instead, I step back, giving him a mock pout. "Fine," I say, my tone velvet-soft. "But you owe me for every second I'm not on my knees, showing you exactly how good staying in could've been."

"Whatever you want," he says, his tone laced with promise before slapping my ass lightly. "Now go. Don't keep me waiting."

I roll my eyes but can't help the smile that tugs at my lips as I head toward the bedroom. His gaze lingers on me the entire way.

As I close the door behind me, the smile slips from my face, replaced by unease. Eamon doesn't do anything without a purpose, and whatever tonight is about, it's clear it's not just a simple dinner.

Still, I don't push him. Not yet. He'll tell me when he's ready, or he won't. Either way, the truth will come out soon enough.

Ruairi

The report comes in while I'm finishing up in my office, and it's worse than I imagined. The shipment meant to solidify my foothold in the Midlands is gone, reduced to nothing but twisted metal and scorched earth. I grip the edge of my desk, my knuckles whitening as the details are relayed.

"They blew the whole damn thing to hell," Ronan says grimly, standing across from me.

"How?" I demand, my voice tight, though I already know.

"Controlled charges," he replies. "Set on the containers themselves. Whoever did it wanted to send a message loud and clear."

It's not hard to guess who's behind it. This is Eamon O'Sullivan's response to the warning I sent him. It's a declaration of war.

Losing the shipment is going to cause all kinds of problems for my Syndicate with my contact in the north. The deal we had would provide their faction with enough weapons to solidify their position and tip the balance of power in their favor. Now, with nothing to show for it, not only have I lost their trust, but I've also handed them a reason to question my leadership.

But it's not the loss of the shipment that twists my stomach into knots. It's Aoife. The thought of her getting caught in the crossfire of this escalating violence turns my blood cold.

I straighten, shoving the fear aside. "We'll hit back harder," I say, though my voice lacks its usual authority. "But first, I need to make sure Aoife isn't anywhere near this madness."

It's just past midday when I arrive at Cian O'Leary's office. The hallway leading to it hasn't changed much over the years. There are the same framed photographs and the same muted carpet that muffles every step. I know this space well. I used to trail behind my da as a boy, legs half the length of his, watching the back of his coat sway as he led meetings I was too young to understand.

Back then, Cian's office had felt impossibly big. I remember sitting on the edge of a leather chair, back straight, feet barely brushing the floor, doing everything I could to look like I belonged among the men speaking in clipped, measured tones. I wouldn't fidget. Wouldn't speak unless spoken to. I was there to observe. To prove I was watching, learning, becoming.

And Cian saw that.

He never talked down to me. Never laughed when I tried to mirror the gravity of my father or asked questions meant for a man twice my age. He'd offer a nod, a quiet "Good question," or pass me a sweet from the dish on his desk like it was a shared secret between us, one that said, *I see you trying, lad. Keep going.*

That respect, however quiet, stayed with me.

Now, as I step into his office as a man no longer trying to belong but already entrenched in this world. I find the room just as I remember, precise, still, and expectant.

"Ruairi," he greets, standing and extending a hand. "This is unexpected."

"We need to talk," I say, ignoring the pleasantries.

Cian's brows knit together as he waves me to sit. "What's going on?"

"Aoife," I say, cutting straight to the point. "She's working at The Emerald Briar."

Cian's expression shifts as recognition flashes in his eyes. "O'Sullivan's place."

I nod, watching his reaction closely.

"What the hell is she doing there?" Cian asks.

"She's trying to prove a point," I reply carefully. "Aoife wants me to let her work in our Syndicate. She thinks this is how she'll make me see her as capable."

Cian leans back in his chair, a faint smirk tugging at his lips. "Your father always said she was stubborn."

"She needs someone to pull her back from this mess," I say, fixing him with a pointed look.

His smile fades, replaced by a more serious expression. "You're asking me to go to Dublin?"

"Yes," I say without hesitation. "You're smart, steady. She needs that right now. Convince her that you're the better choice and get her to come home."

Cian's eyes narrow, the lines around them deepening as he studies me. He doesn't answer right away. Instead, he leans back in his chair, steepling his fingers like a man carefully weighing risk against reward.

"She's young," he says finally. "There's a significant age gap between us. People might talk." A note of dry amusement threads his voice, though his expression stays unreadable. "And not kindly."

I don't flinch. "Let them."

"Even if I were willing, what makes you so sure Aoife would go along with it?" he asks. "She didn't seem so receptive that night at dinner."

"She doesn't have to want it. Not yet," I say, voice steady. "She just needs to be seen with you. That's how it starts. The idea gets planted, and over time, she'll come around. She's smart—she'll see what you have to offer. She'll realize you're the best choice."

Cian drums his fingers against the armrest once then stills. His gaze sharpens, thoughtful. "I'm not sure how I feel about manipulating the girl," he says slowly. "She's your sister, Ruairi, not just a piece to move around on a board."

"This isn't manipulation," I say evenly. "It's influence. A nudge in the right direction. Aoife will make the decision herself. I'm just helping her see the right one."

A beat passes. Then Cian gives a slow, deliberate nod. "All right," he says. "I'll do it."

"Good." I stand, clapping a hand on his shoulder. "Keep me updated. And don't let her slip through your fingers."

Cian smiles, the familiar confidence I've always admired in him returning. "Don't worry. I'll take care of it."

As I leave Cian's office, I allow myself a brief moment of hope. The pieces are moving. The board is shifting. But as I step out into the cool afternoon air, a nagging unease coils low in my chest.

Eamon O'Sullivan isn't the kind of man who lets go easily. He doesn't chase women for fun, and he sure as hell doesn't keep them around without a reason.

And Aoife, she's spent her whole life protected, kept far enough away from the fire not to feel the heat. She thinks she's in control now, finally making her own choices. But she has no idea how deep this game runs or how quickly it can swallow her whole.

Cian

THE CITY HUMS WITH ITS USUAL CHAOS, THE STREETS of Dublin alive with the sound of impatient horns and the rhythmic chatter of passersby. But none of it touches me, not really. The noise is distant and insignificant compared to the sharp clarity of my thoughts.

Ruairi's request lingers in my mind like the aftertaste of something forbidden—unexpected but not altogether unpleasant. He wants me to go to Aoife. To be seen with her. Shape perception. Plant ideas.

He may as well have handed her to me.

I met her once, years ago. She couldn't have been more than seven or eight, all wide eyes and wild hair, bouncing into her father's office like she owned it. She was a distraction then. Nothing more than a bothersome child interrupting conversations she didn't understand. I barely looked at her.

But now? Now she's a woman. And not just any woman. She walks with pride and speaks with that sharp-tongued defiance that's all fire and bite, like she knows what she's doing. But beneath it, there's something else.

She's naïvé—untouched. Preserved like a secret. Hidden away

by men who thought they were protecting her. Shielding her. All they really did was keep her ripe.

And Ruairi, the fool, just handed her over like she's a pawn in his game. But Aoife Quigley isn't a piece to be moved. She's something to be claimed.

Broken in.

Ruined.

And if anyone's going to do it, it'll be me.

Ruairi thinks he's using me to control her.

What he doesn't realize is he's handed me something far more interesting.

I step into The Emerald Briar, its polished floors gleaming under the soft glow of chandeliers. The air's clean and inviting, carrying a subtle blend of citrus and bergamot mingled with hints of sandalwood and a trace of white tea. It's a scent that speaks of quiet luxury, perfectly complementing the opulent surroundings. Eamon O'Sullivan has always known how to project power.

It doesn't take long to find her. Aoife stands behind the front desk, her uniform crisp and professional, but there's something about the way she holds herself. A subtle defiance and a spark in her green eyes.

She's no longer hidden away, unknown by those in our world. She's transformed into something far more powerful, more dangerous. A force that cannot be ignored. For a moment, I wonder if Ruairi truly understands what he's unleashed or if he's blinded by the illusion that he can still control her.

When her gaze lifts and locks onto mine, surprise flashes across her face. It's fleeting, gone almost as quickly as it appeared and replaced by a polite smile. But I see the way her fingers pause over the keyboard, the subtle shift in her stance.

"Cian?" she says, her voice smooth but edged with curiosity.

"Aoife," I reply, letting her name roll off my tongue with a familiarity that makes her blink. "What are the odds?"

Her smile falters for a fraction of a second before she catches herself. "What are you doing in Dublin?"

I shrug, slipping my hands into my pockets as I lean casually against the counter. "A cousin's wedding, if you can believe it. I figured I'd stay a few days. Enjoy the city."

She studies me, her gaze scrutinizing, but her tone remains light. "And you just happened to check into this hotel?"

I laugh softly, the sound easy, but calculated. "A coincidence, I swear. Though I have to say, seeing you here is the best surprise I've had all week."

Her lips press into a thin line, and she glances down, typing something on her computer. "Well, welcome to The Emerald Briar." Her tone is polite—detached.

Then, after a brief pause: "And your last name?"

"O'Leary," I say smoothly, watching her for any sign that it registers. "Cian O'Leary," I add, savoring the way her posture stiffens ever so slightly. That tells me all I need to know. She remembers.

But she doesn't look up. Not yet. Just types. Efficient. Controlled.

When the card is programmed, she slides it across the counter toward me, her fingers brushing the polished wood.

"If there's anything you need during your stay," she says, her voice cool as she finally meets my gaze, "let me know."

"Oh, I'll let you know," I murmur, my voice dropping just enough to make her look up.

She meets my gaze, tone cool. "Does that line usually work for you?"

My smile is slow and deliberate. "Only when I mean it."

I pick up the key card, letting my fingers brush where hers just were. "And I always mean it with you," I reply, letting my gaze linger on her for just a beat too long before pushing off the counter.

As I walk away, I can feel her eyes on me. Unsettling her was almost too easy.

Stepping into the elevator, I turn to face her, catching her gaze and holding it as the doors begin to close. Her expression is unreadable, but the fire in her eyes is impossible to miss. A silent promise that this game is far from over.

Aoife doesn't know it yet, but this is no coincidence. She's walking into something carefully constructed—layered with intention, steeped in silence and patience. She thinks she's here to prove something to her brother, to take her place, to finally step out of the cage she was raised in. What she doesn't see is the trap being laid at her feet, velvet-lined and waiting. She believes she's carving out a piece of this world for herself when, in truth, she's already been written into someone else's design.

After all, even the brightest stars can't outshine the shadows that surround them.

Aoife

THE WEIGHT OF WHAT I'VE CAUSED KEEPS ME TANGLED in a mix of guilt and defiance. The whispers of unease are always there, growing louder with every escalation in Ruairi and Eamon's war. What started as calculated maneuvers, quiet power plays behind the scenes, has spiraled into outright hostility. The cracks are impossible to ignore now. Attacks on supply lines, ambushes in the dead of night, and casualties that neither side will openly admit, but both are quietly counting.

I didn't want this war. I didn't want blood spilled, lives lost, or alliances shattered. But I also can't bring myself to stop it. Not yet. For most of my life, Da kept my identity a secret. He looked at me like I was a fragile doll to be kept on a shelf, away from the world.

I'd hoped Ruairi would be different. That he'd see me for what I've become. That he'd give me the chance to show him everything I've learned while I was away. The languages I picked up. The connections I made. The way I watched, listened, and studied. Proving every step of the way that I could be more than a name. More than a sister.

But he didn't. So now I'll show him another way that I've earned my *rightful* place in the Syndicate.

If forcing his hand means standing by while he and Eamon tear each other apart, then so be it. I refuse to back down, even if the guilt gnaws at me. Because so does the fire of my defiance. I won't sit quietly on the sidelines, waiting for permission to act. That time has passed.

This war will end, but it will end on my terms.

My day takes a darker turn when Cian O'Leary walks through the hotel doors. He claims he's here for a family wedding. A convenient excuse, too convenient. I don't buy it, not for a second.

As soon as he disappears in the elevator, I pull out my phone.

Aoife: Cian's at Eamon's hotel. He says it's for a wedding. What the hell is he really doing here?

The reply is almost immediate.

Ruairi: I don't know. Why don't you ask the man you're sleeping with?

I grit my teeth, fingers flying across the screen.

Aoife: You think this is a joke? He's on your payroll. I have no doubt he's here doing your bidding.

Ruairi: Then handle it. You're the one in the thick of it. Or is this too much for you, Evie?

The nickname twists in my chest, a reminder of when things were simpler between us before our lives splintered into this mess. But now, it feels like a taunt, a jab meant to remind me of how he sees me—little Evie, his helpless twin sister, playing at being something more.

Aoife: You really think you're so clever, don't you? Sitting up there on your throne, pulling strings like a puppeteer, while I clean up your messes.

Ruairi: My messes? Last I checked, you're the one who crawled into bed with my enemy. If anything, I'm cleaning up after *you*.

Aoife: Don't you dare put this on me. If you hadn't shut me out, none of this would be happening. You started this war the second you decided I wasn't good enough to stand beside you.

Ruairi: And you're proving me right every step of the way. This isn't a game. You're out of your depth, and you're going to get people killed.

Aoife: No, *you're* going to get people killed because you refuse to see the bigger picture.

Ruairi: And what's that, Evie? That you're some kind of mastermind now? Spare me.

Aoife: Your arrogance is going to destroy us all.

Ruairi: Funny, I was about to say the same thing about you.

The screen blurs under the weight of my fury. My fingers clamp tighter around the phone, rage coiled and simmering just beneath the surface. The urge to throw it across the room and hear its satisfying crack as it hits the wall nearly wins. It takes all my self-control to not get in the car, drive straight back to Belfast, and force him to look me in the eye. Force him to see me not as his sister, not the obedient girl he thinks he can control, but as the woman I've become.

But I know better. Ruairi won't hear me until he's ready. And right now, he's too blinded by control, by legacy, by fear of what I might become if he lets go.

So I swallow the fury and let it settle in my bones.

Because when I come for my place, he won't be able to ignore me anymore.

Aoife: Keep underestimating me, Ruairi. I dare you.

I hit send and slide my cell back into my pocket, my hands trembling with a mix of rage and frustration. Ruairi doesn't reply. We're at a stalemate, as always. Even still, something about his silence feels like a victory, however small.

After my shift, I return to the penthouse and find Eamon in his office on the phone. He doesn't see me right away, giving me a rare opportunity to observe him. He's leaning against his desk, one hand gripping the edge while the other holds his phone to his ear. His white button-down is wrinkled and untucked. The top few buttons are undone, revealing a hint of his chest. His tie hangs loose around his neck like he gave up on maintaining appearances hours ago.

He looks tired. Stressed. The weight of this war with Ruairi is etched into the tension in his shoulders. His usual controlled demeanor is fraying at the edges. For a moment, I see not the unshakable leader but the man beneath who's carrying more than he lets anyone see.

As if sensing my presence, he turns his head and looks up. The transformation is instant. His body visibly relaxes, and he lets out a breath as if my presence has eased some of the pressure weighing him down. Without hesitation, he raises his hand and motions for me to come in.

The knowledge that Cian is in Eamon's hotel and that Ruairi is likely involved twists my stomach in knots. I'm not sure how much to tell him or how much he already suspects. But this is Eamon. He'll see right through me before I even say a word.

As I step into the room, his focus shifts entirely to me, his intense gaze narrows as I approach. Without missing a beat, his voice remains calm yet firm as he speaks into the phone. "I'll handle it tomorrow. I need to go." He doesn't wait for a response before ending the call and setting the phone down on the desk, his full attention now fixed on me.

"What's wrong? You're tense."

"It's nothing," I say, but the words sound unconvincing even to me.

"Don't lie to me, Aoife," he murmurs, his voice soft but commanding. "What's going on?"

I hesitate, my teeth worrying my bottom lip as I weigh my words. "One of my brother's men checked in earlier," I finally admit. "He says he's here for a wedding."

His expression hardens instantly, his jaw tightening as he processes the information. "And you think that's bullshit?"

"I know it is," I say, my voice surer. "He not only works for Ruairi, he's the man my brother tried to set me up with. Now he just happens to show up here?"

"It's definitely not a coincidence. If he's here, he wants something." Eamon takes a deep breath, his hand sliding up to rest at the small of my back, grounding me. "Did he say anything else?"

"No," I reply, shaking my head. "He stuck to his story. But it doesn't sit right."

He watches me closely, something dark tightening behind his eyes. "What's his name?"

"Cian O'Leary," I reply.

His jaw clenches, and he pulls me a fraction closer, his grip possessive but steady. "If he's here for Ruairi, I'll deal with him," he says, voice low and laced with quiet determination. "But if he's here for you..."

He doesn't finish. He doesn't have to.

The threat hangs between us, a promise cloaked in silence.

I shiver, not from fear, but from the intensity of his protectiveness. The way his body tenses when he hears Cian's name. The way his eyes darken like he's already thinking five steps ahead.

"I'll handle it," I say firmly. "Cian doesn't know I'm on to him, and I can use that. I'll find out what he's really doing here."

Eamon's gaze lingers on mine for a beat, and then he nods, slow and deliberate. "Then you make him less careful."

He moves to his laptop and pulls up the security feed, his fingers moving with practiced precision. It doesn't take him long to find what he's looking for.

"He's at the bar now," he says, voice low and dangerous. "Perfectly settled. Comfortable. That's when men make mistakes."

He turns the screen toward me, and I see Cian sitting casually, with a drink in hand and a relaxed posture.

"You want to find out what he's really after?" Eamon continues. "Let him think he's still in control. Let him underestimate you. Let him talk. The more you pretend to play his game, the closer you get to taking him off the board."

"This is how we get to Ruairi," he says, softer now but no less lethal. "Cian doesn't even realize he's the first crack in your brother's foundation. Let him think he's winning. Then we start pulling everything out from under him piece by piece until there's nothing left."

I swallow hard, adrenaline buzzing beneath my skin. For a brief moment, doubt crosses my mind, but I bury it quickly. This is what I signed up for, what I've fought for.

"If Cian's here to stir up trouble, I'll find out exactly what he's planning." My voice is steadier than before. I meet Eamon's gaze without flinching. "I won't just play the game. I'll win it."

"That's my girl," he murmurs, pride threading through the quiet rasp of his voice. But there's heat behind it, too.

He steps closer, his gaze locked on mine. "Just remember, winning comes at a cost. Don't let him get close enough to make you bleed." His fingers brush my jaw, deceptively gentle. "But the second he crosses a line, I end it. No hesitation."

I nod, though I know I won't let that happen. "Understood."

"Good," he says, his voice softening slightly as his hand moves to cup my cheek. "I'll never allow any harm to come to you."

For a moment, the tension between us shifts, replaced by something far more vulnerable. I lean into his touch, letting his warmth steady me before I turn to get changed.

Once I'm in our bedroom, my uniform is the first thing to come off, discarded in a heap on the floor without a second thought. Stepping into the closet, I choose a sleek black dress that clings to my curves. The fabric glides over my skin, the hemline teasing just above my knees, while the neckline dips low enough to demand attention without giving too much away. I pair it with stiletto heels that make my legs look impossibly long and complete the look with a touch of red lipstick.

When I step back into Eamon's office, his attention snaps to me immediately. His gaze rakes over me, slow and deliberate. He doesn't bother hiding his approval.

"You're killing me," he says, his voice a deep rumble.

Feigning innocence, I reply, "It's not for you." My tone is light but teasing.

He leans back against his desk, crossing his arms over his chest. "That dress says otherwise," he counters, his eyes lingering on me in a way that sends a rush of heat through me.

I let out a soft laugh, shaking my head as I step closer. "You're impossible."

"Can you blame me? You're stunning," he says, pushing away from his desk and closing the distance between us. His hand glides over the curve of my breast, slow and deliberate, his touch a whisper through the thin fabric. My nipples tighten beneath it, a sharp ache blooming in response. "You look lethal," he murmurs like he wants to worship and destroy me in the same breath.

"Good," I reply, my voice even though every nerve beneath his touch comes alive, aching for more.

"Don't forget who you are, Aoife. You're not just a pretty face at a bar. You're the woman who could burn this whole place down if you wanted to."

His words hang heavy in the air, sinking into my skin and settling in the pit of my stomach. *The woman who could burn this whole place down.* There's a strange power in hearing him say it. In the way he sees me. To Eamon, I'm not someone he needs to protect or control. He recognizes I'm a woman capable of chaos and destruction.

I lift my chin slightly, meeting his intensity with my own. "Don't worry," I say quietly, the hint of a smile tugging at my lips. "I haven't forgotten."

"So, what's your plan?" Eamon asks, the playfulness gone from his voice, replaced with something harder.

"To make him underestimate me," I reply, meeting his gaze without flinching. "He already sees me as naïve. I'll let him keep believing that while I get close enough to find out what he's really doing here."

His jaw ticks, a flash of something dark crossing his expression. "And how close is close?"

"As close as I need to be," I say evenly. "He won't see it coming. I'll use exactly what he expects from me—sweet, compliant, harmless. And when he lets his guard down, I'll be ready."

Eamon doesn't speak at first. Just studies me with that stormy quiet I've learned to recognize as anything but calm.

"If he so much as lays a finger on you," he growls, eyes dark, "I'll bury him myself."

"I'm not letting him do anything," I reply. "I'm controlling the narrative."

He steps closer, not touching me, not yet, but close enough that I feel the heat of his restraint. "Just remember who you belong to when this game ends."

"I don't belong to anyone," I say, though my voice softens around the edges. "But I'll always choose you."

For a moment, silence hangs between us, heavy with unspoken words. Eamon's hand brushes my arm before trailing down to take my hand. "You're not in this alone," he murmurs, his voice low and laced with meaning, "You have me and my Syndicate behind you."

"I know." With that, I slip out of his grasp and head for the door, feeling his gaze on me the entire way. The air feels heavier with every step, but I don't stop. If Cian's here to stir trouble, I'll find out, and I'll make damn sure he regrets it.

Aoife

THE LOW HUM OF CONVERSATION AND CLINKING glasses greet me as I step into the hotel bar. The warm glow of pendant lights reflects off polished wood. The faint scent of whiskey and hops lingers in the air.

I spot Cian immediately. He's nursing a whiskey at the far end of the mahogany bar. He looks effortlessly at ease, his dark suit crisp despite the late hour. A glass of whisky sits in front of him, half empty. My heels click against the floor as I make my way across the room.

He glances up as I approach. "Well, this is unexpected," he says, a slow smile spreading across his lips as I slide onto the stool beside him.

"Is it?" I ask lightly, catching the bartender's attention with a wave of my hand. "I figured you might be here."

His brow arches, curiosity dancing in his expression. "What gave me away?"

I don't answer immediately, instead ordering a Guinness. A choice that earns me an approving nod from the bartender and a chuckle from Cian.

"Aoife Quigley, drinking a Guinness," he says, leaning back

slightly, his eyes lingering on me. "I never would've guessed that'd be your drink of choice."

I let a smile tug at my lips as I angle my body toward him. "And you? Whiskey, I assume? Neat because you like to keep things simple."

His grin widens. "You already have me figured out."

"Do I?" I ask, tilting my head slightly, feigning innocence.

"So, tell me, what brings you here?" he asks, his tone light. But the calculating intensity in his eyes tells me he's assessing everything. "It's a long way from the protective reach of your family."

I shrug, taking a sip of my beer before answering. "I have some friends in the area, and honestly, I needed some breathing room from my brother's overbearing drama."

Cian lets out a low laugh, shaking his head. "Let me guess, Ruairi isn't exactly thrilled with letting you make your own decisions."

"He's convinced he knows what's best for everyone. It's exhausting," I say, rolling my eyes for effect. "I had to get away before he smothered me completely."

"And you picked this hotel? Out of all the places you could've gone?"

"A friend invited me to a party here," I say, crafting my lie with ease. "While I was here, I saw a hiring notice. Figured I'd take a chance and apply. I didn't think I'd actually get the job, but they hired me right away. They even included my room as part of the package."

Cian's expression is thoughtful, but I can see the hint of skepticism in his eyes. He doesn't trust coincidences, and neither do I.

"Interesting," he says, his tone measured. "Sounds like you've landed on your feet."

"Luck, I guess," I reply with a slight shrug, taking another sip of my beer.

He studies me for a moment longer before setting his glass down. "Let me buy you dinner," he says, his voice smooth. "I'm afraid we didn't get off on the right foot last time we shared a meal."

I pretend to hesitate, glancing toward the restaurant before nodding. "Sure, why not?"

As we stand, he places a hand on the small of my back, guiding me toward the restaurant with a possessive ease that sets my nerves on edge. I let him, though, leaning into the act, playing my part. His touch is firm, deliberate, as if staking a claim.

Once we're seated, the conversation flows easily. At least on the surface. Cian orders a bottle of wine without asking for my opinion, a bold move that feels in line with everything about him. I don't comment. Instead, I pretend to study the menu as he shifts the topic back to the hotel.

"So," he says, leaning back in his chair, his tone casual but his attention focused. "Do you know much about the owner of this place?"

I glance up, feigning mild curiosity. "The hiring manager mentioned it," I lie smoothly. "Éanna, Eirnin, or something like that. Why?"

His lips curl into a small, knowing smirk. "You're working here, staying here, and you don't know who signs the checks?"

I shrug, my eyes returning to the menu. "Not everyone's as suspicious as you. Besides, everything's direct deposit these days. I don't even see a physical paycheck."

Before he can respond, the server arrives with the wine, presenting the bottle with a flourish. Cian nods in approval, and they pour a small taste for him to try. He swirls it expertly before taking a sip, his expression shifting to one of satisfaction.

"This will do," he says, gesturing for the server to pour.

The wine is rich and velvety, its warmth lingering on my tongue as I take a sip. The server lingers just long enough to take our orders before disappearing, leaving us alone once more.

Cian leans forward slightly, resting his elbows on the table, his expression suddenly more serious. "You don't find it strange that this hotel, with this particular owner, just happened to hire you? Seems like an odd coincidence, don't you think?"

I raise a brow, pretending to fumble slightly. "I'm not sure I follow. What's so strange about it?"

He watches me closely as if waiting for me to slip. "The owner," he says slowly, as though revealing a secret. "Eamon O'Sullivan. Does that name ring any bells?"

I tilt my head as though trying to place it. "Eamon?" I echo, dragging out the name like I'm racking my brain. "That might be the name she said. Why does it matter?"

Cian chuckles, clearly enjoying my act of cluelessness. "Eamon O'Sullivan is your brother's enemy. They've been at war for months now. You really didn't know?"

I widen my eyes, putting on a perfect show of surprise. "Why would I," I ask, shaking my head. "You worked for my father and now my brother. You know as well as I do that I've never been involved in that side of things."

He leans back, clearly pleased with himself, and takes another sip of wine. "Well, now you know. And maybe now you'll understand why I find it interesting that you're working here. You can't tell me it's a coincidence, Aoife."

I force a dry laugh, waving my hand dismissively. "You're overthinking this. My brother doesn't tell me anything. He thinks I'm too weak to handle any of it," I say, letting frustration creep into my tone. "I didn't even know this guy existed until just now. Honestly, I don't care what Ruairi and Eamon are fighting about. Let them sort it out. It's not my problem."

My nonchalance seems to convince him, his shoulders relaxing as he nods. "Fair enough," he says, lifting his glass in a toast. "To new beginnings and whatever trouble they bring."

To new beginnings," I echo, with the faintest smile, clinking my glass against his.

Throughout dinner, I put on a show, laughing at his jokes, leaning in just enough to keep his attention, and letting my gaze linger on him a moment too long. By the time we finish, I can tell he's hooked, convinced that I'm nothing more than a bored, sheltered woman trying to escape her brother's shadow.

As we walk back toward the elevators, his hand once again finds the small of my back, his touch even more possessive this time. He leans in, his voice low. "Come to my room for a drink."

I pause, letting just enough hesitation show to make it believable. Then I smile. "Sure. Why not?"

Even as I say it, I can already picture Eamon's reaction when he finds out. He's going to lose his mind. But I'll deal with that later. Right now, I have a role to play, and I'm going to play it perfectly.

Eamon

THE SECURITY FEED GLOWS ON THE SCREEN IN THE penthouse, giving me a perfect view of the restaurant. Aoife sits across from Cian, her posture relaxed, her smile easy, and her movements deliberate. She's playing her part flawlessly, but watching it unfold twists a knife in my chest.

Cian leans closer, his body language screaming flirtation. His hand brushes hers, his smile practically dripping with charm. I can't hear what they're saying, but I don't need sound to know he's laying it on thick. And her? She's letting him, keeping him hooked. It's part of the plan, but it doesn't make it any easier to watch.

I sit back in the chair, forcing my hands to stay loose on the armrests instead of curling into fists. The key to control is restraint, and I've mastered that. Or so I thought. Because right now, every muscle in my body is coiled tight, screaming for me to storm down there, stake my claim, rip her away from him, and end this game entirely.

Movement catches my eye as they leave the restaurant together, his hand resting low on her back. My eyes are glued to the screen as they walk to the elevators. The anticipation builds as

I watch the doors close, knowing she'll be safe in the penthouse in just a few minutes.

I follow their ascent, not missing how Aoife looks up at the camera, knowing I'm watching. The elevator stops, the doors open, and they both step out on his floor.

Sitting forward, I release a low growl as I stare at the screen. My mind races, trying to piece it together. "What the hell are you doing, Aoife?" I ask aloud as I switch to the view of the corridor.

They stop outside his room, and I watch the scene play out. Cian holds his room card against the digital lock. She's going to his room. My fists clench, and the familiar cold anger starts to bleed into my veins.

I don't trust him. Not for a second. He's dangerous, and we both know he's not here by accident. Even without evidence, I know Ruairi's hand is in this. Cian is a pawn, and Ruairi sent him here to test her. To test me.

Every instinct I have screams at me to act, to go down there and rip the door off its hinges. But I know I can't step in. This is about Aoife and the Syndicate she should be leading. I have to let her handle this.

Tension drives me to my feet, the phone gripped tight as I start pacing the room. If I can't go to her, I'll make damn sure she's protected. I call my head of security in the hotel, barking orders. "I want at least two men on Cian O'Leary's floor immediately. Keep them discreet, but I want them stationed near his room. Now."

"Yes, sir," he replies.

"If anything happens, you call me. Immediately." He barely manages a response before I hang up and dial Seamus. "What's the update on the Callahan situation?" I snap, not bothering with a greeting.

There's a pause on the other end before Seamus rattles off information about the latest skirmish. I'm only half-listening. My thoughts are still on Aoife.

"Eamon," Seamus says cautiously, clearly picking up on my mood. "Is something else going on?"

"No," I snap, cutting him off. "Just handle the Callahan's. Do your damn job, and stop questioning me."

He hesitates again, and I can hear the tension in his voice when he speaks. "Alright, but you seem—"

"Enough," I say, my voice low and dangerous. "I don't need commentary. Get it done."

Before he can respond, I hang up, tossing the phone onto the desk. The walls of the penthouse feel like they're closing in around me. It's too quiet despite the storm raging inside me. I force myself to sit, to review reports, to occupy my hands with anything that might keep my mind from spiraling.

But none of it works. My eyes dart to the clock, counting the minutes, the seconds, until the door finally opens.

The sound of her heels clicking against the floor sends a wave of relief through me, followed quickly by the heat of residual anger. I stand, watching as she walks in, calm and collected like she didn't just light me on fire by going to his room.

"Aoife," I say, my voice sharp.

There's a fiery intensity reflected in her emerald eyes when she stops and meets my gaze. My fists tighten at my sides, but I force my next words to come out steady.

"Tell me everything."

THE ELEVATOR DOORS SLIDE SHUT, TRAPPING US IN A confined space filled with electric tension. Silence hums between us, thick and charged. Leaning casually against the wall, I watch her in the polished reflection—stealing glances I don't bother to hide.

The soft curve of her profile. The way her dress clings to her body, skimming her hips like a second skin. Every breath she takes draws the fabric tighter across her chest, teasing the rise and fall of her breasts. She's perfectly indecent in all the right ways. Every subtle shift of her body is a provocation. Intentional or not, it doesn't matter.

Aoife Quigley.

Patrick's hidden treasure. The daughter he kept tucked away like a secret too dangerous to share. How he managed to shield her from the world for so long is beyond me—but now she's here, mine for the taking.

Ruairi's sister. A line that should give me pause. A name that should stop me.

It doesn't.

He wants this—wants me with her. Thinks I'd be a safe

choice. Trustworthy. Established. Predictable. He doesn't know how very wrong he is.

Her presence sets something off inside me. A hunger that's more than mere lust. It's possession. It's obsession. Her innocence is disarming, but I know better. She wears it like a costume. There's something sharper beneath that polished surface. Something that wants to be seen. Longs to be touched. Craves to be ruined.

She's playing the part of the good girl. But there's a darkness in her eyes. A flicker of something feral, something waiting. That thought alone is enough to make me hard. The ache is immediate, sharp, and dangerous. She has no idea what she's doing to me.

Or maybe she does.

And if she does, God help anyone who tries to touch her but me.

The elevator doors slide open with a soft chime, and I motion for her to step out first. She does, wordless, her movements smooth and unhurried. Each step deliberate, like she knows I'm watching.

And I am.

My gaze trails the sway of her hips, the way the fabric of that dress hugs her curves with every breath she takes. It's a quiet kind of torment.

The corridor stretches ahead, but all I see is her, this woman I've been handed like a carefully wrapped gift. My room is at the end of the hall, and the closer we get, the more tightly the anticipation coils beneath my skin.

Not nervousness. Not hesitation.

Need. Possession.

She doesn't know what she's walking into. Not really. But soon, she will.

Once inside, I close the door behind us and loosen my tie, watching her as she takes in the room. Having her here, alone with me, is almost too perfect. She's supposed to be untouchable. The thought of ruining her is intoxicating.

Ruairi sent me here with a clear purpose—to turn her head and draw her close. He underestimated just how compelling she is and how much I'm willing to bend the rules to take what I want.

"Make yourself comfortable," I say, my voice low.

She moves slowly, perching on the edge of the couch, her hands smoothing over the hem of her dress. Going to the bar, I pour two drinks, letting my eyes roam over her body with open intent as I speak. "You know, Aoife, you're full of surprises. I never would've imagined someone like you working in a place like this."

She smiles softly, her eyes dropping shyly. "It was a whim," she says. "I have no experience. I really didn't think they'd hire me."

I take a step closer, handing her a glass, my fingers brushing hers deliberately. "I doubt they could say no to you," I reply, letting the words hang in the air.

Her cheeks flush, and I sit beside her, our legs pressed close together. The warmth of her presence is intoxicating, and I can feel myself leaning in, drawn to her like a moth to a flame.

"You're different than I expected," I murmur, letting my hand rest on the back of the couch behind her.

"Different how?" she asks, her voice soft, her eyes meeting mine.

"Innocent," I say, my gaze dropping to her lips. "Untouched."

Her cheeks deepen in color. It's enough to drive me insane. My hand lifts slowly, fingers brushing along the curve of her jaw, trailing down to the soft, delicate line of her neck. Her skin is warm beneath my touch, and the way she leans into it sends a pulse of heat straight through me.

"Do you know what you're doing to me?" I murmur, my voice dropping to a husky whisper as my thumb grazes the corner of her lips, lingering there.

She glances down and quietly gasps when she sees the unmistakable bulge straining against my trousers. Then, she quickly looks away, biting her lip. Her reaction only makes the fire in me burn hotter.

"I'm not sure what you mean," she whispers, her voice carrying the perfect touch of shyness, her lips parting as if she's at a loss.

I let my thumb trail back along her jaw, tilting her face just enough so she has to look at me. "I think you know exactly what I mean."

She stays quiet, and the tension between us crackles like a live wire. I can feel the restraint pulling at me, telling me to tread carefully, to not push too hard, not yet. But the temptation is maddening, and it takes everything I have to pull back, to keep myself in control.

If she's going to play innocent, I'll let her, for now. But Aoife Quigley has no idea just how dangerous that game can be.

"How did your father manage to hide you away for so long?" I ask.

"Boarding schools mainly," she replies. "After I graduated, he let me travel."

I take the opportunity to press her for more. "Travel? Where to?"

"Paris, Tokyo. Wherever I wanted to go." Her tone softens as she speaks.

I let her talk, offering a few questions here and there to keep her going, all the while studying her every movement, every word.

When there's a lull in the conversation, I strike. "Why not work for Ruairi? Surely, he could use someone as capable as you."

Her expression hardens, her guard slipping for the briefest moment. "Because he won't let me," she says flatly. "He thinks I'm too weak, too inexperienced. He doesn't see what I'm capable of."

I lean forward, my interest piqued. "And what are you capable of?"

"More than he'll ever give me credit for," she says, her voice soft but laced with steel. "I'm not some fragile thing to be tucked away, no matter how much he wants to believe that."

I lean in closer, drawn in by the fire simmering beneath her carefully composed exterior. "He's the fool for not seeing it," I murmur, my voice low, testing the waters.

She gives a quiet, bitter laugh. "Ruairi doesn't do foolish. He does calculated." She glances at her phone, frowning slightly. "It's late. I should be going."

I stand as she does, not letting the moment slip away. "Do you have work tomorrow?" I ask, my voice casual.

She glances at me, brushing a strand of hair behind her ear. "No. I'm off," she replies.

"I'd like to spend the day together," I say, my words laced with purpose.

She hesitates, her lips pressing together. "What about the wedding?"

"The wedding's the day after tomorrow," I say smoothly. "I came early to handle some business for Ruairi. Maybe you'd like to accompany me?"

She studies me for a long moment. "If I do, you have to promise Ruairi won't find out."

I smile, placing a hand over my chest. "You have my word. He'll never know."

"Alright," she says softly. "Tomorrow, then. I'll meet you in the lobby."

As she turns to leave, I step in just enough to shift the air between us. My hand grazes her lower back as I lean in, brushing a kiss against her cheek. Not rushed. Not innocent. A promise wrapped in restraint.

Her breath catches, barely, and then she's gone, the door clicking shut behind her.

The taste of her lingers on my lips, subtle but undeniable.

She's not what I expected.

But one thing's for sure, she will be mine.

Aoife

THE PENTHOUSE IS QUIET AS I STEP INSIDE. THE ECHO of my heels fills the expansive space as I make my way through the expansive space, heading toward Eamon's office. The door is slightly ajar, and I find him standing by the windows, his silhouette illuminated by the city lights below.

He turns around as I step into the doorway, his dark eyes locking onto mine. "Aoife," he says, his voice low.

I set my clutch on the nearby table and meet his gaze, my posture calm even though the fire in his eyes is enough to make anyone else squirm.

"Tell me everything," he says, his tone leaving no room for hesitation.

"It went fine," I say simply.

"Fine?" he asks, his posture tense, his fists clenched at his sides. His eyes are dark and burn with frustration. "Do you have any idea what you put me through tonight?"

"I told you I could handle it," I say evenly.

"You went to his room," he says, his voice low but no less biting. "Do you know how insane that is? I couldn't watch you. I had no idea what he was doing, what he was planning."

I sigh, crossing my arms as I meet his gaze. "You said you

trusted me," I remind him. "You said I was strong enough, smart enough to handle this. Was that a lie?"

"I do trust you," he snaps, running a hand through his hair, clearly struggling to rein in his temper. "It's him I don't trust."

"And you think I don't know that?" I counter, my voice rising slightly. "You think I walked into this blind? I knew exactly what I was doing."

Eamon takes a step closer, his jaw tight as he stares down at me. "You took a risk—a big one. I don't know what I'd do if anything happened to you."

His words carry tenderness, but I push it aside, refusing to back down. "You're starting to sound like Ruairi," I say, my tone cutting.

His eyes narrow, his expression hardening. "It's not the same," he growls. "I'm not trying to keep you out of anything. I'm not trying to control you. I care about you. I want you to be safe."

"And I appreciate that," I say, softening my tone just slightly. "But if this—" I gesture between us "—is going to work, you're going to have to trust me. Completely. I need to know you believe I can take control of a situation."

Eamon hesitates, the tension in his jaw giving away his internal struggle. I can see the protectiveness warring with his respect for me.

"You said you trust me," I repeat as I cross the room, closing the space between us. "Prove it," I murmur, my voice dropping, taking on a seductive edge.

His blue eyes burn into mine as tension coils in every muscle of his powerful frame. "Aoife—"

I don't let him finish. My hands slide up his chest, over the hard planes of muscle beneath his shirt, until I reach the collar. Pulling him down toward me, I capture his lips in a kiss that's anything but gentle. It's demanding and forceful. A statement of control.

Eamon groans against my mouth, his hands gripping my waist, but I'm quicker taking control as I press him back. His knees bump the edge of the oversized black chair, and I push him down without hesitation. His chest rises and falls in sharp, ragged breaths, restraint unraveling beneath my touch. There's no resistance. Only surrender.

I climb onto his lap, my knees bracketing his thighs, my black dress riding up slightly as I settle over him. His hands instinctively move to my hips, trying to take control, but I catch them, pinning them in place. Leaning in until my lips are at his ear, I whisper, "Tonight, I'm in charge."

Eamon's eyes, full of desire, darken as they lock onto mine. His hands flex under my grip, his need to touch me battling with his willingness to obey. "I'll play your game, Aoife," he says, his lips curving into a wicked smirk. "But don't forget, when it's my turn, you won't stand a chance."

A thrill races through me at his words, but I don't let him see it. Instead, I grind against him, feeling the hard evidence of his arousal pressing into me. He groans low in his throat as his hands tighten beneath mine.

"Let's see if you can survive tonight first," I tease as I lean down to kiss him again, this time slower, drawing him further into my control.

My fingers glide down the front of his shirt, slow and deliberate, slipping open one button at a time. Each inch of exposed skin reveals the hard ridges of his chest, warm beneath my touch. His breath deepens, chest rising with anticipation as my lips skim his throat, leaving a trail of heat in their wake.

"You're not used to this, are you?" I ask.

"Used to what?" he manages.

"Not being in control."

His mouth sets into a hard line, but his eyes stay locked on mine, burning with unspoken agreement. I smile, leaning in to brush my lips against his collarbone before easing off his lap.

My fingers toy with the hem of my dress, pulling it up slowly, just enough to show the curve of my thighs, before dragging it higher, over my hips, then up and over my head. The dress falls to the floor in a silken pool, leaving me in nothing but my black lace bra and matching knickers.

Eamon's eyes are glued to me, dark and hungry, his chest rising and falling with each shallow breath. I revel in the power that surges through me, knowing I have this strong, commanding man completely at my mercy.

Reaching behind me, I unclip my bra, letting the straps slide down my arms in a slow, deliberate tease. The fabric falls away, and I bring my hands to my breasts, cupping them, letting my fingers tease and play as I watch him struggle to hold himself back.

"Do you like what you see?" I ask, my voice dripping with confidence.

His groan is deep, guttural as his hands grip the arms of the chair like it's the only thing keeping him from lunging at me.

"More than you know," he says, his voice hoarse.

I take a step closer, my hands moving to the buckle of his belt. He sits perfectly still, watching as I undo it, the metal clinking softly in the quiet room. But as I reach for the button of his pants, his hand darts out, grazing my wrist.

I pull back immediately, shaking my head with a sly smile. "No touching."

He lets out a low growl, his head falling back against the chair.

I chuckle, relishing the control, the way his restraint only adds to his tension. "Pull your pants down," I command, my tone firm but laced with seduction.

For a moment, he hesitates, his pride warring with his desire. But then his hands move to his waistband, and he does as I ask, pushing his pants and boxers down, freeing his arousal.

"Good boy," I purr, stepping closer until I'm standing between his legs.

I drop to my knees in front of him, the cool floor pressing against my skin as I look up at him through my lashes. His eyes are wild, blazing with a mixture of frustration and raw need, but he doesn't move. Doesn't dare break my rule.

I wrap my hand around his hard length, stroking him slowly,

teasingly, as I let my tongue dart out, grazing the tip. His head falls back, and I take him fully into my mouth.

The sound he makes sends a thrill through me, a rush of power that fuels me as I set a slow, deliberate pace. My hands hold his hips, keeping him firmly in place as I take him deeper, my tongue swirling, teasing, drawing out every shudder, every gasp.

"Fuck, Aoife," he groans, his voice raw and broken, his hands gripping the chair so tightly his knuckles are white.

I revel in the effect I have on him. The way this man, so powerful, so in control, has completely unraveled under my touch. I let him feel it all, the heat, the pressure, the deliberate strokes designed to drive him to the edge.

When his breathing grows ragged and his body tenses beneath me, I pull back slightly, my lips brushing against him as I murmur, "Not yet."

He groans again, his head falling forward, his dark eyes meeting mine with a pleading intensity.

"Please," he breathes, his voice thick with desperation.

"Please what?" I ask, my tone light, almost mocking, as I lean in closer, my lips hovering just out of reach. "You're going to have to be more specific."

His jaw clenches, his pride warring with his need, but I can see the moment he gives in. "Please," he says again, his voice rough, filled with raw hunger. His jaw tightens as he forces the next words out, his pride all but shattered. "I want your pretty lips wrapped around my cock. I want to watch you take me in your mouth. I need to come down your throat and hear you moan while you do it."

The graphic confession sends a jolt of heat through me, power coursing through my veins as I watch him unravel. A slow, wicked smile tugs at my lips as I lean in, brushing my fingers lightly along his jaw before trailing them down the hard lines of his chest.

"Was that so hard?" I murmur, my voice laced with teasing confidence.

His eyes blaze as they lock onto mine, his lips parting with a sharp intake of breath. "You're a fucking goddess, Aoife Quigley," he growls, the words raw and reverent, spoken like a man who's completely undone.

I chuckle softly, savoring the way his body trembles under my touch, the tension in his muscles a testament to the hold I have over him. His need is palpable, a storm I control with nothing more than a look, a touch, a whispered word.

I let the moment linger before taking him fully once more. The rhythm is slow at first, deliberate, coaxing him further into submission until I feel him begin to shake, his control slipping entirely. When his release overtakes him, his body shudders with the force of it, and my name spills from his lips. Not as a command but as a plea, a prayer answered only by my touch.

As I rise to my feet, his gaze follows me, full of something raw and unspoken. I lean down, brushing my lips against his ear.

"Now you see what happens when you trust me," I whisper, my voice soft but full of power.

"You win," he says finally, his voice hoarse but carrying a hint of amusement.

But before I can revel in my victory for too long, his hands shoot out, gripping my waist as he stands in one fluid motion. A surprised gasp escapes as he effortlessly hoists me over his shoulder, his hand resting firmly on the back of my thighs.

"Now it's my turn," he growls, his voice dark and full of promise. "Let's see if you can handle what happens when I'm in charge."

My breath catches, heat surging through me as he strides toward the bedroom, every step purposeful. I let him take me, a thrill coursing through my veins at his possessiveness, his strength.

There's no protest, no fight—I don't want to stop him. Instead, I smile to myself as I realize something undeniable. As much as I love the control, there's a raw kind of pleasure in surrendering it to him, like stepping into the fire and daring it to burn.

Aoife

Eamon had been up early, leaving with nothing more than a quiet, "There's something I need to take care of. Be safe today." There was no lecture, no overprotective warnings, just a simple acknowledgment that I could handle myself.

I attempt to get a little more sleep, but the sunlight streaming through the penthouse window feels relentless. Giving up, I decide to get moving. It's a new day, and I'm ready to play my part. I slip into tight black leather pants that hug my curves and a silky, low-cut white blouse that's just provocative enough to keep eyes on me for all the wrong reasons. My black ankle boots add a slight edge to the outfit—sexy, but not trying too hard. I pull my hair back into a long, sleek ponytail and check my reflection in the mirror. Perfect.

When I step into the lobby, I spot Cian leaning against a pillar, scrolling on his phone. Casual confidence oozes from every pore. His gaze snaps to me the moment I approach.

"You look incredible," he says, his eyes lingering just a little too long.

I let a small, shy smile cross my lips. "Thanks. You don't look so bad yourself."

He offers me his arm. "Ready?"

"Always," I reply, my voice light and playful.

The drive is quiet at first, the air thick with anticipation. I focus on the scenery outside, but Cian's occasional sideways glances don't go unnoticed. He thinks I'm here because I'm infatuated with him. That's fine. Let him believe what he wants, for now.

The meeting place is a warehouse on the outskirts of the city, blending seamlessly with its industrial surroundings. From the outside, it looks ordinary, like all the rest. It's the kind of place you wouldn't think twice about, just another cog in the city's bustling trade. A sleek black car is parked near the entrance, its polished exterior standing out in the otherwise utilitarian setting.

Inside, the air smells faintly of sawdust and grease. Along one wall, there's a table and a few metal chairs—a makeshift meeting area that's just out of the main flow of work but still in plain sight.

Two men stand off to the side, their sharp suits a stark contrast to the gritty, industrial backdrop of the warehouse. They exude a cold authority, their postures rigid, arms loosely crossed as they wait assumingly for Cian. He approaches them with the ease of old acquaintances.

"Boys," he says, his tone warm but calculated. "Hope I didn't keep you waiting too long."

His words are smooth, almost disarming, but there's a sharpness beneath the charm that suggests he's playing his own game.

"Who's the girl?" one of them asks, his eyes rake over me like I'm something to be bought and sold.

"Her name doesn't matter," Cian says, his hand pressing lightly against my lower back. "She's with me."

The way they watch me makes the hairs on the back of my neck stand on end, but I don't give them the satisfaction of a reaction. Cian jerks his chin toward a seat off to the side, but I'm not here to be sidelined, and I don't take orders.

Instead, I cross the room with slow, deliberate steps, swaying my hips, and slide onto the edge of the table, ignoring the chairs completely. The cold metal seeps through the leather of my pants, but I don't show a hint of discomfort. Leaning back on my palms, I cross one leg over the other, the motion tugging my blouse just enough to keep their attention locked on me.

Their expressions are a mix of curiosity and calculation as if they're trying to decide what role I play in all this. I flash them a small, confident smile as if I'm completely oblivious to their scrutiny.

"Take a seat," Cian says, his tone firm but laced with amusement. "In a chair."

Offering a casual shrug, I slide off the table and move to one of the chairs. The men eventually turn their attention back to Cian, though I know I've made an impression.

They speak with ease, their tones confident, their body language relaxed. No tension, no unnecessary caution.

With a disinterested expression, I cross my legs and lean back as if the discussion is nothing more than background noise. Let them think I'm just a pretty face here to kill time. It makes it easier to listen without drawing attention.

While they talk and share details about the shipment, timing, and security, I pretend to scroll on my phone, all the while absorbing everything. They don't so much as glance my way. Which is exactly why they don't notice when I snap a few discreet photos, angling my screen just right.

Ruairi might've set this in motion, but after I bring this information to Eamon, he'll stop it before my brother can do anything about it.

The deal wraps up, and Cian leads me back to the car, his hand lingering on the small of my back as we walk. Once we're inside, he starts the engine, but instead of pulling away, he turns to me.

"That little show you put on in there," he says, his voice low. "Every man in that room was watching you, and not one of them was thinking about the deal."

"Oh?"

"They wanted you," he continues, his gaze dragging over me like I'm something he owns. "Fergus even asked if I'd share you. Said a woman like you shouldn't be wasted on just one man."

My stomach churns, but I keep my voice calm. "I didn't notice," I say, then add, "and for the record, I'm not yours to offer. Or anyone's."

Cian's lips twitch in amusement. "You've got this ability to wrap men around your finger without even trying."

Leaning in just enough to close the space between us, my voice drips with sweetness. "Wrap men around my finger? That's quite the compliment."

His gaze darkens. "You'll have us all on our knees begging for a taste."

I let my fingers trail idly along the edge of my seat as if I'm considering his words. "You think so?" I ask, my tone teasing. "Maybe you're just easy to impress."

Cian lets out a dark, humorless laugh. "It's not about being impressed. It's all you. There's something about you that gets under a man's skin and makes him desperate. Makes him want to risk it all to have you."

I bite my lip just enough to make it look innocent. "Well, maybe I like a little danger, too."

Cian's grin widens, sharp and predatory. "Oh, Aoife, you don't just like danger—you *are* danger. And that's what makes you irresistible."

His eyes linger on my lips, and for a moment, the tension in the car feels suffocating. He thinks he's in control, that he's playing me.

"You've got men like me ready to burn everything down just to keep you," he adds, his voice low and possessive, the words dripping with intent.

"Careful, Cian. Playing with fire might get you burned."

"Maybe I want to get burned."

I keep my expression playful, teasing, while inside, I'm counting how many ways I'll use his desperation against him.

A slow breath leaves him, his grin spreading with quiet satisfaction like he's already won. I keep my gaze steady, my smile soft and inviting. *Let him believe that. The more power he thinks I have, the easier he'll be to manipulate.*

As we pull away from the warehouse, Cian's grip on the steering wheel is loose, relaxed. He's in a good mood, smug even. He's confident today went exactly as he planned.

After a few minutes of driving in comfortable silence, I glance at him. "So, where are we going?"

"You'll see," he replies, his eyes never leaving the road.

"That's not an answer."

He glances my way. "Just trust me. Consider it a celebration."

"A celebration?" I ask, playing along.

"Of our future," he says. "And whatever else might come of it."

I let out a small laugh. "That's vague."

"You'll like it."

I lean back against the seat, watching the sights blur past the window as I pretend to let myself be charmed. Eventually, he slows the car, parking along a quiet street, and turns to me with a glint in his eye.

"Come on," he says, pushing open his door.

After stepping out of the car, I take in my surroundings, following him through the winding streets. We turn down a narrow alley—Love Lane. It's tucked away and bursting with vibrant murals, hand-painted tiles, and scribbled love notes left behind by strangers. The colors pop even in the gray Dublin light, bright splashes of red and blue standing out against the damp brick.

Cian watches me as I trail my fingers along the artwork, pretending to be lost in the charm of it all.

"Fitting, don't you think?" he says, stepping closer.

I glance at him with a playful smile. "You think bringing me to a place called Love Lane is subtle?"

"Nothing about me is subtle. I thought you would've figured that out by now," he says, slipping his hands into his pockets.

As we walk, Cian watches me more than the walls. "You know, they say if you leave a note here, it seals your love forever," he muses, voice laced with amusement.

I glance at him over my shoulder. "Is this where you tell me you believe in that kind of thing?"

"I believe in making memories." Before I can respond, he pulls out his phone. "Come on, we need a picture. Something to remember the day by."

"Didn't peg you for the selfie type."

He just smiles. "There's a first time for everything."

I let him position us in front of the wall and make sure my smile is bright. He holds his cell phone in front of us, capturing the moment—the illusion of something real. Cian tucks his phone away, a hint of satisfaction in his voice. "We're not done yet," he says.

Taking my hand in his, Cian leads me over cobblestone streets that are alive with music, laughter, and the low hum of conversations in different accents to Temple Bar. A place that always pulses with energy.

"Now this," he says, gesturing around, "is what Dublin is all about."

I glance at him, amused by the pride in his voice. "And here I thought Dublin was only business to you."

"Not always. Sometimes, you have to enjoy the finer things in life."

We step into the pub with its dim lighting, old wooden beams, and walls lined with framed records and whiskey bottles. The air is thick with the scent of aged liquor and firewood. We're seated right away and Cian orders for us without asking my opinion.

Several minutes later, the server returns with two lowball glasses, each filled with a generous pour of whiskey—dark, smooth, and meant to burn slow.

"Try it," he urges, watching me closely.

I take a sip, letting the heat spread through me, licking a stray drop from my bottom lip. Cian's eyes darken, his gaze lingering far too long, but he says nothing. He doesn't have to.

I shift in my seat, setting the glass down with a soft clink. "I thought the Syndicate's business stayed in Belfast," I say casually, picking up my fork.

"It usually does," he says finally, his tone easy—too easy. "But sometimes lines blur. Borders shift. And someone has to make sure everything still runs smoothly."

"So, Ruairi sent you up here?" I probe.

Cian's eyes stay on his plate for a beat too long before he lifts them to meet mine. "Not exactly," he says, dabbing at the corner of his mouth with his napkin. "I offered. Figured since I was coming up for the wedding anyway, I might as well make myself useful."

He smiles like it's the most natural thing in the world, but there's something behind it—something too polished.

Before I can dig deeper, he gestures toward my plate. "Eat before it gets cold. The chef here has a way with seabass it'd be a shame to let it go to waste."

Just like that, the conversation shifts steered cleanly away from business and back into safer territory.

We finish the rest of the meal with wine and practiced smiles, the kind that don't quite reach the eyes. He keeps the conversation light. Trivial stories and surface-level charm. And I let him. I know better than to press too hard all at once. Whatever Cian's really doing in Dublin, he won't give it up over dinner.

But that doesn't mean I'm not watching. Listening.

The check comes and goes, and I rise from the table, already filing the evening away in my mind—every glance, every answer he didn't give.

"One more picture," he says, lifting his phone. "Gotta document the whole day."

I move closer to him and pose just right, letting the warm pub lights cast a golden glow over my skin. He takes a few pictures and studies the screen for a second before showing me.

"We look good together, don't we?"

I laugh softly, tucking a strand of hair behind my ear. "I suppose we do."

And we do—on the surface. Cian's the kind of man people call distinguished. Sharp suit, clean lines, expensive taste. Conventionally handsome in a way that photographs well. But he's much older, closer to my father's age than mine.

I still don't understand why Ruairi thinks this makes sense. I wasn't looking for an arranged marriage, and I'm sure as hell not interested in being paired off for politics.

But none of it matters.

Because I've already made my choice.

And it isn't Cian.

He slides his phone into his pocket, but his gaze lingers. "This is just the beginning, Aoife."

I give him a slow smile, keeping my expression playful, but my thoughts drift elsewhere.

Eamon knows I spent the day with Cian. I told him it was strategic—an opportunity to gain trust and maybe learn something useful.

But that wasn't the whole truth.

What I didn't tell Eamon was that Cian planned to bring me to a Syndicate meeting. And I went.

Eamon's going to ask questions about where we went and what we did. And he isn't going to like the answers. Even after last night, after I proved I wasn't afraid to take control, I know exactly who Eamon is. He allowed it, let me have that moment, but that doesn't mean he's the kind of man to sit back and let things happen.

Eamon O'Sullivan is a man who takes. And I have no doubt he's going to take back control the first chance he gets.

By the time we return to the hotel, night has settled over

Dublin, the city pulsing with quiet energy. I'm exhausted—tired of the masks, the small talk, the game. But Cian isn't done.

After the elevator doors close, he reaches out and hits the button, bringing it to a stop. "Come back to my room," he says, voice low, each word weighted. There's no mistaking his meaning.

Before I can respond, his lips are on mine. Letting my hands rest lightly on his chest, I kiss him back. It's calculated, deliberate. Glancing up at the camera blinking in the corner, I'm certain Eamon's watching. I can only imagine how he's reacting.

Cian finally pulls away. "You're full of surprises, Aoife."

I let out a soft, breathy laugh as I reach around him, pressing the button to restart the elevator. A long moment later, the elevator slows to a stop on Cian's floor, the doors sliding open behind him, but he doesn't step out. Instead, he lingers, his gaze locked on mine, dark with desire.

"You sure you won't come with me?" he asks. "Seems like a shame to end our evening here."

"Tempting," I murmur. "But I think I'll have to pass. I have to work the early shift tomorrow."

"Another time, then."

"Goodnight, Cian," I say as the doors slowly slide shut, sealing him on his floor.

As the elevator ascends, I slip my keycard from my pocket, swiping it for access to the penthouse. In the silence, I touch my lips, my mind racing.

Cian thinks he's smart. He thinks he's clever.

But he's nothing compared to me.

Let the games begin.

Eamon

I STAND JUST INSIDE THE PENTHOUSE DOORS, FISTS clenched tight. My mind replays the scene in the elevator, the way Cian's hands lingered on her, the way she kissed him back.

Calculated. It was fucking calculated.

But that doesn't matter. It doesn't fucking matter.

She's been gone all day. Didn't tell me where she was going or what she was doing. I willingly let her walk out the door, knowing she'd be spending the afternoon with Cian. But seeing his hands on her. His lips against hers ignites something primal in me. A fury I can't contain.

The handle turns a second before the door swings open, and Aoife steps inside. She stops short the second she sees me. Her expression falters with mild surprise, maybe the slightest hint of guilt. But she recovers quickly.

"I didn't know if you'd be home yet," she says, shrugging off her jacket like nothing's wrong.

I don't move. "Where the hell have you been?" My voice is low, barely restrained.

She lets out a soft sigh, tossing her purse onto the counter. "Out."

Her flippant attitude grates against the edge of my restraint. "Out?" I take a step toward her, gaze burning. "You were gone all fucking day, Aoife. And I saw the kiss."

She shrugs. "It was nothing."

"Nothing?" My jaw tightens as I grab her wrist before she can walk past me. "You kissed Cian in my fucking elevator, and I'm supposed to believe it was nothing?"

She yanks at her arm. "Let go of me."

"Not until you tell me what the fuck is going on."

She glares up at me. "Cian brought me to a meeting. Business for Ruairi."

My grip tightens involuntarily. "You went to a Syndicate meeting? Without telling me?"

She scoffs. "I didn't realize I needed your permission."

I inhale sharply through my nose, temper dangerously close to snapping. "This isn't about permission. It's about the fact that you went to a meeting involving the Syndicate with no protection. Do you have any idea how reckless that was?"

She crosses her arms, eyes flashing with defiance. "Now you sound just like my father and Ruairi."

I don't think I pull her against me. My hands lock around her waist, forcing her body flush against mine. "Did they ever do this?" Before she can fire back, my mouth crashes against hers.

She gasps against my lips but doesn't pull away. My hands tighten on her hips, my body reacting to hers. When I finally break the kiss, my breathing is uneven, but my grip stays firm. "Do their bodies respond to you like this?" My voice is rough, raw.

She swallows, eyes locked on mine. "Of course not."

Something dark comes over me, and an idea forms before I can stop it.

"You're sure you want to play with the big boys?" I ask, my voice quieter now, more controlled.

She doesn't hesitate. "Yes."

I nod once. "Fine. Then let's go."

"What?"

"We're going out."

"It's late and I'm exhausted. I just want to go to bed."

"I don't care," I say flatly. "You're coming with me."

She watches me for a long moment, searching my face for a clue, but I'm already on my way to the door. With a resigned sigh, she grabs her jacket and follows me out.

The drive is silent. My hands grip the steering wheel, my jaw ticking as I stew, unsure if this is the right move. I don't know where the fuck my head is at. Only that I need her to see the danger, the darkness in whatever game she's playing with Cian.

The low buzz of her phone vibrating against her thigh snaps me out of my thoughts.

I glance at her out of the corner of my eye. Her expression shifts, frustration creasing her brow as she reads the messages. She exhales sharply, her fingers tightening around the phone.

"That better not be him," I growl.

She rolls her eyes and turns the screen toward me. "It's Ruairi."

I glance down. My blood boils when I see the image. A picture of her and Cian at Love Lane. "What the fuck were you doing there?" I ask, my voice deadly quiet.

She sighs. "Walking. Talking. Pretending."

My knuckles go white. "Pretending?"

"Yes, Eamon," she huffs. "I was playing along. Trying to get information."

I force myself to breathe through my nose, steadying the anger coiling inside me. "And what information did you get?"

It lasts barely a breath, a fraction of a second, but I catch it. She shifts slightly in her seat before answering. "Not much of anything. Just that he met with some guys. I couldn't hear what they were saying."

"Alright," I reply, keeping my voice even.

Turning away from me, she crosses her arms as she looks out the window like she's already done with the conversation. The rest of the drive is silent. I don't push her. Not yet. But I will. Because if Aoife thinks she can play this game with me, she's about to learn I don't lose.

Ruairi

Seamus sits across from me, flipping through the pages of a report I already know by heart. The numbers are steady. Our shipments are moving as they should, but none of it holds my attention right now.

My phone buzzes on the desk. I glance down and see Cian's name flash across the screen.

Cian: Spent the day with your sister.

He got her to go out with him already. That was fast. I knew Aoife wouldn't outright refuse him, not if she wanted to stay close and keep her little games going, but I didn't expect her to play along this quickly.

Cian thinks he's winning her over. And maybe she's starting to see reason. Starting to realize where her loyalty should be. Or she's playing him.

Either way, I need to keep him thinking he's in control. If I give him any reason to second-guess himself, he might back off, and I need him to keep going. I need to get Aoife back here where she belongs.

Ronan looks up from his report, catching my expression. "Something interesting?"

I school my features as I say, "Cian took Aoife out."

Ronan raises a brow. "That right?"

I nod. "Seems she didn't put up much of a fight."

He exhales slowly, studying me. "And you're alright with that?"

I shrug. "Why wouldn't I be?"

"He's old enough to be her father," Ronan mutters.

Ruairi leans back, unfazed. "Maybe that's what she needs. A strong hand. Someone who won't let her get lost in all that fire she's carrying."

Ronan scoffs, disbelief edging his voice. "You really think she's going to fall in line?"

I lean back in my chair, fingers drumming against the desk. "We'll see."

Ronan shakes his head, but he doesn't push. He knows better.

Instead, he turns his attention back to the report, flipping a page with deliberate ease. I wait a beat, then pick up my phone and type out a response to Cian.

Ruairi: Didn't expect you to move that fast.

I hit send. Let's see how confident he really is.

His response is almost immediate.

Cian: She didn't put up much of a fight.

I laugh under my breath. That doesn't mean shit.

Ruairi: Good. Keep her close.

A moment later, my phone buzzes again. I glance down to find an incoming message with pictures attached. When I open them, my stomach tightens.

The images are of Aoife and Cian at Love Lane, smiling as if they belong there together. Another one at the restaurant, heads tilted close, her expression soft, playful.

I stare at the photos for a second longer than I should. I still don't believe it—don't trust it. But for a moment, I wonder. Maybe even hope that it could be this easy. Then, I shake off the thought. It was nothing more than an afternoon out.

I type out my next message.

Ruairi: Looks like you had a nice little outing.

Cian: Little outing? Didn't feel like a little outing when she was all over me in the elevator.

I'm still trying to process the first message when the second one comes through, landing like a punch.

Cian: The way she kissed me? Damn near had me thinking about fucking her right there in the elevator.

A muscle in my jaw ticks. I force my fingers to stay steady as I type.

Ruairi: You're not there to get in her bed. If I find out you laid so much as a finger on her, I'll make sure you don't live long enough to regret it. Do your job and stay focused.

A few seconds pass before Cian responds.

Cian: Relax. I know what I'm doing.

The screen blurs at the edges as I reread his words, a slow burn building behind my eyes. If Cian forgets his purpose, I won't hesitate to remind him exactly who he's working for.

Ruairi: I'll relax when she's back in Belfast, where she belongs.

Then, I turn my attention to my sister, forwarding her the picture and typing out a single message.

Ruairi: What game are you playing at?

I wait. She doesn't respond.

A muscle in my jaw twitches as I fire off another.

Ruairi: First, you whore yourself out to O'Sullivan and now to Cian? You think that earns you a seat at the table?

Still nothing.

I throw my phone down on the desk, exhaling sharply. Fine. If Aoife wants to ignore me, so be it. This changes nothing. In fact, it only proves what I already know. O'Sullivan has his claws in her deeper than I thought.

My fingers resume their restless rhythm against the desk, tapping in time with the pulse of growing irritation. The photos

Cian sent remain on the screen, each one more infuriating than the last, especially with Aoife still ignoring my messages. It shouldn't come as a surprise. Defiance is in her nature. She's always pushed, always tested the edges to see how far she can go before someone dares to pull her back.

But this time, she's in over her head. Aoife doesn't see what's happening. She doesn't understand that she's sinking deeper into a war she has no business being in. Fine. If she won't come home willingly, I'll make sure she has no choice.

I glance up at Ronan. "We're going to push harder," I say, my voice low and cold.

Ronan watches me as if he's waiting to see just how far I'm willing to take this. "What are you thinking?"

I lean forward, keeping my voice steady. "Hit the cash drop headed for his London connection."

Ronan's brow lifts slightly. "That's his expansion play. You really want to blow that up?"

"He's been lining it up for months," I say. "New territory, new allies. That money legitimizes the move. Take it out, and you don't just cost him power. You embarrass him."

Ronan nods slowly, the corners of his mouth tightening. "That'll hurt."

"Good," I murmur. "It's time O'Sullivan feels the consequences of dragging my sister into this."

He shifts in his chair, weighing his words before speaking. "You're pushing this right to his doorstep. The closer you bring the war to O'Sullivan, the more likely Aoife gets caught in the crossfire."

I slam my fist against the desk, my patience snapping. "Then make sure she doesn't."

Ronan doesn't flinch, but his eyes darken. "You're so set on dragging her back to Belfast, but every time you pull shit like this, you make it harder."

I push to my feet, closing the distance between us. "I don't need a fucking lecture from you. Just handle it."

For a moment, neither of us moves. The tension between us is like a silent challenge lingering in the air. A muscle ticks in his jaw, but he gives a stiff nod. "Fine."

Without another word, I grab my phone and storm out of my office, the weight of my decision settling deep in my bones.

My sister wants to stay in O'Sullivan's world.

Let's see how she handles it when I start burning it down.

Aoife

THE CAR RIDE IS SILENT, THE AIR THICK WITH THE weight of everything that's happened tonight. Eamon's hands grip the wheel too tightly, his jaw locked, eyes fixed on the road ahead, but he hasn't said a word. I had every intention of telling him about the meeting and giving him exactly what he needed to strike Ruairi. But then he freaked out and dragged me out of the penthouse. And now we're in the car, going God only knows where.

As if that wasn't bad enough, Ruairi's text messages made it even worse. I scroll up, rereading his hateful words.

First, you whore yourself out to O'Sullivan and now to Cian? You think that earns you a seat at the table?

The message stares back at me. Ruairi's always been controlling, but this is a low he's never stooped to. His words cut deeper than I care to admit.

And then there's Cian.

I glance at the pictures again, the ones he sent right to Ruairi. I knew he couldn't be trusted. This only cements it. He played his part perfectly today, acting like I was something special, all while feeding Ruairi exactly what he wanted him to see.

Bastard.

I shove my phone into my pocket and cross my arms, staring

out the window. The city lights have long since faded, replaced by winding roads and endless stretches of dark countryside.

"Where are we going?" I ask.

Eamon doesn't look at me. His hands stay steady on the wheel, his expression unreadable. "You'll see."

The vague answer grates on my nerves. "Eamon."

He doesn't flinch, doesn't give me any indication that he even heard my voice. We continue on the main road until he makes a turn onto a narrow dirt path. Up ahead, looming against the night sky, stands an old castle.

I frown. "What the hell is this?"

Eamon shifts the car into park and finally turns to me. "One of my holding sites."

I glance up at the castle, a cold sense of unease curling around my spine. Holding site. I don't need a translation for that. "Why are we here?" I ask.

"You said you wanted to be in this world," Eamon says and watches me for a long moment. "If you're having second thoughts, just say the word, and we'll go back to the penthouse."

I square my shoulders, my tone firm. "I already told you I'm all in."

He nods slowly like he's measuring my conviction. "Tonight will prove to me, and everyone else, that you mean it."

My chest tightens, but I keep my face neutral.

Eamon steps out of the car, and I follow, my boots crunching against the gravel. The castle is even more imposing up close. It rises tall and unyielding, its jagged stone walls looming against the night sky. The narrow windows are dark and empty, like hollow eyes carved into a cold, watchful face.

A few of Eamon's men linger near the entrance, their heads snapping up in surprise when they see him.

"Didn't expect you here, boss," one of them says, his brows lifting.

Eamon's voice is firm, unwavering. "I'm handling things in person tonight."

The men exchange glances, but no one questions him.

I swallow hard, my nerves creeping in, but I push them down. This is what I wanted.

Eamon doesn't slow. "Follow me."

He leads me deeper into the castle, past spiral staircases, and arched stone doorways, the air growing colder with each step. We stop at a stretch of unmarked wall, indistinguishable from the rest of the corridor.

Eamon presses his hand to a carved stone near the base. With a faint click, a section of the wall shifts, grinding open just enough to reveal a narrow passage beyond. A hidden doorway. Without a word, he steps through.

I hesitate. Eamon notices.

He smirks, stepping onto the first stone step. "Having second thoughts?"

I lift my chin. "No."

He watches me, reading me like he always does. "You can still turn back. It's not too late."

Brushing past him, I descend the stairs first, ignoring the way my heart hammers in my chest.

The underground level is worse. The air is damp and heavy with the scent of moisture, old stone, and something faintly metallic—like the ghost of blood long since washed away. The only light comes from a few exposed bulbs swaying slightly. Their glow flickers erratically, casting distorted shadows that seem to shift and stretch out like reaching hands.

The hum of electricity buzzes faintly, almost drowned out by the slow, rhythmic drip of water somewhere in the distance. The uneven floor is slick in places, the moisture seeping through the cracks, making each step feel like I'm sinking deeper into something I can't escape.

We turn into a room, and I see him. A man sits in a chair in the middle of the space, his wrists bound behind him, his face bloodied and swollen from the beating he appears to have already taken. I swallow hard, keeping my expression blank as Eamon steps beside me.

"This," Eamon says, his voice calm, almost casual, like we're discussing the weather, "is one of your brother's men."

My stomach twists.

"He was caught skulking around my docks," he continues, his gaze never leaving the man slumped before us. "We found the explosives in his bag. Tucked beneath crates, rigged to go off the moment my shipment arrived."

A cold chill works its way down my spine.

"Not just spying," he adds, almost as if he's explaining it for my benefit. "He wasn't here to gather intel. He was here to make a statement. To send a message from Ruairi."

He turns his head, finally looking at me. "So now we'll send one back." He steps closer, boots scraping against the cold stone floor. "Do you know how we'll do that, Aoife?" he asks, still staring at the bruised and bloodied figure.

My throat tightens, but I manage the word. "He needs to die."

Eamon's gaze darkens with approval. "Good girl."

I don't flinch when he reaches out, tucking a loose strand of hair behind my ear. His touch is light, almost tender, but there's nothing soft about the moment.

Then, he steps back and unholsters his gun. I watch, frozen, as he holds it out to me.

"You're going to pull the trigger."

The weight of his words crash over me.

I stare at the gun. At the man in the chair. At Eamon.

This is it.

This is the moment where I take control of my future.

If I back down now, neither Eamon nor Ruairi will ever take me seriously. I'll never have a place in the Syndicate. I'll never be more than Ruairi's twin or Eamon's girlfriend.

This is my pit. My pendulum swings above me. And I will not be the one left waiting beneath its blade.

My pulse pounds in my ears.

Eamon leans in, his whispered words meant for only me to hear. "It's not too late to decide this isn't for you."

I know what he's doing. He's pushing me, giving me an out.

But I don't take it.

Instead, I wrap my fingers around the gun, raise it, click the safety off—

Eamon

She went to a fucking Syndicate meeting without telling me.

Without guards.

Without backup.

I already have no respect for the bastard, but this? This was careless. Dangerous. I should kill him just for putting her in danger.

Bringing a woman to a meeting like that was reckless enough, but bringing Aoife Quigley? He should've known better. Her name alone makes her a target. And if the wrong people realize who she is, what she is, she's dead.

Instead, she let O'Leary lead her straight into the fire.

And those fucking pictures.

I don't know what pisses me off more. The fact that she spent the day with him and let him stick his tongue down her goddamn throat in *my* elevator or the fact that he sent them straight to Ruairi like she's some kind of trophy.

Every part of me is teetering on the edge. And that's why we're here. I need her to back out. To realize this isn't a game. That what happens down here isn't something she can walk away from unchanged.

But she doesn't.

My voice is harsh as I push her to give up. "Having second thoughts?"

Her chin lifts, defiant. "No."

I watch her closely, reading every emotion she doesn't think she's showing. The tension in her shoulders, the way her breath hitches before she catches herself and forces it under control.

"You can still turn back, Aoife," I say, my voice quieter now but no less firm. "It's not too late."

Silently, I plead with her to take the out. To admit that this isn't what she wants. To prove that some part of her still values self-preservation over proving a point.

Because if she does this, if she goes through with what I'm about to ask of her, there's no undoing it. No coming back.

But she doesn't.

Her jaw sets, her spine straightens, and without a word, she pushes past me, her shoulder knocking into mine as she descends first, her steps steady despite the slick stone beneath us.

It's a challenge. A silent fuck you.

I exhale sharply, dragging a hand down my face before following.

That was it. Her last chance.

And she walked right past it.

The underground level closes in around us. The heavy air presses against my skin like something living. The scent of rot and damp stone mingles with the metallic sting of blood. I try to take a deep breath, but it sticks in my chest. My fingers flex at my sides before curling into fists, the tension winding through me like a coiled wire.

I've done this more times than I can count. I know the steps, the process, the outcome. But tonight is different. *She* makes it different.

My pulse thrums in my ears, too fast, too loud. I roll my shoulders and crack the tension in my neck, but it does nothing to shake the apprehension that gnaws at me.

I might be making the biggest mistake of my life.

But my plan is already in motion. There's no stopping it now.

Aoife doesn't speak as I lead her through the dimly lit corridor, past the heavy oak doors and jagged stone archways that have stood for centuries. Until we come to the holding room.

We step inside, and I know the exact moment her eyes find him. Aoife stops beside me, her reaction controlled—but I see it. The hesitation. The unspoken questions.

I silently question what the fuck I'm doing bringing her down here.

"This," I say, keeping my voice even, "is one of your brother's men."

She stiffens.

"He was caught skulking around my docks," I continue, keeping my eyes locked on the man in front of us whose time left on earth is quickly growing short. "We found the explosives in his bag. Tucked beneath crates, rigged to go off the moment my shipment arrived."

"Not just spying," I add. "He wasn't here to gather intel. He was here to make a statement. To send a message from Ruairi. So now we'll send one back. Do you know how we'll do that, Aoife?" I ask, turning toward her.

Her throat works as she swallows. Her answer is quiet. "He needs to die."

My gaze darkens with approval. "Good girl."

I reach out, fingers brushing a loose strand of her fiery red hair behind her ear. She doesn't flinch, doesn't move away.

Then, I unholster my gun.

I don't miss the slight tension in her shoulders, the almost imperceptible shift of her weight.

I hold the weapon out to her. "You're going to pull the trigger."

She stills. The air around us grows impossibly heavy as if the castle itself is watching, waiting.

This is it.

The defining moment where she either backs down, proving Ruairi right, or she takes the next step, knowing there's no coming back from it.

I wait, hoping she sees the steep cost.

Hoping she decides it's too much to pay.

But then, her fingers close around the grip.

She raises the gun, clicks the safety off, and pulls the trigger.

The gunshot shatters the silence, echoing through the chamber. The man jerks once, then slumps forward, lifeless.

I don't look at him.

I look at her.

Waiting for the breakdown. The guilt. The regret.

But she doesn't fall apart.

She doesn't even waver.

She lowers the gun and turns to me, her expression unreadable as she hands it back. Like it's something she's done a hundred times before.

A Íosa Críost.

After holstering my gun, I take Aoife's hand and guide her out of the room. My men's eyes follow as we pass, their usual indifference replaced by unspoken respect for the woman at my side.

I knew she was strong. I knew she was relentless.

But this?

She's a goddess. And Ruairi is a fucking fool.

As we step outside into the night air, the significance of what just happened settles in my chest.

I'd be honored to run my Syndicate with her by my side. But her heart is set on Belfast. On the Syndicate that boasts her family's name.

And after tonight, I know she's more than capable of running it.

Eamon

THE PENTHOUSE IS QUIET WHEN WE STEP INSIDE. AOIFE moves like nothing's changed. She kicks off her boots, stretches her arms over her head, and walks toward the kitchen like she didn't just put a bullet in a man's skull.

But I know better.

I watch her closely, waiting for the cracks to show. The hesitation. The reality of what she did finally catching up to her.

She catches me staring and lifts a brow. "What?"

"Are you alright?"

She rolls her eyes. "That's the third time you've asked me that."

Leaning against the island, I cross my arms. "Because you just killed a man."

"He was sloppy and got caught." She shrugs. "He got what he deserved."

"That's not the point."

She turns to face me. "Did you fall apart after your first time?"

I don't answer right away. Instead, I reach for the bottle of whiskey on the counter, twisting off the cap with deliberate ease. The amber liquid swirls as I pour, filling both glasses nearly to the brim and slide one across the island to her. Lifting mine, I take a long pull before setting it back down.

She takes a slow sip. Her gaze never leaves me as she patiently waits for my answer.

"It was my birthday."

She blinks. "What?"

"My first kill," I clarify. "It was my birthday present."

Her expression hardens. "How old were you?"

"Thirteen." I smile, but there's no humor in it.

The glass nearly slips from her fingers as the weight of my words sinks in. "Jesus, Eamon."

"My father said it was time for me to become a man," I continue. "I barely understood what that meant. But, I was his son, heir to the O'Sullivan Syndicate, and in our world, you don't question things like that."

I don't know why I'm telling her something so personal. Other than the men who were there that night, I've never told this story to anyone.

"My mother was furious when she found out," I say, my voice rougher now. "She didn't want this life for me. She wasn't born into this life and didn't understand it."

Aoife's brows draw together. "Then how did she end up with your father?"

I let out a breath, glancing toward the window. "Mom was a university student in London when they met. My father was there for business. She didn't know who he was, only that he was charming."

Aoife exhales a quiet huff of breath before lifting her glass to her lips. "Sounds familiar."

I glance at her, my brow furrowing. "What?"

Her sparkling green eyes meet mine from over the rim of her glass. "Sounds familiar. You charmed me before I knew who you were."

A smile tugs at the corner of my mouth. "The difference is, you knew better."

She rolls her eyes but doesn't argue. "Didn't stop me, though."

No, it didn't. And God help me, even if she'd tried to walk away, I never would've let her.

"She always said she should've known better, but by the time she realized, it was too late. She loved him."

Aoife watches me carefully. "And he loved her?"

"In his own way." I nod. "But it wasn't enough to change him. And she learned to live with that."

She sighs, setting her glass down.

After clearing my throat, I push forward. "After I did it, after I pulled the trigger, I threw up."

"You were a child," she whispers, the words barely audible.

I nod slowly, letting the weight of the memory press down on me. "In my father's eyes, I wasn't. Not anymore."

She shakes her head, disbelief tightening her features. "That's—"

"Part of life," I say quietly. "Part of being the heir to the Syndicate."

Her eyes soften, sympathy creeping into her expression, but I don't want it. Sympathy doesn't change what happened. It doesn't undo who I became that day.

"My father wasn't impressed," I continue. "Said it was part of the process."

"I don't care what your father said." Her voice is soft but fierce. "You were a child, Eamon. He had no right to put that sort of burden on your shoulders."

Her words land harder than I expect. A direct hit.

Aoife's sitting here after putting a bullet in a man's head because I put her in that position. Because I tested her. I wanted to see if she'd break. And yet, she's the one fighting for me. For the part of me that should've been protected, the part I buried so deep I stopped believing it even existed.

I don't deserve it. I don't deserve her.

But fuck if I don't want to keep her anyway.

"Then, as if that wasn't enough, he took me to his mistress. He told me that was part of becoming a man, too."

Aoife stiffens. "That same night?"

I nod once.

She hesitates for a second before asking, "Do you have a mistress?"

It's not an accusation. Just curiosity. But the question still twists something in my gut.

I straighten, my answer leaving no room for debate. "No."

She studies me, looking for any sign of a lie.

"I would never cheat on you, Aoife." My voice is firm, confident. "That's not who I am."

She nods slowly, accepting my answer.

I take a step closer, watching her carefully. "Are you really okay?"

She meets my gaze. "I am."

I reach for her, my fingers grazing her arm. "Listen to me. If you ever feel like you're slipping, like the memory of tonight is too much, I need you to tell me."

She swallows. "I won't."

"You might. And if you do, I'll be right here." I tighten my grip slightly. "I know what happens after you take a life. I've taken a lot of them. If you need to talk, if you need to—" I pause, forcing myself to breathe. "Just know that you don't have to do this alone."

She looks at me for a long time, something unspoken passing between us.

I almost say it. The words rise in my throat, heavy and unspoken—*I love you*.

She means more to me than I ever intended, more than I know how to handle. It burns in my chest, fierce and terrifying.

But the words never come.

Instead, I reach for her, fingers brushing her cheek before I gently tilt her chin up. My lips find hers, not out of hunger, but need—desperate, aching, real.

She melts into me, her body molding against mine, her hands sliding up my chest before curling into the fabric of my shirt. I kiss her slow, deep, drinking in the taste of whiskey on her tongue.

Sliding my fingers into her hair, I tilt her head back further, claiming her, making sure she feels it. That this isn't just about need. It's about her. About the way she fought for me without even realizing it. About the way she's become a part of me.

I walk her back toward the bedroom, never breaking the kiss, only pulling away long enough to strip her out of her clothes. Her breath comes faster, her eyes filled with desire as I tug her top over her head.

"I need you, Eamon," she breathes.

"Shh, *mo chroí*," I murmur, brushing my lips along her jaw, down the column of her neck. "I've got you."

She trembles beneath my touch, her bare skin warm against my palms as I push the leather pants past her hips, letting them pool at her feet. She steps out of them, standing before me in nothing but lace, her body a fucking masterpiece.

My control frays, snapping thread by thread.

Dragging my knuckles down the curve of her waist, I lower myself to my knees, pressing a slow kiss to her stomach before hooking my fingers under the waistband of her knickers. She watches me, her breath catching as I pull them down, exposing her completely.

She's wet, already so fucking wet for me, and I groan as I grip her thighs, guiding her back onto the bed. She parts her legs without hesitation, her trust in me absolute, and fuck if that doesn't wreck me.

"You're so perfect," I murmur against her skin, trailing kisses up her stomach as my hands explore her curves, gliding over her ribs and then rising to cup her breasts. My thumbs brush over her nipples, drawing a soft gasp from her as she arches into my touch.

Positioning myself at her entrance, I push in slowly, inch by inch, savoring the tight, wet heat that wraps around me.

Pressing my forehead to hers, I hold still, savoring the moment. The way she feels wrapped around me, the way her body takes me like she was made for this—for me.

"You okay?" I rasp.

Her lips part, her breath shaky. "I need you to move, Eamon."

I do, fucking her slow and deep. My hips roll in a rhythm that has her whimpering, gasping, and clinging to me like I'm the only thing keeping her tethered to reality.

Each thrust is deliberate, a silent vow, a claim, a fucking prayer.

Because this is more than just sex.

This is me telling her that I see her, that she's not alone. That she's mine.

She clings to me, eyes locked on mine like I'm the only thing anchoring her to the earth. I start to move slowly at first. Her legs wrap around me, drawing me in deeper, her body meeting mine with a desperate rhythm.

Every thrust pulls another sound from her lips—needy, breathless, broken. And I drink in every one.

Her nails dig into my back, marking me. Her hips rise, seeking more friction, more pressure. I give it to her, adjusting the angle, grinding against her with each roll of my hips.

She tilts her head back, her moans growing louder, her body tightening around me. "Don't stop. I'm so close."

"I know, *mo chroí*," I whisper, kissing the corner of her mouth, her jaw, her throat. "Let go for me."

She shatters beneath me, a soft cry breaking free. I keep moving through it, chasing my own release, hips snapping harder now, more erratic, until the pleasure crests and crashes through me. I bury myself deep one last time, groaning her name as I come, every nerve on fire, every thought obliterated except her.

When it's over, I don't move. I stay pressed to her, our bodies slick and tangled together. My hand finds hers between us, fingers lacing tight.

I should tell her. I should say the words that have been clawing their way up my throat. But instead, I hold her tighter, pressing my lips to her hair. And I let her fall asleep in my arms, knowing she's mine.

Aoife

THE ROOM IS DARK. THE ONLY SOUND IS THE SOFT rhythm of Eamon's breath beside me. My body is still relaxed from the way he touched me—claimed me. For the first time in weeks, I feel at peace—wrapped in the scent of him, the strength of his arms.

But peace never lasts.

The shrill ring of Eamon's phone slices through the quiet, yanking us both from sleep. His muscles tense beneath me as he reaches for it, his voice rough with sleep as he answers.

One second. That's all it takes. One second for his entire body to go rigid.

He swings his legs over the side of the bed, his posture instantly alert. "I'm on my way."

I push up onto my elbows. "What's wrong?"

He's already up, yanking on his clothes and grabbing his gun. "Obsidian's on fire."

The words are like ice down my spine.

"I'm coming with you." I shove the sheets back, reaching for my clothes.

He stops me with a hard, unyielding don't test me look. "No, you're not."

"Eamon—"

"No." His voice is final, but I don't care.

"It might be your club," I argue. "But I have a right to know what's going on."

He closes the space between us, gripping my chin, forcing me to meet his gaze. "You're staying here. My guards will be stationed outside. Under no circumstances do you leave."

I go to argue again, but something dangerous flashes in his expression. "For once," he murmurs. "do as you're told." His fingers tighten just slightly. "I wouldn't survive if anything happened to you."

Then he kisses me, hard and quick, before turning and striding out the door.

I don't move, standing there in the dim light of the bedroom, my pulse hammering in my throat. *I wouldn't survive.*

I don't have time to process what they mean before a cold sensation prickles up my spine, the unmistakable whisper of dread curling around me. This was no accident.

The phone rings once, twice—then connects.

"Are you responsible for the fire at Obsidian?" I ask, skipping any kind of greeting, my voice sharp with accusation.

"I don't know what you're talking about," Ruairi says, too calm. Too practiced.

"Don't play dumb with me," I shoot back. "People could've been hurt."

"You're right," he says coolly. "And if you don't break things off with your boyfriend and come home, they will be."

A slow, simmering rage spreads through my chest like wildfire.

"I can't believe how cruel and heartless you are," I breathe.

"I'm not the one tearing this family apart," he snaps. "That's on you."

There's a beat of silence before his voice lowers. "Come home, Aoife. Walk away from him before someone gets killed."

My breathing falters, unsteady and shallow. I know Ruairi. He's not bluffing.

I should be afraid. I should be devastated.

But instead, something colder, stronger rises in me.

Resolve.

"If you're waiting for me to fall into line and obey," I say, my voice like steel, "you're going to be waiting a long fucking time."

Without waiting for his response, I end the call, dress quickly, and head for the door. The moment I step out, two of Eamon's men move to block my way.

"Boss said you're to stay inside."

"We all know I don't take orders from your boss." My hands find my hips, stance defiant, chin lifted just enough to make my point clear.

The two men exchange a glance, clearly torn between their orders and the reality of who they're dealing with.

One of them straightens, setting his jaw. "It's for your safety."

"And you think standing here playing gatekeeper is going to keep me safe? That's adorable." The sarcasm rolls off my tongue as I cross my arms, letting the weight of my glare do the rest.

The other guard shifts slightly, but neither moves to stop me as I step forward.

"Miss Quigley," the first one says, his voice strained with warning.

"Unless you're planning on physically stopping me, you should move out of my way."

They exchange glances, but neither makes a move.

"That's what I thought." I brush past them and step into the elevator, catching one of them already reaching for his phone, no doubt to call Eamon.

My pulse is steady and my spine straight as I press the button for the lobby.

Good. Let him know I'm coming.

This isn't just his war anymore. It's mine.

When the doors open, Eamon's waiting there. His stance is rigid, his face carved from stone. He doesn't yell. He doesn't have to. The fury radiating from him is enough to make the air feel charged, electric.

I don't give him the chance to speak first. "I spoke to Ruairi. I needed to know if he's responsible for the fire."

Eamon's nostrils flare, his jaw clenching. "And?"

"He acted like he didn't know what I was talking about," I reply.

His expression darkens into something lethal. "Do you believe him?"

I lift my chin. "No. He threatened more violence if I don't break things off with you and go home."

Eamon's silent for a moment. "And what do you want?" he asks, the tension in his body coils tight.

I meet his gaze without hesitation. "Ruairi needs to understand that no amount of threats will break me." I take a step closer, closing the distance between us. "I choose you, Eamon," I say, my voice softer but no less fierce. ""It's not about defiance. It's about choice. And I won't let my brother, or anyone, take that from me."

I see the war raging inside him. "I've been holding off on going after him," he finally says. "Out of respect for you. But this? This changes everything." Eamon clenches and unclenches his fists at his sides. "He brought the danger too close. We could've been in that club. You could've been hurt."

My stomach twists. "Did anyone—?"

"All the guests made it out," he says. "But one of my men is in the hospital with severe burns."

Guilt knots in my chest. "I'm so sorry."

"No. This is not on you." His voice is firm. "This is on him, and I'm going to make sure he fucking pays."

I shift my weight, unsure of my next move. Eamon watches me, his deep blue eyes missing nothing as I press my lips together, debating whether or not to say anything.

"Spit it out, Aoife," he snaps, his voice rough with exhaustion and frustration. "Whatever it is, just say it."

I exhale quietly. "When I got home earlier, I was planning to tell you something," I say, my voice tight. "Before everything happened."

His focus sharpens instantly. "What is it?"

"The meeting was about a weapons shipment Ruairi's expecting." I pull my phone out of my pocket. Unlocking it, I scroll for a second before holding it out to him. "I was able to get some pictures."

Eamon takes the phone from me. He's quiet as he scrolls through the images. The men at the table. The paperwork. A few blurry shots of what looks like manifests. "The pictures aren't perfect, but it's something."

A slow satisfaction curls in his expression. "This is good, *mo chroí*," he says, meeting my eyes. "Really fucking good."

Relief floods through me, but I push it down before it can show. After everything that happened tonight, I wasn't sure what to expect, but it wasn't this.

He hands the phone back, his fingers brushing against mine. "Thank you."

I nod and look away. I don't know if he realizes it, but those two words mean so much.

Before I can process it, he grips my shoulders and turns me back toward the elevator. "And now you're going back upstairs."

My blood boils. "You can't just send me away like a child."

"Watch me." His voice drops lower. "And if you come back down again, I'll make sure you can't sit for a week."

"Really? That's your big threat?"

His eyes glint with something dark. "Would you like a demonstration?"

My pulse flutters, but I narrow my eyes. "I hate you."

He smirks. "No, you don't."

Then he grabs my chin, kisses me hard, and steps back. "I'll be up as soon as possible," he says, stepping back, allowing the doors to slide shut between us.

As soon as I'm alone, I lean back against the wall and take a deep breath. It feels like the walls are closing in on me. I should be trying to stop this war. I should call Ruairi and beg him to back down.

But I won't.

Because this isn't just about Eamon. This is about me.

This is about proving that I'm more than just Ruairi's twin sister—more than someone he thinks needs protecting. My brother needs to accept me. Needs to understand that I'm not going anywhere.

If he pushes, I'll push back.

If he sets fire to my world, I'll walk through the flames.

Eamon

THE NIGHT AIR IS THICK WITH THE ACRID STENCH OF smoke, the remnants of the fire still clinging to the wind. The building smolders, embers glowing in the blackened ruin of my club.

I stand in the wreckage, watching as the last of the firefighters pack up their gear. Their work is done.

"I appreciate your help," I tell them, my voice steady despite the rage curling beneath my skin.

They nod, offering clipped assurances before driving off, red lights flashing against the wet pavement.

"Boss," Kiernan says, approaching fast, his phone already in hand. "We've got a problem."

That phrase has never meant anything good.

"The cash drop," he continues. "The one for your London contact. It never made it. They hit it en route. Lit the entire haul up like a fucking bonfire."

The words land hard. A quiet moment passes as the full weight settles. That shipment was weeks of planning. Months of positioning.

"You're sure?"

"Saw the photos myself." Kiernan hands over the phone. The screen shows a grainy shot of charred crates and soot-blackened bills scattered across asphalt. No survivors. No salvage.

I stare for a beat too long, the quiet rage inside me hardening into something far more dangerous.

"That drop was meant to solidify London," I say, my voice low. "He didn't just steal from me. He made a statement."

The words barely leave my mouth when Seamus steps forward, a long, slim box in his hands. Matte black, tied with a blood-red ribbon. "This was delivered to the hotel," he says, his voice tight. "Addressed to Aoife. The front desk called it in right after the fire started. Said a courier service dropped it off. No sender."

My pulse slows as I take the box from him. Slipping the ribbon free, I lift the lid. Inside, nestled in black tissue paper, is a single black rose.

Elegant. Wilting at the edges. Dying.

A piece of paper is pinned to the stem with a thin silver needle. I pluck it free, unfolding it with careful fingers. The words are scrawled in ink, deliberate and precise.

"A heart consumed by fire cannot be reclaimed."

Seamus's jaw tightens. "Someone doesn't like that she's with you."

A chill runs through me, and my hand tightens around the note, crumpling the paper.

My first instinct is to say his name, to confirm what we all suspect. But suspicion isn't proof. My mind races through the implications, the message behind the message. Finally, I say what I believe to be true. This wasn't just business. This was personal.

"This has Ruairi Quigley's name written all over it." My voice is sharp, cold. "He's trying to force Aoife to go back to Belfast."

Seamus shakes his head. "And you're still keeping her here?"

I clench my jaw, already knowing where this is going.

He scoffs, running a hand over his face. "Christ, Eamon. You've lost shipments, men, and now this. For what? A woman?" He lets out a harsh laugh. "Pack her bags and send her back to him. No pussy is worth this much fucking trouble."

The rage that's been simmering beneath my skin boils. I turn on him, my vision sharpening, my body poised like a predator ready to strike. "Say that again."

Seamus tenses, reading the danger in my stance. But he doesn't back down. "You know I'm right. This isn't just about her anymore. Quigley's not going to stop until he's buried you or you bury him."

I take a slow step forward. "Then I'll bury him." My voice is low, lethal. "And if you question me again, if you so much as speak her name with that fucking tone, you'll be buried, too."

The others shift uncomfortably, waiting, watching.

Seamus holds my gaze, weighing his options. He knows me. Knows I don't bluff.

After a long moment, he gives a single nod. "I'm with you."

I turn back to the smoking ruin of Obsidian.

For weeks, I've played Quigley's game. Not anymore.

"We're done playing tit for tat," I say, my voice steady, final. "We're going after Ruairi himself."

The words hang heavy in the air, pressing down like unseen hands at my throat. The darkness ahead is deep, yawning, stretching wider with each breath. There's no turning back, no escape. If I want a future with Aoife, I have to end this.

But hope is a cruel thing. It lingers in the space between certainty and ruin, whispering that there's still time, still a way out.

There isn't.

There's no peace for us while Ruairi draws breath, no future untouched by blood or betrayal. The way ahead is narrowing— each cruel choice is suspended between damnation and the dark unknown. The pressure builds, tightening, constricting, something unseen yet inescapable, forcing me forward.

It's him or me.

The descent has begun.

Aoife

"Please, Aoife," Bridget begs. "Come home. At least for a visit."

"I already told you," I say, pinching the bridge of my nose, trying not to snap. "I'm not coming back."

She blows out a frustrated breath. "I can't stand seeing you and Ruairi torn apart like this. Over a man."

Like this is some petty feud, some childish grudge I'm holding because of Eamon.

"It's more than that," I say, my tone sharper than I intend.

"Then explain it to me," she pleads.

I take a slow breath, forcing down the bitterness in my throat. "Ruairi sent Cian to Dublin."

Bridget goes silent.

"When he showed up, I gave him the benefit of the doubt," I continue. "I spent the day with him, just to see what he was playing at. And then he sent pictures of us to Ruairi like I was some kind of trophy to be won."

Bridget inhales sharply. "Oh, Evie—"

"And do you know what Ruairi did in response? He sent me the most vile, hateful messages. He called me a whore." My voice cracks. "And when that wasn't enough? He set fire to Eamon's club."

Bridget gasps. "He what?"

"Obsidian, Eamon's club. He ordered it to burn while people were inside." My stomach twists at the memory. "One of Eamon's men is in the hospital with severe injuries. Innocent people could've died. And for what? To make a point? To control me?"

Bridget's quiet for a long moment.

"I'm sorry," she finally whispers, and I hear the sincerity in her voice. "You have to understand that your brother is worried about you. He'd do anything to keep you safe."

I close my eyes, pressing my fingers against my temple. Why does everyone keep excusing him? "That doesn't make it okay, and where I appreciate the apology, it doesn't change anything," I say, my patience fraying. "Not until it comes from him."

She's about to say something else, but a voice from the front desk interrupts me.

"Sorry, Brie. I have to go. I'm the only one here today."

She sighs. "Okay. Just promise me you'll think about it, alright?"

I don't answer before I hang up, shoving my phone into my pocket as I step back behind the desk.

A man stands there, waiting, dressed like he belongs in a boardroom, but everything about him screams back alley.

"Welcome to the Emerald Briar. Are you here to check in?"

"I have a meeting with Mr. O'Sullivan," he says, his voice carrying the unmistakable weight of business.

"Who can I tell him is here?" I ask, keeping my voice professional and polite.

"Jerry Callahan," he replies.

I nod and pick up the phone, dialing Eamon. When he answers, I keep my voice neutral. "Mr. O'Sullivan, there's a Mr. Callahan here to see you."

Eamon doesn't ask questions, just says, "Tell him to wait at the bar. I'll be down shortly."

After hanging up, I offer the man a polite smile. "He asked that you wait in the bar."

As he moves toward the lounge, I busy myself behind the desk, going through routine tasks until Cian strolls over. He leans casually against the counter, giving me a slow once-over. "A girl like you shouldn't be wasting her time behind a desk."

I don't bother hiding my boredom. "Oh? And what exactly should I be doing?"

"Something much more fitting." His grin widens. "Something where your looks won't go to waste."

"You mean like sitting around looking pretty while some man tells me what to do?"

Cian chuckles. "Now, would that be so bad?"

I roll my eyes. "Sounds boring."

His smirk lingers. "I'd make sure you weren't bored, *mo bhanríon*."

I swallow down my disgust at the pet name. "Is that supposed to make me swoon?" I ask, my tone dripping with sarcasm. "You're going to have to try harder than that, handsome."

Then, I let my eyes rake over him, taking in his attire. "By the way, shouldn't you be dressed for a wedding? Or is crashing them more your style?" I ask, my tone dry.

He shrugs, a grin tugging at the corner of his mouth. "Bet you won't believe this."

"Try me." I cross my arms, unimpressed.

"The bride got cold feet. Called the whole thing off at the last minute."

"No way," I gasp, clutching my chest like I'm seconds from swooning. "What a shocking turn of events."

"Swear on my life." He shifts, pressing his forearms on the counter. "Which means I'm here, with no obligations, for the rest of the day. Thought maybe you and I could do something about that."

"And what exactly did you have in mind?"

He pauses, letting his gaze drift over me, slow and suggestive.

"Ditch work and come out with me. One night, just us, before I have to slip away in the morning."

Before I can come up with an excuse, a familiar presence moves behind him.

Eamon.

He steps up, his expression unreadable. "Is everything okay here?"

Cian turns, momentarily caught off guard, but recovers just as quickly. His grin is all confidence, his tone light but deliberate. "No trouble at all. Just trying to convince this one to run off with me for a few hours."

"I don't believe we've met." His movement is controlled as he extends a hand. "Eamon O'Sullivan—owner of the hotel."

Cian takes it without hesitation, matching his confidence. "Cian O'Leary," he replies, his confidence unshaken. "Didn't realize I'd get the pleasure of meeting the man in charge."

Eamon holds his gaze for a beat longer than necessary before releasing his grip. "Pleasure," he says, though his tone makes it clear it's anything but. "Careful, though. Not everything that looks good is meant to be touched."

Cian doesn't waver. If anything, his smirk deepens, like he's enjoying whatever game he thinks he's playing. "I'm sure you know how it is. When you have something this good, it's hard to walk away."

Eamon doesn't react right away. Instead, he studies Cian until his mouth curves into something that resembles amusement. "That so?" His voice is almost casual, but there's a lazy sort of challenge beneath it. He glances at me, his gaze lingering just long enough to make a point before looking back at Cian.

"Can't say I know the feeling," he continues, his tone light but deliberate. "When something's really yours, you don't have to chase it down." He smiles, slow and easy, but his eyes stay cold. "It stays exactly where it belongs."

Cian doesn't miss a beat. "Evie and I have been close for years. Her father approved the match long ago," he says, adjusting his cuff like this conversation is nothing more than a formality. "I know she's up here in Dublin trying to spread her wings, but I want to take her back home. Get married right away."

Eamon's gaze slides to me. "That true, *Evie*?"

I open my mouth to answer, but Cian cuts in smoothly. "She's shy. Doesn't like to talk about relationship details in public. I'm sure you understand."

"Of course." Eamon nods slowly. "You're a lucky man, then, to have someone as special as her." His lips curve into a smile that doesn't quite reach his eyes. "I wouldn't want to stand in the way of young love."

My stomach twists. What the hell is he doing?

"As a matter of fact," Eamon continues, "why don't the two of you have dinner in my restaurant? On the house."

My breath catches. "That's far too generous, and I—"

"I insist," Eamon interrupts. "And don't worry about your shift. I'll have someone cover for you."

Cian grins. "That's very kind of you."

Eamon takes out his phone, already typing, his attention seemingly elsewhere.

"I can wait until someone gets here," I offer.

"No need," Eamon replies, not bothering to look up. "I wouldn't dare keep your betrothed from whatever grand plans he has for tonight."

Speechless, I force a tight smile. "Cian, do you mind if I change out of my uniform first?"

"Of course," he says.

As I gather my things, Eamon stays making small talk with Cian. His questions are casual and polite. Just a man making conversation. But I know better. He's asking all the right things, pulling at the threads of whatever story Cian's spinning.

And Cian? He doesn't hesitate. Lie after lie rolls off his tongue with practiced ease.

"I'll meet you in the restaurant," Cian says as I walk toward the elevator.

I nod but say nothing, keeping my expression carefully neutral until the door shuts behind me in the penthouse.

My phone buzzes.

Ruairi: Bridget told me she invited you home to see Saoirse, but you declined.

Aoife: After your last message, of course I said no.

A few seconds later, his response comes.

Ruairi: I was out of line.

Aoife: You think?

Ruairi: We miss you. We want to see you.

My fingers hover over the screen. For a moment, I consider giving in but decide on a different approach.

Aoife: I'll come if Eamon can accompany me.

Ruairi: I will not have that bastard in my home.

Aoife: Then I'm not coming.

Ruairi: You need to stop playing games, Evie. Walk away from him before it's too late.

Aoife: Or what?

His response comes fast.

Ruairi: You'll see just how dangerous things can get.

A threat. A promise.

Ruairi: You don't want to test me on this.

I'm done with his *warnings*. His attempts to control me. If Ruairi thinks he can scare me into submission, he's wrong.

He doesn't get to decide where I go, who I trust, or who I let into my bed. Let him rage. Let him threaten. I won't bend for him, especially not when I've just started to stand on my own.

My gaze flicks to my phone again, but this time, it's not Ruairi I'm thinking of. It's Eamon. I tap out a message, fingers steady.

Aoife: What game are you playing? Giving me time off to have dinner with Cian?

Eamon's reply comes quickly.

Eamon: An opportune moment. You spend more time with him. I control the variables. I also wanted to see if he knew about us.

Aoife: And?

Eamon: He doesn't. Clearly, Ruairi doesn't tell him everything.

If Eamon wants to play games, I'll raise the stakes.

A slow smile curls at my lips.

I slip into a deep burgundy dress—the color of temptation and defiance. The fabric hugs every curve, the hem skimming high on my thighs, daring anyone to look too long. A pair of razor-thin heels with crimson soles complete the look. Dangerous, elegant, and impossible to ignore.

When I step into the restaurant, all heads turn. But there's only one reaction I care about.

And when my eyes find Eamon's from across the room, I know I've won. His jaw tightens. His grip on his drink flexes. But he can't do anything, or he'll give us away.

Cian's jaw nearly hits the floor. "No more shy and innocent tonight?" he asks, voice husky.

"I thought I'd try something different," I say as I slide onto the seat across from him.

Cian's practically drooling. Subtlety clearly isn't his strength. But it's not his attention I'm after. My eyes slip over his shoulder to the man behind him.

Eamon O'Sullivan is seething. And I'm enjoying every second of it.

Eamon

Jerry Callahan's voice grates in my ear, his tone tinged with impatience. He's demanding something—money, a favor, respect he hasn't earned. I should be paying attention, should be shutting him down, but my focus is elsewhere.

Across the restaurant.

On her.

The woman wrapped in a short, red dress that clings to every damn curve. The moment she steps through the door, the entire room shifts. Conversations falter, glasses pause mid-air, and men openly stare. Murderous rage courses through me, and I force myself to take a slow sip of whiskey. I knew playing with her was like playing with fire. I just didn't think she'd be so blatant about it.

O'Leary sits back in his chair, the picture of arrogance, like he's already won. Then, he leans in and says something to her, and she laughs lightly. His fingers brush her hair back. Each move is calculated and intentional.

The urge to storm across the room and rip him away from the table by his collar simmers low in my chest. But I stay rooted, forcing myself to play the part.

Jerry shifts beside me, catching my line of sight. "Christ," he mutters, letting out a low whistle. "That's a sexy piece of ass."

I don't look at him. Don't take my eyes off Aoife.

"I'd kill for a taste of what's between those legs. Bet it's just as pretty as the rest of her." He chuckles darkly, taking a sip of his drink. "Think she's looking for some fun tonight?"

"She works the front desk," I say evenly, voice smooth and disinterested.

"I thought she looked familiar. Bet she knows how to be real accommodating."

Keeping my expression unreadable, I warn, "I'd be careful where you point your appetite."

Jerry snorts, unfazed. "Relax, man. Just talking." He raises his hands in mock surrender, but there's a glint in his eyes like he hasn't decided if he's scared or amused.

It takes everything in me to play along, to keep my pulse steady, when all I want to do is slam his face into the bar. Instead, I glance back at the table, watching as Aoife crosses her legs, deliberately slow, her dress riding up just enough to keep every man in the room interested.

Including *him*.

The whiskey burns as I swallow it down, my restraint hanging by a thread.

Let her test boundaries, bend the rules, and pretend it's just a game.

Because once you step into the dark, it stains you. And Aoife's already wearing my mark.

Aoife

A server approaches the table, carrying a bottle of the restaurant's finest champagne. "Compliments of the owner," he says, pouring two glasses before setting it on the table and leaving.

My stomach tightens as I glance across the restaurant.

Eamon sits at the bar, his posture relaxed, although I know he's anything but. He lifts his glass in a mock toast, a slow, knowing smile playing on his lips.

I keep my expression blank, refusing to give him the satisfaction of a reaction.

Cian glances over his shoulder, then lets out a low chuckle as he picks up his glass. "And what do you suppose that's about?"

Offering an innocent smile, I ask, "What's what about?"

Cian leans back in his chair, swirling the champagne in his glass. "O'Sullivan sending over a bottle of his best. Toasting you from across the room." His voice is laced with something suspicious.

"Perhaps he's just being a good boss." I shrug. "You talked to him more than I ever have. Did he say anything to you after I left?"

Cian hums, unconvinced. "I don't trust him," he says. "Do you know he started a war with Ruairi?"

"Ruairi doesn't tell me anything about the Syndicate. And I didn't even know my boss was involved in that world until you told me the other night," I say, a trace of defensiveness creeping into my voice despite my best effort to sound calm.

His eyes search mine, looking for any sign of a lie. "You sure about that?"

"What Ruairi does with the Syndicate has nothing to do with me." My voice is steady, matter-of-fact. "And unless my job suddenly involves having to make backroom deals, I don't see why any of it matters."

Cian seems convinced, for now. He lifts his glass again, but instead of drinking, he asks, "Have you heard anything about the fire at Obsidian?"

My fingers rest against the cool stem of my glass, trying to read between the lines of why he's bringing it up. A quiet unease coils in my chest. If Cian had a part in it, he'd never admit it. But if he suspects his name's being whispered in the wrong corners, he might be here to get ahead of it. To see just how much I know.

I keep my expression neutral. "Only what the other employees are whispering about?"

"And what exactly are they whispering?" he asks.

Cian meets my eyes, his stare lingering a second too long before an easy smile curves his lips. "Just curious."

Then, without missing a step, he changes course. "Come back to Belfast with me."

The shift is so abrupt it takes a moment to register.

"Why would I do that?" I ask. "I just got to Dublin."

His tone is measured, but his eyes give him away. "I don't think it's safe for you to stay here. Not with everything going on between your boss and your brother."

"I'm sure my boss doesn't know I'm related to Ruairi, or why else would he have hired me?" I say, trying to sound confident even as doubt creeps in. "He wouldn't take the risk, especially if things are as tense between them as you say they are."

Cian's brow lifts slightly, his voice low. "You really don't know, do you?"

"No," I admit, eyes narrowing as I study him, "but I'm sure you can tell me why Ruairi's going after him?"

He hesitates, swirling the liquid in his glass before finally responding. "I'm not sure how much I should say."

"Really? That's interesting, considering you brought me to a Syndicate meeting, but now you're hesitating to answer a simple question?" I sit back.

Cian's lips press into a thin line. He still doesn't answer.

I sigh, shaking my head. "I thought you were different. But I see that you're content treating me the same way Ruairi does," I say, letting just the right amount of frustration seep into my voice. "Like I'm too naive to understand. Like I should sit back and let the men handle things."

I pick up my napkin and toss it onto the table. "I should've figured. I mean, you *do* work for my brother. Why would you be honest with me? Why would you see me as anything other than a weak woman who needs protecting?"

The chair screeches across the floor as I stand. "I don't need another man like that in my life."

Before I can turn, Cian's hand closes around my wrist, his grip forceful as he pulls me back down into my seat.

"You don't know anything about me," he says, his voice quieter now, almost coaxing. "But I'd like to change that."

I watch him carefully. "And how do you plan to do that?"

His hand drifts under the table, fingers skimming up my leg, his touch bold.

I don't react. Not outwardly.

He leans in close, the heat of his breath ghosting over my jaw, deliberate and intimate. "Ruairi didn't try to set us up, Aoife. He *chose* me for you. Gave his blessing like it was already done." His voice is velvet-wrapped steel, smooth but unmistakably possessive.

"So let me show you why. Let me show you what it means to belong to a man who knows exactly how to handle you."

I smile slightly, meeting his gaze. "Dating me is one thing. Spending the night with me? That's something else entirely."

His fingers trail higher. The urge to push him away burns under my skin. But I stay still, letting him think he's in control while I draw him further into my web.

"We need to be smart," I murmur. "Think our moves through. Keep Ruairi's blessing."

Finally, he exhales, pulling back with a reluctant nod. "I want you to understand what's really happening, Aoife," he says, studying me like he's weighing his options. "Ruairi wasn't ready to take over."

I don't react, but my pulse quickens.

"He's making decisions that aren't in the best interest of the Syndicate." He pauses, letting the words hang between us as if he's waiting for me to challenge him.

I don't. Instead, I give him exactly what he wants, my curiosity. "And what would you do differently?"

"Your brother's weakness is his temper. He reacts instead of thinking things through and responding. He's making reckless mistakes." His lips curl as he sits back. "I'd make sure we're running things right. No reckless feuds. No emotional decisions."

Cian lets out a soft, humorless laugh, his eyes never leaving mine. "No."

He leans forward slightly, voice dropping. "Because I'm not just here to take something from Ruairi."

A pause. Calculated.

"I have a proposition."

My brows lift. "Go on."

"I want to take over the Syndicate," he says smoothly, "and I want to run it with you."

The words land like a weight in my chest. For a moment, I can't tell if it's ambition or nausea twisting in my stomach.

He says it like it's inevitable. Like I've already agreed. What he doesn't see is the way my nails press into my palms beneath the table, how hard I work to keep my face still.

He thinks I'll be flattered. Empowered.

But all I feel is the cold, calculating truth settling into place.

He doesn't want me as a partner. He wants me as leverage. As a crown to place on his stolen throne.

But I've worn prettier masks than this. And I've played far more dangerous games.

"You're a smart young woman, Aoife," he continues, his voice carrying a hint of admiration. "Too smart to be working a front desk. You're a Quigley. That makes you royalty. You should be doing something deserving of your name."

I let my lips part slightly, as if mesmerized, as if no one has ever seen me like this before.

"I know you want more. You've been pushing to prove yourself, and your brother still won't let you in. You belong in this world. And with me? You'd have power. Real power," he says as if he's offering me the world in silk and chains.

I inhale slowly, as if overwhelmed. "What about Ruairi?"

"If he willingly steps down, he'll be offered another position in the Syndicate."

I sit back, crossing my legs, like I'm genuinely thinking it over.

Cian lets the silence stretch, his eyes never leaving mine as he waits for my answer. Then his phone vibrates on the table. He glances at the screen and then back to me.

"Excuse me," he mutters, pushing back his chair. "I need to take this." He stands, adjusting his jacket. "Wait here for me?"

I give him a small smile, nodding. "Of course."

The moment he's out of sight, I push away from the table. My heart hammers as I walk briskly across the restaurant toward a side entrance.

Jerry Callahan's still there, slouched in his seat beside Eamon. As I pass, he whistles low, turning slightly toward me. "Leaving already, sweetheart?" he drawls, his voice as sleazy as the way he looks at me. "Shame. You looked bored out of your mind with that old bastard." He leans in just a little, voice dropping to something rougher, darker. "I could show you a much better time tonight. Something slow, hard, and worth remembering."

I stop and turn in his direction, ready to put him in his place, but before I can get a word out, Eamon moves. The punch lands hard and fast, Jerry's head snapping back before he even registers what's happening.

Eamon's guards react immediately. One grabs me, yanking me back, while the other hauls Jerry out of his seat. Everything moves in a blur. I don't fight as I'm led through the kitchen to a back entrance and ushered into the elevator. By the time I step into the penthouse, I'm fuming.

I don't know what pisses me off more. Cian treating me like some delicate thing he can manipulate, trying to lure me back to Belfast with half-truths and veiled warnings. Jerry thinking he could say whatever he wanted like I was just another pretty face in a tight dress there for his entertainment. Or Eamon thinking I need him to fight my battles.

I cross my arms, pacing the room, my anger burning hotter with every step. I had it handled. I always do. But now? What if Cian gets wind of my boss starting a brawl over me? He's going to ask me more questions. Questions I don't have good answers for.

I've been playing this game carefully, staying close enough to Cian to pull information without tipping him off. But if he starts connecting dots, if he suspects there's something between Eamon and me, then it's over. He'll shut down.

And then what?

Blowing my cover now means losing the one advantage I have in this war. And for what? Because Eamon couldn't keep his damn hands to himself? Because he needed to throw a punch to mark his territory?

Frustration coils hot in my chest as I stop pacing and press my fingers to my temples. Rage and disappointment throb behind my eyes. I don't need anyone stepping in for me—*not* Cian, *not* Ruairi, and *especially not* Eamon.

He thinks he's protecting me. What he's really doing is under-estimating me.

Let them all circle like vultures, mistaking me for something fragile. They forget—it's not the damsel they should fear. It's the reckoning she brings.

Eamon

THE RESTAURANT IS SILENT. NOT THE COMFORTABLE kind that settles over an upscale place like this after a lull in conversation. No, this is the brittle, stunned silence that follows violence where it doesn't belong.

Jerry Callahan groans as he's dragged toward the exit, his nose a mess of blood, his pride shattered right along with it. My men flank him, shoving past stunned patrons, muttering apologies to no one in particular.

I exhale slowly, rolling my shoulders back, ignoring the weight of a hundred eyes on me. It wasn't my most subtle move, but I regret nothing.

I'm about to walk out when a familiar figure strolls back into the dining room.

Cian.

His gaze sweeps the restaurant, then locks onto his table, where he finds an empty chair. His smile fades.

He turns, eyes narrowing as he approaches me. "Where is she?"

Taking my time adjusting my cuff, I finally ask, "Who?"

His expression twists with irritation. "Aoife. Where the fuck is she?"

I finally look at him, letting a slow, mocking grin curve my lips. "Do you mean the girl from the front desk? *Your* date? Shouldn't you know where she went?"

Cian exhales sharply, his patience obviously fraying. "Cut the shit, O'Sullivan." He lowers his voice just enough to keep the conversation between us. "You're too smart to not know that she's *the* Aoife Quigley."

I don't blink, playing at indifference.

Cian studies me, eyes narrowing before he presses on. "You're in a war with her brother, and now you've got her working for you? That's a bold fucking move." His voice drops even lower. "If you know what's good for you, you'll fire her. Tell her to pack her shit and send her back home where she belongs."

A veiled threat. A demand wrapped in concern.

I let the silence stretch between us, watching as he waits for my reaction, smug in the belief that he's just given me valuable information. He handed me her identity like a fool. Either he's sloppy or he's testing me.

Then I step in closer, lowering my voice. "Is that a threat?"

He still wears a smug expression, but there's tension beneath it now. "Just some friendly advice. You're smart, O'Sullivan. You don't want to make an even bigger enemy of the Quigleys."

"And you don't want to make an enemy of *me*."

His jaw twitches. But I don't give him the chance to respond. Instead, I turn and walk out of the restaurant.

By the time I step into the penthouse, I'm ready to put this entire night behind me. Except the second the door closes, I realize I've walked straight into a storm. Aoife's waiting for me, arms crossed, eyes blazing with fury.

"You started a fight over a man hitting on me?" she snaps. "Are you serious?"

I shrug off my jacket, keeping my movements slow and measured. "He deserved it."

Her laugh is sharp, incredulous. "I can take care of myself, Eamon."

I turn to her, my temper flaring despite myself. "And you're going to tell me this is how you *take care* of yourself?" My gaze drags over her. "Walking into that room dressed like this. Making sure every bastard in there was looking at you like you were theirs to take?"

She doesn't flinch. Doesn't back down. Instead, she takes a step toward me, her chin tilted up, her eyes dark and playful. "You're the one who told me to have dinner with him," she reminds me, her voice slow, deliberate. "I figured I'd play the part."

She takes another step closer, slow and predatory, forcing me to hold my ground. Then, she leans in, her mouth just shy of my jaw. "Cian put his hands on me, you know. Dragged his fingers dangerously high." Her voice is barely above a whisper, enough to set my blood on fire. "And he wanted me to spend the night with him."

Red-hot rage explodes in my chest, sharp and unrelenting.

I grip her wrist, yanking her flush against me, my voice a low growl against her ear. "I don't give a fuck what information Cian has." I pull back just enough to meet her eyes, making sure she understands me. "That was the last fucking time he, or anyone else, touches what's mine."

I don't give her time to speak, to argue, to push me further. I crush my mouth to hers, swallowing the sound she makes—a gasp, a curse, a challenge. Maybe all three. Her nails rake down my chest, not in protest but in provocation, and it only fuels the fire already roaring through me.

This isn't soft. It's not sweet.

It's anger and want, betrayal and need, all twisted together into something dangerous.

I spin her around before she can catch her breath, pressing her hands to the back of the couch. Her body arches, instinctively knowing what I want, what I need. My fingers drag up her thighs, bunching her dress at her waist, exposing the curve of her ass. She doesn't resist. Doesn't flinch.

She's waiting for it.

"Is this what you wanted?" I rasp, my voice rough, barely human. "To make me lose control?"

She doesn't answer, not with words. She pushes back against me, a silent demand that makes something primal snap inside my chest. "Always pushing," I growl, pressing her back against the marble, pinning her beneath me.

I tear at the thin scrap of lace keeping her from me, my fingers sliding against her slick heat. Aoife lets out a strangled sound, her body jerking, but I don't give her time to adjust. I slide two fingers inside her, thrusting deep and fast, my thumb pressing against her clit as her body tightens.

"Tell me," I demand. "Tell me who you belong to."

"You," she breathes. "I belong to you."

My belt hits the floor with a hiss, the zipper a sharp rasp that cuts through the thick air between us. I shove my pants down just far enough, then grip her hips, grounding myself in the feel of her beneath me.

I enter her in one hard stroke, burying myself deep.

She cries out, raw, wrecked, but doesn't pull away. Her body welcomes the punishment, the depth, the fury in every motion. I move with a rhythm that has nothing to do with grace. It's a claiming. A warning. A confession I'm too fucked up to say aloud.

I fuck her hard, relentless, chasing every moan, every sharp inhale, until she shatters around me. Her body trembles, clenching tight. I drive into her twice more, then I'm gone, a guttural sound ripping from my throat as I empty myself inside her.

For a moment, the only sound is our ragged breathing.

Then Aoife lifts her head, that wicked little smirk back in place. "Guess I won that round."

I let out a low chuckle, fingers tracing lazy patterns on her bare thigh. "You really think this is a game, *mo chroí*?"

Her smirk deepens. "Isn't it?"

"Games have rules." I press a slow kiss to her throat before pulling away. "And eventually, someone loses."

Aoife

AFTER EAMON FUCKED ME OVER THE ARM OF THE SOFA, he carried me to bed and ruined me all over again until my limbs were weak and my body trembled. Until I was too spent to do anything but cling to him. Even now, I can still feel him on my skin, the bruises his hands left, the ache between my legs, and the delicious exhaustion that threatens to pull me back under.

The bed shifts slightly, a hand trailing lazily down my spine. "I didn't think you'd wake up," Eamon murmurs, his voice rough with sleep, but there's amusement laced in it. "I almost had you convinced to stay unconscious."

I hum, stretching slowly, wincing at the soreness in my limbs. "You tried."

His chuckle is low, pleased. He presses a kiss to my bare shoulder before pulling away and getting out of bed.

By the time I open my eyes again, he's near the window, already dressed, buttoning the cuffs of his sleeves. He moves with easy efficiency, but there's tension in his shoulders. "I have to go out of town," he says, glancing at me.

I push up onto my elbows, my voice still thick with sleep. "Why?"

He meets my gaze, unreadable. "Business."

I sit up, keeping my expression neutral. "Can you be any more vague?"

He doesn't take the bait. "Seamus and a few of my men will be here while I'm gone."

"To keep me safe or to keep me in line?"

"Both," he answers, stepping closer.

I hold his stare, then ask, "How long will you be gone?"

He exhales, adjusting the watch on his wrist. "Hopefully, no more than a few days."

I watch him carefully, searching for anything he's not saying. "That's all you're going to tell me?"

"It's all you need to know," he says, leaning down and trailing his fingers along my jaw before tilting my chin up. "Please, *mo chroí,* behave yourself while I'm gone."

Without breaking eye contact, I reach up, brushing a hand over his chest. "I always behave."

His chuckle is low, amused but not convinced. He presses a quick, firm kiss to my lips, then pulls away. "I'll be back soon."

I watch as he leaves, the door clicking shut behind him. The moment he's gone, I reach for my phone.

Time to set things in motion.

Aoife: I'm in.

The response is immediate.

Cian: Where'd you disappear to last night?

Aoife: When my boss started that fight, I got scared and left. Went back to my room and crashed.

Cian: Probably for the best.

Aoife: So, what's the next move?

There's a pause before the bubbles pop onto my screen.

Cian: I don't want to put it in text, and there are too many people around for me to call. It's not safe. Once I'm back in Belfast, I'll be in touch.

I stare at the message, unease prickling beneath my skin. It's too vague. Too convenient.

Whatever game he's playing, I won't be left on the sidelines.

I've spent enough time watching from behind locked doors, told I wasn't ready, that I didn't belong. But I've seen enough. Learned enough. And I'm done waiting for someone else's plan to unfold.

If Cian wants to keep secrets, let him. It's time I start putting my own plan into motion. And that begins with Ruairi. We need to talk, not as brother and sister, but as two people who want the same crown.

Whether he's ready for that or not.

Aoife: We need to talk.

Ruairi: About?

I stare at the screen, knowing I have to word this perfectly.

Aoife: I'm tired of this war between us. I miss my family. We need to find a way forward. A truce.

There's a long pause. I'm not sure he's going to respond.

Ruairi: Not at O'Sullivan's hotel.

Aoife: Name the place.

Ruairi: The Cobblestone Tavern. 7 PM.

I'm familiar with the small pub. It's public enough to be safe and private enough for a real conversation.

Aoife: I'll be there.

The stage is set. Now, I need leverage. There's tension between Seamus and Eamon. I don't know the details. I don't need to. If there's friction, there's opportunity.

Making my way downstairs, I find him exactly where I expect, in Eamon's office. His broad frame is leaning over the desk, scanning through something on the computer.

He doesn't look up when I step inside. "You lost?"

Stepping forward, I reply, "Not at all."

His sigh is slow, irritated. "What do you want, Aoife?"

I close the door behind me and lean against it. "I need your help."

That gets his attention. He straightens in his seat, his eyes narrowing.

"My help?" His tone is edged with surprise. "And why would I do that?"

"Because you're smarter than the rest of them."

Seamus scoffs, arms crossing over his chest. "Flattery's not going to get you what you want."

I tilt my head, offering him a softer smile. "It's not flattery if it's true."

He watches me, waiting for the catch. I sigh, letting just a hint of vulnerability slip into my voice. "Look, I know you don't trust me, and I can't blame you." I glance away briefly as if hesitating. "But I want to prove myself. I want to help."

Seamus narrows his eyes. "Help with what, exactly?"

I take another careful step forward. "Ruairi. This fight between him and Eamon. It's spiraling. It's going to get worse, and we both know that." I pause, lowering my voice even more. "I want to stop it before it does."

"Keep talking," he says.

"I know I don't have power in this world," I continue, keeping my tone even, steady. "Not yet. But I have information. Connections. And I'm in a position to move between both sides in a way no one else can." I meet his gaze, my expression sincere.

He lets out a slow breath. "And what exactly do you want from me?"

Ruairi

BRIDGET WATCHES ME FROM ACROSS THE ROOM, ARMS crossed, her expression tight with concern. "What else did she say?"

I sigh, running a hand through my hair. "She asked to meet. Said it was time to put an end to this." I exhale, forcing down my frustration. "She needs to cut ties with O'Sullivan. Whatever this is between them, it ends tonight."

Bridget shakes her head. "That's not what's important right now."

"Like hell it's not. That bastard is using her. If she stays wrapped up in his world, it won't end well for her."

My wife crosses her arms, stubborn as ever. "The most important thing is getting her home. Everything else will fall into place the way it's supposed to."

"It almost sounds like you don't care if she's with him."

She holds my gaze, unwavering. "I don't."

"You can't be serious."

"If he treats her well, if she's happy, who are we to stand in the way?"

I shake my head, my hands clenching at my sides. "No. That's not how this works."

She gives me a skeptical look but doesn't push. Instead, she asks, "When will you be home?"

I grab my keys off the counter. "I'm staying the night in Dublin. I'll be back first thing in the morning."

Bridget nods, but I can see the worry still written all over her face. She doesn't press me further, just watches as I crouch down next to Saoirse, who's sitting on the floor, stacking her wooden blocks with the kind of focus only a toddler can manage.

I brush a hand over her curls, watching as she sets one block carefully on top of another. "You be good for your mammy while Dada is gone."

She nods solemnly, then looks up at me with big, curious eyes. "Where go?"

I tap her nose lightly. "I'm going to bring Aunt Evie home, *a stór*."

"Auntie E home," she repeats, like she's reminding me of my own task.

I chuckle, pressing a kiss to her forehead. "That's the plan, love."

She thinks about this for a moment, then holds up a block. "Take?"

A small smile tugs at my lips as I take it from her tiny hand. "For luck?"

She nods, very serious. "No lose it."

"I won't," I promise, tucking it into my pocket.

Satisfied, she goes back to her blocks, stacking them with a determined little hum.

Bridget steps closer as I stand, smoothing a hand over the front of my jacket like she's fixing something, but really, it's just an excuse to touch me before I go.

"Come home in one piece," she murmurs, voice softer now.

"That the best you've got?" I ask a hint of amusement in my voice.

She huffs, shaking her head, but there's warmth in her eyes. "Don't make me say it, Ri."

I exhale a quiet chuckle, brushing my knuckles softly on her cheek. "Wouldn't dream of it."

Her lips twitch, but she doesn't argue. Instead, she squeezes my arm, fingers lingering just long enough to say what she won't.

"Always," I murmur and press a kiss to her cheek, then turn for the door, tucking the wooden block into my pocket before I go.

I have a long ride ahead before I reach Dublin, plenty of time to figure out my next move. How to handle Aoife and what to say to make her listen. She's always been stubborn, always pushed back any time she felt cornered. There's no avoiding the real issue —she's not going to back down on working in the Syndicate.

The thought alone makes my grip tighten on the wheel. It's not only about keeping her safe, though that's a part of it. However, my sister is a capable young woman. She can shoot with the best of them, and I've seen her sparring skills. She'd give anyone a fight, but she shouldn't have to.

The things I've seen and had to do—I don't want that life for her. I never have. I want to keep her kind and loving. The world I live in is dark. The last thing I want is for it to twist her into something she was never meant to be.

But I can't tell her any of that. She'll shut down. If I refuse to give her a place in the Syndicate, she'll dig her heels in to spite me. And if I try to dance around the subject, she'll know I'm lying.

I need to be careful and play this right. Because getting her home is only half the battle. The real fight will be making sure she stays.

By the time I reach Dublin, I have a plan I think we can both live with. A compromise. Something that gives her just enough of what she wants without putting her in the kind of danger she doesn't fully understand.

I pause outside the pub, looking through the window to assess the situation. As head of the Syndicate, I know better than to walk in blind, especially here, in O'Sullivan's territory. I didn't bring guards with me. A deliberate choice. If I want Aoife to trust me, I can't treat this like a battlefield.

Still, that doesn't mean I'm careless. I scan the nearly empty space, noting the exits. A handful of patrons scattered around. A couple of men sit hunched over their drinks near the bar. They appear lost in their own conversations. Nothing immediately sets off alarms, but I keep my guard up as my eyes land on Aoife.

She's already here, sitting at a small table tucked in the back corner. Her fingers lightly trace the rim of her glass. She looks lost in thought, but there's tension in the set of her shoulders, in the way her foot taps absently against the floor. In the quick, darting glances she keeps throwing toward the door like she's waiting for something. Or bracing for it.

After taking a measured breath, I step inside.

My footsteps are heavy as I walk across the wooden floor. "Aoife."

She looks up. "Ruairi."

It's been months since I've seen her in person, though that hasn't stopped us from fighting through texts or over the phone. Every conversation we've had has been laced with resentment. I expected tension when we finally sat face-to-face, and I was right. It lingers between us, thick and unyielding, filling the silence of every unspoken word.

She offers a tight smile. "Thanks for meeting me."

I nod. "How've you been?"

"I'm doing well." Her voice is steady, confident.

And looking at her now, I almost believe it.

We may be twins, but in my eyes, she's always been my little sister. The one who needed protecting, the one I had to keep safe.

But the woman sitting across from me isn't the innocent little girl I remember. She's composed. Self-assured. Controlled.

It should put me at ease. Instead, it unsettles me.

That's all she says before a server approaches, setting a pint of Guinness down in front of me and another in front of Aoife. He follows it with a bowl of hearty Irish stew, the rich scent of beef and potatoes filling the air.

I glance at her, my brow raised.

She lifts her glass. "I ordered for us."

I huff a quiet breath, shaking my head as I pick up my pint. "Thanks," I mutter before taking a drink.

Aoife doesn't say anything else before picking up her spoon, stirring the thick stew in front of her, and taking a bite. I follow suit, scooping up a spoonful, the rich, savory broth warming me from the inside.

For a few minutes, we eat in silence. The only sounds between us are the clink of metal against ceramic and the low murmur of conversation from the bar. It's almost normal. Almost like we're just two people sharing a meal instead of a brother and sister poised on opposite sides of a war.

Aoife shifts slightly, wrapping her hands around her glass. "How's Bridget?"

"She's fine."

"And Saoirse?" she asks, looking up at me.

There's no malice in her voice, no challenge in her expression.

"She's good," I say after a moment. "Growing too fast."

Aoife nods, fingers idly tracing the condensation on her glass. "I bet."

I set my spoon down, refocusing. "Enough small talk. We need to talk about why you called me here."

"Of course," she says, leaning forward and resting her elbows on the table. "Let's talk."

I keep my voice level carefully measured. "Cian seems to think you and he felt a connection while he was here."

Her lips twitch, but it's not quite a smile. "He was very charming", she says lightly.

"I hope that opened your eyes to everything you could have. Everything you've been missing."

Aoife swirls her spoon through the last remnants of stew, then looks up. "Maybe you're right."

That stops me cold. I expected resistance. Some sarcastic jab or fire in her eyes. But there's none of that. Just calm. Until she keeps talking.

"But if I come back, it's on my terms."

My brows draw together. "What terms?"

She doesn't hesitate. "I want a seat at the table. I want a real place in the Syndicate."

I exhale slowly. "You're not ready for that."

"You've never even let me try," she snaps, heat finally cracking through her composure. "You kept me locked away like I was some secret. Some weakness."

"That's not what this is about."

"Yes, it is." She keeps her eyes locked on mine. "I want in. And I want to be with Eamon."

The air in the room shifts—heavy, volatile.

My hand curls around my glass, knuckles whitening. "You want what?"

"I'm not choosing between love and loyalty," she says, quiet but fierce. "I've played the obedient sister long enough. I won't do it anymore."

Anger flares white-hot in my chest. "He's dangerous."

"So am I," she says, with a smile that doesn't reach her eyes.

I stare at her, trying to bite back the heat rising in my chest. She doesn't flinch. Doesn't look away. The girl I used to protect with everything I had isn't sitting across from me anymore. This woman, this version of her, is fire and defiance wrapped in velvet.

"You think he sees you as an equal?" I ask, voice low. "That man doesn't love you, Aoife. He sees a Quigley. A tool. A weakness to use against me."

"If that's what he sees, then maybe we understand each other better than you think.

I open my mouth, but nothing comes out. For once, I don't have the right words to fix this.

"You're throwing away everything we built."

She doesn't blink. "No. I'm building something of my own."

Before I can stop her, she steps back, brushing her phone off the table. "Excuse me," she says smoothly. "I need the loo."

And just like that, she turns and walks away.

I sit there in stunned silence, the weight of her words crashing down around me. My little sister. My last piece of family. Already halfway out the door, and I'm not sure there's a damn thing I can do to stop her.

Minutes pass. Too many. I start to wonder if she used this as an opportunity to slip out the back. I take another slow sip of my beer, unease creeping in, my instincts humming.

Just as I shift to glance over my shoulder, someone stumbles past, knocking into my chair. I barely register the movement before I feel it—a quick, sharp prick at my neck.

I jerk, reaching up, but it's already too late.

A familiar voice murmurs near my ear. "I'm sorry, Ri."

My vision sways, my limbs going sluggish. I force my head to turn, to see for myself who it is.

Aoife stands holding the syringe.

"What the hell—" The words barely leave my mouth before the world tilts, the edges of my vision darkening until everything goes silent.

Aoife

THE QUIET RUMBLE OF THE ENGINE FILLS THE SPACE between us. In the back seat, my brother lies unconscious, his hands bound, his chest rising and falling in deep, steady breaths.

I did this.

The thought should break me.

It doesn't.

It coils around my spine, cold and sharp, like a blade I never meant to wield. But I did. I pressed it to the soft belly of loyalty and sliced clean through.

This isn't the act of a dutiful sister. It's a betrayal carved from necessity, born from years of being kept small. He would've never handed me the crown. So I took the throne in the only language this world understands—force.

The weight of it sits heavy, but not unfamiliar. Not unwelcome. Maybe this is what power tastes like. Metallic. Quiet. Inevitable.

Somewhere deep in the marrow of me, a voice whispers that this is the beginning of my descent. That once you tie up your own blood, there's no return from the abyss.

But maybe the abyss is where I was meant to rule.

I tighten my grip on my lap, my nails digging into the fabric of my dress. My mind drifts back to earlier today in Eamon's office.

Seamus lets out a slow breath. "And what exactly do you want from me?"

"I need your help kidnapping my brother."

He stares at me for a long moment. Then, he laughs, shaking his head. "You're out of your fucking mind."

I expected that reaction and I'm prepared to state my case. "I'm trying to convince Ruairi to let me run the Syndicate with him," I explain, keeping my voice even. "But he refuses to listen. He's left me with no choice but to take drastic measures."

Seamus leans back in his chair, arms crossing over his chest. "And you think I'd help you why, exactly?"

I meet his gaze, unwavering. "Because once I have control, I'll put an end to this war between the Syndicates. And that means Eamon stays safe."

That makes him pause. He exhales slowly, studying me with calculating eyes. "You've got some balls. I'll give you that."

I stay quiet, letting him think it over.

After a moment, he asks, "Why not go directly to Eamon?"

"Because this isn't his fight. If I want to prove I'm capable, I need to do this on my own. I need to show that I can use the resources available to me. That I know how to do this."

Seamus pushes back his chair and stands, taking his time as he walks toward me. He gets close enough that I catch the faint scent of whiskey and gunpowder on his skin. I force myself to hold my ground, even as every instinct warns me to step back.

"I don't trust you. You're the reason this war started in the first place," he admits, leaning in just a fraction more, his voice darkening. "I've told Eamon to get rid of you more times than I can count."

My pulse kicks up as I counter, "And yet, here I am."

That earns me a short, humorless chuckle. "Yeah," he mutters. "Because for some goddamn reason, Eamon sees something in you. Something worth keeping."

Seamus considers me for another long moment. "Fine. I'll help you. Not because I like you, but because if you really have the power you claim you do, this war ends, and we can all get back to business as usual."

His expression hardens, and his next words come like a threat wrapped in steel. "But make no mistake, Aoife, if you turn on Eamon, if you backstab me or fuck this up in any way, I'll kill you myself."

The weight of his words settles between us. But I don't show a hint of doubt.

Instead, I extend my hand. "Then I guess we have a deal."

Once I set the meeting with Ruairi, all it took was a few calls. The owners of the Cobblestone are loyal to Eamon. They locked their doors and closed for the day. Not patrons, not strangers. Most were the pub's staff mixed with several of Eamon's foot soldiers who were told to play a part. The bartender pouring drinks, the old man in the corner nursing a pint—they were all in on it.

Ruairi never saw it coming.

And now, he's heading toward a fate he could've never predicted. A trap set by his own sister.

Seamus drives in silence, focused on the road ahead. He hasn't asked me if I'm sure about this. Maybe because he already knows the answer.

I sit straighter as the castle comes into view, its towering stone silhouette cutting against the night sky. The gates open before us, and the moment we roll inside, guards are already stepping forward to help.

Ruairi doesn't stir as they lift him from the car. His head lolls to the side, his body slack as they carry him inside.

I expect them to take him to one of the holding rooms in the underground area that Eamon brought me to. But instead of going to the hidden staircase, we move deeper inside the castle. Until we reach a heavy metal grate embedded in the floor.

I freeze.

One of the guards steps forward, flipping a switch. A mechanical hum fills the air as a lift lowers from the ceiling.

Ruairi is loaded onto the crude device, and it's lowered into a hollowed-out pit. The guard pulls out a knife and cuts through the ropes that bind him. Then, he's lifted back out, and the grate is slammed shut over the hole, locking Ruairi inside.

I take a breath, schooling my features into something calm and controlled. Then, I wait. Minutes stretch before a low groan echoes from below.

Ruairi stirs. His movements are sluggish at first as he fully regains consciousness. He jerks upright as his eyes snap open, taking in his surroundings. Slowly, he pushes himself to his feet and looks up. I know the moment his gaze lands on me.

"What the hell is going on, Evie?" he yells. His voice echoes off the cavernous walls.

"I was hoping you would've seen reason. That I wouldn't have had to resort to this."

He glares up at me, his hands clenching into fists. "Are you fucking crazy?"

"No, Ruairi. I know exactly what I'm doing."

He exhales harshly, pacing beneath me like a caged animal. "Do You think locking me up is going to get you what you want?"

"The ball's in your court now," I say and fold my arms as I stare down at him. "Agree to let me run the Syndicate with you, and this ends right now."

His laugh is harsh and humorless. "You're crazy." His voice hardens. "And after this, you'll never run the Syndicate with me."

I let out a quiet hum, tapping my finger against my arm. "We'll see about that."

Seamus steps up beside me, arms crossed, as he watches the pit below. "I don't know what's more fucked up. The fact that you pulled this off or the fact that you think it's going to work."

I don't take my eyes off Ruairi, who's pacing below. "I wouldn't be here if I wasn't sure."

He studies me for a long moment. "You've got ice in your

veins. I'll give you that," he mutters, rubbing a hand over his jaw. "But if this backfires? If he doesn't cave?" He pauses, his voice dropping lower. "What's your next move then, *princess*?"

I don't let the nickname or the skepticism in his tone shake me. "He will cave," I repeat, my voice steady. "Because the alternative is worse."

I turn on my heel and address the guards. "Cut the lights."

A second later, the room is swallowed in pitch black.

Ruairi's curses follow me as I make my way through the castle with Seamus following close behind.

Neither of us speaks as he starts the drive back to the hotel. I keep my gaze fixed on the window, watching as the dark countryside blurs past, nothing but twisted trees and moonlit fields bathed in shadows, all the while telling myself I did the right thing. That I had no choice. But the doubt lingers, quiet and insidious.

It hits me in the silence between breaths. This isn't a step forward—it's a fall. And the pit I've thrown him into may be the one I can't crawl out of.

Cian

I STRIDE THROUGH THE HALLS OF RUAIRI'S BELFAST office, a smug grin tugging at my lips. I've got something worth boasting about, and I want to see how he reacts.

Spending time with Aoife in Dublin had been productive. Perhaps not in the way Ruairi was hoping, but he doesn't need to know that. I'm here to plant the seed, to make him think I'm getting closer to her in a romantic sense. If he believes I'm just another suitor, he won't see what's really coming.

But when I push open the door to his office, he's not there. Ronan, his second-in-command, sits behind his desk.

"Where's the boss?" I ask, keeping my tone casual.

Ronan sets down a stack of papers, leveling me with a look. "He's off on business."

"Business?" I echo, brow lifting. *That's news to me.* "He didn't mention anything to me."

"I'll give him a call," I reply, already reaching into my jacket for my phone.

"He said he didn't want to be disturbed," Ronan cuts in, his voice sharper this time—final.

My hand stills. That's interesting. Ruairi doesn't just go off the radar like this.

"I have information on Aoife," I say, letting the words hang. "And he's going to want to hear it."

Ronan smirks like he sees right through me. "If there's anything worth knowing, I'm sure Ruairi will find out for himself. He went to Dublin to meet with his sister."

That stops me for a beat. Ruairi and Aoife are together? That's not what I expected to hear.

I force an easy grin. "That right?"

Ronan just shrugs. "That's what I said, isn't it?"

I hold his gaze a moment longer, but he doesn't give me anything else. Pushing off the doorframe, I offer a lazy nod. "Guess I'll have to catch him later then."

What the fuck is going on? I need answers, now. I fire off a text.

Cian: Did your brother make it safely to Dublin?

Aoife: How do you know he was here?

Cian: It's my job to know, lass.

Aoife: We had dinner earlier.

Cian: What did you two talk about?

Aoife: Family stuff. I'm making it look like I want to repair our relationship so he won't see you coming for him.

Cian: You're fucking brilliant. We're going to make one hell of a power couple.

Aoife: We'll have everyone on their knees begging at our feet.

I stare at Aoife's message, my grip tightening around my phone.

We'll have everyone on their knees begging at our feet.

My pulse kicks up as a slow heat coils in my chest, dark and consuming.

Power is a seductive thing, but power with her? That's something else entirely. A kingdom built on blood and loyalty, on whispered secrets and bodies left in our wake. And Aoife, sharp, clever, deadly, will be right beside me.

Desire coils low in my gut, thick and insistent. The thought of her, dangerous, untouchable to everyone but me, sinks deep into my veins like a drug. My cock hardens at the idea of her by my side, dripping in power and mine to ruin.

Ruairi has no idea. He thinks he can control her. But I see her. I see ambition coiled around her spine like a serpent ready to strike.

She's the storm that unmoors kingdoms, the ruin men carve altars for. And I'll kneel first, knowing I'm the one who lit the match.

Ruairi

THE LIGHT OVERHEAD FLICKERS ONCE BEFORE plunging me back into darkness. I exhale sharply, pressing my hands against my thighs, trying to anchor myself with something solid, something real, as the void stretches around me.

I don't know how long I've been down here days, maybe. Weeks. It's been long enough that my body no longer flinches at the sudden shifts between light and dark. Long enough that the cycles have begun to blend together, stretching time into something shapeless. Long enough, that exhaustion seeps into my bones, dragging at the edges of my mind.

They're trying to break me.

I know that.

What's worse is Aoife orchestrated this.

I've spent every moment in this pit trying to reconcile what she's done. Trying to piece together how my own twin, the person who was supposed to stand by my side no matter what could betray me like this.

She set the trap.

She gave the order.

And then she abandoned me here.

Not once has she come to face me.

Not to explain. Not to justify.

The guards come and go, shoving scraps at me just enough to keep me breathing, too little to keep me strong. But Aoife remains absent. And somehow, her silence cuts deeper than any blade.

A door groans open above, the iron hinges creaking against the silence. My head snaps up, muscles coiling as I hear the steady click of heels against the stone.

Finally.

A shadow moves above the grate, and then my sister steps into view.

She looks down at me with the same cold expression she wore the night she drugged me and put me in this God-forsaken pit.

I stumble to my feet, muscles stiff from disuse. Anger lashes through me like a second wind. "You finally decided to show your face." My voice is hoarse, rough from too many days of silence. "Tired of hiding behind O'Sullivan's men?"

She doesn't rise to the bait. Instead, she remains quiet, studying me like she's assessing the damage.

"Are you ready to talk?" she asks, her voice infuriatingly calm.

"That depends. Are you ready to tell me what the fuck you think you're doing?"

She doesn't answer. Instead, she steps forward, lifting her hand. I hear it before I see it. The sound of something shifting, the scrape of metal against stone.

And then a rope begins to lower.

My body goes rigid as I track its slow descent. It sways slightly in the dim light, thick and sturdy, just within reach but not quite low enough to grasp without jumping.

I look back up at Aoife, my blood running cold as I realize what this is.

She's giving me an opportunity. A false one. An illusion of salvation. The idea that I could escape if only I reached far enough or climbed high enough.

This isn't an offer. It's a test.

I meet her gaze, and for the first time since this started, I see something darker in her expression.

Not regret. Not guilt.

Conviction.

A quiet, unshakable certainty, like she's already decided how this ends. Like she believes she'll win.

And that terrifies me more than anything else.

I grit my teeth, forcing my voice to remain steady. "What is this, Aoife?"

She crosses her arms, her nails tapping against her sleeve. "A choice."

My breath comes slow, controlled. "A choice," I repeat.

"You can climb if you want. Try your best to escape." She pauses. "Or you can agree to what I'm offering you."

I glance at the rope again, at the way it sways just out of reach.

And I understand. This isn't about me climbing out. This is about seeing how far I'll go before she cuts the rope. My own flesh and blood is dangling hope in front of me to see how desperate I really am.

I step closer, staring up at her.

"You think this is going to change my mind?" I hurl the words upward, my voice cracking under the strain. "You think this will make me bend?"

Aoife's expression doesn't waver. "I think you have a decision to make."

I let out a slow breath, my jaw ticking as I roll my shoulders back.

I don't reach for the rope. I don't move at all.

Instead, I hold her gaze and say, "You should've just killed me, Evie. Because after this, there's no coming back."

She turns to leave, but I step forward, my voice cutting through the space between us.

"You better hope I die in here," I snarl. "Because if I get out, *when* I get out, I'm coming for you."

She pauses just long enough for hope to claw its way up my

throat. I almost believe she'll turn back. But she doesn't. Her heels strike the stone, each step hammering the coffin closed.

She pauses for just a second. Long enough for me to wonder if my words hit their mark. Then, without a word, she keeps walking. Each click of her heels grows fainter with each step she takes until there's nothing.

The lights cut out, ripping her from me, drowning everything in darkness.

I stand in the black, reaching for a rope I can no longer see. For a salvation that was never mine.

And I wait.

For the darkness to take me whole.

Aoife

I TAKE A SLOW SIP OF MY TEA, THE WARMTH DOING little to settle the unease curling in my stomach. Outside, the late afternoon light spills through the curtains, too golden, too bright, like it's trying to peel back the layers and expose something I don't want to face. Maybe it is. I called off work and spent the day in the penthouse. I needed space to think. To figure out my next move.

It's been weeks since I locked Ruairi in the pit, but it feels like a lifetime. Every hour gnaws at me, pressing heavier against my chest, making it harder to breathe, harder to think. I haven't laid a hand on him. I haven't needed to.

The darkness does the work. The silence. The slow, merciless bleed of time.

I know what it does to a mind. I know what it strips away. And I know what it's doing to him. I don't want to break him.

I only need him to bend. To see that I'm right, that I deserve my place at his side. That we're stronger together than apart.

If he would only surrender, I could end this. We could stitch back what's been torn open. But deep down, I know the truth—some wounds never heal.

And some fractures run too deep to mend.

My phone rings, cutting through the silence and making my stomach twist.

Glancing at the screen, I see that it's my sister-in-law. A cold rush of dread spikes through me as I answer.

"Hey," I say, forcing my voice light.

"Hey," Bridget echoes. Her voice sounds even, but there's a brittleness underneath.

"Everything okay?" I ask, pretending not to notice.

"Have you talked to Ruairi lately?" she asks.

I shift the mug in my hand, gripping it tighter. "Not since we had lunch a few weeks ago. Why?"

"He said he'd be home the next morning," she explains, the words tumbling out now. "But he never came back. I thought maybe he was still with you."

I keep my voice steady. "No, I haven't seen him since we had dinner."

She hesitates. "Did anything happen between you two?"

"Nothing out of the ordinary," I say, making my voice casual. "He wouldn't hear me out. We argued, and I left him at the pub."

"For the record, I don't think Ri is right keeping you in the dark. You have just as much right to this Syndicate as he does."

There's a pause, then she asks, "So, I guess this means you're not coming home?"

My chest tightens. "I was willing to compromise," I say carefully. "I told Ruairi I'd come home for a visit as long as Eamon could come with me, but he refused."

Bridget sighs. "Try to see this from his point of view. Eamon's his enemy. You're asking him to welcome the man he's at war with into his home."

"Eamon wasn't his enemy until Ruairi made him one," I say, defensiveness creeping into my tone.

"I don't want to fight with you. That's not why I called." She goes quiet. "I'm really starting to worry about Ruari. I've been calling and texting him," Bridget explains. "At first, I thought he just needed space, but it's been too long."

I exhale slowly like I'm thinking. "Why didn't you reach out sooner?"

"I didn't want to make things worse if you and he needed time," she trails off, uncertain. "You know how your brother can be."

"Cian mentioned that there was some trouble brewing with one of their Derry contacts," I say, thinking aloud. "They wanted Ruairi involved directly. Maybe he decided to handle it while he was here. It would make sense."

"You really think so?" she asks a thread of desperate hope in her voice.

"It's possible," I say. "You know how he is when he gets something in his head. He shuts everyone out until it's done."

"Yeah," she says, but she doesn't sound convinced.

"Maybe check with Ronan," I suggest, shifting the weight off myself. "If anyone knows where Ruairi is, it'll be him."

"Okay," she says, latching onto the suggestion. "I'll give him a call."

"Let me know what you hear," I offer like I'm not choking on the lie.

We hang up, and I set my phone down on the counter, staring at it like it might come to life and expose me for what I really am.

A liar.

A traitor.

A Quigley.

I press my palms to the counter, forcing a breath into lungs that don't want to obey.

I chose this path. There's no turning back now.

Even if it damns me.

Even if it tears everything I love to pieces.

Eamon

THE TIRES GRIND SOFTLY AGAINST THE ASPHALT, THE low thrum of the engine filling the quiet as I lean back in my seat, phone pressed to my ear.

"Give me an update," I say, my voice clipped.

On the other end of the line, Seamus exhales. "Everything's running smooth. No major disruptions."

I nod to myself, glancing at the road ahead. "And Aoife?"

A beat of hesitation. "She's been occupied."

"Occupied how?"

Before Seamus can answer, a sound filters through the call. Faint but distinct. A deep, metallic clang. Then another. The unmistakable sound of a grate opening and closing.

My entire body goes rigid. I know that sound.

Gripping the steering wheel tighter, I sit up straighter. "Where are you?"

He stays quiet for half a second too long.

"Seamus," I snap, my patience wearing thin.

"I'm at the castle," he finally admits.

"Why?"

Another pause. Then, with a casualness that I don't fucking buy, he says, "Aoife's holding her brother here."

The words hit me like ice water. "What the fuck did you just say?"

Seamus fills me in on how Aoife set Ruairi up and how she's keeping him in the pit. How she's trying to make him break. He's careful with his words, hoping to turn me against her, to plant doubt in my mind.

But it doesn't work.

I hang up mid-sentence and immediately dial Aoife.

No answer. I don't leave a message. Instead, I make a sharp turn, cutting through the traffic, and head straight for my castle.

The moment I step inside, the air shifts. It's heavy, charged. There's a dark energy to the place. Then I hear it. The slow, deliberate grind of metal against stone.

I follow the sound, moving silently through the dim corridors, until I step onto a shadowed balcony that overlooks the vast chamber below. From here, I have a perfect view.

Aoife stands at the edge, poised like a blade, sharp enough to draw blood with a single look. She doesn't flinch. Doesn't hesitate.

Every movement is measured, deliberate. A symphony of control so precise it makes my chest tighten. Power clings to her, thick and electric, humming in the air like the static before a lightning strike.

I should be furious with her. And I am. She went behind my back and made this move without me. She's playing a dangerous fucking game, and she didn't trust me enough to tell me. Despite that, I'm rooted in place, watching her with a hunger I can't seem to bury.

There's something almost holy in the way she commands the space—destructive and beautiful all at once.

She's ruthless. Untouchable.

With a slow, almost casual movement, she reaches for a lever embedded in the stone wall. A deep, mechanical groan echoes through the chamber. The sound of old gears grinding to life. Metal scraping against metal.

I shift my gaze downward, watching as the walls of the pit begin to move. Not fast. Not sudden. But deliberate.

Ruairi notices it, too. He steps back, his stance tensing as he glances around, realizing what's happening. The walls are closing in, forcing him toward the center. Toward the rope that still sways, taunting him from above.

The stone mechanisms controlling the pit are ancient, buried deep beneath the castle's foundation. I've never bothered with them, never had a reason to. The holding rooms below have always served my purposes well enough. But Aoife's unearthed them. She's awakened something long forgotten, bending this place to her will, making it hers.

I watch as she keeps her hand on the lever, adjusting the speed. Not fast enough to be immediate. It's slow enough to sink into his mind. To make him feel his options narrowing with every passing second.

Ruairi lets out a low curse, his fists clenching at his sides. "This is a fucking joke," he snarls. "What do you think you're going to prove by doing this, Evie? That you're more powerful. That you actually *deserve* a place in my Syndicate?"

Aoife doesn't rise to his anger. She simply watches as the walls inch closer.

Ruairi steps toward the rope and then stops himself. He's weighing his choices, trying to decide whether it's better to wait or act.

She's already won. Ruairi just hasn't realized it yet.

I stay in the shadows, watching the way she moves, the way she controls the room, the way she's turned the tables on her brother. When she finally steps away from the pit, I back up, slipping into the shadows as I make my way down from the balcony.

The castle is a maze of stone corridors and forgotten passageways, but I know them well. I move quickly, my footsteps soundless against the worn floor as I follow the winding path that will bring me to her.

By the time I reach her level, she's already walking away. She's calm. Unshaken. As if she didn't just tighten the walls around her own brother like a vice.

Stepping out from a darkened hallway, I cut off her path.

Aoife stops short, her breath hitching for just a fraction of a second before she schools her expression. Her gaze lifts to meet mine. "You're back."

"And you have some fucking explaining to do."

Aoife

My pulse kicks up, but I force my expression to stay neutral. Eamon steps closer, the dim light catching the sharp angles of his face. His jaw is tight. His eyes dark and unreadable. I don't know how long he's been here or how much he's seen, but I know one thing for certain.

I've been caught.

Keeping my voice steady, I say, "I can explain."

He doesn't say anything, just stares at me, his silence heavier than anger. I force myself to keep my breathing even as I continue.

"Ruairi refused to listen. Refused to back down, so I did what needed to be done," I say carefully. "I had to do this to show him that I'm not someone he can ignore."

Eamon exhales sharply, dragging a hand through his hair. "And you couldn't have told me first?" His voice is low and controlled, but there's something simmering underneath it.

Anger. Frustration. And something else. Something darker.

His gaze drags over me, slow and deliberate. Not just assessing—possessive.

Heat coils low in my stomach.

I see it now. It's not just anger. It's a different kind of hunger.

"You used *my* men," he says, his voice like gravel as he steps closer, forcing me back toward the stone wall behind me. "You brought him to *my* castle. And you did it all without saying a fucking word."

"You were out of touch, and it needed to be done." My breath comes faster now, my body hyper-aware of how close he is. "I handled it."

He lets out a dark chuckle. "Oh, I know you handled it. I stood there and watched you close the walls in on him." His fingers lift to my jaw, tilting my chin up, forcing me to meet his gaze. "I should be furious with you, Aoife."

I swallow hard. "You are."

His grip tightens just enough to make me gasp. "Not nearly as much as I should be."

Then his mouth crashes against mine.

I gasp into the kiss, my fingers clutching at his shirt as he presses me harder into the wall, his body flush against mine. His hand slides down, gripping my thigh, hiking it up against his hip.

"Inside," he mutters against my lips, pulling away just long enough to drag me toward one of the rooms.

I barely have time to register which one before the door slams shut behind us. Then he's on me again. His hands shove beneath my dress, fingers digging into my bare thighs, lifting me with ease as he presses me against the heavy wooden door. His mouth is all heat and hunger, devouring me, claiming me.

"You like this, don't you?" he murmurs, his voice dark and dangerous. His teeth graze my throat before he bites down. I arch against him, a whimper slipping from my lips.

"Like what?" I pant, already breathless and craving more.

"Power," he growls, dragging his tongue along the mark he left. "The way it feels when you have complete control."

His words send a shiver down my spine because he's right.

I fucking love it.

I don't get a chance to respond before he turns, carrying me across the room and tossing me onto the massive wooden table in the center. He grips my ankles, yanking me to the edge, spreading me wide beneath him.

"You think you can do whatever the fuck you want without consequences?" he asks, his eyes dark and predatory. Then, his fingers slip beneath the thin lace of my knickers. With one tug, he tears the fabric and tosses it to the side.

"Maybe," I whisper. "What are you going to do about it?"

His answering smile is pure sin. "I'm going to remind you who you belong to."

His hands are on me, rough and unyielding, as he slides his fingers through the sensitive flesh between my thighs, teasing, taunting, keeping me just on the edge without giving me what I need.

"Eamon," I breathe, my hips rolling into his touch, desperate for more.

But he takes his time, tormenting me, dragging this out just long enough to make me ache. Without warning, he thrusts two fingers inside me. I cry out. My back arches off the table as he curls them, hitting the spot he knows will break me.

"You get off on this, don't you?" he murmurs, his lips tracing along my jaw as he finger fucks me, his pace ruthless. "Manipulating your brother, running circles around men who think they're stronger than you."

I bite my lip, clenching around him, my breathing ragged.

"Look at me," he orders.

I force my eyes open, meeting his gaze.

"Tell me. I want to hear you say it, *mo chroí*," he says, his voice low.

"I love it," I admit.

A wicked smile curves his mouth as he drags the head of his thick cock against my slick folds. Then, he pushes in, slow and brutal, sinking into me inch by inch until he's seated deep.

My head falls back against the table, a broken moan slipping from my lips.

Eamon doesn't move, doesn't thrust. He holds himself there, a deep, merciless stretch that has me writhing beneath him.

"You love being the one pulling the strings," he murmurs, his breath hot against my skin. "Making kings and monsters kneel without ever lifting a blade."

A soft, desperate sound escapes me as he finally moves, a slow, punishing grind that has me clenching around him, chasing friction, chasing more.

But Eamon is relentless. He drags it out, fucking me slow and deep, drawing out every whimper, every plea I try to swallow.

"You want to be worshipped for it, don't you?" he taunts, his hand sliding up my body to wrap around my throat, a dark promise against my pulse.

"You deserve to be worshipped, *mo chroí*."

He pulls back almost all the way, the loss so sharp I nearly sob, then slams into me hard enough to rattle the table beneath us.

My cry is swallowed by his mouth crashing against mine, a brutal claiming kiss that leaves no doubt. I'm his. And he's going to break me apart piece by piece, not because he wants to ruin me.

Because he knows I'm meant to be ruined by him.

"Fuck, Aoife," he groans, dropping his forehead against mine. "You drive me fucking insane."

I scrape my nails down his spine, biting his shoulder as he pounds into me, the room filled with the sound of skin against skin. The raw, desperate rhythm of us.

My orgasm builds fast, spiraling tight, my body already too far gone from his teasing earlier. I feel the tension in Eamon's body, the way he's forcing himself to stay in control.

But I don't want him to keep control. I want him to see him fall apart. I want him to break with me.

"Don't hold back," I whisper, my lips brushing against his ear. "Give me everything, Eamon."

His body tenses, and then he snaps. His grip tightens on my hips, his pace turning erratic, wild, ruthless. I cry out as pleasure crashes through me, my walls clenching around him, pulling him deeper as I shatter beneath him.

He groans my name as he chases his own release, spilling inside me and filling me completely.

For a moment, the only sound in the room is our ragged breathing. Then, slowly, he leans back, his fingers tracing along my jaw.

"No more secrets," he murmurs, his voice rough. "No more going behind my back."

I force my expression to stay soft. "I promise."

Even though I know there's more I'm not telling him.

Cian.

The name tastes like ash on my tongue. It festers in the back of my mind, a rot I can't cut out.

I press my lips harder against Eamon's, burying the lie between us like a blade hidden beneath silk.

Because some truths are too dangerous to speak aloud.

Some betrayals must be buried deep enough to rot before they're unearthed.

And this one—this one swings lower with every beat of my heart until all that's left between us is ruin.

Aoife

The phone rings and I brace myself.

Bridget's voice comes through, unsteady, raw. "Aoife, please tell me you've found something."

I close my eyes for a second, gripping the edge of the counter. "We're doing everything we can."

She exhales shakily. "No one knows anything. No one's seen him. He can't have disappeared. Ronan's losing his mind, and I—"

"Eamon has his men looking for him, too." The lie slips from my lips effortlessly, even as guilt gnaws at my insides. "We'll find him, Bridget."

"Eamon?" she snaps, skepticism thick in her voice. "They're at war, Aoife. Why would he lift a damn finger to help?"

My pulse kicks up. "Because I asked him to," I say smoothly. "He knows how much this matters to me."

Bridget makes a sound of frustration. "And you believe him?"

"I know you don't trust him, but I do. And I swear to you, he's doing everything he can."

"I don't know what to think anymore." A long pause lingers between us, thick and suffocating. Then, her voice drops, quieter, almost broken. "It's been weeks with no news. I need him back," she whispers. "I need to know I'm not going to be alone in this."

"You're not alone," I promise.

"You don't understand, Aoife. I'm pregnant."

The words hit me like a punch to the gut. My mouth opens, but nothing comes out.

"I haven't told him yet," she continues in a whisper. "I was waiting for the right time. And then he disappeared. What if he never comes back? What if—"

"Stop," I cut in. "I swear to you, he's coming back. Eamon and I are doing everything in our power to find him."

Silence stretches between us. Then, finally, she whispers, "Okay."

"I'll call you as soon as I hear anything," I promise.

"Please," she murmurs, her voice still shaking. "Please find him."

"I will," I whisper, the guilt of my deception crushing me.

As soon as we hang up, I drop the phone onto the counter and press the heels of my hands against my eyes.

I hate this. I hate lying to Bridget. I hate knowing I'm the reason she's crying. I hate knowing that right now, Ruairi's sitting in a cold, dark pit, being worn down by my choices.

But I can't stop it. Not yet.

A quiet movement behind me makes me stiffen. I turn to see Eamon standing in the doorway. "What happened?" he asks, his voice low.

"Bridget called." I swallow, willing the emotions away. "She's pregnant."

His brows lift slightly. "Fuck."

I nod, pressing my lips together. "She begged me to find him."

Eamon watches me for a long moment before stepping closer. "What do you want to do?"

"What do you mean?"

"If you want to let him go, I'll order my men to release him right now," he says simply. "It's your call."

A part of me wants to say yes. To end this. To stop lying, stop twisting myself deeper into an unwinnable game.

For a moment, the words teeter on the edge of my tongue, trembling there like a secret I don't dare speak aloud.

But then I see Ruairi, in my mind's eye, staring at me with that same stubborn, unyielding glare he's worn since we were children.

Not the boy who once stood between me and the monsters.

The man who would walk blindly into their jaws now if I let him.

But I can't. Not yet.

Mercy is a luxury I can't afford. Not when the walls are already closing in, not when every decision I've made has been another stone in the tomb I'm building around us all.

The game isn't over yet.

And until it is, I have to be the one holding the blade.

"No." I meet Eamon's gaze. "I'm not letting him out until he gives in."

"Then he stays where he is. You have my full support. And that of my men."

"Thank you." I press onto my toes, brushing my lips against his in silent gratitude. He deepens the kiss, his fingers skimming along my waist, grounding me, but I pull back before I let myself fall too far into him. "I need to get to work," I murmur. "My boss doesn't take kindly to employees who are late for their shifts."

Eamon smirks, his hands still resting on my hips. "Sounds like a real hard-ass."

"The worst," I tease.

Amusement flickers in his eyes. "Maybe you should quit. Find a boss who treats you better."

I hum, pretending to consider it. "Tempting. But I think I'll keep this one. He has his perks."

"Oh yeah? Like what?"

I lean in, letting my breath graze his lips before I pull back at the last second. "Wouldn't you like to know?"

Before he can catch me, I slip from his grasp and disappear through the door, leaving him wanting.

Downstairs, I duck into the back office before starting my shift and pull out my phone. I need answers, and there's only one person I can get them from.

I dial Cian.

He answers after two rings. "Aoife. I wasn't expecting to hear from you so soon."

"I wanted to check in," I say smoothly. "Have you gotten any updates on my brother?"

"There's been no sign of him. No one's seen or heard a thing."

"And you checked with your contacts in Dublin?" I ask, probing deeper.

"I did. They weren't even aware he was in the city," he confirms.

I keep my voice carefully controlled. "I see."

"I suspect your boss had something to do with it," he says, letting the accusation hang between us.

"Eamon? You really think he'd do something to Ruairi?" I ask, letting just the right amount of shock seep into my tone.

"Come on, lass," Cian says, amusement laced in his voice. "You know what kind of man O'Sullivan is. He's ruthless. Strategic. You think it's a coincidence that your brother walked into his city and suddenly vanished?"

I let the silence stretch, like I'm considering his words. "I don't know," I murmur. "I can't believe Mr. O'Sullivan would hurt him. Not with me here."

"That's exactly why he would," Cian says. "To prove a point. To show both you and Ruairi who really has control."

"I mean, I have heard things." I keep my voice low as if I'm wary of saying too much. "The staff whispers about him when they think no one's listening. They say he's been disappearing a lot lately. Taking secret meetings. Avoiding questions."

Cian hums in approval, like he's satisfied I'm starting to see things his way. "See? It all adds up."

"What do you think we should do?"

"I already have a plan in motion," he says smoothly.

"What plan?" I ask, alarmed.

"It's not something I want to discuss over the phone," he says. "I'm coming to Dublin tomorrow. We'll talk then."

I hesitate, then let out another breath. "Okay. Tomorrow."

"That's my good lass," he murmurs.

The line clicks dead before I can respond.

My stomach twists, a knot pulling tighter with every breath.

Cian believes I'm his.

Ruairi's exactly where I need him—shackled in the dark, blinded by trust he should have never given me.

The walls tighten with every breath, the air thick with the stench of inevitability.

I can feel it pressing closer — the slow, grinding crush of my own making.

This was never a game.

It was always a death march.

And I chose it.

One wrong step and the ground will open beneath me, dragging everything I love into the grave I've been digging with my own two hands.

But I won't flinch.

I won't falter.

There's already blood soaked into the stone.

Before this ends, there will be more.

The only question is whose.

Cian

THE SLEEK BLACK CAR ROLLS TO A STOP IN FRONT OF the hotel, and Aoife slides into the passenger seat. Her short skirt rides up higher as she crosses her legs and pulls the door shut, the movement casual yet calculated.

"Where are we going?" she asks, her voice holding a guarded edge.

"Somewhere private," I reply.

The city fades in the rearview mirror, and the roads get rougher the farther we go. I take us toward a warehouse by the docks, a place I've recently acquired, the kind where no one looks too long or asks the wrong questions.

As the city fades behind us, Aoife shifts in her seat. "I have something to tell you."

I glance at her, arching a brow. "What is it, lass?"

"Ruairi's gone because of me. I'm the reason he disappeared." Another beat of silence, heavier now. "I'm holding him," she finishes, her voice steady but tight.

My grip flexes and then relaxes as I take a slow breath. Then, I let out a short laugh, one without an ounce of humor.

"You're fucking what?" I turn my head slightly, catching the way she watches me, calm and composed, like she didn't just drop a fucking bomb in my lap.

"I have him," she says smoothly.

I shake my head as I focus back on the road. "And when, exactly, were you planning to share that little detail with me, lass?"

"I was hoping I could convince Ruairi to see reason first," she says, her voice tight. "It would've made it easier to carry out the plan if he was on our side. But I haven't had any luck." She lets out a frustrated breath. "I wanted to tell you in person. This isn't the kind of thing you say over the phone."

"Right. Convenient." I let the word hang in the air, watching for a crack in her expression.

"It's the truth," she says without hesitation.

I scoff, shaking my head again. "And here I was, wasting my time thinking O'Sullivan had something to do with his disappearance."

Aoife lifts her chin, a flash of defiance in her voice. "Seems like I solved the mystery then."

My fingers drum against the wheel. Being caught off guard isn't something I tolerate easily. Still, I can't help but be impressed.

"What's your endgame?" I ask.

She leans back against the seat, her fingers toying with the hem of her skirt. "Payback."

Side-eyeing her, I respond, "Oh yeah? That simple?"

"Ruairi's underestimated me my entire life. Kept me out of the Syndicate. Treated me like an afterthought. I wanted to show him that I'm not someone he can control," she explains. "I had the opportunity, so I took it."

A slow grin spreads across my face. "You're fucking dangerous, Aoife."

"And you love it."

"I do," I say, letting my hand drift over the gear shift, grazing my knuckles up her thigh.

She doesn't flinch or pull away. She lifts a brow, challenging.

"I don't know whether to be fucking impressed or pissed off," I admit.

"Why not both?"

I watch her for a second longer. "You're something else, Aoife Quigley."

A beat of silence stretches between us before I speak, keeping my tone casual. "Where is he?"

She hesitates. It's quick. Barely noticeable. She's not ready to give me that information.

"Aoife, you and I both know the only way this ends is with Ruairi gone. You already have him. All we need is to finish it."

She exhales slowly, looking out the window for a moment before speaking.

"There's something else I haven't told you," she confesses.

I arch a brow, waiting.

She sighs, feigning uncertainty, like she's weighing whether or not she should say it. "Since the night at the restaurant, Mr. O'Sullivan's been pursuing me."

The question leaves my mouth like a low threat. "Has he now?"

She nods. "I've gone out with him a few times. Trying to get close. To learn whatever I can from him."

"You're a mastermind, lass," I say, a grudging edge of admiration in my voice.

"I wanted to play with him a little first," she adds, a sly smile curling on her lips, her eyes gleaming with mischief. "See how much he would let slip if he thought he was winning me over. Find out just how far he'd be willing to go to take out Ruairi."

"You're fucking ruthless, you know that?" I murmur, unable to hide the low, dark laugh that rumbles from my chest.

"You wouldn't want me any other way."

She's right. I slow the car as we approach the docks, parking in the shadow of the warehouse. "I just had a thought," I say, slow and calculated. "With you inside O'Sullivan's Syndicate, we don't have to stop with Ruairi."

"What are you saying?" she asks.

"Think about it," I smirk. "When Ruairi's out of the picture, we take his Syndicate. But why stop there? We could take both of them."

She meets my gaze. "You want to take out Mr. O'Sullivan, too?"

"You and I together, Aoife." I reach out, trailing a finger along her jaw, watching her reaction. "We could rule it all."

She doesn't pull away. But she doesn't agree either.

Leaning back, I rest my arm against the window. "I've already put things in motion. With you having access to O'Sullivan, it makes my plans that much easier. Soon, we won't have to worry about either of them."

"And what exactly have you put into motion?"

"Now, now. You know better than to ask me that." My fingers tap lazily against the steering wheel. "Let's just say some wheels are already turning. And with you right where I need you, those wheels are about to crush everything in their path."

I shift my body, turning slightly toward her. "You trust me, don't you?"

Aoife tilts her head, her lips curving into something between amusement and intrigue. "Sounds messy."

"A necessary mess," I counter smoothly. "You're not afraid of getting your hands dirty, are you?"

She drags a nail along the hem of her skirt. "You know I'm not."

"Fuck, Aoife," I say, my voice deepening. "You have no idea what you do to me."

Before she can respond, I lean in, claiming her mouth. My fingers slide up her thigh, gripping hard enough to remind her exactly who she's dealing with.

She lets it go on just long enough to tease before she pulls back slightly, her breath uneven but controlled. "Where are we?"

"Why don't I show you?" Stepping out of the car, I move

around to her side, opening her door. "Welcome to the beginning of our empire."

Aoife takes in the warehouse, her gaze sweeping across the vast space like she's already envisioning what it could be. "It's a bit rough around the edges," she says as she takes a few more steps inside.

"So was your father's empire when he took over. This place needs the right hands to shape it into something unstoppable."

She turns, looking at me with a slow, knowing smile. "Good thing you have me, then."

Fucking hell. I drag a hand over my jaw. "You really do know how to keep a man on his toes."

She smirks a glint of mischief in her eyes. "What's the fun in being predictable?"

I lean closer, letting my voice drop. "Predictable's never been what I want from you."

"I can see it now," she says as she walks further into the space. "The two of us, running everything. No Ruairi. No O'Sullivan. Just power."

"You sound like you're already convinced."

She exhales a quiet laugh, trailing a hand along the rusted edge of a shipping container. "I didn't go through the trouble of taking Ruairi to stop now."

Her confidence is fucking intoxicating.

"That's what I like to hear," I say, stepping in and closing the space between us.

"But if I'm in, I'm all in." She meets my gaze, unwavering. "That means no secrets, no half-truths. If we're doing this together, I have a voice in every step. After all, I'm the one who has access to both Ruairi and Mr. O'Sullivan."

Fuck me.

A slow, dark grin curves my lips as my fingers trail along her jaw, tracing the line to the hollow of her throat. "You have no idea how much that turns me on."

Aoife

Cian walks ahead of me, gesturing around the warehouse like he already owns the city. Like this place is just the first piece of his inevitable empire.

"We need to move soon," he says, turning back to me. "I don't want to waste any more time. O'Sullivan has had his grip on Dublin for too long."

He's power-hungry, so I don't have to push. All I have to do is stand to the side and wait. Sure enough, he dives right in.

"Here's what I'm thinking," he starts. "We hit him when he's vulnerable. Catch him in transit. Somewhere outside his comfort zone. Maybe when he's heading to one of his properties. We block the road, force him out, take him before his men even know what's happening. Simple, clean, effective."

Simple. Clean. Effective. It takes everything in me not to let my amusement show.

Cian thinks he knows what he's doing, but I can already see the flaws. He has no understanding of Eamon's security and no grasp of the way his operation runs. He's thinking like a thug, not a strategist.

But I don't let it show.

Instead, I sigh, crossing my arms like I'm weighing the plan. "It won't work," I finally say, shaking my head.

Cian's brows knit together. "What do you mean? Of course, it'll work."

I exhale, letting my voice take on a mix of confidence and experience. "I've been working at the hotel for months. I've watched how Mr. O'Sullivan moves. How his security operates. He's never alone. If you try to box him in, it won't be his blood on the pavement. It'll be yours."

Cian's frown deepens, but I see the shift in his eyes. He knows I'm right.

Stepping closer, I lower my voice. "But there's another way."

That gets his attention.

"Go on," he says, intrigued.

I let a slow smirk curve my lips. "He's interested in me, and I've played into it. If I tell him I'm delivering Ruairi to him, he'll come running. No security. No backup. Just him. And when I get him alone..." I trail off, letting Cian fill in the blanks.

His grin spreads wide. "You're fucking brilliant."

I give a slight shrug like it's nothing. "I know."

Cian's practically vibrating with excitement now. He presses for details. He wants to know exactly how I plan to pull this off.

But I can't give him that. Not yet. Because that would mean revealing Ruairi's location.

So, I lean against one of the rusted beams, exhaling like I'm thinking it all through. "I need a little more time."

"Time?"

"I need time to gain Eamon's trust so I can convince him to come alone. If he has even a shadow of a doubt, he'll bring his men. If that happens, we won't stand a chance."

Cian exhales sharply, running a hand through his hair. He wants to push. I can see it, but I've dangled the perfect scenario in front of him.

In the end, he can't resist.

"Fine," he says after a moment. "But don't take too long. The sooner we do this, the better."

I give him a slow, knowing smile. "Trust me. No one will see it coming."

He grins, stepping in closer, his hands settling at my waist. "You really do have a devious fucking mind, Aoife."

I let him kiss me, let him think he's the one in control.

But the truth is, Cian's already eating out of the palm of my hand.

And he has no idea.

Eamon

Aoife stands at the edge of the pit, her posture deceptively composed. She's always been good at hiding her emotions, too good, but today, something's different. There's a crack in her armor, subtle but undeniable. A slight tightening around her mouth. A flicker of uncertainty in her eyes before she steels herself again.

For the first time since this started, she looks unsure.

Even as she speaks, poised to deliver a far crueler blow than any that came before, there's a hesitation. A weight bearing down on her, dragging at the edges of her bravado. She tries to bury it, to tuck it behind the sharpness of her words,

But I see it. I feel it. However, this isn't the time to question it.

So I keep my distance, watching in silence, letting her command the moment, letting her be the one to decide how far she's willing to go.

She gives a signal, and the guards move into position, activating the hidden mechanisms deep beneath the castle. The sound of ancient stone shifting echoes through the chamber, followed by the unmistakable sound of flowing water. I watch as it begins to trickle in from unseen openings along the walls.

Ruairi doesn't react at first. He's been locked down there for weeks—he's endured darkness, silence, and isolation. But now, he straightens, his body stiffening as he notices the slow, steady rise of the water pooling at his feet.

He glances up, his eyes locking onto Aoife's. "What the fuck is this?"

"You wanted to be untouchable," she says, her voice almost bored. "Let's see how well you do when the water starts rising."

Ruairi snarls, lunging at the rope that still hangs above him. But the effort is wasted as my guard pulls it out of his reach.

"You're going too far, Evie. It's time to end this charade," he yells.

Aoife stands at the edge of the pit, still as a statue, her posture carved from iron. To Ruairi, she must look unbreakable—cold, ruthless, every inch her father's daughter.

But from up here, I see the truth.

There's a tremor she tries to mask. A slight tension in her shoulders, the way her fingers curl too tightly at her sides. Beneath the sharp tilt of her chin and the merciless gleam in her eyes, something deeper stirs.

Guilt. Doubt. Grief.

Ruairi doesn't see it. He only sees the executioner standing above him, ready to deliver the final blow.

But I see the girl bleeding beneath the steel.

The girl fighting not just him—but herself.

Still, I stay silent, letting her have this moment. Letting her bury the pieces of herself she's not ready for anyone else to carry.

The water continues to rise, a black tide devouring the floor, inch by merciless inch. Ruairi shifts his weight, fighting to keep his footing as the pit stirs around him, the current dragging at his legs like a thing alive, hungry for flesh. The water laps at his knees now, cold and unrelenting, seeping through his clothes, clinging to his skin like a death shroud.

He grits his teeth against the chill sinking into his marrow. I hear the falter in his breathing, the crack in his composure he can no longer hide.

He's not panicking yet.

But the pit is patient. It waits with ancient hunger, tightening its grip with every heartbeat, every shallow gasp that tears from his lungs.

I see it in the frantic darting of his gaze, the way he scans the slick, unforgiving walls for an escape that doesn't exist. I see it in the way his hands flex and curl as if he could tear through the stone itself if only he fought hard enough.

But the pit will not be cheated. Soon, it will consume him.

Aoife crosses her arms. "Say the words, and I turn it off."

Ruairi glares up at her. "Go to hell."

Aoife exhales slowly, a shudder of breath that barely stirs the air, then gives a curt nod to the guard stationed at the control panel.

The gears whine and groan, and the pit answers as if awakening to its hunger. The current surges, the water climbing faster now, dark and glistening, alive with malicious intent.

Ruairi curses, the word torn from his throat raw and ragged. He slams his fist against the pit wall, the sound a dull, hollow thud swallowed almost instantly by the rushing water. It floods up around him, icy and relentless, soaking him to the waist, weighing down his limbs with cruel hands.

I watch him grapple with himself, forcing breath into his lungs, counting heartbeats, searching for logic in a place that has none. He's trying to believe this is still a game. That Aoife will break, that someone will call it off, that salvation waits just beyond the next moment.

But salvation doesn't live here. Only the slow, creeping weight of inevitability.

And then I see it—the precise instant the doubt seeps in, threading through his mind like poison in the blood. His gaze stutters, and he loses focus. His hand, mid-clench, falters.

In that fragile, unguarded second, the pit seems to expand its walls, stretching wider, the ceiling climbing higher as if space itself mocks him.

The world tilts, unsteady, dreamlike.

He's not just doubting Aoife now.

He's doubting the ground beneath him.

The air he breathes.

His own mind.

And in that splintered second, the pit seems to close tighter around him, as if it, too, can smell his weakening hope.

"Enough," Ruairi growls. "You've made your fucking point."

She tilts her head, considering. "Have I?"

Ruairi grits his teeth, every muscle in his body straining against the fear rising faster than the water. He clings to the illusion of control, to the lie that he can outlast this. That he can outlast her.

Aoife stands unmoving at the edge of the pit, framed by stone and shadow, as cold and unyielding as the walls closing in around him. Her eyes, once vibrant with life, are hollow now—bottomless wells that reflect nothing back.

When she speaks, her voice carries not rage or cruelty, but something far worse.

Certainty.

"My lips are not thin with judgment," she says, the words falling like iron into the void. "They're firm with resolution. You'll break before I do."

The water surges higher, a black tide swallowing his chest, pressing against his ribs, making every breath a labor. His hands grasp at the stone, desperate, instinctive, leaving streaks of blood where his nails tear against the rock.

"Aoife," he gasps, and this time, her name is an invocation, a prayer to something that no longer listens. His voice is tight, cracking under the weight of inevitability.

But there's no answer.

She doesn't move.

She doesn't blink.

She doesn't exist in the same way anymore.

She stands there as if she's already stepped beyond the mortal world and become something else entirely—an executioner carved from grief, forged in betrayal, crowned in silence.

Time fractures. Seconds stretch and fold, each heartbeat a lifetime, each breath a battleground. The walls breathe with him. The water hums with a hunger older than memory.

There's nothing left but this.

The sister who will not yield.

The brother who will not endure.

And the pit, waiting to devour them both.

If I were a better man, I'd stop this. But I'm not. And I don't. Because I need to know how far she's willing to go before she can't look herself in the eye.

Ruairi shifts, panic stealing the last of his strength.

The water keeps climbing until his heels lift off the floor. For a heartbeat, he floats suspended between the surface and the abyss.

Then, the current catches him. It shoves him backward, spinning him helplessly toward the grate, toward the place where the pit swallows the broken and the drowned.

He flails instinctively, reaching for the stone walls, but the slick surface slides away from his fingers. There's no purchase here. No mercy.

"Aoife," he calls out, voice splintering under the weight of terror.

She doesn't move.

Not at first.

She watches him drift, watches him fight the inevitable, her gaze cold and fathomless. She lets the helplessness root deep. Lets the reality of it hollow him out. The truth that he's no longer a man but a body, another piece of wreckage the pit will claim.

Only after that truth sinks in, after it becomes part of him, does she give the smallest nod to the guard.

The machinery stutters. Groans. The water stops its climb.

Then, inch by agonizing inch, it begins to recede, dragging Ruairi back down toward the floor with it, leaving him sprawled and gasping in the mire.

He sucks in a shattered breath, chest heaving, limbs trembling violently from the cold and from the knowledge he couldn't outlast her.

But it's too late. The pit has already marked him.

And Aoife stands over him, silent, watching as the last pieces of who he was slip away with the retreating tide.

I watch her, too, still and silent in the shadows.

And for the first time, I see it clearly—she doesn't belong to us anymore. She belongs to the darkness.

Aoife steps closer to the edge, looking down at the broken figure gasping in the shallow water.

"You have a decision to make," she says, her voice flat, stripped of anything soft. "Next time, I might not be feeling so generous."

Without waiting for a response, she turns and walks away.

Behind her, the lights in the pit flicker once, then vanish, sealing Ruairi back into the cold, wet prison she's made for him.

I'm waiting for her as she exits the chamber, stepping into the dim corridor. Before she can brush past me, I catch her wrist.

She doesn't look at me.

"You're not here," I murmur, voice low enough that only she can hear.

She tenses beneath my hand, her body going rigid, the truth slicing through her sharper than any accusation.

"I'm fine," she says tightly.

I don't believe her.

Not for a second.

"Is this because you know Bridget is pregnant?" I ask, softer now, careful not to snap the last threads holding her together.

She stills, so briefly, most wouldn't notice, but I do.

Then she shakes her head, a sharp, mechanical gesture. "No."

She won't meet my gaze. And that tells me everything. She's

retreating, folding herself up behind those walls she thinks will keep her safe. But I won't let her.

"Come with me," I say, already steering her toward the car before she can build another excuse.

"Where are we going?" she asks, a hint of exhaustion threading through her voice.

"You need a break."

She gives me a skeptical look, guarded and calculating. But she doesn't fight me. She slides into the passenger seat without a word.

Twenty minutes later, we're standing at the marina, the salt-tinged air cool against our skin, the water whispering secrets in the fading light. Aoife's eyes narrow as I lead her toward a private dock, the water lapping gently against the boats moored there.

"What is this?" she asks, her voice wary.

I smile as I step onto the deck of the sleek yacht, the polished surface gleaming under the last golden light of the day. "This, *mo chroí*, is the Eclipsed Serenity."

She hesitates at the edge of the dock. "This is yours?"

I extend a hand, watching as she eyes it suspiciously before finally stepping onto the deck. She moves cautiously, her steps measured, testing the yacht's stability beneath her feet. The faintest frown tugs at her lips as she glances around, taking in the pristine deck, the soft glow of recessed lighting coming to life as the sun sinks lower on the horizon.

She lets out a breath of disbelief, trailing her fingers along the edge of the built-in bar. "How many bodies have been dumped off this thing?"

"You wound me, mo chroí," I say, pressing a hand to my chest in mock offense.

"Do I?" she murmurs, glancing at me from beneath her lashes, the ghost of a challenge lurking behind her words.

There's a challenge in her voice, one that sparks a slow grin across my face.

I don't answer.

Instead, I pour us both a drink, letting the silence stretch between us like a live wire. When I hand her a glass, her fingers brush mine and linger, just for a breath too long. A tremor, so slight she probably thinks I miss it, runs through her hand before she pulls away.

I bring my drink to my lips, watching as she finally lifts hers, masking whatever cracked through her behind the rim of the glass.

"I never would've guessed you owned a yacht," she says. "You don't step away from work long enough to relax."

"And yet, here I am."

She hums, unconvinced. "So, do you take business calls from the deck? Host meetings with your underlings while the waves crash in the background?"

I chuckle. "You'd be surprised how much business gets done on the water."

She shakes her head in a slow, tired motion, then turns away from me toward the horizon. The last threads of sunlight melt into the sea, staining the water in deep, bruised colors—violet, indigo, the bleeding edge of black.

For a long moment, she just stands there, silhouetted against the dying light, letting the slow, rhythmic sway of the yacht cradle her.

The wind brushes strands of hair across her face, but she doesn't move to tame them. She simply breathes as if trying to remember how.

Out here, surrounded by endless water and fading sky, she finally lets herself be small. Not the girl who taught herself to be untouchable. Not the Syndicate's hidden heir. Not the executioner.

Just a woman standing at the edge of the world, trying not to fall apart.

"How many women have you brought on board?" she asks after a long moment, her voice softer now, as if she's afraid of the answer.

"None," I say.

Her lips part slightly, surprise flashing across her face before she masks it, slipping her expression back behind cool, practiced walls. "Not even one?" she asks, quieter this time.

I shake my head. "This is a part of my life I've never wanted to share with anyone before."

The moment stretches between us, thick and heavy with everything neither of us is ready to name. Maybe she feels it too because she doesn't tease, doesn't deflect, doesn't turn it into a joke the way she usually would.

She just sets her glass down, her fingers lingering on the edge for a breath longer than necessary, then moves past me toward the bow.

Toward the open water, where the horizon stretches into forever.

She braces her hands against the railing, standing at the very edge. I follow, stepping up behind her. My hands find her waist, gentle at first, almost asking permission, and when she doesn't pull away, I draw her back against my chest.

Aoife leans into me, a soft, shuddering breath slipping from her lips as the last light of the sun sinks into the sea.

"It's beautiful," she murmurs, her voice barely louder than the wind.

I press my lips to the curve of her shoulder, tasting salt and warmth. "It is," I whisper.

But I'm not looking at the sunset. I'm looking at her.

She turns in my arms, tilting her chin up, and I see it—the moment she lets go. The moment the walls drop, the fear falls away, and only feeling remains.

And then she kisses me.

It's slow at first, desperate and searching, but then it deepens, her fingers tangling in my hair, her body pressing into mine, heat blooming between us.

I lift her, carrying her inside the cabin and lowering her onto the bed.

I don't rush. Tonight's not about control or power or proving a point.

It's about her—about us.

I take my time, dragging my hands over every inch of her, memorizing the way her body reacts to my touch. My fingers skim along the delicate curve of her waist, the dip of her spine, the soft swell of her breasts.

She's tense at first, every muscle tight, fighting the slow unraveling I'm asking of her. Her breath catches—a sharp, fractured inhale she can't quite hide. For a moment, she holds herself rigid, caught between instinct and fear.

Then, slowly, her body begins to yield.

The tension bleeds out of her muscles, her weight shifting, barely, but enough, leaning into me without meaning to, as if instinct is dragging her somewhere her mind hasn't given permission to follow.

I let my fingers slide lower, toying with the hem of her dress. "Let me see you."

"You want it off? Then do something about it," she taunts, eyes dark with challenge. She wants this, but she wants to make me work for it.

Slowly, I drag the straps of her dress over her shoulders, my fingers grazing the sensitive skin there. Slipping my fingers beneath the lace of her bra, I push the cups down, allowing her breasts to spill free.

My hands find her, slow and sure, but not patient. There's no patience left in me when it comes to Aoife only hunger, only the aching need to know her in ways no one else ever will.

I cup her breasts, the weight of them perfect in my palms, my thumbs teasing over her nipples until they harden beneath my touch. A gasp slips from her lips, sharp and helpless, and she arches into me, silently demanding more.

Dragging my mouth lower, I trace the curve of her breast with the edge of my tongue, savoring the way she trembles when I close my lips around her peak. I suck—slow, deliberate, just hard enough to pull another broken sound from her throat.

As I peel the dress from her body, my knuckles graze her ribs, the flat plane of her stomach, the sharp line of her hips. For a moment, all I can do is look at the way she sprawls across the bed, bare, wild, burning, like a flame no one has ever dared to touch until now.

"Beautiful," I murmur against her skin, the word tasting like a prayer I don't deserve to say.

I trail kisses lower, each one slow and claiming, mapping every inch of her like she's mine to learn and memorize and worship. Her stomach quivers under my mouth, her breath fracturing into uneven gasps as I move lower, lower still.

When I reach the curve of her inner thigh, I slip my fingers beneath the lace clinging to her hips, dragging it down, baring her completely to me. I press a kiss just above the place she aches for me, feeling her tense, feeling her fight the instinct to beg.

Not yet.

I want her undone.

I want her wrecked.

I want her ruined in ways no one else will ever be able to put back together.

"Stop teasing me," she breathes, her voice cracked open, threaded with frustration and need.

Her body is strung tight beneath my hands, every muscle trembling on the edge of surrender. I groan against her, dragging her thighs wider, anchoring her to the bed as my mouth claims her without mercy. I lick, tease, devour until she's gasping, rocking against me, her hands tangled in the sheets as she fights not to fall apart too soon.

"Eamon," she cries, my name falling from her lips like a prayer she doesn't even know she's saying.

I lift my head, fingers slipping into her, slow and deep, stroking her in a rhythm designed to undo her completely.

"Say it again," I rasp, my voice rough, the need clawing up my throat.

She does, broken and desperate. When I finally give her what she needs, she shatters beneath me, her body seizing around my fingers, a raw, helpless moan tearing from her throat.But I don't stop. Not yet. I drive her higher, pull every last tremor from her, wringing the pleasure out of her body until she's boneless and trembling, utterly wrecked in my hands.

Only then do I rise over her, catching her mouth in a bruising kiss, pressing her into the sheets like I could brand myself into her skin. She claws at me, nails dragging down my back, desperate to pull me closer, to pull me inside where she already belongs.

"Tell me what you want," I rasp against her lips, my cock throbbing against her thigh.

She meets my gaze, no hesitation, no fear, only need. "You. Every part of you."

With a groan that rips from deep inside me, I push into her slow, brutal, claiming her all over again. And this time, I lose myself completely.

Every thrust is a vow I don't know how to speak aloud. Every broken sound she makes drives me harder, deeper until there is nothing left but this beautiful act of trying to carve ourselves into each other before the world can tear us apart.

She comes first, her body clenching around me, her cries muffled against my shoulder as she falls apart in my arms. The feel of her shattering, of her holding onto me like she'll drown if she lets go, rips through my control.

I drive into her one last time, spilling into her with a groan that sounds more like a prayer than anything human. Her name is the last thing on my lips as the world collapses around us.

I ease out of her slowly, carefully, the loss like a fresh wound I don't know how to close.

But I don't let her go. I gather her against my chest, anchoring her there, feeling every trembling breath she takes against my skin.

Her fingers trace slow, mindless patterns over my heart until her breathing evens out and sleep finally pulls her under.

But I stay awake, staring into the darkness above us.

And when I'm sure she's lost to dreams, I let the words fall from my mouth, barely a whisper against the quiet. "I love you, *mo chroí*."

I don't want this to end.

God help me. I don't know if I'll survive it if it does.

Aoife

THE SUN BARELY PEEKS THROUGH THE THICK CURTAINS, but I've been awake for hours. Sleep has barely touched me all week. I blame Eamon and our night on his boat.

He was up early, leaving before the first light of day to handle some business, slipping out of bed with a quiet efficiency that should've let me sleep. It didn't. Because the moment the door clicked shut behind him, I was left with nothing but my thoughts about him.

Which is a problem because I should be thinking about the pieces on the board. About the way the walls are closing in around me. Instead, my body betrays me, longing for his hands, his mouth, the feel of him deep inside me.

That should terrify me. I don't have time for this.

I push myself upright, running a hand over my face. There's too much happening, too many moving parts. I can't let myself get distracted. Not when Cian is breathing down my neck, and Ruairi refuses to see me as his equal. My growing feelings for Eamon only complicate an already impossible situation.

My phone buzzes on the nightstand.

I stare at the screen for half a second before swiping to answer. "You're calling early," I say, keeping my voice even.

"Plans have changed," Cian says, cutting straight to the point. "I'm moving up the timeline."

A pulse of irritation flares through me, and I sit up straighter. "That's not a good idea."

"I didn't ask if it was a good idea."

I grit my teeth. "It's too soon. I need more time to ensure everything's in place. If we move too quickly, we risk losing control."

"And I risk losing patience," he cuts in. "You've been playing both sides too well. Maybe a little too well."

My pulse kicks up. "Don't insult me."

"Then don't make me question your loyalty."

I go still, my body locking down around the anger tightening in my chest.

"You don't have to question me."

"Are you sure about that?" Cian's voice carries a mocking lilt designed to peel back my defenses.

"Yes," I answer without hesitation.

A beat of silence stretches between us before he exhales sharply. "Good," he says, voice clipped. "Then I expect you to make it happen."

"I'll get back to you by tomorrow," I say, each word measured, leashing the fury tightening in my chest.

A beat of silence. Then, the slow, deliberate drag of his breath through the speaker.

"Don't keep me waiting, Aoife. You won't like what happens if you do."

The call cuts out. I let the phone fall onto the bed, the sound sharp in the silence, and draw in a slow, fractured breath.

I need a plan.

Now.

Cian is impatient. Ruairi is oblivious. And Eamon has tangled himself through my blood, my bones, and my breath in ways I don't have time to untangle now.

I shove the thought aside, push everything aside except the

gnawing truth clawing at the edges of my mind. If I get this wrong, one, or both, of the men I care about will die.

Because of me.

That's why I kept Ruairi in the pit longer than I should have.

Not for cruelty.

Not entirely.

Once I realized Cian meant to kill him, I needed to keep Ruairi contained. There, in the pit, he was helpless.

He was mine to guard.

Mine to punish.

Mine to save—or not.

And somewhere deep beneath the layers of loyalty and love, in the place where anger rots into something unrecognizable, I wonder if a part of me wanted him there. Wanted him afraid. Wanted him to know what it felt like to drown and beg and break.

Because maybe he deserves it. Maybe he deserves worse.

The thought festers, black and hollow inside my chest.

I don't want to look at it.

I don't want to know if it's true.

But it's there, whispering in the spaces between my heartbeats.

Let him drown

Cian

POWER PULSES BENEATH MY SKIN, SHARP AND ELECTRIC, close enough to taste. I tip my whiskey glass to my lips, savoring the slow burn as it carves its way down my throat, anchoring the hunger coiling tighter inside me.

Everything I've bled for is finally within reach.

Eamon.

Ruairi.

Their men. Their empires. Their power. Soon, all of it will be mine.

And Aoife.

The ring box in my pocket weighs heavier than it should. A solid promise pressing into my thigh, waiting for the moment I'll make it real.

She doesn't know yet. But she will.

I'll slip the diamond onto her finger, and she'll take her place at my side sharp, ruthless, crowned in blood and loyalty. And exactly where she belongs.

Ruairi never understood what she could be.

Eamon only saw how he could use her.

But I see it all.

I see what no one else has the strength to claim.

"

Aoife is a queen.

My queen.

And if she refuses the crown I offer her, if she falters—I'll break her. I'll bury her beside the men too blind to recognize their place.

She'll come through.

She has to.

I'll make her my queen. Or I'll make her a ghost.

The hunger inside me doesn't care which.

It only cares that I win.

The phone vibrates against the desk, a shrill demand slicing through the silence. I let it buzz once, twice, savoring the power thrumming through me before leaning back in my chair, smiling as I connect the call.

"Tell me you have good news," Ronan says.

"I do," I say flatly. "I spoke with Aoife and told her we're moving up the timeline."

"And?" Ronan presses, impatience threading through his voice.

"She'll be in contact tomorrow. Things are moving along," I say, keeping my tone even.

"There's still one problem," he mutters.

I let out a slow exhale, irritation already prickling under my skin.

"What problem?" I bite out.

"The men," he says grimly.

I narrow my eyes. "We already talked about this. We wait until they have no choice but to fall in line."

"And most of them will," Ronan agrees. "But not all."

I know what he's getting at before he even says it. "Seamus," I say, rolling the name over my tongue like a curse.

"You know he won't turn, even when O'Sullivan's gone," Ronan says. "They grew up together. He's loyal. That kind of devotion doesn't disappear because his boss is dead."

I drag a hand over my jaw, weighing his words carefully.

Seamus has always been one of O'Sullivan's most trusted men. Ruthless. Calculated. Deadly. It's what makes him dangerous, but it's also why he'd be valuable if he pledged loyalty to me instead.

"Let me handle him," I say.

"No." There's a sharp edge to Ronan's voice. "Seamus will never be loyal to us. He's a liability we can't have."

Seamus is a relic, a man who clings to the idea that Eamon is untouchable. I take a slow sip of my drink, letting the burn settle before answering. "Then we make an example of him."

"That's not quite what I had in mind," Ronan chuckles.

"What are you proposing?" I ask, already anticipating his answer.

"We let Aoife handle him," Ronan replies, his tone casual like he's suggesting something as simple as moving a chess piece across the board.

I go still. A muscle ticks in my jaw as I carefully set my glass down. "Aoife?"

For the first time in our partnership, Ronan catches me off guard. Of all the ways I imagined he might deal with Seamus, this wasn't one of them. I was ready for blackmail, pressure, or a quiet disappearance. I was prepared to spill his blood myself if it came to that.

But handing him to Aoife? As a test?

The thought sinks into me like rot, slow and cold, spreading through the hollow spaces I can no longer ignore.

I don't move. I don't blink.

I let the stillness hold me together while the poison curls deeper into my bones.

"You're hesitating," Ronan notes, a smug edge creeping into his voice like he's caught me in a moment of weakness.

I force my expression to smooth out and keep my voice carefully measured. "I don't see the point in testing her when I already know where she stands."

"Do you?" he presses. "Because I'm not convinced. You say she's with us, but she's been treading a fine line, keeping both

Ruairi and Eamon within reach. We need to know she's truly loyal to you. To us."

I don't like the idea. Not because I doubt her but because I know exactly what she's capable of.

Aoife isn't weak.

She's sharp enough to cut, ruthless enough to destroy if she chooses to. There's a darkness in her that Ronan hasn't seen yet. One I should fear more than I do.

But forcing her hand now, before she's entirely mine before the last chains settle—it's a risk I can't afford to second-guess.

I drag a breath through my nose, cold and shallow, swallowing the hint of unease in the pit hollowing out my chest. I can't let Ronan see it.

"Fine," I say, at last, my agreement a slow, measured concession. "We'll test her."

He doesn't hear the death already written into my voice. Doesn't realize he's just another piece I'll sweep off the board when the time comes.

He still believes I'll leash her.

Tame her.

Make her kneel.

Fool.

Aoife was never meant for chains.

She was made for the crown.

She was made for blood.

And when I rise, she'll rise with me—not as a pawn, but as the fire that devours everything in our path.

She's the only one left that matters.

The only one strong enough to match me.

The only one strong enough to break me—if I let her.

And maybe I want her to.

Ronan exhales, satisfied. "Good. Let's see where her loyalty really lies."

We end the call, and I roll my shoulders. Reaching into my pocket, I pull out the small velvet box and flip it open. The diamond catches the dim light, burning like ice in my palm. I picture Aoife with my ring on her finger, standing at my side. Not just mine in the way she should have been all along but mine in the eyes of the world.

My blood runs hot at the thought.

Nothing will stop this.

Nothing will stop me from ruling with Aoife. Not Ruairi. Not Eamon, and not Ronan.

Ronan thinks his place at my side is guaranteed. It isn't. I only need him for a little while longer. Long enough to help dismantle the old order.

And when the time comes?

I'll deal with him the same way I'll deal with the rest of them.

Permanently.

Ruairi

THERE'S NO LIGHT TO MARK THE PASSAGE OF TIME.

No clocks.

No sun.

No stars.

Only the slow, rotting crawl of my mind devouring itself in the dark.

I don't know how long it's been since they threw me down here.

Hours. Days. A lifetime.

It doesn't matter anymore.

My body says long enough.

Long enough to starve, to bleed, to unravel.

Long enough to know I won't be leaving this place.

Not alive.

The air presses against me, thick and wet, clinging to my skin like a second, rotting flesh.

The walls breathe.

I swear to God, they breathe.

In and out, slow and patient, like they're waiting for me to give up.

Maybe this is how it ends.

Not with a gunshot.

Not with the clean mercy of a blade.

But with slow, creeping madness—the pit itself swallowing me whole.

And the worst part?

It's *her*. Aoife.

The sister I once swore to protect. The girl who used to wrap her arms around my neck and laugh into my chest. She was never supposed to see this life, let alone become a weapon sharpened by it.

But she put me here.

She watches from above, silent and cold.

She made the pit my grave before the dirt even touched me.

I squeeze my eyes shut, but it doesn't stop the hallucinations.

Doesn't stop the voices.

Bridget's voice—"Come home, Ri."

Saoirse's laughter—"Daddy?"

I reach for them, clawing blind at the walls.

At first, I knew they weren't real.

I told myself it was a memory.

Madness.

The dark playing tricks.

But now? Now I'm not so sure.

I speak to them.

I beg.

I promise.

I lie.

Telling Bridget I'll find my way back.

Telling Saoirse that Da's coming home.

Telling myself I still exist outside this place.

But every time I reach, my hands scrape against the cold, unyielding stone.

And their voices slip away into nothing.

· · ·

I open my mouth to scream, but there's nothing left in me but dust and silence.

The pit whispers. Low and endless, threading through my bones.

Stay. Stay. Stay.

No one is coming. No one ever was.

The dark never forgets.

It only waits.

Then, without warning, a blinding flood of light so sharp it burned through my skull and seared into my retinas until my eyes watered and my head pounded. I tried to block it out, squeezing my lids shut and pressing my palms against my eyes, but it didn't matter. The light was relentless, scorching through every crack.

And then it was gone, and I was plunged back into the suffocating dark.

The cycle repeated. Darkness that stretched on endlessly. Long enough to make me desperate for anything else, to make me yearn for even a sliver of light. When the light came, it was cruel—blinding and unforgiving.

And then there was music. Not real music with a rhythm or melody. No, it was ear-splitting, distorted, droning tones that vibrated through the pit. Sometimes, it blared at full volume, rattling in my skull and making my thoughts scatter like broken glass. Other times, it dropped to a barely-there hum, just enough to get inside my head. The same three notes over and over, cycling in an unholy loop to keep me from resting or slipping away into unconsciousness.

And then silence.

The silence was worse than the sound. Worse than the light. Because when the silence came, I knew she was watching. That was when I sunk to my lowest and started begging. Not for freedom. Not for survival. But for the darkness to take me completely.

For this to end. But it didn't.

Sometimes, Aoife speaks. That's when it's the hardest because she isn't cruel, not in the way I'd expect. She's careful. Calculated. She talks like she's trying to reason with me, like this is all some fucked-up lesson. Like I've forced her hand.

"I could let you out, Ruairi," she told me once, crouched just outside the pit, her voice gentle. "All you have to do is admit you were wrong. Admit I deserve a seat at the table."

"You're not one of them, Aoife," I growl. "No matter how much you want to be."

She only smiled before turning and walking away, leaving me in the dark.

And still, that was nothing compared to the blade.

My fingers twitch at the memory, my wrists raw from where they tied me down, forcing me to stay still while the edge of steel kissed my skin. The cut was shallow, a warning, but the intent was clear. If she wanted to, she could have me killed.

I shudder. I can't let my mind go there. Not now. Not when I need to hold on to the only thing keeping me sane.

Bridget. God, she must be out of her mind with worry. I can picture her pacing our bedroom, her face drawn with exhaustion, her green eyes full of fear, full of the same fire I fell in love with.

And Saoirse. My little girl. She must be wondering where her da has gone and why I haven't come home. Does she ask about me? Does she cry at night? That thought cuts deeper than any blade ever could.

I grit my teeth against the jagged lump rising in my throat, but it's useless. There's no fighting the regret clawing its way through my chest.

I should've told them I loved them more.

Should've kissed Bridget longer before I walked out the door that morning.

Should've read Saoirse one more bedtime story. Held her until she fell asleep.

Should've stayed.

Should've fought.

Instead, I left like I had all the time in the world.

Like there would always be another morning.

Another kiss.

Another goodnight.

There isn't.

There never was.

And now it's too late.

Too late for promises.

Too late for prayers.

Too late for anything but the slow, quiet unraveling of everything I ever was.

There's no escaping this pit.

No climbing free.

No hand reaching down to pull me back into the light.

Aoife's waiting for something.

An answer. A surrender. Maybe even my final breath.

And deep down, in the part of me that's already given up, I think I'm ready to let her have it.

I let my head drop back against the stone, the cold biting into my skull like a silent brand. The darkness swells against my skin, thick and suffocating, seeping into my bones until even breathing feels borrowed.

Maybe this is how it ends.

Not with a scream.

Not with a fight.

Just a slow, silent vanishing.

Swallowed whole by the dark.

Aoife

TONIGHT CHANGES EVERYTHING. I TELL MYSELF THAT over and over as I make my way to Eamon's office, my pulse steady, my steps even. I don't let myself hesitate. I can't afford to.

Eamon glances up when I enter, his brows lifting slightly before a slow smile tugs at his lips like he wasn't expecting me but is damn glad I'm here. "Well, this is a surprise." His expression softens. "What brings you to me, *mo chroí?*" he asks.

I meet his gaze head-on. "Tonight's the night it ends with Ruairi," I say.

He leans back in his chair and crosses his arms over his chest. "You've decided to let him go, then?" he asks, his tone unreadable.

I don't blink. "No," I reply, my voice steady.

"You're going to kill him?" he presses, his eyes narrowing slightly.

"I have no other choice," I say smoothly, keeping my voice even. "I started this. I'll be the one to finish it."

Eamon exhales, slow and measured, before standing. He walks toward me, eyes locked on mine like he's searching for something. "You don't have to do this."

I tilt my chin up. "If I let him go, I'll be seen as weak. And

Ruairi?" I let out a short, humorless laugh. "He won't hesitate to end me the second he gets the chance. That's not an option."

He studies me, silent. For the first time since I stepped into this world, Eamon looks at me like I might've gone too far. But I don't waver. I can't.

"This is for the best," I continue. "It'll devastate Bridget, but at least she'll have closure. She'll be able to move on."

Eamon shakes his head slightly, dragging a hand through his hair. "And after?"

"After, I take my place as head of the Quigley Syndicate." I step closer, voice dropping. "The war between our Syndicates will end."

For a beat, he doesn't move. Then, finally, he inclines his head. "I stand with you," he says quietly, the words heavy with meaning.

The weight in my chest eases slightly. "I need your help to set it up. It has to look like an outside hit."

Eamon nods. "My guards are at your disposal."

"I'm doing it myself," I say, leaving no room for argument.

His expression hardens instantly, his jaw tightening as he closes the space between us. "No."

"He's weak. Worn down. He won't be able to fight me off."

"And if you're wrong?" he counters. "If he overpowers you? I'm not taking that chance."

"I started this," I say, voice low, firm. "I will be the one to end it."

Eamon's eyes bore into mine. "One of my guards goes down first. He'll restrain Ruairi before you get anywhere near him."

I bristle. "Eamon—"

"I'm not fucking budging on this, Aoife." His voice is harsh. "And I'll be down there too."

My hands curl into fists, but I force myself to relax them. "Fine." I take a slow breath. "But I don't want any other guards there."

He hesitates but then nods once. "No one else."

I hold out my hand. "Swear it."

His gaze locks on mine. And then he takes my hand, his grip firm. "I swear."

There. Done.

Before I can second-guess myself, before its weight can sink in, Seamus walks into the room.

"Boss," he says. "There's a situation that needs your attention."

Eamon sighs, his gaze lingering on me a moment longer. "I have to take care of this, but I'll be back. We'll get this handled tonight," he says before he steps past me, heading for the door.

The moment it clicks shut behind him, I pull out my phone and dial. Cian picks up on the first ring.

"It's set for tonight," I say quietly, moving toward the window. "I have him at an old castle on the west cliffs. There's a watchtower just beyond the south wall—unguarded, no cameras. It's the best place to wait."

"When?" he asks, his voice edged with anticipation.

"Be there just after nightfall," I tell him. "Stay hidden until you hear two shots. That's your signal. Ruairi and Eamon will both be handled by then, and you'll know it's safe to move in."

Cian exhales a slow breath. "You've done good, lass."

"I have to go," I say and hang up quickly.

Seamus looms in the doorway, arms crossed, suspicion carved into every line of his face. He doesn't say a word as he reaches back to shove the door shut, then strides into the room, his gaze pinning me in place like a predator stalking its prey.

"You're going to tell me what the fuck is going on."

Eamon

"IT WASN'T A FUCKING ROBBERY," SEAMUS SAYS, HIS voice tight with frustration. "They didn't take a damn thing."

I grab the back of my neck as I stare down at the photos spread across my desk. Six of my men were executed. The cargo burned to ash. Whoever did this wasn't looking for a payday.

They wanted to send a message.

"This was found at the scene." Seamus tosses a folded piece of paper onto my desk. The edges are crisp, untouched by the blood soaking the ground in the photos.

I pick it up, unfolding it slowly.

She builds her empire on the edge of the abyss, blind to the blade above. One will take her. Both will end her.

A slow, burning heat coils in my gut.

They're not threatening me. They're threatening Aoife.

Seamus exhales sharply. "Who the fuck even writes like that?"

Only one person ever has. Ruairi. But he's rotting in a pit, barely able to lift his own head, let alone plan a fucking ambush. So who the fuck else wants her dead?

"Any leads?" I ask, my voice deceptively calm.

Seamus shakes his head. "Nothing solid yet. Whoever's responsible knew what they were doing."

I let the note fall onto the desk, my fingers already reaching for my phone. Whoever they are, they just made the worst mistake of their life. "Until we find out who's behind this, I want you on her. She doesn't go anywhere alone."

He gives a single nod, his expression unreadable. "Understood."

"I will not risk her safety," I grind out.

Seamus exhales, shifting his weight slightly. "She's not going to like it."

"She doesn't have to."

"I'll keep her in my sights."

Without another word, he turns and strides toward the door, his movements efficient, deliberate. He pulls it open, hesitates just slightly, like he wants to say something else, but then steps through and lets it close behind him.

The room is silent again, and I lean back in my chair, dragging my thumb across my lower lip, the taste of blood and iron sharp on my tongue. My mind shifts easily into place. Aoife plans to kill her brother tonight. I should be worried about how it will change her, twist her into something darker.

I'm not.

The truth festers beneath my skin. I don't care who she becomes as long as she's mine. The truth coils through me like a living thing. I crave the monster she'll become. I crave the ruin.

Already, my thoughts are reaching past the slaughter to what waits on the other side. A future built on ash and bone, a throne stitched together from the wreckage.

Ours.

But something stirs beyond the edge of all my careful plans, a shadow I can't yet name, a hand already reaching to tear it all away.

Let them come.

I'll drown the world in blood before I let that happen.

Aoife

THE SECOND I TURN, I FEEL THE ANGER ROLLING OFF Seamus in waves. Controlled but undeniable. He stands just inside the doorway, arms crossed. But his eyes—they burn.

I don't let him sense even an ounce of intimidation. "Something on your mind, Seamus?"

"That depends," he says, voice tight. "What the hell were you just talking about?"

I meet his gaze without flinching. "You're going to have to be more specific."

His jaw flexes. He doesn't take the bait. Doesn't reveal how much he heard or if he saw me on my phone. So, I go with the safest option. "I was going over plans for tonight. Speaking out loud."

"What plans?" Seamus demands, his voice tight.

"Didn't Eamon tell you?" I ask, letting the question hang between us.

"Tell me what?" he presses, suspicion sharpening every word.

I let out a small, deliberate breath as if it's nothing more than an afterthought. "I'm going to kill my brother tonight."

For a moment, something flickers across Seamus's face, shock, maybe even disbelief, but he masks it almost immediately. "You're serious," he says, his voice low.

I lift a shoulder in a careless shrug. "Why wouldn't I be?"

His expression hardens. "Eamon mentioned it," he bites out. "But he's too busy dealing with another attack—one that's conveniently tied to you."

The words hit me like a cold slap. "What?"

"Someone killed six of our best men and left a message for you at the scene. Same kind of shit that used to show up from Ruairi."

My blood ignites. Another attack? A threat meant for me?

My fists tighten at my sides. "Who the fuck is behind this?"

Seamus studies me like he's waiting to see if I'm holding something back. "That's what I'd like to know. Any ideas?"

I take a steady breath. There's only one name that comes to mind. Perhaps he sees through my plans. I pull out my phone and dial, making sure Seamus sees. When Cian picks up, I hit speaker.

"Twice in one day, lass," he muses, amusement lacing his tone. "What a pleasure."

I don't indulge him. "Did you hit Eamon's shipment?"

A pause. Not long, but enough.

"What?" His voice loses its usual smoothness. "No. Why the fuck would I?"

"Then you need to find out who did. If there's a traitor in the Syndicate, someone trying to take advantage of Ruairi being gone, we need to know."

Silence stretches for half a second before he replies, "I'm already working on it. And I'm doing everything in my power to bring your brother home."

Seamus and I exchange a quick glance. Cian's a smooth liar. Even I'm not sure if he's behind the hit or not, but I will damn sure get to the bottom of it.

Still, I'm thankful he seemed to know better than to push back. To question why I was calling him like this and to give Seamus even the slightest reason to doubt me.

"I appreciate it, Cian," I say, not waiting for a response before I hang up.

For a long moment, neither Seamus nor I say anything. Finally, I turn to him. "What do you think?"

"He sounded genuinely surprised," he says. "I don't trust the bastard, but this time, I think he's telling the truth."

So do I. Which is a problem because if it wasn't Cian, who was it? I push the thought aside. Focus. Turning back to Seamus, I ask, "Why are you even here? Shouldn't you be with Eamon?"

His lips twitch slightly, but there's no real amusement behind it. "Eamon put me on you."

I expect irritation to rise, but instead, what slips out is "Thank you."

It surprises me just as much as it does him. Something shifts in his expression, just for a second. Then his voice lowers, steady as steel.

"No one's going to get to you, Aoife." His eyes are sharp, unwavering. "Eamon and I will see to it."

I inhale slowly, taking a moment to sit with the gravity of everything that's happening. "I'm going to need your help tonight."

Suspicion flashes across his face. "Help with what?" His tone is edged with skepticism. "What the hell are you planning now?"

"I can't go into the details right now," I say, keeping my voice steady.

His expression darkens. "Not good enough, Aoife."

I lift a shoulder, playing at nonchalance. "It's all happening tonight, one way or another. You can either help me or stay out of my way."

For a long moment, he studies me. Then he exhales, shaking his head like he already knows he's going to regret this. "Christ." He rubs a hand over his face. "Fine. But if this blows up, I'm not the one cleaning up the mess."

"Noted."

I turn away before he can pry further, but I feel his eyes on me, still searching, still waiting for an answer I'm not ready to give.

Cian

THE CITY ROTS BEHIND US, CRUMBLING INTO SHADOW and ash as we drive. The road cuts through the darkness like a scar, stretching endlessly into the hollow outskirts of Dublin.

Inside the car, the air thickens, poisoned with the stench of old fear and new betrayal. I should be clear-headed, sharp as a blade. Instead, Aoife's voice scrapes through my skull, each word winding tighter, tighter, a noose soaked in oil and fire.

Someone left her a message. A warning. A threat. And I have no name to carve into the bones for it. The unknown festers under my skin, raw and screaming.

Power was never a throne—it was a grave dressed in silk.

And somewhere in the dark, hands I can't see are already reaching to drag me under.

Beside me, Ronan shifts. "Your head's not in the game."

"I'm fine."

"Bullshit."

There's no point in pretending he doesn't see it. Ronan may be an arrogant bastard, but he's not stupid. "Aoife called me earlier."

Out of the corner of my eye, I see his smirk. "Oh? What did the little princess want now?"

"Eamon's shipment was hit," I say flatly, ignoring his comment. "Someone left a message for her. Same kind of message Ruairi used to leave at the scenes of his attacks."

Ronan lets out a sharp bark of laughter.

I glance at him, eyes narrowing. "What the hell is so funny?"

He shakes his head, a grim edge to his voice. "Relax, Cian. That was me."

A cold, slow heat builds in my chest. My fingers tighten around the steering wheel. "You?"

"I ordered it." His voice is casual, like this is nothing more than a simple business move. "It was a test."

"A test," I echo, my tone unreadable.

"We need to be sure she can handle this before we agree to let her into the Syndicate," he continues. "Aoife talks a big game, but I wanted to see how she'd respond. If she'd panic."

Something about this doesn't sit right. Letting her into the Syndicate was never up for debate.

Ronan watches me for a reaction, his snide smile still lingering. I don't trust him. Not fully. But I'm too close now. Everything I've worked for is within my reach. We need to get through tonight, then I'll deal with Ronan.

I force my body to relax. "And? What do you think?"

He chuckles. "I think she's not as soft as you are about her."

I keep my expression blank, but the words spark something deep in my gut. Ronan sees her as a weakness—my weakness. He thinks she's just a spoiled, reckless princess playing at war. That she doesn't have what it takes to stand in this world, to rule beside men like us.

He couldn't be more wrong.

Aoife's stronger than he'll ever be. More cunning, more relentless. She's spent her life clawing for a seat at the table, and unlike him, she doesn't just take power. She ensures no one ever takes it back.

He's underestimating what she's capable of. That'll be his mistake to pay for.

The road stretches ahead, winding through the countryside. We pull off onto a narrow, overgrown path and drive another half mile before I kill the engine.

"We walk from here," I say, already moving toward the tree line. "We can't risk being seen."

Climbing out, we keep our movements quiet as we scan the area. The wind moves through the trees, rustling branches overhead. The scent of damp earth and old stone lingers in the air.

Ronan follows the crunch of our boots muffled by the soft earth beneath us. The castle looms in the distance, its jagged silhouette cutting into the night sky. It's old, a relic of another time with stone walls weathered by centuries, the kind of place that has seen its fair share of blood. A fitting backdrop for what's coming.

We reach the watchtower, the structure looming like a broken sentinel at the edge of the castle grounds. The stones are slick and cold beneath my fingertips, slick with age, with rot, with something older than memory. I press against the wall, scanning the darkness, feeling the weight of it press back.

This is where we wait.

The night breathes around us. The low moan of the wind through the crumbling stones, the hollow call of an owl somewhere beyond the trees. But underneath it, there's a silence so deep it feels alive. Watching. Listening.

The air tightens. The ground shifts.

Something's coming.

Something that won't be stopped.

And when it arrives, there will be no going back.

Eamon

The penthouse is quiet when I step inside. Too quiet.

I make my way toward the bedroom, drawn in by the soft sounds of movement. The door is cracked just enough for me to see inside.

And there she is, standing before the full-length mirror, her body encased in black. Tight pants hug her curves, and a short, fitted top reveals the toned lines of her stomach. Her red hair is pulled back, sleek, severe.

She's beautiful. Deadly. Unstoppable.

Aoife bends slightly, adjusting the waistband of her pants, and my gaze tracks every movement. I should be thinking about what's coming. About where we're going. But all I can think about is her. Somewhere along the way, I stopped seeing Aoife as a tool to wield against Ruairi. I stopped seeing her as an enemy's sister, as a dangerous gamble.

I fell for her.

And now, watching her, that realization is a slow-burning weight in my chest. I should tell her. Should say the words. But not tonight. Not when she's about to kill her own blood.

She lifts her head, catching my gaze in the mirror. A slow, knowing smile curves her lips. "Enjoying the view?"

I step inside, closing the door behind me as I move toward her. "More than you know."

Placing my hands on her waist, I let my fingers press into the fabric, into the heat of her skin beneath it. We're both facing the mirror now, her body fitting against mine like she was always meant to be there.

My lips brush the shell of her ear. "You look fucking lethal. And it's the sexiest thing I've ever seen."

Her smile deepens, but a shadow passes over her face before she quickly schools her features.

"Seamus is waiting with the car," I murmur. "Are you ready?"

She turns toward the dresser, reaching for her heels with a quiet, deliberate grace. One by one, she slips them on the final touch to a masterpiece already carved in perfection.

Straightening, she meets my gaze. "I'm ready."

The ride stretches out in silence, thick and brittle as glass. Aoife stares out the window, her reflection ghosting against the darkened glass, distant and unreadable. Her hands rest carefully in her lap, fingers still, but the tension in her shoulders betrays her.

Every so often, her jaw tightens, the slightest crack in an otherwise perfect mask. She's bracing for tonight. We both are.

Seamus' eyes meet mine in the rearview mirror, but neither of us says a word. This is her moment.

He hasn't always approved of her. Hasn't always trusted her. In the beginning, he warned me against getting too close, constantly reminding me exactly who she was and where her loyalties would lie. But lately, something's shifted. There seems to be an unspoken truce between them.

Maybe it's because he's seen what I have. That Aoife's more than Ruairi's sister, more than a wildcard in this war. She's ready to claim what's hers. And tonight, she will.

We pull into the castle grounds, the tires crunching over gravel, the shadows swallowing us whole. This place was built in blood. Held in power. Steeped in history that would make lesser men tremble.

I've killed here. Men have begged for mercy inside these walls, their voices swallowed by the stone. Their ghosts don't haunt me. I made my peace with death a long time ago. Tonight, another name will be added to this place. But it won't be by my hand.

I step out first, opening her door. Aoife hesitates for only a second before slipping her hand into mine. Her fingers are steady. Her grip is strong as we walk inside together.

She doesn't rush. She walks with purpose, each step echoing off the ancient walls, the weight of history pressing down but never breaking her.

Aoife was never meant to be kept from this world. Not by her father. Not by Ruairi. And certainly not by me.

We stop in the armory, the scent of oil and steel heavy in the air. Aoife steps forward, her fingers brushing over the hilts of the knives and the barrels of the pistols. She's not simply choosing a weapon. She's choosing how her brother's life ends.

She pauses, and something shifts in her eyes. Slowly, she reaches down and lifts a dagger. It's sleek, sharp, and perfectly balanced for a precise, deliberate kill. She tests the weight in her palm, tilting it under the dim light, watching the steel glint as if she can already see it buried in flesh.

I step closer, my voice low. "A gun would be cleaner."

Aoife doesn't look at me as she continues to turn the blade over as if seeing how it belongs in her hand. "I don't want clean."

Exhaling, I reach out, my fingers brushing against her wrist. I'm not seeking to stop her. Just grounding her. "A gun would be safer."

When she finally meets my eyes, there's something dark and

steady in her gaze. "I've already agreed to have him restrained. There's nothing he can do to hurt me."

I exhale, my fingers tightening slightly around her wrist. "I think I don't like the risk."

She gives me a look that's half challenge, half curiosity.

I nod toward the holstered guns on the wall. "One bullet and it's over. No struggle. No second chances."

No way for her to feel it happen.

"I don't want it to be over in an instant," she says, her voice quiet but filled with certainty.

The air between us tightens. There's something intoxicating about the way she says it, about the conviction in her voice.

A better man would tear her away from this edge. He'd take the weight from her hands, carry the blood himself. He'd find another way. But I'm not that man.

All I can do is watch as she steps into the dark and pray there's still something left of her when the night is over.

Darkness greets us as we enter the room above the pit. Aoife lifts a hand, signaling one of the guards. A switch is flipped, and the pit floods with light.

Ruairi flinches, throwing up an arm to shield his eyes from the sudden glare. The movement costs him. A raw, hacking cough wracks his thin frame, leaving him hunched and gasping.

When he forces himself upright, there's still a ghost of defiance in his eyes—fading, desperate, as if he needs to believe he's still dangerous even as his body betrays him.

"Come to gawk, Evie?" his voice scrapes out, raw and splintered, more ruin than threat. "Or have you finally found your spine?"

Aoife doesn't flinch as I take my place beside her, my hands slipping into my pockets.

Ruairi's gaze shifts to me, narrowing. "Well, well. If it isn't O'Sullivan. I would've thought you'd have the balls to do this yourself. But I see now, you're nothing more than a coward using my sister to get her hands dirty for you."

"This isn't my war," I say flatly, gesturing to Aoife. "She's the one in control. She decides what happens next."

For the first time, something flickers behind Ruairi's eyes. Doubt. Wariness.

Seamus and two other guards descend into the pit, carrying a chair on the lift.

Ruairi stiffens. "What the hell is this?"

No one answers him. The guards grab him by the arms, hauling him up and forcing him into the chair. He fights them, but he's weak and is no match. The restraints loop around his wrists and ankles, cinching tight.

Still, he tries to fight, his voice hoarse with rage. "You think this makes you powerful? Sitting up there while your boyfriend's men tie me down like a fucking dog?"

I study her, searching for signs of hesitation. She's quieter than usual. Too still.

Leaning in, I ask, "You sure about this?"

"Yes," she answers without looking at me.

"Please, take the gun," I murmur. "Make it quick."

Finally, she turns her head, meeting my gaze with something cold. "No. I need to feel it, Eamon. I need to feel his life leave him."

Something stirs deep in my chest. Admiration? Concern? A mixture of both?

I exhale slowly, nodding once. "Then I'm with you," I say, my voice low. "I'll be your anchor tonight. And when it's over, I'll be the one who pulls you back from the edge."

The last guard ascends from the pit, leaving only Seamus behind with Ruairi.

Aoife and I step onto the lift. The mechanism groans to life, the walls of the pit closing in around us, the air growing heavier with every passing second.

I nod to Seamus, who stands rigid against the far wall. Aoife hadn't wanted anyone else down here. Maybe she changed her mind. Maybe, deep down, she knew she shouldn't carry this alone. Relief threads through me as we descend. She wasn't as far gone as I'd feared. Not yet.

When we reach the bottom, Ruairi lifts his head, his eyes burning with fury as they land on her. His sister. His executioner.

Then he shifts his eyes to me. "Why are you with her?" he demands.

"To bear witness." My voice is smooth, final, dark with the weight of inevitability. "The blade is already swinging, the pit already open. You were dead the second she let you fall."

Ruairi's jaw tightens, his breath ragged.

Aoife steps forward, dagger in hand.

I watch her, unshaken, unwavering, every bit the queen she was always meant to be. I've never seen anything more powerful.

<h1 style="text-align:center">Aoife</h1>

I SHOULD FEEL GUILTY.

The blade rests in my palm, its cold weight a reminder of what I've chosen to do. What I've become. The room smells of damp stone and fear, the air so thick I can almost taste the tension. Ruairi sits bound in the chair before me, his head slumped forward, his breathing ragged. My twin. My blood. The other half of me, whose shadow I've spent my entire life living in.

And here I am, about to prove once and for all that I'm just as worthy.

The pendulum swings in the shadows above us. Its steady rhythm echoes the pounding in my chest, a reminder of how little time I have. I trace the edge of the blade with my thumb, watching the light flicker across its surface. One slice. One mark to show him I'm not the same girl he's always underestimated.

"Do it," Eamon's voice murmurs from the corner. Smooth, steady, unrelenting. He's the devil on my shoulder, the man who saw in me what Ruairi never could.

Strength. Ambition. Fire.

Ruairi lifts his head slowly, his bloodshot eyes locking onto mine. He doesn't plead. He doesn't flinch. He just stares at me with that infuriating mix of defiance and pity, like he still thinks I'm a child playing at a dangerous game.

"You don't have to do this, Aoife," he says, his voice hoarse but steady. "You're not like him."

I laugh, though it tastes bitter on my tongue. "And what am I like, Ruairi? A good little girl? The obedient twin? The one you keep locked away while you play king?"

His jaw tightens, and I see it—the crack in his armor. My words hurt more than the blade ever could.

"You're better than this," he whispers, his voice softer now. Almost pleading.

But I'm not.

I press the blade against his skin, and he winces, though he doesn't try to pull away. My hand trembles. Not because I can't do it, but because I know this moment will change everything.

"Better?" I whisper, my voice breaking. "Better doesn't survive in our world, Ruairi. You taught me that."

The pendulum swings lower, its hiss slicing through the silence. Eamon shifts in the shadows, waiting, watching.

But tonight, I'm not here to be his equal. I'm here to take the throne.

I tighten my grip, my voice steadier. "You're right, Ruairi."

He blinks, his expression caught between shock and confusion.

"I'm not like him. And I'm not like you either."

Before anyone can react, I spin, the dagger flashing in the light, a streak of silver cutting through the air.

Eamon's sharp intake of breath is the only sound before I lunge, pinning him against the wall with the tip of my knife at his throat. His eyes, dark and unreadable, widen in something I've never seen before.

"What the—" Eamon hisses, his voice cutting off as I press the blade harder against his skin.

"No more games," I say, my voice cold and commanding.

Ruairi struggles against his restraints, his voice ragged with frustration. "Aoife, what the hell are you doing?"

I don't look at him. My gaze stays locked on Eamon, who tilts his head slightly, his lips curling into a slow, dangerous smile. The blade hums with quiet menace, its edge a whisper of promises unspoken. And this time, I'm the one holding it.

Eamon looks between me and Ruairi, a slow, humorless smirk spreading across his lips. "Well played, Aoife." His voice is controlled, but there's venom beneath it.

He thinks I betrayed him.

He looks to Seamus. "End this."

Seamus draws his gun.

For a heartbeat, the pit is silent, only the sound of Ruairi's ragged breathing filling the space. Then Seamus shifts and aims the gun at Eamon.

Eamon tenses, his jaw clenching as he takes in the weapon now pointed at him. "What the fuck is going on?"

I lean in, putting a little more pressure on the blade, but keep my voice steady. "Seamus, untie my brother."

Eamon's head snaps toward me. "He doesn't take orders from you."

Seamus doesn't hesitate. He moves to Ruairi, working at the restraints. Eamon's fury is palpable, but he doesn't move to stop me. Ruairi shakes out his hands as the last of the ropes falls away, his eyes locked on me, suspicion warring with curiosity.

Neither of them understands. Not yet.

I take a slow breath, letting the silence stretch before I finally say, "While the two of you have been busy destroying each other, I've been trying to protect you and the Syndicates."

Ruairi scoffs. "Protecting me? By throwing me in a pit and leaving me to die?" Ruairi chokes on a cough. "You'll forgive me if I don't feel particularly saved."

I ignore the sarcasm, my tone cutting through the room like steel. "Cian has been plotting for months to take you out, Ruairi. He wants our Syndicate for himself."

A shadow of recognition crosses Ruairi's face, but Eamon remains unmoved.

"Not exactly shocking," Eamon drawls.

"That's only the beginning." I level him with a look. "When Cian found out I was working for you, he saw an even bigger opportunity."

Now I have both of their attention.

Lowering the blade and stepping back, I explain, "He decided the Quigley Syndicate wasn't enough. He's been planning to take you out and take your Syndicate, too."

Eamon's entire body stills. His expression remains unreadable, but I know him well enough to realize I just hit a nerve.

Ruairi shifts in his chair. "And how exactly did he think that was going to happen?"

I exhale slowly. "By taking both of you out. And running the Syndicate's with me."

Ruairi lets out a ragged, broken laugh that quickly dissolves into a cough. "Cian wanted you to rule with him? Now that's rich."

I cut my gaze to Ruairi. "It's the truth. And despite having confidence in my ability, I could never let that happen."

Eamon watches me carefully now, his earlier anger shifting into something else. "So you set him up." His voice is quieter this time.

"Cian's at the watchtower. He believes I'm going to end this tonight—kill you both and leave the Syndicates wide open for us."

I let the weight of my words settle, watching as realization dawns on them both. They wanted to believe I was playing their game.

But this was always mine.

Stepping between them, my voice is calm and controlled. "This is how everything is going to go."

Cian

THE SILENCE IS DEAFENING AS I SIT WITH MY BACK pressed against the cold stone of the watchtower, my fingers twitching at my sides. Waiting. Watching. My nerves are razor-sharp, my pulse steady but quick.

Beside me, Ronan shifts, exhaling sharply. "It's taking too long."

I grit my teeth. "She'll come through."

Ronan scoffs. "You're sure about that?"

He doesn't trust her. He never has. Truth be told, I don't know if he's wrong.

Aoife's been at war with Ruairi since their parents died. Ruairi's been a damn fool. He's spent years clinging to a title he doesn't deserve, playing the noble leader while his empire rots from the inside. He thinks loyalty is enough to keep a Syndicate strong. That men follow out of respect rather than fear.

But he doesn't understand the truth. Power isn't inherited—it's taken. And if you're too weak to seize it, you don't deserve to rule.

Ruairi should've known better. He should've seen the asset standing right in front of him. Aoife isn't just sharp. She's lethal. She understands how this world works better than Ruairi ever could. And yet, he shoved her aside. Ignored her. Kept her caged while he played the righteous heir.

Pathetic.

Ruairi doesn't deserve what he has. He never did.

And that's why I've spent months tightening the noose around his throat. Every deal I've made, every lie I've spun, every so-called ally I've flipped, every move has been leading to this. I played the long game, let Ruairi think he was in control, let Eamon believe he was untouchable.

And now? They're both as good as dead.

That leaves Aoife exactly where I need her. She thinks she's in control. Thinks she's playing her own game. She isn't.

I let her fight, let her sharpen her edges against the men who underestimated her. I allowed her to think she was carving her own path when, really, I've been the one guiding her the entire time, feeding her just enough power to make her hungry for more. I let her think this was about respect, about proving herself worthy. But power isn't given, and it sure as hell isn't earned.

It's stolen. Taken with blood and fire.

Ruairi was too weak to see it. Eamon is too blinded by lust to care.

But me? I know exactly how this ends. Because I designed it.

For now, Aoife has a place in my Syndicate. But if the day ever comes when she forgets who put her here, when she stops being useful, she's as expendable as the rest of them. I'll slit her throat just as easily as I'd slit her brother's.

Because in the end, there's only one thing that matters.

Me.

I don't let doubt take root. "She will."

Ronan doesn't look convinced. His hand lingers near his gun, fingers twitching. He's restless. Dangerous.

The night stretches, suffocating, endless. Finally, two gunshots split the air.

Relief crashes through me like a drug and I push off the wall. "That's the signal. Let's go."

We move quickly, cutting through the darkness toward a back entrance that would have once been used for staff back when this place was more than just a relic of power and blood. Adrenaline licks at my veins, sharpening my senses. The castle looms ahead, its stone walls swallowing the moonlight.

No one sees us. No one stops us. Just as planned.

When we get there, the old wood door opens, and Aoife stands there. She's steady. Too steady. Something in her stance doesn't scream victory. It screams calculation. But I ignore the feeling. Instead, I step forward, wrapping my arms around her and pulling her into me.

"It's done?" My voice is quiet, meant only for her.

She nods, letting me hold her. For a breath. A second. Before she stiffens. Her green eyes look up past me. I follow her gaze, turning slightly. She's staring at the man behind me.

Her expression tightens. "Ronan?" Her voice isn't just surprised. It's wary.

She steps back, putting space between us and my stomach knots. "You didn't tell me you were working together."

My throat goes dry. "Aoife, I—"

I don't have the words. I don't know why I didn't tell her. Maybe because I knew she wouldn't like it. Maybe because, deep down, I wanted to keep Ronan in my pocket, separate from her.

She studies me, eyes sharp, demanding an answer I don't have.

Ronan steps forward. "I told him not to tell you."

Aoife's gaze snaps to him. "Why?"

He waves a hand. "Does it matter?"

She doesn't answer.

Ronan doesn't waste a second. "Where are the bodies?"

Her expression smooths. Her unease is gone.

"In the pit." She turns, leading us inside.

The room is dimly lit, the light barely cutting through the thick, oppressive air. The stone walls loom around us, worn by time, stained by history.

Aoife stops at the edge of the pit and gestures down. "There."

I step forward, peering over the ledge. Two bodies lie unmoving below, barely visible in the dark. I exhale. It's over. The power is now mine.

But Ronan doesn't look convinced. He steps closer, narrowing his eyes. "Hard to see from up here."

It all happens so fast. His hand moves. I don't see it coming. Not until it's too late. In a flash, he yanks Aoife against him, his gun pressing into her ribs.

The air leaves my lungs.

"You're a fool, Cian," Ronan murmurs, voice smooth, almost amused. "Too trusting. Too soft. You don't deserve to run a fucking Syndicate."

A slow, burning rage ignites in my chest. My hand moves for my gun—

The shot rings out before I can reach it.

Fire erupts in my chest, stealing my breath and knocking me backward.

Pain. Blinding. Sharp.

My legs buckle. My vision swims. I hit the ground hard, my body refusing to respond.

A sound cuts through the ringing in my ears—a scream.

Aoife.

I don't know if it's rage, horror, or something else entirely, but it splinters through the haze, sharp and jagged. Aoife's fighting. I can hear the struggle, the scrape of boots on stone, the sharp intake of breath—hers or Ronan's, I don't know.

I try to move. Try to do something. But there's only cold. The world fades at the edges.

And then—nothing.

Eamon

The cold stone presses against my back, bleeding the warmth from my body, the weight of the pit folding in around me like a coffin waiting to be sealed.

I stay still. I barely breathe. The air hangs thick and damp, sinking into my chest with every shallow inhale.

I don't know how Ruairi survived down here for weeks.

The walls seem to lean inward, squeezing the space, tightening with every heartbeat.

We're not dead.

Not yet.

But we have to look it.

Above us, Aoife's voice rings out, steady and sure, slicing through the pit's heavy silence.

She's selling the lie.

Selling our deaths.

Then, her tone shifts. A name slips from her lips—Ronan.

I go still. I know that name. Ruairi's second-in-command. A man too ambitious for his own good. I hear the shift in her voice. Her careful control falters, just for a second. That's enough to tell me that this isn't going according to plan.

Ruairi shifts beside me, the sound of his breathing rough and broken, scraping against the pit's heavy silence. He's too weak to stay still, his body hollowed out from weeks of damp stone and darkness wearing him down.

I turn my head, the movement stiff and strained. Ruairi's face is tight, his eyes wide and unfocused, staring into the dark. But I see it—the moment understanding slams into him.

It isn't just Cian. It's Ronan, too. His right hand. The man he trusted to hold the line in his absence. Betrayal cuts through him like a blade, sharp and merciless.

He doesn't speak. He doesn't have to. I feel it in the way the air sours between us.

I don't have time to process it. The world above us fractures in an instant as a gunshot rips through the silence. Aoife's scream follows—raw, jagged, real enough to tear me open.

I go rigid, panic flooding every inch of me.

I can't see her.

I can't see anything.

Ruairi grits his teeth and tries to push himself up, but his body crumples, shuddering against the stone. Grabbing Ruairi, I pull him toward the farthest edge of the pit, pressing him against the wall. Every instinct is screaming at me to act, to move, to do something. But the lift isn't down here. We're trapped.

"Stay down," I order, my voice low, steady. "You're no good to her like this."

His eyes burn with frustration. He knows I'm right.

Above us, footsteps scrape across the stone, fast, heavy. A grunt. A struggle. Then Aoife's voice low and lethal.

"I should've ended you the second I saw your face."

A grunt. The dull thud of impact—bodies colliding.

"You fucking bitch." His voice is furious. "I don't know what O'Leary saw in you."

"A way to get himself killed, apparently." Her words drip with defiance.

Another scuffle. The scrape of boots. The harsh rustle of fabric.

Ronan's breath comes faster, strained. "You always were a handful."

"I guess you should've picked a better hostage," she snaps back.

His voice dips, smug and taunting. "Maybe I should spread those legs and see if you're really worth all this fucking trouble."

A heartbeat of silence, then a sharp, vicious sound. A grunt of pain. His.

Aoife's breathing is hard, unbroken. She's still fighting. Then, the sharp shatter of glass breaking against the stone. A strangled curse. A heavy breath.

She's fighting back. Still moving. Still resisting.

"Where the fuck are your men?" Ruairi rasps.

"They're coming." My voice is low, edged with barely contained fury. "But not fucking fast enough."

Because every second she's up there alone, fighting, is another second I'm stuck down here, unable to put a bullet in Ronan myself.

Ruairi exhales sharply beside me, a mix of exhaustion and frustration. "We need to get out of this fucking pit."

"No shit."

I crane my neck, straining for a better angle, desperate to see something—anything. But all I have are the sounds. The scuffle of boots. The grunt of exertion. Then, a loud, metallic scrape. A struggle. Bodies slamming against something heavy.

"Let go of me, you piece of shit." Aoife's voice tears out of her, ragged and breathless.

"You're making this harder than it has to be."

A new sound leather against skin. A crack. A sharp intake of breath. I don't know if he hit her or if she landed another strike on him. I can't see. I fucking hate this.

"If you think I'm walking out of here with you, you're dumber than I thought," Aoife spits. "You'll be dead before you hit the front gates."

"That so?" Ronan breathes out a low laugh. "Guess we'll find out."

A sharp rustle. The unmistakable sound of a gun cocking.

I push off the wall, instinct taking over. "Seamus, end him!" I bark, my voice cutting like a blade.

Silence.

No answer. No movement.

The pit swallows my voice like a grave swallowing the dead. For a moment, all I can hear is my own breath, ragged and useless. Above us, the chaos that once raged fades into something worse—silence.

No more gunfire.

No more fighting.

Only the sickening truth settling over me like dirt on a coffin lid. Ronan is gone. And he's taken Aoife with him.

A raw sound tears from my throat—rage, helplessness, a vow stitched in blood.

Aoife

Ronan's grip is brutal, his fingers knotted painfully in my hair, yanking my head back with every step. The cold bite of his gun grinds into my temple, a constant, vicious reminder of who holds the power now. He drags me through the hollow, echoing halls of the castle, each footfall ringing against the stone like a tolling bell.

When we break into the night, the cool air slashes against my skin, sharp enough to sting— but the illusion of freedom shatters before I can even reach for it.

I scan the darkness, desperate for something, someone.

Nothing.

Ronan catches the way I hesitate and lets out a low, mocking chuckle, the sound curling around me like a noose. "Looking for your rescue party?" he taunts. "I'm not as fucking reckless as Cian. I knew Eamon's men could be bought, so I made them a better offer."

Dread curls in my stomach. "You paid them off?" My voice is hoarse.

Ronan chuckles low under his breath. "Everyone's loyal until someone offers them more."

He keeps moving, dragging me behind him like dead weight.

My heels sink into the loose dirt, the uneven ground biting at my ankles, yanking me off balance. I stumble hard, hitting the ground with a jolt that rattles through my bones.

Ronan jerks me back to my feet with a vicious pull like I'm nothing more than a rag in his hands. "Take off the fucking shoes," he growls in frustration.

I crouch low, my hands shaking as I force each movement to stay slow and deliberate as my mind races for a way out.

Then, a gunshot.

A sickening thud.

Something warm splatters across my skin.

Ronan jerks violently, his grip loosening a fraction of a second before his full weight crashes into me, slamming me hard into the ground.

The impact knocks the breath from my lungs. I choke on a gasp, shoving at his dead weight, blood slicking my hands as I scramble backward. My heart hammers, and my eyes scour the dark.

And then I see her standing there, frozen in the silver wash of the moonlight, the gun still raised, her hands trembling so badly it's a wonder she hasn't dropped it.

For a heartbeat, all I can do is stare, stunned, unsure if she's even real—or just another ghost conjured by the madness of this night.

"Bridget?" I call, but she doesn't respond. Her eyes pass right through me, unseeing.

Pushing up to my feet, I move carefully toward her. Her whole body trembles. Her eyes are wide and unblinking as tears stream down her face.

"It's okay, Bri," I say softly. "It's over."

She doesn't react. Doesn't blink. She's in shock. Gently, I reach for the gun and pry it from her fingers.

As soon as I take it, her eyes snap to me and widen in horror.

"Oh my God—" her voice is a shattered breath. "Aoife, you... You're covered in—"

Her hands fly to her mouth, her whole body shaking.

"I'm okay," I assure her, cupping her face, forcing her to meet my eyes. "You saved me."

She's still shaking her head. Still staring at the blood.

"Is Ruairi here?"

Swallowing hard, I nod. "Yes."

Her hands grip my arms, her voice desperate. "Take me to him, please."

Before I can move, I hear my name ripped raw from his throat. "Aoife."

I turn as Eamon barrels toward me, his face blanched with fear, his eyes locking on the blood smeared across my skin. He grabs my shoulders hard enough to shake me, his hands trembling.

"Are you—" His voice breaks, and he has to swallow before he can force the words out. "Are you hurt?"

"I'm fine," I rasp, though the lie trembles on my lips. "But we need to get Bridget inside. Now."

Eamon glances between the two of us. There are a thousand questions in his eyes, but he doesn't ask a single one.

I nod. Silent. A promise I'll explain later.

"Come on," I say, taking Bridget's hand in mine. "Let's get you to Ruairi."

Ruairi

The groan of rusted metal grates through the pit as the lift begins its slow descent.

Eamon paces, his breathing sharp, controlled only by sheer force of will. Every time the chains creak, his jaw tightens. I don't tell him to calm down. Because, for once, I'm just as desperate as he is.

Above us, Seamus operates the controls, cursing the old mechanism. The winch creaks under the strain, rust grinding against rust, chains rattling like bones.

Eamon shoves his hands through his hair. "For fuck's sake, Seamus, get it down here faster."

Seamus's voice cuts through the dark, brittle with impatience. "Unless you want to climb, this is as fast as it goes."

Finally, with a shuddering jolt, the lift reaches the bottom. Before the gate even slides open, Eamon hauls me up, gripping my arm as he drags me off. I stumble, my body weak, unsteady, slower than I've ever been.

The lift lurches, a sickening jolt, then starts its agonizing crawl upward.

"Fucking hurry," Eamon growls at no one in particular. His

fists are clenched at his sides, and his breathing is ragged and shallow.

The moment the platform scrapes against the top, he doesn't hesitate, shoving the cage door open. Without a word or a glance in my direction, he takes off, chasing after Ronan and Aoife.

I don't have the strength to go after him. All I have is Seamus, who steadies me, his grip firm but careful as he helps me into a nearby chair. Then, he grabs a bottle of water from a nearby crate. "Drink," he says, pressing the bottle into my hand. "There's food here," he offers. "The guards had supplies."

I shake my head. "Not now." I don't say that the thought of eating makes my stomach turn. Twisting off the cap, I take a long swallow. The water is lukewarm, but it soothes the raw burn in my throat. "What the fuck happened? Where were you?" I rasp, the words scraping their way out.

Seamus exhales, dragging a hand down his face. "It fell apart the second we got into place."

My stomach turns. "Explain."

He doesn't argue. He just starts talking, his voice raw with barely contained fury. "The guards turned on me," he spits. "The ones who were supposed to have my back."

He drags a hand down his face. The motion is jerky, almost violent.

"I barely made it two steps before they were on me. They took my weapon like I was nothing while they held me down like a fucking dog." His hands clench into fists at his sides. "Then, they locked me in one of the upstairs rooms and left me there, helpless, while everything went to hell."

A slow, cold rage coils up my spine, tightening with every word.

Seamus grits his teeth. "The lock was old. Rusted. It took longer than it should've to pick it." His voice is low, edged with frustration he can't hide. "But the second I broke free, I ran straight down here."

"But by then, Ronan already had her."

The words taste like acid.

Seamus meets my gaze, steady and unflinching. "Eamon's on them," he says. "He'll bring her back."

Before I can respond, a gunshot cracks through the night. Seamus and I both freeze. My pulse slams into my throat. We exchange a look one neither of us wants to acknowledge.

What the hell just happened?

Who took a bullet?

Seamus paces. I watch him for a long moment before speaking. "Go."

He stops, turning to me. "What?"

"Go after them."

Seamus crosses his arms. "Not happening."

I grit my teeth. "I'm no good to anyone right now. I can't fight. I can barely fucking stand. But you can."

Seamus doesn't budge. "I'm not leaving you here. You think I trust any of those bastards not to come back?"

I open my mouth to argue, but he cuts me off.

"I get that you want to help her, but I'm not risking you just to chase after something Eamon already has handled."

I clench my jaw, glaring at him. And yet, I can't deny it. Seamus isn't just loyal to Eamon. He's loyal to Aoife.

It guts me to realize I didn't see the ones closest to me for who they really were.

Ronan. Cian.

Both of them turned against me. And I didn't see it coming. I was too fucking blinded by war. Too caught up in the fight with Aoife. Too focused on Eamon as the enemy. The weight of it settles like a stone in my gut.

The silence stretches. Each second feels like an eternity until, finally, the door opens. Eamon steps in first. His gaze sweeps the room, locking onto Seamus before landing on me. Behind him are Aoife and Bridget.

I freeze.

Bridget's breath catches. Her eyes widen in disbelief.

"Ruairi?" Her voice trembles. "Is that really you?"

"It's me, *a ghrá*," I say softly, my voice thick.

She doesn't move. Like she's afraid if she does, I'll disappear.

When I open my arms, she rushes into them. Her hands grip my face, her body pressing into mine, desperate, needing to feel that I'm real.

"What happened to you?" she breathes, her hands skimming over me.

I hold her tighter, pressing my face into her hair. But I don't tell her. Not now.

Not yet. Instead, I meet Aoife's gaze.

Eamon's holding her tightly against him. My sister, the fiercest thing I've ever known, is shaking in his arms like she might come apart if he lets go. She's covered in blood. Brain matter. Bits of the man who thought he could control her. She's wearing the aftermath like war paint, but this isn't a victory.

It's survival.

Eamon's hands are steady around her, his hold protective, firm. He murmurs something low against her temple, but I can't hear the words.

She doesn't respond. She's not crying, but she's far from okay. And all I can think is, how the fuck did it come to this?

I was so busy waging a war that I thought I had to win. Too busy pushing Aoife away, telling her she wasn't strong enough, worthy enough to have a place in the Syndicate. I never saw the storm my sister was becoming.

And now? Now, she's standing in the wreckage of all of it.

Bridget pulls back, her eyes pleading. "What happened?"

I stroke her hair, breathing her in, feeling her warmth against me.

"We'll talk about it later," I say softly. "The only thing that matters is that we're together."

And that we're all still standing.

For now.

Aoife

Seamus is pacing near the entrance, phone
pressed to his ear, his voice low and clipped. "Castle grounds," he
says. "Use the south entrance." He pauses, listening, then adds, "I
want them gone before sunrise."

I know who he's talking to. The clean-up crew. The kind of
men you don't find in the yellow pages.

Bridget's wrapped around Ruairi, holding onto him like she
can keep him whole if she holds him tight enough. Her voice is
soft but insistent. "You need to go to the hospital."

Ruairi shakes his head, slow and deliberate. "No."

"You can barely stand," she presses, her voice breaking.
"Ruairi, please. They need to do scans. Check you for internal
bleeding—"

"No hospitals," he says again, forcing the words past cracked
lips. "Too many questions."

Bridget's frustration flashes across her face. "I don't care about
questions. I care about you staying alive."

Before Ruairi can snap back, Eamon steps in.

"I'll call my physician," he says calmly.

Bridget turns toward him, uncertain. "Is he a *real* doctor?"

"He's treated me for years," Eamon says, his voice steady with conviction. "I trust him with my life."

Without waiting for confirmation, he calls the doctor. His voice is low, clipped, giving him only the bare essentials. He ends the call, sliding the phone back into his pocket. "He'll meet us at my penthouse."

Bridget looks back at Ruairi, searching his face for any sign of agreement.

Ruairi gives a single nod. "We'll go."

Bridget doesn't like it, but she doesn't argue. She hooks her arm under Ruairi's, helping Seamus guide him toward the exit.

Eamon turns to me, his hand coming to rest on my lower back. "Come on," he says gently. "Let's go home."

Seamus drives, his hands white-knuckled on the wheel, his reflection in the rearview mirror hollowed by guilt and dread he doesn't bother trying to hide.

Bridget keeps her arms around Ruairi. He's slumped against her, racked with violent coughs, every breath a ragged wheeze. Tears streak her face as she pleads with him again, her voice shaking. "Please, Ruairi. Let us take you to the hospital."

"No hospitals," he rasps, his voice barely above a breath. "No questions."

Bridget's face twists in frustration. "You need real medical care, Ri—"

"I said—" His voice shatters mid-sentence, breaking into a fit of coughing that wracks his entire body. When he forces his head up again, his glare is fierce, stubborn, daring anyone to argue.

She exhales loudly but doesn't push anymore. Instead, she presses her forehead against his temple, her eyes squeezed shut as if trying to hold back tears.

The air inside the vehicle is thick, weighted with everything that's happened.

I can still feel it. The blood drying on my skin. The gunshot ringing in my ears. The weight of Ronan's body collapsing onto me. My fingers twitch, itching to scrub it all away.

Eamon shifts beside me. He hasn't let go of me since we got into the car. His hand is firm on my thigh, grounding me. But I still feel like I'm unraveling.

Staring out the window, I watch as we leave the castle behind.

We don't speak. What the hell is there to say?

Seamus pulls into the hotel's underground garage. The second the vehicle stops, Eamon's already moving.

"Come on," he murmurs, his voice meant only for me. "Let's get you upstairs."

The elevator doors slide open. Two of Eamon's guards are already waiting. They move without needing orders and step forward to help relieve Seamus of Ruairi's weight.

The elevator shudders as it begins to rise, every second stretched thin under the weight of what we've just survived. Ruairi's breathing is ragged, each shallow gasp cutting through the suffocating silence. Bridget doesn't let go of him. Seamus keeps a steady hand on his shoulder, holding him upright.

The floors tick by too slow, too loud. When we finally reach the penthouse, the doors slide open, and I'm hit with the heavy scent of antiseptic. Dr. Kearney stands just inside the doorway, his sleeves already rolled up, a small medical kit open beside him, his expression focused. He's ready for whatever damage Ruairi's broken body will reveal.

His eyes sweep over my brother and then land on me. "Is she hurt?" he asks, taking in the blood-streaked across my face and arms.

I don't answer. I'm not sure I could if I tried.

"She's not injured," Eamon answers for me, his arm tightening protectively around my waist. "The blood's not hers."

Dr. Kearney nods once. "My things are set up in the guest room. I'll start with him." He gestures for the guards to bring Ruairi through the hall. Bridget follows them wordlessly, her hand never leaving her husband's back.

The second we're alone, Eamon turns to me, his expression softening. "Let me take care of you."

I nod.

He doesn't say anything else as he laces his fingers through mine and leads me down the hall to our room. Once we're inside, he closes the door and turns to me. His gaze darkens, skimming over my ruined clothes, over the dried blood, the grime. The evidence of everything that happened tonight.

I feel it, heavy on my skin. It clings and suffocates me. But I don't react. I don't know how.

Eamon moves with care. His hands find the hem of my shirt, but he doesn't rush. He undresses me gently, his fingers unhurried, as if he's peeling away layers of something fragile.

The fabric is stiff with blood as he pulls it over my head. It lands on the floor with a quiet thud, but the sound feels deafening. His fingers skim down my arms, dragging away the remnants of tonight. My pants follow, sliding down my legs, pooling at my feet.

I stand there, bare, cold despite the warmth of the penthouse, despite Eamon's hands on me.

His brows pull together, concern flashing across his face. He cups my cheek, his thumb dragging over my jaw. "Aoife."

I blink but don't answer. I can't. Something inside me has gone still—too still.

Eamon exhales sharply as if he was hoping for some kind of response.

When he steps back, his hands go to his own clothes. The soft rustle of fabric fills the heavy silence between us, but I barely hear it. Everything feels muted like I'm underwater.

His shirt drops to the floor first, followed by his belt and pants. I don't even register the way he watches me as he strips, steady and unblinking. I can barely see him through the haze choking my vision.

Then he's there, solid and real, his arms wrapping around me without a word. He lifts me easily like I weigh nothing. Like my broken pieces aren't a burden he's afraid to carry.

The bathroom light cuts through the darkness, too bright, too clean. It feels wrong, like shining a light on a corpse. The water hisses from the faucet, roaring in my ears.

Eamon steps into the shower with me, still holding me close.

The first blast of heat scalds my skin, but I don't care. Pain is something. It means I'm still here.

Red stains the water the moment it touches me. It streaks down my arms in thick rivulets, smears against my legs, and pools at my feet. I stand there, watching it swirl down the drain, endless and slow, like no matter how much washes away, more will keep coming.

The coppery stench clings to me—thick, nauseating. It seeps into my hair, my nails, my skin. Into my bones. Into whatever's left of me.

And then it hits me, sharp and brutal. It isn't just Ronan's blood slipping from my body.

It's everything.

Cian's betrayal. Ruairi's war.

Every lie. Every wound.

The last pieces of who I was.

The girl who thought she could survive this and come out clean.

The girl who believed survival meant something.

She's gone.

What's left now is something empty. Something ruined.

The nausea claws up without warning. I double over, retching hard. Eamon catches me instantly, his arms steady and warm, grounding me when I have nothing left to hold onto.

He doesn't flinch. Doesn't pull away. Not even when I shake so violently my teeth clatter against each other.

The strength bleeds out of my legs, and I collapse. Eamon comes down with me, slow and careful, lowering us both to the slick tile floor. He pulls me against him, his chest bare and solid beneath my forehead.

"I've got you," he murmurs against my hair.

"I don't think I've got me," I press my face against him and just breathe—or try to.

My lungs stutter, my breath coming in ragged, shallow gasps that won't quite fill me. But Eamon's arms stay firm, wrapped around me like he's trying to shield me from the whole collapsing world.

Something inside me gives way.

Everything I've held inside, the pain, the exhaustion, the fear, the rage, spills out in a broken sob that I can't hold back. I curl into him, terrified that if I let go, they'll be nothing left of me.

He doesn't tell me it's okay. Because it's not.

He rocks me gently, steady against the trembling that I can't control. His lips brush the crown of my head, soft and reverent, and he murmurs into my hair words low and fierce, meant for me and no one else.

"I've got you, *mo chroí*," he whispers. "You're not alone. Not now. Not ever."

His fingers stroke slowly down my back, over the curve of my bare shoulders, tracing every broken piece as if learning how to hold them together.

"I'll carry this with you," he breathes. "Every scar. Every burden. I'm not letting you face it alone."

I don't know how long we sit there, the water pouring over us, washing away everything except the ruin left inside me.

When the sobs finally subside, when my chest aches from the force of it all, Eamon's voice breaks through the quiet. "Why didn't you come to me?" he asks, low, rough.

I inhale, the sound sharp in the wet air between us.

"Aoife." He tilts my chin up, gentle but insistent, forcing me to meet his gaze. "Why didn't you let me help you?" His thumb brushes my cheek. "You were never meant to carry this alone."

My throat tightens painfully, but it's not grief now. Not rage. It's something rawer. Bare.

"I had to prove it," I whisper, my voice nearly drowned by the hiss of the water. "To Ruairi. To you. To myself. That I could handle it. That I could be the one to run the Syndicate."

Eamon exhales slowly, brushing a strand of soaked hair from my face. "No one survives this life alone," he murmurs, steady and sure. "Letting the people who love you carry you isn't weakness."

My breath stutters.

Love.

I blink up at him, the word slamming through my heart louder than the roar of the water in my ears. "You said the people who love me," I whisper, almost afraid to believe it.

His fingers trail the line of my jaw, so tender it breaks something new inside me. "I love you," he says like it's the simplest truth in the world. "I've loved you from the moment I ran into you on that beach."

A broken sound escapes me—half a breath, half a sob.

I don't deserve this.

I don't deserve him.

The words rise, desperate to spill free, but he presses a finger gently against my lips.

"Don't," he whispers. "Don't apologize for surviving."

Tears burn behind my eyes. Tears I thought I'd emptied already.

I shake my head, my heart splitting open. "I love you too, Eamon."

He kisses me then, not rough, not claiming, just infinite. He kisses me like a prayer, like a vow whispered to the wreckage of who I used to be.

When he finally pulls away, it's only to lift me carefully to my feet, his hands never leaving my body, as if letting go might break me again. His fingertips move over my skin, slow and reverent, washing away the blood, the grime, the weight of everything I had to become to survive.

It's not just a touch.

It's devotion.

It's worship.

It's love—unconditional, unflinching, and eternal.

He says nothing as he moves, and he doesn't need to. Every stroke of his hands is a silent vow. *I'm not going anywhere.*

The water runs clear now.

The blood is gone.

But I'll never forget the woman who stepped into this shower or the one Eamon cradled in his arms while she shattered.

Because she isn't the same anymore.

And maybe that's the point.

He wraps a towel around me like he's shielding something sacred, pulling me into his arms once more. I press into him, feeling the steady, patient beat of his heart against my cheek.

And for the first time in a long, long time,

I allow myself to feel safe.

Not the girl I was.

Not yet the woman I'll become.

Just me, broken and breathing, held together by the only man strong enough to stay.

Aoife

THE ENDS OF MY HAIR CLING TO MY NECK, STILL DAMP from the shower, curling in uneven waves. I follow Eamon into the kitchen, my bare feet brushing against the cool tile, every step pulling me a little further from the wreckage I left behind.

The silence between us hums low and steady, not heavy like before. Something quieter, something I can breathe inside. Eamon's presence fills the room, steady and sure, holding back the darkness I'm not strong enough to face alone.

For now, it's enough.

Seamus is already there, sitting at the table, a mug of tea in one hand, his phone in the other. He glances up as we enter, his face lined with exhaustion but sharp with focus. "Cleanup's underway," he says, his voice all business, cutting straight to what matters.

Eamon crosses his arms. "Any word on my men?"

"Located," Seamus replies. "They're en route back to the castle." He glances between us. "Do you want to handle it personally?"

Turning to Eamon, I say, "It's okay if you need to go."

Eamon doesn't take his eyes off Seamus. "No. You handle it."

Seamus gives a short nod, no questions asked.

The conversation is interrupted as Dr. Kearney steps into the room, his white sleeves rolled to the elbow.

I straighten instinctively. "How is he?"

Dr. Kearney looks to Eamon who gives a slight nod, his permission to speak freely.

"Severely dehydrated. Malnourished. His vitals are stable for now, but his body's been pushed past its limits," Dr. Kearney says, his voice clipped but controlled. "He's showing early signs of pneumonia. He'll need aggressive rest, a high-protein diet, and time. With proper care, I expect a full recovery, but it'll be a hard road."

He doesn't come out and say it, but I recognize that as doctor-speak, for *he's lucky to be alive.*

Behind him, Bridget appears in the doorway, her arms crossed tight against her chest. Her eyes find mine, but there's no warmth, no welcome. Only a shuttered stare that makes my stomach knot.

I search for something to offer, some small way to make it better. "Would you like some tea? Or something to eat—"

She cuts me off, her voice sharp, final. "Ruairi's asking for you."

I flinch, a breath catching in my chest. Whatever bridge once stood between us has already burned.

Before I can respond, Eamon brushes his hand gently against the small of my back and leans in to press a kiss to my temple. "Go. I'll make sure Bridget has whatever she needs."

With a final glance at my sister-in-law, I turn and walk down the hallway. My pulse thrumming harder with each step. The guestroom door is cracked, but I still knock.

"Come in," Ruairi calls.

Easing the door open, I step inside slowly. Ruairi's propped against a pile of pillows, and IV snakes from his left hand, the line a stark reminder of how close he came to breaking. Clean clothes hang loose on his too-thin frame. The shirt swamps his shoulders, the sleeves falling past his wrists, but he's upright—barely.

He looks tired. Pale. Older.

I hover in the doorway, unsure.

"Come sit," he says

Each step toward him drags, the weight of guilt pressing harder with every breath. I lower myself into the chair beside his bed, unable to look at him, my gaze fixed on my trembling hands instead.

"Evie," he says quietly.

And that's all it takes. Whatever was holding me together shatters, and the tears spill over before I can stop them.

"I'm sorry," I whisper, my voice splintering under the weight of it. "I'm so sorry for everything. For what I did to you. I—" I choke on the words." I thought I was doing what I had to. I thought I was protecting us. But it all got so... complicated."

"Stop." His hand moves toward mine, and without thinking, I let him take it. His grip is weak, but the effort behind it is all strength. "Why did you do it?" he asks, his voice raw, barely above a whisper.

I swallow hard, my throat burning. "Because you wouldn't listen," I say, the words trembling out of me. "You wouldn't let me in. I needed to prove I was smart enough—strong enough. I thought if I showed you, you'd finally believe in me. I didn't mean for it to go this far."

Ruairi lets out a slow, shuddering breath, the sound cutting deeper than any accusation. "You're right," he says, his voice threaded with something dangerously close to regret. "I kept pushing you away. I told myself it was to protect you. But truthfully? I didn't want things to change. I didn't want you to change them."

His eyes meet mine, and for once, there are no walls, no shields. "That's on me."

I stare at him, my heart breaking all over again.

"When we met at the restaurant," he says slowly, something bleak passing through his expression. "I was ready to offer you a place in the Syndicate." He scrubs a hand over his face, frustrated, tired. "But then we fought. And I let pride get in the way," he admits.

He lets out a broken laugh. "Turns out I'm just as stubborn as you are."

A breathless sound escapes me. Something between a laugh and a sob. "We're twins," I manage, my throat tight. "Comes with the territory."

For the first time, Ruairi's mouth tugs into the ghost of a smile. But the moment shatters in the next breath.

"Did you tell Bridget?" I ask quietly.

Before he can answer, a voice slices the room clean in two.

"Did he tell me what?"

We both turn. Bridget stands in the doorway, shoulders stiff, her eyes sparking with fury barely held in check.

Ruairi stiffens. "It's nothing—"

"It's not nothing," I cut in, standing before I can think better of it. I move toward her, my heart hammering so loudly I can barely hear my own voice. "I'm the reason Ruairi disappeared."

Bridget's face drains of color. "What are you talking about?"

"It's complicated," I say, the words tumbling out in a rush. "I don't know if I can explain it all. But I set things in motion. I thought it was the only way to prove I was capable."

Bridget's mouth hardens. Her voice sharpens to a blade. "You think that justifies it?" She whips toward Ruairi, her fury cutting clean and deep. "You were right not to trust her."

"No," he says, firm despite the rasp in his throat. "I was wrong." He turns to me, his voice steady. "She saved my life."

The words linger between us like smoke, impossible to clear, impossible to forget.

And then, softly but without hesitation, he adds, "And if she still wants it, I'd like her to run the Quigley Syndicate with me."

Bridget recoils like he struck her. "What?" she breathes.

I blink, caught off guard by the weight of it. "I'd love to," I say carefully, cautiously, "but only if it doesn't cause problems between you two."

Bridget says nothing, her expression locked tight, unreadable.

Ruairi answers for her, quiet but unyielding. "It won't."

The knot in my chest tightens. "I accept," I say, my voice steady, "but on one condition."

Bridget's eyes narrow. "You're not really in a position to make demands."

Ruairi cuts her a look that shuts her up instantly. "Let her speak."

I take a breath, every word feeling like a choice I can't take back. "The Quigley and O'Sullivan Syndicates need to start working together. You and me, Ruairi. And Eamon."

His jaw tightens, the bitterness surfacing for a moment before he forces it down. "You're really staying with him?" he asks.

"I love him," I say simply, letting the truth settle between us.

Before Ruairi can answer, another voice slices clean through the tension.

"And I love her," Eamon says from the doorway, his voice low, lethal in its calm. He steps forward, each move deliberate, placing himself at my side like he was built to belong there.

"I won't let you take her from me," he says, his hand settling on the small of my back. His eyes stay locked on Ruairi, cold and unblinking. "She's mine no matter what you decide. And I don't make a habit of losing what's mine."

The air between them crackles, silent and deadly.

I lay my hand gently over Eamon's, grounding both of us, feeling the tension vibrating under his skin. "Let's give him some time," I murmur, trying to steer us back from the edge. "Let him rest."

Eamon doesn't move for a beat, his body coiled tight, still staring Ruairi down. Then, finally, he grunts a low "Fine," but the weight behind it promises anything but peace.

With his hand still firm on my back, he guides me from the

room, leaving Ruairi behind, swallowed by the silence and the fractures we can't undo.

And as the door shuts softly behind us, I know nothing between us will ever be the same.

<h1 style="text-align:center;font-style:italic">Ruairi</h1>

THE MOMENT THE DOOR CLICKS SHUT BEHIND AOIFE and Eamon, Bridget turns on me. Her arms are crossed, her jaw tight, and her eyes blazing with something that looks like betrayal wrapped in heartbreak.

"Are you out of your mind?" she snaps. "You're offering her a position in the Syndicate? After everything she did to you?"

"I get it. You're angry. I am, too. Part of me, anyway. But if I'd kept my word to her." I exhale slowly, trying to keep my voice level. "If I'd given her the place she rightfully deserved, none of this would've happened."

She shakes her head, eyes filling with tears. "You don't get it. You weren't here." She begins to pace.

"I begged her to help find you. I told her how scared I was. How lost I felt. I bared my soul to her, and the entire time, she was lying. She knew exactly where you were. Aoife was the reason you were missing."

Bridget's voice cracks and I feel the sharp twist of guilt slice through my chest.

"Even when I told her I was pregnant," she whispers, "she still didn't tell me the truth."

Everything in me stills. "You're pregnant?"

Bridget turns her face away, blinking hard. "I found out a few days before you disappeared. I was planning to tell you when you came back from meeting with Aoife, but you never came home."

My breath leaves me like a punch to the ribs. "Jesus, Bridget." I lift my hand, gesturing for her to come closer. She hesitates, only for a heartbeat, then crosses the room and climbs onto the bed.

She curls into me like she always does. Her head finds its place on my chest, and I wrap my arms around her, holding her close, breathing her in. Grounding myself in the fact that she's here, that we're both here.

That we survived this.

"How did you end up at the castle?" I ask.

She shifts, her cheek brushing against my chest. "I went to your office." Her voice is quiet. "I didn't know what I was looking for. Maybe just a place where I could still feel you. But Ronan was there."

My entire body goes rigid.

"He didn't see me," she continues. "The door was open just enough. He was on the phone. I don't know who he was talking to, but I heard enough to make my blood run cold."

She pauses.

"He was talking about working with Cian on some plan to take you out so he could run the Syndicate. But then he said Cian was a reckless idiot who didn't deserve to lead anything. He told whoever he was speaking to that he had his own agenda. Ronan's plan was to kill Cian, Eamon, and Aoife."

A cold, bitter chill slices through me.

"How did you find out about the castle?"

"Ronan mentioned they were supposed to meet Aoife at a castle in Dublin that belonged to Eamon. He gave all the details, including how many of Eamon's guards he'd have to pay off to leave. That's when I left."

She pulls back just enough to meet my eyes.

"I called in a favor with Malachy Flynn. He was the only

person I could think of," she says quietly. "I asked him to find the location."

I exhale, stunned. "You went there thinking Aoife was walking into a trap?"

"Yes." She nods before continuing, "I didn't know you were there. I thought maybe I could stop them," she says, voice trembling again. "Maybe I could keep Aoife alive. If I'd known she was the one who orchestrated your disappearance—" She swallows hard. "I don't know if I would've spared her when I pulled the trigger."

"I'm so sorry you went through that alone. I can't imagine what it felt like. But I need you to believe me. Aoife didn't mean to hurt you like that," I say, my voice low and steady, even if I don't fully trust it myself.

"I find that hard to believe," she says, her words sharp enough to sting, even through the tears. "Why didn't she tell you? Why not come clean and let you handle it?"

"Because she felt that she needed to prove her worth to me. That if she had come to me for help, I would've seen her as incapable. And honestly, she might've been right. I was too busy treating her like a child. Like she didn't belong."

I pause, brushing her hair back gently.

"What she pulled off. The risks she took. Aoife proved she's strong enough. Smart enough. And the Syndicate? It matters to her as much as it matters to me. That's why I offered her the place she rightfully deserves."

Bridget doesn't answer right away.

"I don't know if I can forgive her," she murmurs. "Not now. Maybe not ever."

"I'm not asking you to right now," Ruairi says quietly, the words scraping out like they cost him. "Give it some time. For now, step back and let me figure out what's best."

She hesitates. Then nods. "I'll try. But I'm not going to pretend this didn't wreck me."

"I know." I kiss the top of her head. "Let's talk about something else." A small smile tugs at the corner of my mouth. "Like the fact that you're carrying our child?"

She pushes up on her elbow, her expression softening. "Yeah. Like that."

"How far along are you?"

"Fourteen, fifteen weeks. I haven't had a proper checkup yet."

"We'll fix that." I grin. "I hope it's a son."

She laughs softly. "Of course you do."

I reach for her hand and thread our fingers together, but before I can say anything else, a yawn pushes its way up through my chest.

Bridget smiles, brushing her thumb across my knuckles. "Sleep. You need to rest so you can get better and we can go home."

"I want that more than anything," I murmur as my eyes begin to drift shut. I'll never take for granted the feeling of Brie lying beside me.

The safety. The quiet. The peace.

Eamon

THE DOOR CLICKS SHUT BEHIND US, SEALING RUAIRI and Bridget inside their own storm—acceptance, rage, whatever comes next for them. It's not ours to carry anymore.

The penthouse hums with silence.

The doctor is gone. Seamus is gone.

There are footsteps. No voices.

Just us.

Aoife moves ahead of me down the hall, her wet hair clinging to the back of her shirt, still damp from the shower.

She's silent but not retreating. Not lost.

She's dangerous now.

She's ruined and radiant all at once.

I close the bedroom door behind us, the sound sharp in the quiet, final in a way that sinks deep into my bones.

When I turn, I see her—truly see her.

Not the girl I met.

Not even the woman who survived.

Someone new.

Someone forged in blood and ruin and fire.

And I know, without a doubt, without fear, that whatever life we have left, I will spend it standing beside her.

"Eamon," she says it like my name is a confession. A surrender. An invitation.

I cross the space between us in three strides. My hand wraps around the back of her neck, and I kiss her deep, slow, and hungry. I kiss her like I own her. Like I always have. She moans into my mouth, her fingers already curling into the front of my shirt.

"Take it off," she breathes against my lips. "Now."

I obey without hesitation. My shirt falls away, hers right after, fabric whispering against skin. Her bra loosens under my fingers, sliding down her arms. My hands find her instinctively, cupping her breasts, teasing her nipples, tracing every inch of her bare skin. Like I have to learn her all over again. Like I'll never get enough.

A soft gasp breaks from her when I ease her backward, her knees brushing the edge of the mattress. She falls into it with a helpless little sound, her red hair spilling like fire across the pillows, wild and untamed. I'm on her a breath later, following her down, my mouth never straying from her body.

I trail kisses over her collarbone, down the trembling lines of her ribs, across the hollow of her waist, worshipping every fragile, furious piece of her like a man who nearly lost it all.

She trembles, but it's not fear. It's need.

Slowly, reverently, I strip her, my hands never straying far from her skin. Every inch of her feels like a miracle pressed into my palms, a silent reminder of everything we almost lost. My teeth graze along her thigh as I slide her knickers down her legs, the taste of her already teasing the back of my throat.

"You have no idea what you do to me," I murmur against her skin, dragging my tongue up the delicate line of her inner thigh. "How impossible it is not to fall apart at your feet every goddamn second of the day."

She arches toward me, breath hitching, a silent plea. "Please, don't stop," she whispers, voice broken and aching.

Lifting my head, I catch her gaze—steady, raw, endless. "I'm not stopping, *mo chroí*," I promise, the words rough against the thickness in my throat. "I'm just beginning."

Her thighs part under my hands like a prayer unfolding, and I settle between them like a man finding the only place he's ever belonged. The sight of her wrecks me, already wet and ready for me. I lower my mouth to her, savoring that first taste like it's oxygen after nearly drowning.

Her fingers dive into my hair, desperate for more, but when her hips arch to meet my mouth, I grip them firmly, holding her in place, making her take every slow, aching stroke on my terms. Building her higher until she's cursing my name through gritted teeth, her whole body strung tight.

When she gasps for me, wrecked and desperate, I finally give her what she needs. My mouth closes around her clit, sucking slow and deep, every vibration against her making her body jolt and writhe.

"That's it, *mo chroí*," I breathe into her, voice breaking against her skin. "Fall for me. Break for me."

She trembles, thighs clenching around my head, breath hitching so sharply it punches through the silence. Two fingers slip inside her, curling just right, dragging a ragged moan from deep in her chest.

"So fucking perfect," I whisper. "And so fucking mine."

Her body bows off the bed, a raw offering. I take everything she gives, everything she is until there's nothing left but the wild hammering of her heart against my hands, against my mouth, against every shattered piece of me that only she could ever make whole.

I drink her in like she's holy.

Because she is.

She tugs at my hair, her voice wrecked, desperate. "I need you. Now."

I move over her, slow but sure, lining myself up with her slick entrance. One smooth thrust, and I'm inside her, deep, buried to the hilt, where I was always meant to be.

We go still. For a heartbeat, I hold her against me, feeling every tremor still working through her body, every shuddering breath. My heart pounds against hers, frantic and reckless, like it's trying to tear its way into her chest. Like it's trying to lose itself in her.

Neither of us speaks. There are no words big enough for this—for what we lost, for what we fought for.

Because this isn't just sex anymore. It's not about dominance or control or chasing release. It's about every goddamn thing we survived to get here.

Every choice. Every broken, bleeding moment that led us to this.

I press my mouth to her temple, my lips lingering there, breathing her in like she's the only thing keeping me tethered to the earth.

Aoife shifts, her hand sliding up my spine, curling into the back of my neck like she needs the connection as much as I do. Her skin is damp, hot, alive beneath my palms, and when she exhales, it feels like she's giving me something sacred.

Then, her legs wrap around my hips, tight and desperate, anchoring me to her like she's afraid the world might tear us apart again if she lets go. I start to move, slow and deliberate, savoring every inch of her.

She gasps my name, her nails dragging down my back, branding me with every desperate scratch. I thrust deeper, harder, setting a rhythm that's less about fucking and more about staking a claim.

Aoife meets me stroke for stroke, her body greedy for it, for me, her mouth pressing frantic kisses against my throat, my jaw, anywhere she can reach. Every moan, every breathless whisper, every shattered gasp is a prayer that only I get to hear.

"You're mine," I growl into her skin, my voice breaking with it.

"Yours," she sobs against my mouth. "Always."

I drive into her harder, rougher, chasing the edge we both know is coming fast, brutal, inevitable. Her body locks around mine, trembling, burning, and when she comes, she shatters completely.

Beautiful, wild, and fucking mine.

The second she breaks, I follow, groaning her name into her skin like it's the only truth left in me. The world falls away, and for the first time in a long, long time, there's nothing but this.

Nothing but her.

Nothing but us.

We collapse together, tangled and trembling, breathless and wrecked, but still here.

Still standing.

Aoife presses her hand to my chest, right over my heart. "We made it," she whispers like she's almost afraid to believe it.

"We did," I say quietly, the finality of it settling between us.

She tilts her head, eyes catching the low light, soft but blazing with the fire they never managed to kill. "What now?" she asks, voice steady, certain.

I drag my thumb across her lower lip, slow and reverent, savoring the feel of her.

"Now," I murmur, "we rebuild everything they tried to burn to ash."

A slow, wicked smile curls her mouth, the kind that promises kingdoms rising from ruin. "Together," she breathes.

"Always."

The world tried to break us.

Tried to scatter us into dust.

But we didn't bend.

We sharpened ourselves into something deadlier.

We became the blade.

And now, in the ashes of everything they destroyed, we rule.

Epilogue

AOIFE

The paper is old now—yellowed, delicate, the ink faded to a ghost of itself. I stand in Ruairi's office, staring at it, framed behind glass like something sacred. A scrap of lined notebook paper, written in my messy, childish scrawl.

We promise to run the Quigley Syndicate together, side by side.

The words are stained with our blood where Ruairi, with all the recklessness of a boy who thought pain proved something, sliced both our fingers open and pressed them to the page. The mark we left that day, raw and clumsy, outlasted everything.

We didn't understand what we were promising.

Not really.

But somehow, that scrap of paper survived where so much else didn't.

Through the betrayals.

Through the wars.

Through the nights we bled and fought and lost too much.

I turn away from the glass, my footsteps echoing through the hollow quiet of Ruairi's office. The house is still, heavy with the ghosts of what it took to survive. Some mornings, it feels like they press close to the walls, breathing down my neck, waiting to see what we'll do with the world we stole back.

Outside, the sky hangs low and silver, bleeding pale light across the Belfast hills like a wound refusing to close. I step onto the patio, the cold stone biting into my bare feet, a steaming mug of tea clutched tight between my hands.

Across the wide stretch of grass, Eamon runs with two small, shrieking girls tumbling in his wake. Saoirse, almost four now, has her mother's stubbornness and my brother's fiery, defiant eyes. Maeve, who's just shy of two, trips on the uneven ground. Eamon scoops her up, spinning her high against the washed-out morning until she erupts in wild, breathless giggles.

Uncail Eamon. That's what they call him. A man who's ordered more deaths than most could imagine, brought to his knees by sticky fingers and ungoverned joy. A wolf who let himself be tamed—only for them.

I sip my tea, letting the heat anchor me against the chill pressing in from the hills. My heart is quiet now. Scarred but full.

Bridget still doesn't trust me. Not fully. Maybe she never will. She's never said the words aloud, but I see it sometimes in the hesitation between her smiles, in the shift of her gaze when she thinks I'm not looking. The wound I carved between us never truly healed. It simply stopped bleeding.

I don't blame her. I kept her husband in a pit and made choices she'll never be able to understand. Time has softened the edges of that wound. The rage has faded. The sharp grief dulled. But we're not who we once were. We walk beside each other now, not hand in hand, but close enough.

I love her daughters like they're my own. I'd lay my life down for them. And Bridget knows that. If nothing else, she knows that.

Today, she's bringing two more into the world, twin boys that will be born into a legacy forged in blood, stitched with loyalty, and the bone-deep will to survive.

Ruairi called me this morning. "She's almost there," he said, voice tight with nerves he didn't bother trying to hide. "I wish you could be here."

But we all agreed that Eamon and I would stay with the girls. Today's meant for laughter, for running feet and high, shrieking joy. For letting them have a few stolen hours untouched by the darkness we carry.

Even if it's only for a few hours.

Our world is quieter now. Not peaceful. Not safe. But settled the way a grave settles after the earth stops mourning.

The Quigley and O'Sullivan Syndicates remain separate in name, but in practice, we rule Ireland side by side. Two empires, woven at the seams.

I hold Dublin in my hands. Ruairi commands Belfast. And Eamon—he grips everything else in his fist like a blade he's never once considered dropping.

Our love doesn't live in soft glances or whispered *I love yous* at sunrise. It breathes in shadows. It sharpens itself in silence. It's loyalty worn like a second skin, a weapon drawn without hesitation.

It's not gentle. It's not sweet. It's not safe. It's a fire that devours, daring even the gods to look away. A love born of blood and strategy, of secrets we never needed to confess, of sins neither of us would repent for even at the gates of hell.

I once read: *We loved with a love that was more than love.* And now, I understand. Because what exists between Eamon and me is not tenderness. It's something older, deeper. Something brutal. Immortal.

We're no longer merely man and woman. We're a kingdom of two crowned in ruin, built on the bones of every soul who tried to tear us apart.

He's the darkness I chose. And I'm the blade he welcomed into his hand. We sharpen each other until nothing remains but steel and devotion. We trust no one but each other.

And when the time comes, if it comes, we'll bleed for each other. We'll die for each other.

But not today. Not while the girls are laughing. Not while the sky still dares to soften for us.

Today, there is no blood.

Today, there is power.

Today, there is love—raw and undefeated.

And I would choose this life again.

A thousand times over.

With him.

Always.

The End

Trapped in a marriage built on lies.

Haunted by a love that never died.

Alessia's freedom was never free—and Antonio's about to learn what it'll cost to protect her.

Beneath the Shadows is a dark mafia reimagining of Poe's *The Cask of Amontillado* you won't forget.

Start reading today **Beneath the Shadows** https://geni.us/ BeneaththeShadows

About the Author

Tara Conrad is the author behind sizzling and passionate love stories that ignite the senses. Her novels celebrate the fiery intensity of desire. They're known for having a blend of deep emotional connections, relatable characters, and captivating plots that ensnare readers from the very first page to the last.

Tara's the mother of four incredible, kind, and talented adult children. She also has one son-in-love who will always be her favorite. She's also Nana to the more perfect little boy- E.J. He's the little owner of her heart.

Tara's married to her soulmate and Dominant, George. They are about to celebrate their 30th anniversary and are more in love today than yesterday. George encouraged Tara to start writing, and with each passing day, she's more thankful for his insistence that she tell her stories and his partnership on this journey. There's no one else in this world she'd ever want by her side. He is her happily ever after.

Acknowledgments

First, I want to thank my husband for coming up with the idea to do a Poe retellings. It was not on my radar, but as soon as we started talking about it, I knew it had to be done. Thank you for being my partner on this incredible journey.

I have to thank my kids: George, Jacob, Kayla, Rebekah, Jonathan (my son-in-love), and Bryanna (my bonus daughter). Your constant encouragement and love help make this possible. I love that you are all such an invested part of this with me.

Baby E- You are Nana's everything. I love you with my whole heart. Thank you for allowing Nana to see that world through your innocent and loving eyes. We're going to buy lots and lots of broom brooms after this book releases. <3

To my readers: None of this would be possible if it wasn't foreach of you. I love getting your social media messages and emails. Thank you so much for coming to my signing so I can hug you. I hope you fall in love with Antonio and Alessia's world, and I hope to see you at a bookstore very soon!

~Tara

Find Tara's Books Here

www.ingramcontent.com/pod-product-compliance
Lightning Source LLC
Chambersburg PA
CBHW060613300726
48975CB00005B/1546